TWILIGHT TEARS

KULIKOV BRATVA
BOOK 2

NAOMI WEST

MAILING LIST

BOOKS BY NAOMI WEST

Zakharov Bratva

Diamond Devil

Diamond Angel

Zaitsev Bratva

Ruby Malice

Ruby Mercy

Aminoff Bratva

Caged Rose

Caged Thorn

Tasarov Bratva

Midnight Oath

Midnight Lies

Nikolaev Bratva

Dmitry Nikolaev

Gavriil Nikolaev

Bastien Nikolaev

Sorokin Bratva

Ruined Prince

Ruined Bride

Box Sets

Devil's Outlaws: An MC Romance Box Set

Bad Boy Bikers Club: An MC Romance Box Set

The Dirty Dons Club: A Dark Mafia Romance Box Set

Dark Mafia Kingpins

Read in any order!

Andrei

Leon

Damian

Ciaran

Dirty Dons Club

Read in any order!

Sergei

Luca

Vito

Nikolai

Adrik

Bad Boy Biker's Club

Read in any order!

Dakota

Stryker

Kaeden

Ranger

Blade

Colt

Tank

Outlaw Biker Brotherhood

Read in any order!

Devil's Revenge

Devil's Ink

Devil's Heart

Devil's Vow

Devil's Sins

Devil's Scar

Other MC Standalones

Read in any order!

Maddox

Stripped

Jace

Grinder

—

TWILIGHT TEARS

I'm pregnant with the *pakhan's* baby…

And he has no intention of letting me out of his sight.

I used to like surprises.

Not anymore.

Because every surprise lately has been worse than the last.

Surprise! A blind date with a mob boss ruined my life.

Surprise! I ended up pregnant with his baby.

Surprise! I got captured by his enemies, watched his sister take a bullet for me…

And now, I'm locked in a cell with a monster at the door and Yakov nowhere in sight.

He'll come for me.

He has to…

Right?

I can only hope he does.

Because the shadows in the corner are creeping closer and closer...

And if I want my babies to make it to their first breath—Yakov is the only one I can count on.

Unless he's decided I'm not worth his love anymore.

TWILIGHT TEARS *is Book 2 of the Kulikov Bratva duet. The story begins in Book 1,* **TWILIGHT SINS.**

1

LUNA

I've never felt safer.

I roll over and Yakov is lying on his side, smiling at me. It's rare to see his full smile. The one that crinkles his eyes and makes my heart beat faster.

"You've been asleep for hours," he whispers.

"How would you know? Have you been watching me?"

"Always." He curls an arm around my stomach and tucks me into his embrace.

"You're freezing!" I yelp. I try to scramble away from him, but he holds me tight against him. My body recoils at his touch even as goosebumps bloom across my skin. "Are you sick? Your hands are like ice cubes!"

"Everything is fine, Luna."

"I don't feel fine." I roll over, but the bed is empty now. I'm shivering, my teeth chattering as I call out for him. "Yakov? ... Yakov?"

I wake myself up, Yakov's name clawing its way out of my dry throat. My lips are stuck to my teeth and my tongue feels like a stone in my mouth. I've never been so thirsty in my entire life.

I must be sick. That's why Yakov is taking care of me. Lying awake next to me.

Except... Yakov isn't next to me.

I run my hands down my arms. My skin is rough with goosebumps and I'm naked except for my underwear.

My body protests as I sit up. My head swims and blackness creeps in on the edges of my vision. *What is happening?*

Then the room solidifies and I see the cement walls. The stained mattress under my pale legs. The barred cell door. The last few hours —*days? weeks?*—come back to me in a rush.

Mariya falling back into the grass, shot.

The hood they yanked over my eyes.

The zip-tie cutting into my wrists as I flopped around helplessly on the floor of a van.

Akim Gustev smiling at me.

More goosebumps prickle my skin at the memory of his dark black eyes and thin smile. *I'm going to die in here. But first, I'm going to suffer.*

My stomach lurches, but strength I didn't know I had left propels me to the end of the bed. I lean over the rusted metal frame and retch. The last little bit of moisture left in my body rolls down my cheeks in the form of tears as my stomach tries again and again to empty itself.

But it's already empty. It has been for a long time.

How long have I been here without food? Without water? I'm dehydrated and starving, but the fog in my head is from a lot more than that.

When my stomach settles, I flop back against the cement wall and think. I have a shifting, hazy memory of waking up to a needle in my arm...

The man holding the syringe was speaking Russian. He laughed as I slapped weakly at his hand. Then—darkness.

How many times have they drugged me since? How long have I been unconscious? What did they do to me while I was out? What if—

Breathe.

I curl my arms around my middle and drop my forehead to my knees. *Breathe. That's it. Breathe.* That's the only thing that brings me peace— focusing on one breath in, one breath out, again and again. Eventually, the goosebumps ease and my heartbeat slows.

But I'm still curled up and still shivering when a door squeals and loud voices echo off of the cement.

Footsteps. More voices. I strain to understand what they're saying before I realize they aren't speaking English.

I draw my legs to my chest, trying to cover myself as much as I can as a man stops in front of my cell. He's tall, nearly taller than the cell door, and almost as broad, too. His dark eyes crawl over my skin. Then his beefy hand reaches through the bars. I flinch, expecting him to unlock the latch and venture inside. The only thing worse than being trapped in this room would be being trapped in this room with *him.*

But he doesn't touch the lock.

Tucked into his massive hand is a small glass of water. It looks like a toddler's sippy cup compared to his thick fingers.

"Drink," he barks in a thick Russian accent.

I keep my knees to my chest and lean forward to grab the cup, but he pulls it back out of reach. A sick smile twists his mouth.

They aren't going to let me die with dignity.

I want to refuse the cup on principle and stay seated on the bed, but every cell in me is screaming for even a drop of water.

So I uncurl myself, stand up, and reach for the cup.

Again, he pulls it back, his eyes lingering on my bare breasts.

More goosebumps spread across my skin that have nothing to do with the cold. My stomach flips like I'm going to be sick, but I force myself to stand still. To meet his gaze. When I lift my chin, looking directly into his dark eyes—that's when he finally hands me the glass.

The moment the cup is in my hands, I no longer give a fuck about dignity. *Water. I need water.* So I drain the glass in one swallow. My tongue swirls around the lip, absorbing every drop.

"More," I beg, holding the cup out to him. "I need more. Please."

My legs are so shaky that I fall to the floor and my knees crack against the frigid cement. I feel the vibration in my skull.

The man curls his lip like he's disgusted. But he isn't disgusted with himself or what his boss has done to me—he's disgusted with me for begging.

If I wasn't so scared for my baby, maybe I'd be disgusted with myself, too. But I'll do anything for my baby. Whatever it takes to get out of here, I'll do it.

The man leaves without another word. The show is over…

For now.

Once I'm sure the cup is drained of every last drop of water, I crawl back to the mattress. It's thin and stained, but it's better than the floor. I curl up on my side and resume my shivering. Sleep comes to me in fits and starts. In those scant seconds, I dream of Yakov.

He isn't angry in my dreams. Not like the last time I saw him. He's smiling and tender. He cradles me against his chest and wraps his hands around my stomach. In my dreams, he knows about our baby.

If I don't get out of here, dreams will be the only place where he knows. The only place where we can be together.

I close my eyes and try to stay there.

2

YAKOV

It's been an hour since my brother bled out on the sidewalk and the man who killed him is laughing outside of a club.

The asshole has a big grin on his face as he holds up two fingers and mimes pulling a trigger. *The* trigger. The one that sent a bullet searing through my brother's chest.

He's retelling the tale like it's the world's greatest fishing story. He thinks he bagged a big one.

He has no idea what's waiting for him.

It was easy enough to find him. I drove around to Akim's clubs until I saw the black car. Then I looked for the scar. The raised white twist of skin that runs from his temple to his jawline. If I had a memorable marking like that, I'd wear a ski mask before I go around murdering people.

It doesn't matter now. That scar is going to look like a beauty mark when I'm through with him.

I'll keep him alive long enough to ask about Luna. That's where all of this started, anyway. Nik was trying to help me. I denied it over and over again, but he knew what Luna meant to me. He knew it before I did.

So I'm not going to let his sacrifice go to waste. I'm going to torture Akim's man for information and then I'm going to gut him for what he did to my brother. For the way his friends shot my sister on my fucking property. For Luna... wherever she is.

Akim ripped apart my family limb from limb tonight. He probably thinks he's won. But now, I'm a man with nothing to lose.

I'm going to be his worst fucking nightmare.

The man with the scar claps his buddy on the back and then saunters around the side of the club. I pull around the block, stopping for drunk girls in heels to stumble across the street. Then I turn off my lights and park at the corner of the alley.

He's sauntering away from me with his hands in his pockets, heading towards a black SUV parked behind a trash can. When I climb out of the car, I hear his laugh echo off the bricks.

"What do you think Akim will give me for taking out Yakov's second?" he asks. "Maybe I'll ask to give Yakov's woman a ride."

"If there's anything left of her," the other man snorts. "Akim is keeping her close. Maybe he'd consider it if you bring in Yakov himself to watch."

If there's anything left of her. I'm teetering on the edge of sanity, rage sizzling under my skin. I'm out of my body—out of my fucking mind —as I thunder down the alley after my brother's murderer.

He laughs again. Probably for the last time. "It's not out of the question. I'm on fucking fire tonight."

"Fire will be if you're lucky," I say, raising my gun.

The men turn around as I aim and shoot.

First, a shot through the scarred man's right thigh. By the way he buckles, I know I broke his femur.

"Fuck!" The other man turns to run, but I shoot him through the side, the bullet likely tearing through both his lungs. But he's still moving on the ground.

I click my tongue in disappointment, stalking towards the scarred man.

"On a good day, I could hit a man through the heart from this distance with one eye closed." He's scooting across the gravel to escape me. As if I'd ever let that happen. I shoot through his other thigh. "Today has not been a good day."

He howls in pain, but chokes on the sound when I kick him hard in the chest. He falls back and I can't stop myself. I rear back and kick him hard in the side of the head. Shit breaks inside him.

His eyes flutter and then he's gone. Still breathing, but unconscious.

"You weak son of a fucking bitch. You didn't deserve to breathe the same air as my brother." I grab him by his hair and drag him towards my car. "Soon, you won't be breathing at all."

It's the third bucket of ice water I dump on him that finally gets a reaction.

"There he is." I throw the bucket at his chest, dying to break the plastic over his skull. "Rise and fucking shine."

He shakes water off his face and looks around. His eyes are wide, terrified, confused.

Then he remembers.

"Do you know what you're doing here or have the multiple concussions left you confused?" I hiss in his ear.

It's been over an hour of this. Breaking my knuckles across his face until he blacks out and then dousing him with water to wake up. Each time, it takes him longer to come to. Each time, I have to force myself not to sever his head from his body while he's unconscious.

"Tell me where she is and this ends," I growl.

He snorts, blood dribbling down his chin. "You're going to kill me either way."

He's right. Of course he's right.

I sigh. "Here I was hoping you would beg for your life."

"I know better." He looks up at me through blackened, swollen lids. "I know what I'd do to anyone who touched my brother."

Before I can think, I punch him again. My fist aches. I probably have a broken finger. Maybe several. Usually, the pain helps. It centers me. But right now, all I can think is that I'm still here to feel pain. I'm here to hurt and bleed.

And Nikandr isn't.

I slam my fist into the man's skull again, letting the impact of the blow radiate up my arm into my shoulder. "Tell me where she is and this ends. Tell me where Akim took her and I'll kill you quickly."

"I'd rather die slow than die a traitor," he spits past a row of broken teeth. "I'm no rat."

I pull out my blade and walk a circle around his chair. "But you are. You're no better than a fucking rat, scurrying away while your brothers died."

"*You* killed them," he snaps.

I press the blade to the back of his ear. "And *you* were laughing before their bodies were even cold. Don't talk to me about my brother. You have no fucking idea what the word means."

Before he can say anything else, I slice through his ear. The cartilage lands on the floor with a satisfying *thwack*. Even more satisfying is the moan the man tries to stifle.

"I don't even know your name," I realize with a start. A laugh bubbles out of me. The echo of it off the high warehouse ceilings sounds as untethered as I feel. I drag the tip of the knife across the scar on his cheek. "Anyone ever call you Tony Montana?" He winces away from the knife, blood pouring down his neck and soaking the collar of his shirt. "Get it? *Scarface?*"

"Real original," he mumbles.

I plunge the knife through the thick pad of his cheek.

He tries to scream, but he can't. Not with the blade in his mouth and blood pooling in the back of his throat. He chokes and sputters until I pull the knife free.

"That felt pretty original." I wipe the knife clean on my pants. "I've never stabbed a man in the face before."

"I'm not going to tell you anything. Just fucking kill me," he burbles, blood foaming between his cracked lips.

The door behind me opens. I glance back and see Isay walking towards me. He hesitates for only a second when he sees the bloody heap of a man in front of me.

"I gave him matching scars," I announce. "He looks better this way. More balanced."

Isay clears his throat. "Very nice, sir."

Sir. Nik never called me "sir." He should have. Our father would have insisted. *Blood or not, a leader is a leader. Demand respect.*

I turn to face my new second-in-command. "What is it?"

"The hospital called." He holds up my phone. I gave it to him before I came into the warehouse. I didn't want any distractions. "Your sister is finished with surgery. She's awake."

"I'm busy."

Isay looks at the man behind me. It must be bad, because his face puckers like he's going to be sick. There's real fear in his eyes when he looks at me. Like I'm a wild animal who might pounce at any second.

I might.

"She's asking for you." Isay lowers his head. "And Nikandr."

She doesn't know. Mariya still has no idea Nik is dead. I want to let her live in that version of reality for as long as possible. But it isn't fair. She's right about what she told me; she isn't a kid anymore.

Someone should tell her. *I* should tell her.

"I guess it falls on me to deliver the bad news. Did you hear that, Scarface? My sister doesn't know you killed her big brother."

He is lolling in his chair, close to unconscious again.

"Fucking pussy," I say over my shoulder to Isay. "He can't handle even a little torture."

Isay smiles, but it's thin. He steps further away from me. He thinks I've lost my mind. And he's right.

I have.

With one quick arc, I plunge my knife into the soldier's throat and twist. The blade grinds against bones and hot blood spurts over my fingers and down my wrist. He gurgles and chokes, sinking down in his chair like a deflated balloon.

Nikandr would have kept this man alive. He would have tortured him for days—weeks, if necessary—to get the answers we need.

But Nik isn't here.

I'm the only one left.

3

LUNA

There is no window in my cell. Not even a peek of daylight to help me know what time it is or how long I've been here. The only thing that helps me mark time is when a guard arrives with a sip of water.

By the fourth swallow of water in fuck knows how many hours, I don't care that I'm naked or cold. There is only thirst.

I claw at the cup like an animal. The guards seem to like that, the way I paw at their hands to get a drink.

I don't care what they like. I don't care who they are. When the fifth small glass of water is thrust through the bars of my cell, I don't even look at who is standing on the other side. I lunge for the water and tip the glass back—only to find it empty.

I crumple to the floor, sweeping my hands on the cement in case I somehow dropped it. In case it spilled and I didn't realize.

"I bet Yakov loved this," a deep voice sneers. "The sight of you on your knees."

I look up to find Akim grinning down at me.

For the first time in hours, I forget about water. I stand up and muster up the tiny amount of moisture in my mouth to spit at him. "Go fuck yourself."

His smile widens. "You should watch your tongue. Babies can hear their mothers while they're still in the womb. Did you know that?"

It takes a second for me to register what he's saying. *What it means.*

He must be able to read the shock on my face, because he grins viciously. "Did you think I wouldn't find out?"

"But how did you—?"

"The same way I have you here," he snarls. "Because I always get what I want, Luna. Always."

A shiver works down my spine. "What are you going to do to me?"

"Be careful," he warns. "Don't ask questions you don't want to hear the answer to."

My heart races; my lungs tighten. I can't breathe. I gasp for air, trembling all over. "Don't do this to me." I hate the way my voice squeaks out of me, high-pitched and terrified. But I can't help it. "Yakov doesn't even—He was going to leave me. We're in a fight."

In the few moments of clarity I've had since I was abducted, I came up with a plan. I'd convince Akim that Yakov doesn't care about me. Whatever it took to get out of here.

But now...

"I hate to be reductive, darling, but you're just the wrapping paper on the real present now." Akim looks me over, admiring my "wrapping" with pitch black eyes. "You are carrying Yakov Kulikov's one and only offspring. That makes you my new best friend."

"Is it normal for you to imprison and torture your best friend?"

"Only if it furthers my plans," he says with a lazy shrug. "I hate to break it to you, but you aren't special. Plenty of people have died in this cell before you came along. More will follow. It's the way of the world."

"It doesn't have to be."

He arches a brow as if he's curious, but there is no light in his eyes. "What are you proposing?"

My stomach churns before I can even get the words out. But I dip my chin and look up at him. "Whatever you want."

His eyes scrape over me again, but it's different from the way the guards look at me like they're rabid animals looking for a haunch to bite. Akim's gaze is calculated.

I'm not a naked woman in front of him—I'm a pawn. I'm the tool necessary to make Yakov suffer. Now that he knows I'm pregnant, I've become even more precious to him.

"Nothing you say—*or do*," he adds with a grimace, "will change what's going to happen to you."

"You say it like it's fate. Like it won't be you doing it to me."

"It is fate in a lot of ways," he says thoughtfully. "Yakov and I have been heading towards this moment for years. I'm not going to rush my way through it. I need to savor it."

I drop down on the edge of my thin mattress, too weak to stand another second. "Are you here to kill me?"

"Not yet."

I blow out a shaky breath. "How are you going to do it?"

"I told you not to ask questions you don't want the answer to."

"Will it be bad?" I ask anyway.

I don't want to beg again. Not if it won't do any good. I want to be prepared for what's coming so I can face it with dignity.

"I'd promise not to make you suffer, but I would be lying," he replies, tilting his head to the side to study me. "Especially if Yakov is there to watch. If he's there… it will be bad for you, Luna. You'll be in agony. But that's the only way I'll be able to enjoy my revenge."

He thinks Yakov is going to come for me. It's a tiny drop of good news in a sea of shit. But even if Yakov gets to me, Akim will kill us both.

My body clenches. I twist towards the corner and throw up the tiny amount of water in my stomach. It's a few drops, if that.

When I wipe my chin and sit back up, Akim is gone.

4

YAKOV

I hit the elevator button with a swollen, bloodied finger. I washed my hands in the hospital lobby bathroom until the water ran red, but there's still blood under my fingernails and in every crease of my knuckles.

Going home to change wasn't an option. Not when every man in my Bratva is scouring the streets for Luna. I should be out there looking for her, digging up more leads, following her trail before it goes cold.

The only thing that could pull me away from that is Mariya. She deserves to know about Nik. That he's gone. That he isn't coming back.

A wide-eyed nurse behind a half-moon desk on the fourth floor points me towards Mariya's recovery room. Her hand shakes and she tries to hide it by tucking it behind her back. I must look as bad as I feel.

But I forget about all of that when I walk into the room and see Mariya slumped down in a hospital bed.

She looks over at me, her eyes narrow slits. "I know, I know," she grumbles weakly. "Hospital blue is not my color."

She wants me to laugh, but none of this is funny.

"Hospital blue is better than bloody red."

I should know. I've seen a lot of it today.

"Yeah, you're probably right." She chews on her pale lips to disguise how her chin wobbles with emotion she doesn't want me to see. "Have... have you found her?"

I don't have to answer. As soon as she looks at me, she knows. Her face crumples, fat tears rolling down her cheeks.

"If there's anything else you can remember, I need to know now," I tell her. "Anything at all. What the men looked like, the color of the van... *anything.*"

Her brow furrows as she thinks. "I was so busy fighting that I didn't see their faces. By the time Luna was out there, I was on the ground... I was fading in and out."

My fists clench. I came so close to losing every single person I care about tonight. The reminder of that failure doesn't do anything to douse the anger burning low in my gut. Sitting here next to Mariya's bed is hard enough without wanting to storm through the door and set fire to every fucking thing I touch.

"I should have taken care of her. I—I tried." She hiccups, tears coming faster now. "I did what you would have done, Yakov. Because... because Luna was... she was pregnant."

The confession tumbles out of her. She buries her face in her hands.

"Luna didn't want me to tell you because she wanted to do it herself, but she was scared. She was afraid you didn't care about her anymore. I wanted to tell you, but I thought the two of you would work things out. Now, Akim has her and—"

"I know."

Instantly, Mariya lifts her face. "You know what?"

"I know about the baby. Dr. Mathers told me."

She blinks, emotions flickering across her face too quickly to track. Then, without warning, Mariya leans forward and slaps me across the face. She winces immediately, grabbing her own arm.

"You're going to hurt yourself," I warn her.

"I'm trying to hurt *you*! If you knew she was pregnant, why didn't you come back for her?"

I grit my teeth. "Nik and I rushed back to the mansion as soon as we realized what was going on. We got there as fast as we—"

"Before that," she says. "Why weren't you there for her *before* that?"

I've asked myself the same question too many times to count tonight. "I didn't know. I found out right before everything happened."

Dr. Mathers dropped the bomb on me on the way to Akim's nightclub. I wanted to turn around. I wanted to go back to Luna. But I stuck with the plan. I kept driving away from her, which gave Akim exactly what he wanted.

I should have gone back to her the moment I knew she was pregnant. I never should have pushed her away in the first place.

I thought I was keeping her safe. Keeping myself safe.

Love is loss. It's the one thing I've always known to be true. If I let myself love Luna, I knew I would lose her. But I tried not to love her and I fucking lost her, anyway. So what the hell is the truth now?

Fuck if I know.

Mariya is still staring up at me, waiting for a response that I don't have. "When I see her again, I'll make things right," I say. "When I see

Luna again, I'll make sure she knows that I'm always going to take care of her."

Mariya blinks back tears. She's about to say something when a loud beep issues from somewhere close behind her.

"What is that?" I check the monitors and machines, but nothing looks unusual. "Are you okay?"

She tries to reach around to the table next to her hospital bed, but it's too far away. Then she starts to slide to the edge of the bed.

I grab her good shoulder. "If you stand up, I swear to God I will—"

"What?" she challenges. "Shoot me? You're too late. Someone already beat you to it."

"This shit is not a joke, Mariya."

"It is if you laugh." She smiles, but gently lies back in bed. "Fine. You get the phone then. It's been going off since the nurse brought it to me."

I grab the phone from the table and am about to hand it to her when I freeze.

This isn't Mariya's glittery purple phone case.

I tap the home button and have to grip the edge of the hospital bed to keep from dropping to the floor at the sight of my brother's face on the screen.

"What is it?" Mariya gasps.

"Nik's phone," I manage. "You have Nik's phone. How do you have this?"

I didn't grab it from his… *body*. It's hard to even think the word. But that's what he is now. A body.

I wasn't thinking clearly in the minutes after he was shot. I left him there on the sidewalk, phone in his pocket, gun in his hand.

So how is his phone *here*?

"I told Nik it was cringe to have a picture of yourself as your home screen, but I guess it all worked out. A nurse from the operating room recognized him from when he was down there with me," she says. "She brought it to me."

"How did a nurse have his phone?"

"I guess it was in his pocket," she says with a shrug.

A million questions burn through my head, but all I can think is... "You know."

"Know what?" she asks, frowning.

"You know Nik was... That he was shot."

She nods solemnly. "Yeah. Bad luck for the Kulikov family tonight."

"'Bad luck'?" I snap. "Our brother just died and you think it's 'bad luck'?"

Mariya's face goes pale. "He *what?*"

"Fuck me." I drag a hand through my hair. "This isn't how I wanted to tell you. I thought—Fuck, I don't know what I thought. I don't know what is going on. But I was with Nik when it happened. The only reason I left him on the street is because I had to go after Luna. He told me to go. But he didn't suffer. You should know that. It was quick."

"Wait. I don't understand. How did he—You're saying he died on the street?" she asks.

"The guy got one lucky shot off. He was aiming for me, but Nik took a stray. I'm sorry, Mariya."

She doesn't look sad; she looks confused. "You think he's dead?"

"He *is* dead. I saw him get shot."

"But did you see him die?"

I sigh. "I told you, I had to leave him to find Luna. I didn't have a choice. He wanted me to leave."

"Yakov, answer the question," she says, eyes burning into mine. "Did you see him die?"

I'll never forgive myself for Nik dying alone. Not as long as I live.

"No," I admit. "No, I didn't."

"Then I have some really good news for you." Mariya squeezes my hand. "An ambulance brought Nik in a few hours ago. He is in surgery. The nurse updated me when she brought me his phone."

"Nik is…"

"Alive," Mariya finishes with a soft smile. "He's still alive."

5

YAKOV

Nik is alive. I roll the words around in my mind, but they don't sink in.

"But I saw him," I breathe, shaking my head. "I saw him bleeding out just like…"

Like our father.

When Nik was lying on the pavement, blood pooled around him, there was only one way that could end. I'd seen it before. I'd been in that *exact fucking spot* before, holding someone I loved as they bled out. Nik couldn't survive.

"He's alive," Mariya repeats. "The nurse told me."

I turn to the door. "I need to see him."

I'll bust into the operating room if I need to. No one is going to get between me and my brother. I have to lay eyes on him. I won't believe he's still breathing until I do.

Then the phone chimes in my hand. A shrill *beep-beep-beep* I've never heard before. Nikandr always keeps his phone on vibrate.

I almost forgot about the phone, even though it's what started all of this.

"It's been doing that for an hour," Mariya complains. "But I don't know his passcode. I can't turn it off."

I want to ignore it. Mariya can deal with some beeping while I go make sure our brother is alive. But he's supposedly in surgery anyway. I have time.

I sigh and tap in his six-digit code while Mariya gawks at me. "You know his password?"

"It was for emergencies."

Like when he gets shot and is unconscious in an operating room.

"Well, isn't that sweet," she muses. I detect a hint of jealousy, but I'm too busy scrolling through the long list of notifications.

There are calls from the hospital—probably from the nurses when Mariya was in surgery. Our mother has texted a few times. I'll figure out what to tell her way later. Maybe never, if I can help it.

But far and away the most notifications are from a tracking app. It's the same message over and over. ***New location for Little Sis.***

"Who is blowing up his phone?" Mariya asks.

"You are, actually."

She holds her empty hands up. "It's not me."

"It's a tracking app. Nik had it installed after—"

"A tracking app?!" She swipes for the phone, but I pull it away. "You put a *tracker* on me?"

"We had to because *you* snuck out and got yourself kidnapped."

"Yeah, I did. But then we agreed that was a mistake. I wouldn't do it again."

"And we made sure of that." I wave Nik's phone in the air to highlight my point.

"This is such an invasion of privacy! I cannot believe you two!"

I expect Mariya's location to be pinging at the hospital. But the red dot labeled **LS** is way north. Nowhere near the blue dot showing our current location.

"It doesn't matter anyway. This cheap fucking app is broken."

"Why? It doesn't work?"

I flip the screen towards her. "It's showing you aren't even in the city."

She cackles. "That is karma. It's what you get for lying."

"It doesn't make sense, though… Nik has been tracking you for over a week. Why is it messing up for the first time tonight?" I zoom in on the dot. It's some residential street between North Hollywood and Van Nuys. I hold out my other hand to Mariya. "Give me your phone."

Mariya taps the nonexistent pockets of her hospital gown. "I'd love to, but I'm traveling light today."

"Where did you leave it?" I look around the room, but I don't see her purse or anything beyond her IV pole and the machines.

"At the house, I guess. I thought I had it on me, but I—" She stops suddenly, frozen with wide eyes.

"What?"

Mariya looks up at me. She's barely breathing. The heart rate monitor behind her beeps along a little faster with every passing second. "I had my phone in my jacket pocket."

I scowl. "And?"

"And Luna was cold." Her eyes are glazed over like she's somewhere else entirely. Reliving the moment. "We were on the stairs and I was going outside to check on what was happening. I didn't want to be restricted in case I had to fight. Luna shivered, and I... I gave her my jacket."

The phone chimes again. Suddenly, it's the most beautiful sound I've ever heard.

New location for Little Sis.

But it isn't Mariya's location.

"It's Luna," Mariya whispers, voicing exactly what I'm thinking.

The little red dot flashes. It's a lighthouse in the shitstorm of this day. It's Nik... Nik saving the fucking day, even while he's downstairs with a hole in his chest.

I press a kiss to my sister's head and sprint for the door. "I have to go."

"Be careful!"

I can't promise that. This lead might be a dead end, maybe even literally. But I have to chase it. I have to do whatever the fuck it takes to save Luna and our baby.

6

YAKOV

I fly down the highway. It's late, so traffic is light. Isay and as many men as we could muster are minutes behind me. As much as I want to slam on the gas, get to the location pinging in the tracker app as quickly as possible, and charge in to save Luna, having backup is the best way to make sure she gets out safely.

If she's still alive.

Mariya's phone is in a shitty part of the city. The kind of neighborhood where screams and gunshots don't raise any alarm bells. Akim could keep Luna there indefinitely. He could torture her—*kill her*—and no one would ever know.

My chest aches at the thought. *What if I'm too late? What if she's already gone?*

More questions like that circle around my head. Each time I bat one away, another one takes its place.

I pull out my phone and am halfway to calling Nikandr just to quiet the noise in my head when I remember he can't answer.

Swallowing down a bitter taste, I call the hospital instead.

Mariya's nurse gave me her direct line before I left the hospital and it doesn't take much pushing to get her to connect me to the nurse in Nik's operating room.

"Mr. Kulikov?" a soft voice says. "You are the patient's brother?"

"Nikandr Kulikov is my brother, yes. Tell me what's going on. Where is he?"

"Your brother is still in surgery," she explains. "He will probably be there for a few more hours, at least."

"Is the surgery going well?"

"It's going as expected," she says.

"What the fuck does that mean?"

She sighs. "Your brother's injuries were extensive. There are a lot of variables. The doctor is doing everything possible to save him."

There it is. Nik is still fighting for his life. Even in the hospital, it isn't over.

Mariya smiled while she told me Nik was alive. She said it like it was good news. And it is... in a way. It's better than him being dead. But I *saw* the blood pumping out of his chest. I *saw* the way his eyes rolled back in his head, the way he went limp.

He shouldn't have survived that. The fact that his heart is still beating doesn't mean anything.

"What are his chances of survival?"

"I really can't say, Mr. Kulikov. Things are still ongoing and could change."

"Tell me," I grit out.

"If you want more information, I can let you speak to the doctor. He'll be available soon and then—"

"Now," I bark. "Fuck protocol. Tell me what his chances are."

There's a long pause before her voice comes over the line again, softer this time. "Your brother coded three times on his way to the hospital. He lost a lot of blood and was without oxygen. We are doing everything we can to save him, but there's a lot we still don't know."

"How long was he without oxygen?"

"We don't know," she says softly. "He was dead when the EMTs found him. They brought him back."

I left him there. Nik was bleeding out on the sidewalk. I thought he was dead; I didn't think he stood a chance; and so I left him. And now, he may never come back. If I'd stayed and given him CPR, would things be different?

"I'll call you as soon as we know anything," the woman says. "Your brother is in good hands here."

I hang up without a word. There isn't anything to say. I have no control over whether he lives or dies. Not now. The only thing I can control is what happens next.

I have to focus on saving Luna.

The tracker app takes me through dark residential streets. Tall grass grows out of the cracks in the pavement. Rusted cars on blocks line the gutters. There are empty lots between the rundown houses like missing teeth.

When I'm a block away, I park along the curb and wait.

It's the hardest thing I've ever done. To sit in the dark, staring at the blacked-out windows of the house where Mariya's phone is. The house where Luna might be.

But I wait for backup to arrive.

There's a white van parked in the driveway. Behind the house, taking up most of the backyard, is a two-storey garage. It's the newest building on the block by decades. And there's a light on inside. I see the yellow glow through a gap in the upstairs blinds.

She's in there.

I feel it the same way I know I would feel it if Luna was already dead. The space in my chest where she's taken up residence would be empty. But it isn't empty—it *burns*.

The thought that keeps my ass in the car and also has me dying to break down the garage door this second is that Akim wouldn't kill Luna right away. To get the most out of his revenge, he'll keep her alive and torture her. He'll make sure she suffers so he can make sure I suffer.

That fact makes every second that Isay and the rest of my men aren't here absolute hell. Fuck only knows what Akim is doing to her in there.

If he knows she's pregnant, things will be even worse. Akim won't just hurt Luna; he'll kill our baby, too.

I grip the steering wheel with white knuckles. I never thought I'd become a father, but the role has settled on my shoulders easily. Without even trying, my thoughts have shifted to doing everything humanly possible to protect my child. I want to shield Luna and our child from every bad thing in the world.

And I will. Or I'll die trying.

7

LUNA

I'm still in my cell. I think I've always been here. I can't remember anything else.

As I look around, the room gets darker. The single bulb hanging from the ceiling is watery like I'm looking at it through a fog. The edges of the room are dark. Monsters lurk there, so I curl myself into a tighter ball in the center of the bed.

But I'm not scared of the monsters. It's the grasping hands reaching through the bars that terrify me.

The hands reach for me. Broken, bleeding fingernails scrape across the cement floor.

I shrink away from the barred door of the cell, but the room shrinks smaller and smaller. I'm shoved forward, closer and closer to the hands until there is no escape. Until they tear at my skin and my hair and my belly...

I wake up with a gasp. I'm shaking against the wall, as far away from the door as possible.

When I was first locked in this cell, I'd drift to sleep and be back at the mansion or tucked against Yakov's chest. My mind was trying to escape this room and whatever Akim has planned for me. When I fall asleep now, though, Yakov isn't there. Not anymore.

Even in my dreams, I'm still in this cell. There is no escape.

But at least I'm alone. I never thought I'd be grateful to be alone, but it's better than my nightmares.

Then I hear the cell door creak open. My relief shatters as the hinge whines and puts my entire body on high alert.

I have to squint to make out the dark shape slipping through the door and crossing the small cell to loom over me. I bolt upright, my heart slamming against my ribcage.

"Relax." The man's voice is grating. "Don't scream."

My throat is so dry I couldn't scream even if I wanted to. *And I want to.*

"Akim said no one would come in here," I rasp. It's a lie—Akim didn't promise me anything. But I can tell that this man doesn't have any good reason for being here.

The only reason anyone has come into my cell so far has been to bring me small drinks of water or a handful of crackers. Even then, the men handed everything through the bars.

This man's hands are empty.

"As far as Akim knows, no one *has* come in here." He touches my arm and I flinch away. He chuckles. "This can be our little secret."

"Akim won't like this."

He twirls my hair around his finger and then pushes it back over my shoulder so he can see more of me. I feel his eyes on me, burning across my chest like acid. "I already told you: what Akim doesn't know won't kill him."

But it could kill me.

I slap his hand away. "Don't touch me."

Before I can lower my arm, he snatches my wrist out of the air. His grip is crushing. I whimper as he twists my arm, turning me to face him.

"Don't make things more difficult for yourself," he growls, lowering his face to mine. His skin is pockmarked and oily. I smell alcohol on his breath. Up close, I can see the red tinge in his eyes.

"This won't be our secret. I'll tell Akim what you did."

Akim might not even care. Maybe he'll think this soldier was onto something and open my cell door to every soldier in his Bratva.

Without warning, the man draws his hand back and slaps me across the face. My head snaps to the side, heat exploding across my cheek. Tears burn in my tired eyes.

The man lowers his lips to my stinging cheek. "And I'll tell Akim that you tried to escape and I had no choice but to teach you a very, *very* hard lesson."

My wrist is still pinned to the cement wall. My face burns. Even on a good day, I wouldn't be able to fight this man off. And today is the furthest possible thing from a good day.

"Look at me," he demands.

I keep my head where it is, my eyes pinned to the ground. I can barely breathe, let alone follow orders. Every ounce of my energy is devoted to blacking out. To slipping out of my body while this man does whatever he's going to do.

It's the only way I'll survive. *Dissociate or die.*

He grips my chin with sweaty fingers and roughly forces my face to his. "I said, *Look at me.*"

He slaps me again. My head snaps in the other direction. I feel the heat on my cheek, but the pain is far away. Like it's happening to someone else.

Good. Fade away. Just like that.

If I don't fight, maybe this will be over faster. If I stay still and quiet, maybe he'll take what he wants and leave. Maybe he won't hurt my baby.

His hand wraps around my throat as he twists me back onto the mattress. The bed is flimsy already, but the metal frame screams under his added weight.

"You should be grateful," he hisses, unzipping his pants. "I could torture you instead."

"You already are," I whisper softly.

Based on the way his fingers dig angrily into my thigh as he shoves my legs apart, I know I said the wrong thing. I press my lips together hard and vow not to say another word. I vow not to cry.

I won't give him the satisfaction.

8

YAKOV

Isay stares at the house at the end of the block, his brow furrowed. "There aren't any guards posted outside."

In the fifteen minutes I've been watching the house, I've only seen one man step out onto the porch. A cigarette glowed orange between his fingers. After a few minutes, he went back inside. Otherwise, it's been quiet.

I try to tell myself that's a good thing. If there was something to see, this place would be crawling with men. Akim would want a crowd.

"Akim wasn't expecting us to find him," I guess. "Not this quickly, at least. But thanks to Nik, we did."

"Thanks to Nik," Isay repeats. He turns to me, shoulders squared. "What's the plan?"

"There is no plan. We'll have to do this on the fly. We're going to do whatever the fuck is necessary to get Luna and Akim out of there alive."

Isay frowns. "You want to get Akim out alive?"

"Yes." I grind my teeth together. "I plan to take my time killing him."

Isay fights back a shiver and nods. "Consider it done, sir."

Under different circumstances, I'd spend the time to formulate a plan. I'd have Nik observe the house for a few days. We'd see who comes and goes and at what times. The time of attack would be selected carefully and we'd have a plan with several backups in case shit went sideways.

But Nik isn't here.

There isn't time for any of that, anyway. Not when Luna's life hangs in the balance. So, five minutes later, I lead my men down the street. We circle the house and, on a silent count of three, we move in.

I kick in the front door as windows on either side of the house shatter. Two men on a sunken-in couch in the living room are dead before they can even stand up. Gun still smoking, I move through a narrow connected dining room and into a kitchen. Another man is dead on the floor. Isay kicks him out of the way and we search, moving from room to room, clearing them as we go.

"She isn't here," Isay calls to me.

"Garage," I command, tipping my head towards the back door. "That's where she'll be."

We moved in so quickly that no one in the house was able to raise the alarm. The yard is quiet and dark except for the crunch of gravel under our feet as we walk from the back door to the wide rolling door of the garage.

"Here," Isay calls, beckoning me over to a side door on the right. "You should enter here first. We'll follow you through the larger door."

The door is held closed with a flimsy lock. Forget kicking it down—I could blow it down.

It's a trap, I think. *Akim is setting a trap again. Just like last time.*

Or he's overconfident. He's holding the woman I love in a shitty garage with no guards out front because he underestimates me.

I weigh the two options, but it's not a choice. One means I take a risk and try to get Luna back. The other means I turn and leave.

And there is no fucking chance I'm walking away.

I kick hard just to the left of the handle and the door shatters inward.

Without taking a step, I take down two of Akim's soldiers where they stand stupid in the middle of the concrete pad. Then the garage door rolls open.

It's a barrage of gunfire and yelling, but Akim's soldiers don't stand a chance. They aren't prepared. They had no idea what was coming for them. I almost feel bad.

Then I see Akim.

The bleached blonde asshole is running from cover to cover on his way to the back door. I forget everything else as I beeline directly for him.

A bullet whizzes past my head close enough that I feel my hair move, but I don't stop.

He's here. That means Luna is here, too.

"Cover him!" Isay barks from behind me. It's something Nik would say.

It makes sense. Nik has been training Isay for the last two years. I'm sure my brother said something along the lines of, *"Yakov will try to kill himself. Don't let him."*

But running at Akim has nothing to do with killing myself and everything to do with not letting that rat slip through my fingers.

Akim peeks his head over the top of a table just as I reach the other side of it. I flip the table over on him. He tries to get out of the way, but he doesn't move fast enough. The heavy wooden table pins him to the floor by his chest.

Just to be sure he doesn't go anywhere, I shoot him in the kneecap.

The bullet through his right leg echoes off the high ceilings. The front half of the garage is two storeys tall. But there are metal stairs along the back wall. And a door.

Akim follows my gaze to the door and shakes his head. "She isn't here."

I scan his face, trying to see if he's lying. He wouldn't be here if Luna wasn't. *Unless it's a trap.*

"There's no use lying now." I press down on the table, crushing him under the heavy wood. "Your men are dead."

Bodies litter the room. A dozen at least. There could be more.

"You'll never find her." Akim lets loose a strangled laugh.

She's here. Where else would she be?

I motion for Isay. He appears at my side. "Tie him up. I'll come see him at the clean-up shed later."

Isay and two other men lift the table and are on Akim before he can even think about running.

"I've heard about the famous clean-up shed." Akim laughs hysterically. "You think you're going to torture answers out of me? I'll die before I tell you anything."

The clean-up shed is a warehouse more than a shed. In the decades the building has been in my family's possession, it's been everything from a storehouse for stolen cars to a meeting spot for illicit deals. Now, it's a place to torture enemies and dispose of their bodies.

Akim will be the latest in a grand tradition—whether he likes it or not.

"I don't want answers from you, Akim. The time for that was over the second you put your hands on my woman. Do you know what I do to people who hurt what is mine?"

He's sagging between two of my men, balancing on his one good leg. "I thought you didn't want answers from me?"

Faster than he can blink, I shoot him in the other kneecap. He lets out a scream before he can stifle it.

"The last man who touched Luna is nothing more than a pile of spongy bones decomposing in a barrel of acid. By the time I'm done with you, you'll be begging for his fate."

Akim holds my gaze, but his face is pale.

I wave at Isay. "Get him out of here. I'll deal with him later."

Once I've saved Luna.

If I'm not already too late.

9

LUNA

My body is clenched tight, so the man has to wrestle to part my legs. I give him as much resistance as I can, but I'm weak and malnourished and pregnant and he's none of those things.

When he wins the first struggle, he reaches for the waistband of my underwear. It's the only piece of clothing I have left. The last barrier between us.

I squeeze my eyes closed and drift away. I try to slip back into one of my earlier dreams. *Me and Yakov curled up on the couch in his living room, Gregory purring on my lap.* I'm so focused on the dream that I can feel the vibration of Gregory's purrs. I can hear the rumble of it.

Or, wait—no…

I open my eyes to see that the man isn't looking at me anymore. He's frowning, eyes unfocused as he listens to…

Gunshots.

That kind of violence could be normal for these people. Maybe there's in-fighting all the time. What's one more dead body on any of their consciences? Not that they have any in the first place.

But I can't help hoping it's Yakov.

Akim must have paid for the best soundproofing money could buy. Whatever is happening downstairs sounds muffled, but it's rattling the bars of my cell.

"What the fuck?" the man on top of me mumbles.

Then the chaos suddenly explodes into the hallway outside my cell.

Men are shouting somewhere far below us. Just the echoes are loud enough to make me cover my ears. Then footsteps. Massive, pounding steps getting closer with every second.

The man on top of me scrambles to get off the bed and stand up, but he isn't fast enough. He's still kneeling between my spread legs, grappling with the zipper of his pants, when a shadow falls across the doorway.

I feel him before I see him.

Maybe it's because I'm dehydrated and half-delirious, but I swear the newcomer glows. There's a bright light shimmering around his broad shoulders. Warmth radiates off of him. He's like an avenging angel, all violent wrath and fearsome light.

"Yakov," I breathe. It's the first full breath I've taken in too long to even count. The first moment I've actually allowed myself to trust that he would come for me.

"Shit!" The man tries to clamber to his feet, but Yakov is already there.

"Get your hands off of her, you worthless piece of—" His last words are lost in the sound of the man's skull shattering against the metal corner post of the bed frame.

When the rapist showed up outside of my cell, I thought he was massive. But Yakov throws him around like he's nothing.

I crawl to the corner of the mattress and curl my body in tightly. I don't want to get in his way.

Yakov drives the heel of his foot into the man's neck again and again. Then he kneels next to his body and slams his head against the floor until there's nothing left but blood.

When Yakov looks up at me, his pupils are so big I can't see the green of his eyes. His face is flushed and he's breathing heavily.

He's the most beautiful thing I've ever seen.

Only then do I let myself jump at him and bury my face in his neck. I can't believe he's here. "Yakov."

"You're alive," he whispers. His hands slide down my spine from all the blood coating his fingers.

He smells like iron and sweat. I hold him tighter. "You're here."

"Of course I'm here," he growls. "I haven't stopped looking for you since you were taken. I was never going to stop."

I shiver against him and he silently takes off his shirt. He pulls it over my head, sliding my hair out of the collar and draping it over my shoulder.

There's blood staining the front, but I don't care. It's warm from his body and smells like him. Akim would have to peel this off my cold, dead body if he wanted to undress me now.

Suddenly, I dig my fingers into Yakov's arms. "Where is Akim?"

He brushes my tangled hair behind my ears. "I got him. You don't need to worry about him anymore."

"He's dead?"

Yakov's face darkens. "He wishes."

At one point, I might have argued for mercy. *Murder isn't a solution. Violence breeds more violence. An eye for an eye makes the whole world blind.* All that bullshit.

But now? Fuck that. I hope Akim suffers every single second until his last breath. I hope even his last breath is painful.

The shadow in Yakov's eyes says he will make sure that happens.

"No one is ever going to touch you again." Yakov smooths his thumbs over my cheeks. "I'm going to take care of you, Luna. You and the baby."

It takes a second for the words to sink in. I blink up at him. "What?"

"I know about the baby. Dr. Mathers called me before... before everything happened."

I just witnessed Yakov murder a man with his bare hands, but *now,* my heart is racing. "I was going to tell you," I blurt. "I wanted to tell you. I tried. But I didn't know how. I didn't know—"

He presses his thumb against my lips. "It's okay, Luna. The only thing that matters now is that I'm going to take care of you both. Always."

Tears blur my vision. I press my forehead to his bare chest and Yakov kisses the top of my head. If I woke up right now, I wouldn't be surprised. This is like a dream. I could stand here forever. I don't need anything else.

This is it for me. *He* is it for me.

I'm about to tell him when something else occurs to me. "Mariya!" I gasp. So much has happened over the last few hours that I wasn't thinking about her.

"She's okay," he reassures me quickly. "She was shot, but she's okay. I was in her hospital room an hour ago."

I exhale. "Thank God. I wanted to save her, but I couldn't. They were coming for me."

"I saw it on the tapes." His jaw clenches. "I wouldn't have blamed you for running right past Mariya to escape. But you stopped."

I squeeze his hand. "She's your sister, Yakov. Of course I stopped."

His hand curls tightly around the back of my head and he presses a kiss to my forehead. "I need to get you to a hospital."

"I'm okay."

"You're not okay until every doctor in the building looks me in my eyes and stakes their fucking lives on the fact that you are okay," he says. "Don't even try to argue with me."

I know he's right. I'm probably dehydrated. And someone should check on the baby. I just want nothing more than to be back home in the mansion. I don't want to be in another strange room surrounded by people I don't know.

"I can't believe we're all okay," I murmur.

I feel Yakov tense. His entire body goes rigid.

I jerk back. "We are, aren't we? Everyone is okay?"

"Not everyone." His lips are pale.

I don't even want to ask. It's selfish, but I want to stay in this moment with him. I want things to be okay for five fucking seconds. But I say it anyway.

"Who?"

He looks away from me. "Nikandr."

"Is he...?"

"It's not looking good."

Before I can say anything else, Yakov scoops me into his arms and walks me out of the cell. I want to see if he's okay and ask more about what happened to Nikandr, but it's beyond obvious that he doesn't want to talk. So I wrap my arms around him, clinging to him like my life depends on it.

I have the feeling he's clinging to me just as hard.

10

YAKOV

"She's slightly dehydrated, but otherwise, she is the picture of health." The middle-aged doctor smiles at Luna. That smile dims when he turns back to me.

"If she was the 'picture of health,' she wouldn't be dehydrated," I say slowly, grinding the words out between clenched teeth.

I haven't been able to relax. Even when Luna was sitting in the passenger seat next to me, Akim's fucked-up torture house shrinking in the rearview mirror, I couldn't let go of the feeling that something was wrong. I still can't.

Luna touches my arm. Her fingers are cold. "I feel okay, Yakov. Really."

"How many more doctors are you planning to cycle through tonight?" Mariya groans from her hospital bed on the other side of the room. There's a thin curtain pulled around her half of the room, but I can see the glow of her phone against the wall. "They've all said the exact same thing and some of us are trying to sleep over here."

"As many doctors as it takes to not get some sugar-coated, bullshit answer."

"I don't think their answers are bullshit," Luna says with a nervous chuckle for the doctor's sake.

The doctor nods. "I'm giving my honest assessment, Mr. Kulikov. Luna is perfectly—"

"And you aren't even sleeping," I interrupt, ripping Mariya's curtain back. "You've been on your phone since I gave it back to you three hours ago."

Mariya narrows her eyes at me. "I have a lot to catch up on *since I was shot.*"

She's going to play that card for a long, long time. I don't even care. At least she's alive and conscious to play it.

Snarling, I tug the curtain closed again and turn to the doctor. "I want Luna admitted until she's the *actual* picture of health. I want her picture to be in fucking textbooks as a perfect specimen. Do you understand me?"

Dr. Andrews furrows his thick brows. "The notes from her emergency room visit show she was given a saline bag upon arrival. From this point forward, normal rehydration at home would be satisfactory to—"

"I'm not paying for 'satisfactory.' I want her to be fucking *perfect.*"

Luna curls her arm around my elbow, holding me tight. She's in the same pale blue hospital gown Mariya is wearing, with my sweater layered on top. She wanted more coverage, which makes sense, considering she was naked when I found her. "I feel great, Yakov. I'm fine."

I curl her around me and tip her chin up with one finger. "I'm not taking any more chances with you."

Her face softens. "I'm going to be okay."

"I know." I look over her head to the doctor. "Because the good doctor here is going to personally make sure of it."

The man's mouth presses into a firm line. Then he nods. "Of course, Mr. Kulikov. Whatever you need."

He scurries off to make arrangements and I settle Luna back into her hospital bed.

"One of the best obstetricians in the country is going to be here to see you tomorrow."

"They already told me the baby is okay," she insists. "You heard the heartbeat."

I snort. "I heard a bunch of static that could have been a whale call for all I fucking know. I want to make sure everything is fine. Dr. Jenkins is flying in tomorrow."

Her eyes pop. "He's *flying* in?"

"He owes me a favor," I shrug.

Truthfully, hundreds of thousands of people are going to owe me a favor. Dr. Jenkins has me to thank for funding his multi-million-dollar research study.

"This is too much, Yakov. I'm fine. Really. I was only there for... It wasn't even a full day."

She says it like she can't quite believe it all happened so fast. I can't, either. It felt like we were apart for so much longer.

She blows out a shaky breath and I know that, in her mind, she's back in that cell. Just for a second.

For the same second, I'm there with her. I see Akim's fucking goon on top of her. I feel the way his skull gives way as I smash it across the concrete.

Luna told me in the car that no one touched her, but if I'd been even a few minutes later…

I grab her wrist and hold it, feeling the reassuring thrum of her pulse against my palm. "It doesn't matter how long it was. You shouldn't have been there in the first place. I'm never going to let you be in that position again."

"It wasn't your fault. You know that, right?" she asks softly. "None of this is your fault."

"I know. There's only one person to blame." I lay her hand gently across her stomach—across our baby. "I have to go."

Luna knows what I'm saying. Where I'm going.

"Be careful," she whispers solemnly.

As I'm leaving, Mariya calls out, "Kick Akim in the balls for me, please and thanks."

I got the call that Nikandr was out of surgery in the middle of Luna's second exam in the emergency room. If I'd told her, she would have shoved me out the door and insisted I go see Nik immediately. But I didn't want to leave her.

Honestly, I don't want to go see Nik, either. Not like this. I said goodbye to him once tonight. That was more than enough. I don't want to have to do it again.

The nurse stops me outside his door. "The doctor isn't here right now. If you want to know more—"

"I want to see him," I say, pushing past her.

She lingers in front of the door. "I can't stop you, but you should know what you're walking into."

It might be easier if I don't know. Hope would be easier without the facts. But I nod. "Fine."

"The surgery went well," she explains, "but he's in a medically-induced coma. He was without oxygen for… well, we don't know how long. It left him with some swelling on the brain. The coma will help him heal. He's under ice blankets for the same reason."

"Is he brain-dead?" I grit out.

"The doctor will run more tests tomorrow. We can't rule anything out." She steps out of the doorway. "He's on life support now. He can breathe on his own, but this is more reliable."

Because he coded three times on the way to the hospital.

Because he was dead on the sidewalk for who knows how long while I was racing across the city.

Because I left my own brother to die.

The room is solid gray in the dimmed lights, broken up only by the blue glow of the machines around him. Medications and fluid bags hang from the IV pole next to him. There are monitors strapped to him and needles inserted beneath the skin. A clear tube runs into his mouth, the machine behind him hissing as it inflates and deflates his chest at an even rhythm.

I barely recognize him. If it wasn't for his shock of dark hair and thick brows, I wouldn't even know it was Nik. Everything I associate with my little brother—his wide smile and booming voice—is gone.

I drop down into the plastic-covered recliner next to his bed and listen to the machines keeping him alive.

I try to be grateful, but I'm so fucking angry. At myself for leaving him there. At Akim for not giving me a choice.

"This is fucked, Nik," I mumble, running my fingers through my hair. "You shouldn't be here like this. It should be me. I was the target. That bullet was meant for *me.*"

I pause like Nik might say something. He always has something to say. Most of the time, I can't shut him up even when I want to. Now, I'd give anything to hear some fucking wisecrack.

"You'd say it's your job as my second to take a bullet for me, but it's my job as your brother to make sure you don't have to. I wouldn't have let you come with me if I thought there was a chance you wouldn't—" I stop and pass my tongue over my teeth. "Fuck this. We'll have this conversation when you wake up. Because you're going to wake up. You're going to fight and pull through."

Nik still doesn't move. Doesn't blink. I know he can't because of the medication, but I've never seen him so still.

"Mariya told me to kick Akim in the balls for her," I say with a soft, exhausted chuckle. "I'm sure you'd come up with something more creative. Hell, maybe Akim will still be alive when you wake up. You can kick him yourself when that day comes."

If it ever comes. The fact that it might not is what forces me up and out of my chair.

Luna was right. None of this is my fault.

There's only one man to blame.

Time to pay him a visit.

11

YAKOV

The clean-up shed is dead quiet. The only light comes from a flickering streetlamp two blocks down. Otherwise, nothing.

No one to raise any warning flags.

No one to hear the screams.

I pass by two guards at the front door with nothing more than a quick nod. They're not necessary. The only way Akim is escaping the shed is through death. But unlike him, I plan for the worst-case scenario. There is no way I'm letting him get away now. Not after everything he has done.

Isay put Akim in a soundproof room in the center of the warehouse. No windows, only one door in and out. He's bound to a metal chair that is bolted to the concrete floor. There's a drain positioned directly beneath him. It's about to earn its keep.

When I walk through the door, Akim is sagged down in the chair. I think he's asleep at first, until he lifts his head slowly, a dazed smile stretched across his pale face. "I was beginning to think you were going to stand me up," he croaks.

"I had to stop by the hospital."

He pastes on a sympathetic mask. "I heard about Nikandr. It's a shame… that my man wasn't able to kill him. It would have been my consolation prize for losing Luna."

I close and lock the door behind me. I don't want any interruptions for what's about to come next.

"I understand what you saw in her," Akim continues. "I mean, I knew shit had to be serious when I heard you were out on a date. Yakov Kulikov, the Bratva bachelor himself, on a date? Un-fucking-believable. Any woman who could tie you down had to be magnificent. But I still didn't expect *her*."

The way he says it, his lips wrapping slowly around the word, makes me want to rip his tongue out of his mouth. Fuck it—I might.

I force myself to put one foot in front of the other and walk away from Akim towards the cabinet of supplies in the corner. I unlock it and reveal a wall of chains, blades, and bats, some still caked in drying blood left over from the men who've occupied that chair before Akim.

"I had them strip her while she was still wearing the hood." His words come a little faster. He's scared, even if he won't show it. "I didn't even need to see her face to understand what you saw in her. I mean, she's built to be fucked. She has the kind of body a man can grab *hold* of, you know?"

Just the thought of Akim touching Luna at all has my hand shifting from a knife towards a bat studded with rusted nails.

"Then they took off her hood." He groans, a low sound deep in his throat. "That face. *That mouth.* If I'd had just a liiittle more time, I would have wrapped those lips around my cock."

My knuckles strain as I grip the handle of the bat. I turn to face him again. "I know what you're doing."

"I'm tied up in a warehouse in the middle of nowhere. What could I possibly be doing?"

He's trying to make me kill him quickly. Akim is smart enough to know he isn't getting out of this room alive. The best outcome for him is for it to be over fast. He wants to piss me off so I lose control.

He smirks, but his eyes shift nervously to the bat in my hands. "Since I won't get the dignity of having any last words passed along to the people closest to me, I'm sure you won't deny me my final fantasy."

"I don't give a fuck about your dignity," I growl. "I care even less about your fantasies. I'm about to deny you your life."

"Funny," he chuckles. "Luna didn't deny me anything. I'm not sure what she told you, but—"

"She told me the truth," I grit out.

No one touched her. She swore it. The man I saw in her bed was the first and only time someone went into her cell.

Yet Akim grins. "Then you already know that I couldn't help myself. I had to taste her. If she's good enough to turn Yakov Kulikov's head, I needed to know what was so special. Believe me, I understand now."

"Bullshit."

He frowns. "So she didn't tell you the truth, then? She must have lied if you don't know what I'm talking about. Because I fucked your woman for *hours*, Yakov."

My blood is pumping. My hand shakes around the bat. "You couldn't keep it up that long if your life depended on it."

"She spread those long legs for me. She *wanted* it," he hisses, ignoring me. "Maybe not at first, I'll admit. But as soon as my cock was inside her—Well, I was glad for the extra soundproofing up there, I'll tell you that. She howled for me."

"You're going to go down with this ship, aren't you?" I shake my head. "All of this for a little revenge? Revenge for revenge, actually. Two steps removed. You went after Luna to get back at me for killing your father after your father killed mine. Do you hear how that sounds? It's insane."

Akim tips his head back, his throat bobbing as he moans. "She felt so good clenched around me. I can't remember the last time I felt a cunt that tight. Is that why you fought your way through my men for her? Because if so, I understand. That's a pussy worth dying for."

I let a long breath rattle between my teeth. "You're going to die because you couldn't leave well enough alone. You could have let me have my revenge and move on. Eye for an eye. Score settled. I never would have looked at you again. Instead… here we are."

Akim meets my eyes. He's hearing every word I say; I know he is. He just refuses to admit it.

"She cried for you when I first locked her up. But by the end, she was crying for *me*." He gyrates his hips, the metal chair legs straining against the bolts on the floor. His voice goes high-pitched. *"Oh, Akim. Harder, Akim. Like that, Akim. No one has ever fucked me this good, Akim."*

It's all lies. It never happened. Akim never touched her.

But he wanted to.

If I hadn't shown up when I did, he would have. After his soldier finished with her.

Who knows how many men Akim would have let into that room? The kind of torture he would have rained down on Luna just to get even with me?

My vision is going dark on the edges. It's tunneling, narrowing until Akim is the only thing I can see.

"I would have let her choke on me if you hadn't shown up," he continues. "I would have fucked your woman until she couldn't take another second. Until she split in fucking half. Then I would have sent her pieces back to you in a coffin. She could have joined your brother. Last I heard, things aren't looking good for—"

The bat smashes against Akim's face before he can finish.

One of the nails punches through his eye. The others drive into his cheek, his temple. Blood pours down his face. He isn't smiling anymore.

My muscles are shaking with the restraint it takes not to rip his head from his body. With the effort required to not kill him from the moment I walked into the room.

But I can release it all now.

I swing the bat right and left, turning his head into fucking pulp. By the fourth swing, he's limp. He isn't moving except when I hit him. But I keep going.

When the bat breaks against his skull, I cut through the rope holding him to the chair and let his body fall to the floor.

A strangled breath forces its way out of his throat. His chest heaves with watery inhales and exhales.

I kick him in the stomach and then lower, nailing him hard in the balls. For Mariya.

Blood is oozing out of his ears and eyes. There's a sizable puddle around his head. But the fucker is *still breathing.*

Nikandr is lying in a hospital gurney, fighting for his life because Akim's man shot him in the chest, yet Akim keeps going.

"Die, you son of a bitch." I kick him in the chest, sending a spray of blood out of his mouth. "Fucking die!"

I kick him in the forehead and feel the snap. The sound of it echoes through the room.

Then, finally, he's dead.

But I'm not done. I keep kicking. I drive my heel into the empty shell of his head until I'm tired. Until I fall down in the chair bolted to the floor and stare at his wasted corpse.

He nearly took everything from me today. Mariya, Luna, my child… Nik. He might still get Nik.

Akim deserved every blow. He deserved worse. But no amount of torture could make up for any of it. Even his death isn't enough.

12

LUNA

I wake up with strong hands on my face. Calloused thumbs brushing over my cheekbones.

Yakov is standing next to my bed, repeating my name over and over again. "I'm here, Luna. You're safe."

He wipes tears off of my cheeks. I didn't even realize I was crying. For a few seconds, even while I'm staring into his stern face, I'm back in that tiny, windowless room.

Then it comes back to me.

"You're safe," Yakov croons again. He folds my hand in both of his. "I'm here."

I'm at the hospital. Yakov is with me. Akim is...

"Where were you?" I rasp. "Where did you go?"

Last night, Mariya said Yakov was going to kill Akim. She said something about a "clean-up shed," but then seemed to think better of it. When I asked what in the hell that was, she wouldn't tell me.

Yakov shakes his head. "It doesn't matter. I'm here now."

"I'm glad you're here. I just want to know what's going to happen to—"

"Dr. Jenkins is here," Yakov interrupts.

"The obstetrician? Already?" The clock above the door says it's only half past seven. "It's early. We were up most of the night. Have you even slept yet?"

"I don't need sleep."

I frown. "Everyone needs sleep."

He waves me off, but there are dark circles under his eyes. When he drags his hand through his tousled hair, I see a speck of dried blood between his fingers.

Last night was hell for me. I was terrified. But Yakov's siblings were shot. Nikandr still might not make it. And Yakov killed at least one man with his bare hands. Probably more, based on the blood I can see and smell on him.

I smooth my hand up his strong forearm. "You've been busy taking care of everyone else. Let me take care of you."

His jaw flexes. "I can take care of myself. I'm fine."

I'm about to argue, but the door to my hospital room opens.

"Knock, knock." A head of light brown hair peeks around the door frame. "Is now a good time?"

Yakov waves him in. "Come in, Doctor."

Dr. Jenkins steps inside, tiptoeing past Mariya's corner of the room. That isn't necessary—she put on noise-canceling headphones three hours ago after the nurse tried to take her blood pressure for the fourth time.

The doctor is tall and thin. He's younger than I expected one of the top obstetricians in the country to be. No older than forty, for sure.

"You must be Luna," Dr. Jenkins guesses with a broad smile. "As Yakov said, I'm Dr. Jenkins. I'm here to see how you and your baby are doing."

My hand shifts to my stomach instinctively. I told Yakov yesterday that I was fine. They used a doppler in the emergency room. We heard the heartbeat. But now that Dr. Jenkins is standing here, I'm nervous.

What if something is wrong?

What if the medications Akim gave me hurt the baby?

What if, what if, what if?

"I'm glad you're here," I admit.

He smiles warmly. "It's normal to be nervous in these early weeks. My job is going to be to ease those worries."

"Check everything," Yakov orders. "I want a full exam of Luna and the baby. Everything you've got."

Dr. Jenkins winks. "You've got it, Dad." He's surprisingly chipper for someone who just got off a plane before eight in the morning.

I'm already in a gown and lying back, so there isn't much for me to do to prepare. I watch Dr. Jenkins wheel in equipment from the hall and arrange different instruments and jellies on the table next to him. Finally, he turns to me with a blood pressure cuff. "Let's get started."

He takes my blood pressure and my temperature. When I think he's done, Yakov makes a disapproving noise and suddenly, Dr. Jenkins is back with a little hammer to check my reflexes.

It's overkill. We all know it. But Dr. Jenkins isn't going to cross Yakov. Not if he owes him a favor big enough to send him across the country on a red-eye flight for a single exam.

After everything Yakov has been through in the last twelve hours, I wouldn't dream of refusing him anything, either. If I can help put his mind at ease by playing along with this over-the-top checkup, then I will.

Finally, Dr, Jenkins leaves the room and comes back with a mobile ultrasound unit. There's a monitor in the center with an array of wands and handheld tools.

My heart instantly jolts into my throat. "We heard the heartbeat yesterday. That's good, right?"

"A heartbeat is rarely a bad thing for us humans," he says with a laugh. "How fast was it?"

I frown. "They didn't say. Should they have told me? Should I have asked?"

"No. Don't worry about it. It's just that in early pregnancy, sometimes, the mother's heart can be mistaken for the baby's. Especially when the person performing the exam isn't trained. The baby's heartbeat will be faster than yours."

"It was someone in the emergency room. I assume they were trained."

"Of course. But it's always good to call in a specialist." He grins and lifts his chin proudly. "That's why I'm here."

Yakov nods in agreement. "We should have gotten you to Dr. Jenkins weeks ago."

"That would have been hard since I didn't know I was pregnant then," I joke weakly.

Dr. Jenkins carefully lifts my hospital gown over my stomach, making sure the sheet is covering me from the waist down. "Is this pregnancy a surprise, then?"

World's biggest understatement.

"It's all been a bit of a surprise." I peek up at Yakov.

He's staring at the ultrasound screen, but he nods. "A happy surprise."

I'm still looking up at his chiseled jaw, grateful to have him standing next to me, when Dr. Jenkins squeezes warm jelly on my stomach.

"Sorry. This stuff makes a mess." He rubs it around with the handheld wand until my entire stomach is covered. Then he looks at the screen, poking and pressing the wand into my stomach. "Let's see here."

I'm not breathing. I can't. Every second Dr. Jenkins spends staring at the screen feels like an eternity.

I was out of my mind with fear and stress all day yesterday. Akim's men tossed me into the back of a van. They drugged me. I was thirsty and hungry and freezing cold. The many, many reasons why something could be wrong with our baby stack up in my mind until I've convinced myself there is no way everything is fine.

How could I have been so fucking naive?

Suddenly, Dr. Jenkins spins the screen towards me. "Say hello to your baby, Luna."

The screen is black with a little white blob in the center. Except it isn't a blob. There's a head and a little body. Tiny arms and bent legs.

It's a baby.

My baby.

Yakov grabs my hand and squeezes.

Our *baby*.

"Hello, little one," I whisper, blinking back tears.

"Twelve weeks." I blow out a long breath. "One more week and I'll be in the second trimester. That's one-third of the way through pregnancy. Can you believe that?"

Yakov is sitting in the recliner beside my bed with the sonogram in his hands. He shakes his head. "No. You don't have even a hint of a bump. Your stomach is flat as ever."

"If you're trying to flatter me, you're doing a very good job."

"I don't do flattery," he says. "I deal in honesty. You're fucking gorgeous. You're beautiful now and you'll be beautiful in a few months, too."

My face warms. "Thanks. Dr. Jenkins said I'll probably start showing in the next couple weeks."

"We'll see if he knows what he's talking about," he says.

"You're the one who flew him across the country to be here. He's the best there is. That means you'll finally trust that I'm fine, right?"

"Probably not."

"You're impossible," I laugh. "I'd be in this hospital forever if you had your way."

He arches a threatening brow. "You better hope that's not what I want. Because I always get my way."

He's joking, but he's not lying. Yakov has a way of getting exactly what he wants out of every situation and person he meets. Even with this whole deal with Akim, Yakov came out on top.

Mostly.

"How is Nik?" I ask.

Yakov glances over his shoulder towards Mariya. She's sitting up in bed with her headphones on, not paying any attention at all to us.

"Sorry," I whisper. "Is it a secret?"

He stands up and slides into the bed with me. His leg presses against mine beneath the thin hospital blanket as he takes up far more than his share of the bed. I'm not complaining.

"No. But I don't want to worry Mariya."

My heart clenches. "That means there is something to worry about?"

"There's always something to worry about," he mutters. "Mariya is still recovering. I want her to focus on resting and getting out of here."

"While you focus on her recovery and how me and the baby are doing *and* Nikandr." I lean my head against his shoulder. "That's a lot for one person to take on."

"Good thing I'm no normal person."

"That is well-documented." I squeeze his bicep. I wasn't sure I'd ever touch him again. Now, he's here and I can't get enough. "Still, you can talk to me, Yakov. I know you can handle everything on your own, but you don't have to."

He sighs. "He's in a medically-induced coma and they aren't sure if he'll ever come out of it. Even if he does, he could be brain-dead. He was without oxygen for... a while. His odds aren't great."

"I'm so sorry."

"It's not your fault."

"It's not your fault, either," I tell him softly. "None of this is your fault. I know I keep saying that, but I just... I'm worried you don't believe it."

"I'm the *pakhan*, Luna. Everything is my fault in one way or another."

"But that's not—"

"Shh." Yakov wraps his arm around my shoulders and pulls me close. He presses a kiss to my temple. "Get some rest. You're tired."

I'm not sure how he knows I'm tired before I do, but he's right. I'm exhausted.

I sink into his warmth and close my eyes. *Does he know I dreamed about this while Akim had me locked in that cell? Being close to him? Being held by him?*

I drift to sleep, his woodsy scent in my nose and wrapped around me.

When I wake up a few hours later, breathless and crying, he's still there. He strokes my cheeks and tells me that he's with me. That he isn't going anywhere.

13

YAKOV

"Son of a mother-bitching fuckbag." Mariya rips her hand away from the physical therapist's with wide eyes. *"Ouch."*

"Sorry. I know it hurts. But these exercises are important to regain full use of your hand."

This has been going on for an hour every day for the last four days. Angela stretches Mariya's hand, Mariya curses up a storm, and then they do it all over again.

Mariya holds her hand protectively against her chest. "You know, I've been thinking about that. What kind of manual labor will I actually be doing? None, right? So what would it really matter if we cut this whole therapy thing short? I won't tell if you won't."

"Suck it up and do your exercises, Mariya," I order. "Angela has places to be."

"We all have places to be," Mariya fires back. "Like my house. In my room. Where no one ever tortures me."

Except when they break through the gates and shoot you in the front lawn.

I swallow down the words. They won't help anything.

Mariya is doing okay. Better than I would have guessed after being gunned down in her own house. I don't want to be the one to remind her how much there is to be scared of.

Angela grabs Mariya's hand while she's distracted and gently stretches her fingers back. Mariya winces, but manages not to explode with creative cursing. Improvement.

"I was going to wait and tell you at the end of the session, but I think you could use the motivation now," Angela says. "I'm going to recommend to your doctor that you are ready for outpatient treatment."

Mariya's eyes go wide. "Really? Like, I can go home?"

"That's not up to me entirely. But as far as I'm concerned, yes. You'll have to talk to your other doctors and see what they recommend for your—"

"She isn't ready."

Angela lowers her head, all of her attention suddenly focused on the exercises. Mariya shoots me a glare. "You may be a know-it-all, but you're not a doctor, Yakov. You don't know what I'm ready for."

"I do know. I've been talking to your doctors."

"*Threatening* my doctors, you mean." She rolls her eyes. "They won't let you keep me here forever."

"They would, actually. For the right price, I can get whatever the fuck I want."

"I feel fine. I'm ready to g—" As the words are coming out of her mouth, Angela bends her fingers in the other direction. Mariya yelps. "Holy shitfuck. Fuck fuck. Ow."

Luna walks out of the bathroom. "Not your most creative combo, Mar."

Mariya uses her good hand to flip her off. "Something about excruciating pain isn't getting my creative juices flowing."

"Which is why you'll stay here until you aren't in excruciating pain," I tell her.

Angela deepens the stretch and Mariya's lips turn white with the effort not to scream profanities. She isn't fooling anyone.

Luna raises her brows at me as she crosses the room. She swapped her hospital gown for a pair of joggers and a matching tank yesterday. It's good to see her looking more normal, but I still grab her hand and help ease her down onto the bed.

Her breath smells like peppermint toothpaste when she leans in to whisper, "What did I miss? Is Mariya almost ready to be discharged?"

"She thinks so. But no."

"Well, what do the doctors think?"

"I don't give a fuck what they think. It's too soon."

Luna flinches at the sharp tone in my voice.

This is all new for me. Anxiety sits like a clenched fist in my chest. But there's fucking nowhere for that energy to go.

I killed Akim. He's dead and disassembled at this point. Give it a week and there won't be a trace of him left on the planet. But it feels like there's something I should be doing. I'm positive that if we leave the hospital, something bad is going to happen.

It's why I told Isay to look into the Gustev Bratva's line of succession. If this mess with Akim proves anything, it's that there is always someone left behind to pick up an old grudge. This feud between our Bratvas is already two generations deep. Why not add a third?

Akim may be gone, but there will always be enemies to face. There will always be someone coming after what is mine.

I won't let myself get blindsided again.

Isay pokes the Salisbury steak on his tray like he's expecting it to move. "Are you actually eating this shit three meals a day?"

"Only when Mariya doesn't break hospital protocol and have food delivered to her room." Which is often. "She always orders me something so I don't take her phone away."

I don't like hospital food any more than the next person, but between taking care of Luna, making sure Mariya doesn't make a break for it, and sitting with Nik, I don't have time to leave to grab anything else. I wouldn't want to.

"I don't blame her," he mutters, shoving the tray away. "It's fine. I'm not here to eat anyway."

"You have information?"

"I have whispers," he says. "Rumblings."

"I'm not interested in rumors. I'm not paying you to keep me up to date on gossip."

"It's not gossip. It's just that a lot of people still don't even believe Akim is dead. They aren't talking about succession because they're waiting for him to come back."

"They can keep fucking waiting. He's gone." I arch a brow, silently asking Isay to confirm.

He nods. "He's gone. I cleaned up the mess. There's nothing left."

Good riddance.

Isay leans in closer. "The word is that now that he's gone, Akim's younger brother is picking up the mantle."

"Pavel?" I frown. "He's not old enough for that. He can't be older than—"

"Just turned eighteen. Last month. He's an adult."

"He's a fucking *child.*"

The last time I saw him, he was eleven. Maybe younger. It was back when our fathers were pretending to play nice with one another. When the idea of an alliance between our families wasn't absurdly out of the question.

Pavel had a round, chubby face and a bag of candy in his sticky fingers. He isn't ready to be a *pakhan.*

"You were only twenty-one when you took over," Isay reminds me.

As if I need reminding.

I shake my head. "It's different. I didn't have a choice."

"Neither does Pavel. If it's not him, then the Bratva goes to his uncle. He'd lose his claim on leadership forever. He may be barely an adult, but that has to be important to him."

I sigh. "Okay. So, what? He's keeping the seat warm until he's ready to actually step up?"

Isay grimaces. "He's doing more than that. The intel I gathered says he's bringing together the men they have left and recruiting more. He's building an army, Yakov... to take you down."

It's not funny, but I laugh. I slam my fist on the table and cackle.

Because it is always fucking something. Some*one*. The world's worst game of Whack-a-Mole.

"I knew it. This is never going to end. The Gustev Bratva isn't going to stop until I eradicate every last one of them. When are they going to take a fucking hint? Now, I have to wipe out a child army?"

"Pavel is young, but we should take the threat seriously."

I nod. "Don't worry. I do. I was eighteen once, too."

And I would have done anything and faced anyone to avenge my family.

If anything, Pavel is even more dangerous than Akim. He has all of the power and none of the experience to know how to wield it.

There's no telling what he'll do.

I'm on my way to Luna and Mariya's room, still thinking about Pavel and how to squash this latest threat, when I realize the hallway is empty.

There is no one standing guard outside their room.

The moment the three people closest to me in the world were all inside this hospital, I fucking locked it down. I stationed men outside of Nik's room in the ICU, more men in front of Luna and Mariya's room, and had eyes watching every entrance or exit to the entire hospital twenty-four-fucking-seven.

But the door to their room is wide open and their beds are empty.

I try to think as my heart races. Mariya is in physical therapy. Angela wanted to take her down to the gym today so they could lift some light weights. One of the guards went with her.

When I left, Luna was taking a nap and Tomek was sitting in the chair just outside the door. *But where the fuck did they go?*

There's only one place I can think of. If she isn't there, no one is getting in or out of this hospital until I find her.

I take the stairs up to the ICU. It's faster than waiting for the elevator. As I barrel through the stairwell door and into the ICU lobby, Nik's nurse is getting off the elevator.

She starts to say hello, but I cut her off. "Where is Luna?"

"I'm sorry. Who?"

I grit my teeth. "Has anyone been in to see my brother recently?"

She frowns. "I'm not sure. My shift doesn't start for another fifteen minutes. If you have questions, you can talk to the night nurse before she leaves and—"

"There isn't time," I snarl.

The woman next to the doors waves the sign-in form at me, but I swipe her badge off of the desk instead. I hold it to the scanner until it flashes green and then shove through the now-unlocked double doors.

"He can't do that!" the woman argues.

I hear Nik's nurse correct her as the doors close behind me. "He can do whatever he wants."

The lights in the ICU are always half-dimmed. Most of the patients are resting or unconscious. Machines hum like cicadas from every room. I'm halfway down the hall before I notice the three dark figures looming outside of Nik's room. One more than usual.

Tomek turns as I approach. "What the fuck are you doing up here?" I snarl at him. "You should be downstairs."

His eyes go wide. "Shit. I should have—Luna wanted to come up here. She wanted to see Nik. I'm sorry, sir. I should have said something."

I ease down, tension flooding out of me. I'm still pissed, but *she's okay.* She's safe.

I jab a finger into Tomek's chest. "From this point forward, I know where she is *at all times.* Do you fucking hear me?"

He stands up tall. "I hear you, sir. It won't happen again."

If he'd let her out of his sight for even a second, he'd be dead. The fact that he escorted her up here and made sure she was protected is better than nothing.

I wave the men back and look through the glass door. The curtain around Nik's bed is halfway open. I can see Luna sitting next to his bed, her legs crossed at the ankle.

Then she swipes at her eyes.

She's crying.

My heart tugs towards her. *Love is loss.* It's what I've always believed. The ugly truth I discovered when my father was ripped away from my mother. *Someone is always left behind.*

Luna reaches out and, navigating the maze of tubes and IVs sticking out of him, grabs Nik's hand. Her thumb brushes over his knuckles. Her lips are moving, but I can't hear what she's saying through the glass.

I don't need to.

What I need to do is everything in my power to protect these people. I won't lose them again.

14

LUNA

Mariya sticks her head through the open car window, her good arm flailing in the wind as she screams, "Freedom!"

"Sit the fuck down, Braveheart," Yakov barks. I bite back a laugh and he turns his scowl in my direction. "Don't encourage her."

"She doesn't need my help to be excitable."

Mariya drops down into her seat, dark hair windblown. "You should try it, Luna! The fresh air feels nice."

"You were in a hospital, not a prison," Yakov grumbles.

Yakov is right, but so is Mariya. After days spent under fluorescents breathing in antiseptic, the fresh air and sunshine feels amazing. Not stick-my-head-out-the-window-like-a-dog amazing. But amazing, nonetheless.

"Maybe later," I say with a smile. "I'm feeling a little nauseous right now."

Yakov's hands tighten on the wheel. "Did you take your vitamins this morning? Dr. Jenkins said you should keep up the B6 supplements throughout the rest of your pregnancy. If you're hungry, I can stop and buy something. Do you want a breakfast sandwich?"

"Yes!" Mariya chimes from the backseat. "Sausage and egg with a hashbrown. And an iced vanilla latte."

Yakov ignores her, flicking his gaze back and forth from the road to me. His green eyes bore into mine.

"I took all the vitamins Dr. Jenkins left for me and I'm not hungry." I smile. "It's just normal pregnancy nausea. Really. I feel great."

He exhales irritably just as Mariya leans forward. "So are we still getting breakfast sandwiches or…?"

Yakov shakes his head. "We're going home."

Home. When Yakov first brought me to the mansion, all I could think about was when I would leave. I was constantly preparing myself to get back to the "real world."

Now, living in the mansion with Yakov *is* the real world. It's where I want to be.

But even then, it isn't *home.* Because when Yakov was avoiding me and I didn't see him for days, the mansion felt cold and empty. I'd never felt more alone.

No, home isn't a place. It's a person.

It's Yakov.

Yakov pulls through the front gates of the mansion, a line of black SUVs rolling in behind us. As soon as I see the wide expanse of grass and the curve of the driveway leading to the front doors, I clench. My chest tightens until it's hard to breathe. I grip the door handle and try to keep a neutral expression pasted on my face even as a movie plays behind my eyes.

I can see the line of dark-clad men walking across the grass towards the mansion like it's happening all over again.

I hear the distant gunshots taking out Yakov's men one by one.

My heart races like I'm back in that night, even though the sun is high in the sky and Yakov is right next to me.

When the car stops, Mariya jumps out and jogs up the steps. "I am going to take a nap in my bed so freaking hard."

"Go ahead," Yakov calls after her. "We'll catch up." He walks around the car and kneels just outside of the open passenger door. "Are you okay?"

"Peachy," I mumble between clenched teeth. I drop my face in my hands. "I take it I wasn't hiding my feelings as well as I hoped."

"You're easy to read."

I groan. "This is so stupid. I'm being ridiculous."

"You're not."

"I am," I insist. "I know I'm safe. I know Akim is dead and no one is coming for me. So why doesn't my body know that?"

His hand spreads out across my thigh. "You've been through a lot, Luna. It's normal to need time to recover from that."

"Mariya didn't need time to recover." I gesture to where she already disappeared through the front door.

"Mariya was born into this world. Plus, she's a teenager. She thinks she's immortal."

"She just got shot," I argue.

"And survived." He rolls his eyes. "As far as she's concerned, that's even more proof. She's going to be impossible to keep track of now."

I smile, but my chest still aches. I can't force myself to step out of the safety of the car. "I'm happy to be back. I *want* to be here."

"I know." Yakov's hand slides up my leg slowly. His fingers brush along my inner thigh. The tingling low in my stomach is a nice distraction from the panic in my brain. "Take your time."

"Keep touching me like that and I'll sit here forever."

"Fine by me." Yakov smirks. It's the first hint of a real smile I've seen from him in days. Maybe longer. "But there's a lot more security around the mansion now. I don't think you want an audience for all the things I'm going to do to you once you're ready."

I'm ready now, I want to say. It's partially true. Where Yakov is concerned, I'm always ready.

But I'm currently so terrified that I can't even stand up and walk into the mansion on my own. Orgasming would be a nice distraction, but I don't want to use Yakov as a distraction.

He's more to me than that. *We* are more than that.

My face is burning hot as I take his hand and let him help me out of the car. I stand on unsteady legs and Yakov presses his lips to my ear. "I've got you, Luna. I'll never let anyone hurt you."

My eyes flutter closed. "I don't think even you can make that promise."

"How many times do I have to tell you?" he asks, pulling back to look down at me. "I can do whatever the fuck I want."

With his chiseled jawline and broad shoulders blocking out the world around me, I'm inclined to believe him.

Yakov helps me up the stairs and into the house. As soon as I'm through the front door, Gregory is making a figure-eight around my ankles. His tail swishes back and forth as he meows at my feet.

Guilt gnaws at my stomach. I was so distracted by everything else that I didn't even think about Gregory.

"Has he been fed? The front door was wide open when I was—" *Kidnapped.* I swallow down the word. "Did he run off? Who brought him back? Is he—"

"He's fine," Hope calls from the hallway.

She's walking towards us, a dish towel thrown over her shoulder. I'm not sure why, but tears fill my eyes at the sight of Yakov's maid. The normalcy of it all is overwhelming. "It's so good to see you."

Hope grins. "I'm glad you're back. Gregory is, too. He spent most of his time yowling at the bedroom door and in front of Yakov's office. He missed you both."

I reach down and scratch behind his fuzzy ears. "I missed you, too, buddy."

Yakov closes the front door and grabs me gently by the elbow. "Come on. You should sit down."

"I'm okay. I actually feel—"

"Hope," Yakov orders, "bring Luna some water. A snack, too."

Hope nods and is already turning towards the kitchen.

"I'm okay. Really. I feel a lot—"

"You need to rest."

Yakov leads me to the sitting room, lays a blanket over my lap, and turns on the television.

And there we stay.

It's nice to slow down with him and not have nurses and doctors interrupting every hour. But it's also… strange. I've never seen Yakov sit still for so long before. He's always busy, running off to some meeting or slipping away to talk on the phone. Now, he doesn't seem to have anywhere else to be.

I suppose that's because Akim is dead. The threat is gone. We're all safe. So now, Yakov seems to have funneled all of that extra energy into never letting me out of his sight.

I can't say I mind.

15

LUNA

Since we got back, we've eaten every meal together, he's taken me on short walks through the garden, and he's slept next to me every night.

"If you two don't move, you're going to fuse to that couch," Mariya warns from the doorway.

"Where have you been?" Yakov asks.

"My room." Mariya narrows her eyes. "Is that okay with you or did I need to ask for permission?"

"You always need to ask for permission."

Mariya snorts. "I don't see why. There are enough guards here that you probably know what I'm up to before I do."

In addition to the extra guards placed at the entrances to the property, a few men take turns doing sweeps of the interior and exterior of the house once every few hours. I'd say it's overkill, but it has actually been really comforting.

"That's the idea," Yakov drawls.

He's watching the television, so he doesn't see Mariya fuming in the hallway. I catch her eye and shake my head. They've both been through a lot. Now that things are calm, they should both be able to enjoy it.

Mariya, however, has other plans.

"I'm not going to live like this, Yakov," she snaps. "We were never under surveillance like this before. This is too much. When Otets was alive—"

"When Otets was alive, the Gustev Bratva was going after him. Not you."

"No one was after *me*. They were after Luna."

I sink down into the couch. If she isn't going to take my advice, the least she could do is leave me out of it. The name of my recovery game the last couple days has been Distraction and Denial.

I figure that if I don't think about the attack, the memories will eventually become hazy. And if I can ignore the fact that an entire criminal organization wanted to murder me just to emotionally torture Yakov, then I'll feel a lot better about bringing a child into this world.

Yakov throws an arm over the back of the couch and turns to face her. "They fucking shot you, Mariya. What more proof do you need?"

"Only because I got between them and Luna. If I'd stayed inside, everything would have been fine."

That's definitely not true. Mariya put herself in the line of fire, but they were coming into the mansion one way or another. If Mariya hadn't fought, she might have been in that cell with me.

"Good. We're in agreement," Yakov growls.

Mariya gives him a cautious look. "We're in agreement about what?"

"That if you stay inside, everything will be fine," he says.

Her eyes flare wide. "What? No! That is not what I was saying."

"But it *is* what I'm saying. If you want to leave the property, I need to be with you. Or I need to assign a guard to go with you."

"Fuck that! You saw the security tapes," she argues. "I was fighting three of Akim's men *by myself* before that coward pulled a gun. I can take care of myself. Especially now that Akim is dead."

"Akim being dead isn't some magic fix, Mariya. You're in even more danger now."

I turn to him. "What?"

The word is out of my mouth before I can stop it.

I thought this was all over. That's why Yakov has been relaxing around the house. It's why he's been spending time with me at home.

We're safe...

Aren't we?

"What the fuck does that mean?" Mariya snaps. "He's dead. You killed him. Why would we be in more danger—"

"Taking down a target like Akim is always going to make more enemies. It never ends."

Mariya's mouth falls open. "I thought..."

She doesn't finish her sentence. How could she? There's nothing to say.

Yakov sounds exhausted. And he's the one who grew up in this world. He was trained for this. *What about me?*

"People are always going to come out of the woodwork to try and take down the man at the top. Unless you want to be collateral damage, I suggest you listen to me."

Mariya doesn't look happy—far from it. But she doesn't argue. After a few seconds, she turns and stomps down the hall to her room.

Yakov lays his head on the back of the couch with a sigh. I should reach out and make sure he's okay. Or offer to talk to Mariya. I should make myself useful. But I can't talk around the lump in my throat. Yakov just dumped a new reality in my lap and I need to sort through it.

I'm always going to be in danger. My child is always going to be in danger. Akim was just the first in a long line of enemies to come. This fight is what our life will be like from this point on. It never ends.

It. Never. Fucking. Ends.

I blink back tears as I stand up. "I'm going to go lie down."

Yakov tenses. "Are you feeling okay?"

No.

"Just tired." I give him a tight smile. I swear there are actual cracks in my flimsy mask.

"I'll come with you."

"That's okay. I'm just going to sleep. You can stay and—"

He stands up and scoops me into his arms before I can finish. "I'm tired, too."

"Not too tired to carry me."

His eyebrow arches playfully, but the emotion doesn't reach his mouth. "I'm never too tired for that."

Yakov carries me to our room and lays me in bed. I dreamed about being here with him. I've always felt safe here in his room. Now, I'm not so sure there is such a thing. Yakov, this life we've built, our child… It could all be taken from me without warning.

I roll onto my side as tears burn in my eyes. Yakov drapes his arm over my waist and I swallow down the sob in my throat. I squeeze my eyes closed and pretend to fall asleep.

16

YAKOV

I reach for my phone for the fifth—no, sixth time. The sixth time in as many minutes.

I can't stop myself.

I know the mansion is under lock and key. There's a guard for every square foot, which is a lot of fucking guards. And yet, I can't stop checking the security cameras to make sure the gates are locked, the house is shut up tight, and Mariya and Luna are safely inside.

I drop my hand. "I'm losing my goddamn mind out here, Nik."

My brother doesn't move. He hasn't moved in days unless a nurse repositions him to redo his IV. But I keep expecting it, anyway.

"You'd be so pissed that you're unconscious right now and can't hear any of this, but it turns out you were good at your job. Gathering intel, plugging holes, and keeping tabs on things. It allowed me to handle other shit. But now..." I shake my head. "All I can think about is how to keep everyone safe."

The worst part of it all is that no matter what I do, I can't change a single thing about Nik's situation. It's too late. Whatever happens from this point on is up to him and his doctors. I just have to sit here… and wait.

Even then, what the hell am I waiting for? He might wake up and be a completely different person. He may never talk again. He could have lasting brain damage that will change everything.

I drag a hand down my jaw. "Apparently, Akim's little brother is rising up to avenge his death. Inconvenient, even if I understand the impulse." My eyes follow the tube out of Nik's mouth, across the bandage on his chest. "I was never going to let Akim get away after what his men did to you. The difference is that Akim deserved what he got. If Pavel wasn't so green, he'd probably see that and back off." I snort and say what I'm positive Nik would say if he could. "Or not. The Gustev Bratva isn't known for their discretion."

The Gustevs have been a problem for years. I thought striking back and answering their attacks with our own would convince them to keep their heads down. But they don't know when to quit.

Now, it isn't just me at risk. It's my siblings. It's Luna. It's the future of our family.

I run my hands through my hair. "I don't know how Otets handled this, Nik. Being a *pakhan* and a husband and a father. He trained me to follow in his footsteps, but he was never scared. He never acted like he was worried about me. But I'm—*fuck*, I'm terrified for what all of this will mean for Luna and our kid."

I stare at the floor between my feet and run through all of my security measures once, twice, a hundred fucking times. I try to convince myself that I'm doing everything I can to control this situation, but it doesn't feel like enough.

I'm not sure it will ever be enough.

I'm still staring at the floor when the door behind me opens. "Oh, Mr. Kulikov," a female voice says. "I didn't realize you were still here."

I look over my shoulder and Dr. Tung is in the doorway. She's an older woman with white streaks in her dark hair. I haven't seen much of her since Nik's surgery, but the nurses keep telling me how busy she is. Apparently, she's the best of the best. Either way, I trust her to take care of my brother. It's just about the biggest compliment I can give.

I glance at the clock and somehow, hours have passed. "Time got away from me," I say.

She gives me a tight smile. "That's okay. It's good to talk to him. The more, the better."

"Can he even hear me?"

"We don't know for sure, but studies show that talking to patients in a coma can only help. Especially when they know the voices. When it's someone they love. That connection can help guide them back."

It all sounds a little woo-woo to me. I turn to face her. "I'm going to ask a question and I need you to be honest with me. No bullshit."

"I'm not into bullshitting," she says sincerely.

"Is there a real chance he recovers?"

Dr. Tung looks at Nikandr. She tilts her head to one side and studies him. "Yes. There's always a chance."

"And there's a chance that the ceiling caves in and I'm crushed under a hospital bed," I snap. "But it isn't likely. What are his chances? Really?"

She chews on the corner of her mouth and then seems to decide something. She looks at me. "I never discount anyone. Miracles happen all the time. But... you should limit your expectations. That's what I can tell you. Miracles happen, but don't expect one."

As soon as I step out of the hospital, my phone buzzes. It's Isay.

"What news do you have for me?"

Something good, for fuck's sake.

"Nothing yet," he says. "But I'm requesting permission to follow Pavel."

I frown. "Why weren't we already doing that?"

Because Nik is in the hospital. My brother would have been following Pavel from the moment he became a threat. He wouldn't have asked for permission. Nik knew what I wanted from him without me needing to say it.

"There was no explicit order given," Isay says. "But now that the threat is credible, I want to learn more about him."

"Yes. Obviously. Gather everything you can. I want to know where he is going, who he is meeting with, and what he is planning," I tell him. "If he so much as pisses the wrong way, I want to know about it."

Isay assures me he'll gather everything he can and report back as soon as possible.

But when I climb in my car, I don't drive home. I drive to the garage where Akim kept Luna. I park down the street and watch the shattered windows, waiting for movement. For some sign that the Gustev Bratva is planning something.

After a few hours, I make the rounds, driving past Gustev-owned clubs and bars. I look for Pavel. If I could take him out now—a quick hit-and-run—it would save a lot of trouble down the road. Maybe it would finally be the end of this feud.

But I don't see him. I don't see anything.

It's after ten when I get back. Luna is still sitting up in bed when I walk through the door.

"You're still up," I observe, closing the door behind me.

"It's hard to sleep when..." She looks at my side of the bed. "I just couldn't sleep."

I stayed away on purpose. Seeing Nik and talking to Dr. Tung didn't exactly put a spring in my step. As much as I wish I did, I don't trust Isay the way I trust Nik. Luna has been through enough that I didn't want to bring her down with all of my shit.

Not that it isn't already too late for that. I've already brought her down. Akim kidnapped her because of me. Now, she's traumatized and can't sleep without me next to her.

"I should have come back sooner." I pull my shirt over my head and ball it in my fists before chucking it into the closet.

"No, I'm fine. I'm okay. You were with Nik, right?" she asks. "How is he?"

"Same. Critical, but stable."

She sighs. "I'm sorry."

"Why? None of this is your fault."

"I know. It's not your fault, either." She pushes the blankets down and shifts to the edge of the bed. She presses her hand flat to my bare chest. "You didn't cause any of this. And you know that Nik wouldn't change anything about that night."

She's right. I know she is. My brother was stubborn. He liked to play the hero. Some petty part of him would love to know he's in a coma for backing me up and following me loyally into gunfire.

None of that helps me, though. It doesn't change a single fucking thing.

"That's good, because he can't. Neither can I. We can't go back and fix it. I can't fix it now, either. There isn't a damn thing I can do to make any of this better."

She rises on her knees and pulls me closer. Her hand is over my heart. "You're making things better for me. You being here... it helps. When I'm alone or asleep, my brain goes right back to that cell. But I can't think about any of that when you're in front of me. You help me relax."

Her eyes are hooded and I'm hard. Instantly.

I want her. Of course I do. But she was in the hospital only a few days ago. She was kidnapped and imprisoned before that. I found her with a half-naked man straddling her in a cell. I'm not going to push her.

"How about a bath?" I ask instead of ravishing her the way every cell in my body wants to do. "That would help you relax."

That's something I can do. A way I can help.

Luna licks her bottom lip. Then she leans forward until her full mouth presses softly to mine. My hand tightens on her waist. It takes every ounce of self-control I possess not to throw her back on the bed and taste every inch of her.

She pulls back slowly. "A bath would actually be amazing."

How about a cold shower? I could go for one of those.

17

YAKOV

"This is a shitty joke, Isay." I kick my feet up on my desk.

It's the first time in almost two weeks that I've been in my office. Gregory must have missed my presence here, because he darted through my legs to get into the room before I could close the door. Now, he's curled in a ball in his bed in the corner.

"It's not a joke, sir. All of the information I have is saying that Pavel has no plans to seek revenge."

"That doesn't make any sense."

I flip through the folder of information Isay put together on Pavel. He was kicked out of three boarding schools for extreme, unwarranted violence. It's not unusual in our world. Pavel was the spare to his brother's heir. That can come with a fuck load of resentment.

My father never made Nikandr feel like a backup in case anything ever happened to me, but a lot of fathers in our world aren't afraid to funnel all of their resources into the eldest son and neglect the others.

Pavel was the useless second son and his parents never let him forget it. But apparently, when I took out their father, Akim stepped up for

Pavel. He covered up his messes with school and gave him a position within the Bratva. Akim was the parent Pavel never had.

And I just killed him.

"Pavel wants revenge," I say flatly. "There's no way he doesn't want to kill me for taking away his brother. I would if I was him."

"All I can tell you is what I'm seeing and hearing. Right now, Pavel has his nose deep in the other Gustev businesses. The raid we conducted to save Luna decimated their highest-ranking lieutenants. He has a lot of rebuilding to do. It doesn't look like revenge is high on his to-do list."

That would be good news... if it was true.

"Keep watching him," I order. "If you hear or see anything strange, I want to know about it."

"Yes, sir."

I hang up with Isay and lean back in my chair.

It doesn't make any sense. I'd love to believe Pavel Gustev has no intention of coming after me for murdering his brother, but I know better. I've been around long enough to know that taking out someone like Akim always has consequences.

I'd like to have a better idea of when I'm going to face them.

I'm thinking, listening to the sound of Gregory purring next to me, when the cat suddenly jolts out of his bed. The fur on his back and shoulders is standing up.

"What is it?" I reach down to pet him, but Gregory darts away and meows at the door.

I open the door to let him out... and I hear it.

Crying.

I don't think—I just move. I sprint down the hallway and throw the door to my bedroom open.

Luna is lying in bed and thrashing. The blankets are churning as she whimpers and cries out. I scan every last corner of the room to make sure there isn't a threat. But the room is empty.

Lune is alone. She's dreaming.

Gregory seems to realize there isn't an imminent threat at the same time I do and disappears down the hall. But I jog towards the bed and grab Luna's hand.

Her fingers are ice-cold.

I press my thumb into her palm and smooth her clenched fist. "It's okay, Luna. It's a dream." I stroke my hand up her arm and down the other.. "I'm here. It's okay."

Slowly, her eyes flutter open. "Yakov?"

"You're okay. It was just a dream."

She blinks up at me like she's amazed I'm in front of her. Then she launches out of bed and wraps her arms around my neck. "You're here."

I should have been there. *She never should have been alone in that cell.*

"I'm here. You're safe."

I lower her back down to the bed and wrap my arm around her waist. She tucks herself against my front and seals her body to mine like she's afraid I'll disappear. There isn't a breath of space between us.

I hold her like that until her breathing levels out and she's asleep. At some point, I fall asleep, too.

Only to wake up to Luna screaming again.

It can't have been more than an hour since the last time she woke up. Her hands are fisted in the sheets. She's bucking against me, fighting to get my arm off of her waist. "No," she rasps. "No, no."

I hold her tighter, my lips against her ear. "It's me, Luna. It's me."

She goes still, but her body is rigid. She feels like a board in my arms.

"Yakov." She sighs, sagging into the mattress. She pulls my arm further around her until my hand is over her racing heart.

"Your heart is pounding."

It should be pounding because I'm inside of her. Because she's falling apart around my cock and screaming for more. That's the only reason this woman should ever be trembling in my bed. The fact that there are other demons tearing her apart is my fucking fault. My fucking failure.

"It was a bad dream. I'm sorry I woke you up."

She readjusts and my hand slides under the neck of her shirt. I feel the curve of her breast against my fingers. Her ass presses back into me.

I'm rock-hard. Sleeping with her against me was too much for my subconscious to handle. When Luna shifts, she brushes my erection. I know she feels it.

"I don't mind." I fight to keep my voice even. "Do you want to talk about it or go back to sleep?"

She slides my hand lower over her chest and grinds her ass against me. "I don't want to talk *or* go back to sleep."

My cock twitches. It would be so easy to take her like this. One zipper, one shift of her panties. It would be nothing.

She needs more time. She isn't ready.

"What do you want then?" My voice sounds huskier than normal.

Luna turns to face me. Her cheeks are flushed as she straddles my hips and settles her ass over my hard length. I can feel every curve of her body through the thin material of my t-shirt.

"I want a distraction."

I grip her hips. I mean to hold her still, but I slide her against me instead. "You're not ready. It's too soon."

"Says who?" she asks. "I'm ready. I want you, Yakov."

Fucking hell. "You're making it hard to do the right thing here."

"Denying us both what we want isn't the right thing." She leans forward and kisses my neck. Her breath is hot against my skin as she whispers, "I'm ready."

I grip her chin and force her pouty lips away from me. "I'm not touching you until I talk to Dr. Jenkins. I need to know this is safe for you and the baby."

"Yakov, I'm fine!"

"When those words come from a medical professional, I'll believe them."

She's still straddling me as she sits up and frowns. "You're really not going to touch me?"

"I'm really not." *No matter how fucking badly I want to.*

Her eyebrow arches. I see the idea spark in her eyes. But I don't understand what it is until she slides down the bed and drags her hands down my thighs. "I didn't hear anything about *me* touching *you.*"

She strokes her hand over the bulge in my pants. I catch my breath and then reach down and catch her wrist.

"Giving you a blowjob will not endanger me or the baby," she argues.

"The danger is that taking your mouth will *never* be enough for me," I growl. "I'll have to take all of you. And I'm not doing that until I talk to—"

"Then call Dr. Jenkins! You're paying him to be on call twenty-four hours a day. Ring him up and ask."

"It's two in the morning."

She uses her other hand to drag my zipper down. My hold on my self-control grows weak as she slips her hand inside my pants and circles my twitching cock. When she parts her lips and takes me deep into her throat, it snaps entirely.

I grab my phone from the nightstand and call Dr. Jenkins.

"Mr. Kulikov?" he mumbles. His voice sounds thick. "Is everything okay?"

"Just a quick question about—" Luna swallows me and hums. The vibrations almost send me into the fucking ether. "—physical activity. Luna's physical activity. Can she… partake?"

Luna smirks and drags her tongue up my underside. She's very proud of herself. Depending on the next words out of Dr. Jenkins' mouth, I'll make sure she pays dearly.

"I don't understand the question," Dr. Jenkins croaks.

I fist my hand in Luna's hair as she dives deep again, bobbing her head faster and faster. "Are there any restrictions to what Luna can do? Physically?"

"Oh. Um, no," he says sleepily. "Her pregnancy is progressing normally. Normal activity is allowed. Encouraged, actually. Staying physical is important for a healthy mom and healthy baby."

The things I want to do to Luna are not "normal." I have plans. Lots of plans.

So I blurt it out. "Can she have sex? Are there any restrictions to what she can and can't do sexually? Will I hurt her or the baby if I fuck her —hard?"

Dr. Jenkins makes a choking sound. Then he clears his throat. "I see. Well, no, there is no concern for her or the baby at this point. As I said, she can participate in any... um... *activity* she would have participated in prior to pregnancy. There is no danger—"

"Good."

I throw my phone on the floor, roll Luna onto her back, and hover over her. "You were playing a dangerous game."

"I think it's about to pay off for me, though." She curls her hand around my neck. "I can't believe you woke Dr. Jenkins up at two in the morning to ask if we can have sex."

"You didn't give me a choice."

I haul my t-shirt up around her waist and kiss my way down her stomach. There's a slight bump now where it used to be flat. Knowing she is growing with my child sparks a level of possessiveness I didn't know I was capable of.

I fold my hands over her stomach. "I love knowing you're carrying my baby. That there's a part of me inside of you."

"I wouldn't mind another part of you being inside me if you—"

I drop down, shove her panties aside, and drag my tongue over her slit. I lick up and down her seam and explore every fold of her until she's rolling against my mouth.

I lap my tongue over her clit and it's instantaneous. Luna explodes, writhing against my mattress for all the best kinds of reasons as I lap her up.

"You taste so fucking sweet," I snarl, crawling back over her.

Her cheeks are flushed and she's breathing heavily. I direct her arms over her head and pull her shirt off.

Her nipples are pebbled. When I flick my tongue over one, she flinches. "I'm so sensitive. I've never come that fast before. I think it's the hormones or—" She rakes her hand through my hair as I suck her breast into my mouth and take bites out of her soft flesh, her collarbone.

"It's that you were made to be fucked by me, Luna."

I pull back and look down at her, golden hair spread out across my pillow. Her blue eyes are glazed from her first orgasm, but they're happy.

She's happy.

She's safe.

She's mine.

I wrap one of her legs over my hip, position myself against her opening, and press in. I slip into her inch by inch, watching as her lips part.

"Yakov," she breathes. She holds me tighter, cinching her leg around my lower back to bring me closer. "Fill me. Please. I want you deep."

I growl against her neck and bury myself to the hilt.

"I've wanted to do this since the moment I heard you were pregnant." I slide out of her and drive in again.

She moans. "I should have told you sooner then."

How many things would be different if she had? I shove the thought away. We crash together again and again until she's glistening with sweat and I'm breathless.

I'm strung tight, ready to fucking explode. "Come for me, Luna." I pin her hands to the mattress and thrust into her, driving her into the pillows. "I want to feel you around me."

Not even a second later, she cries out as her body clamps down.

"Good girl. Come for me just like that."

Pulse after pulse of pleasure moves through her, and I feel every wave. I don't stand a chance. I curse into her skin as I spill into her.

When we've caught our breath, I haul her back against my chest again and hold her until she falls asleep.

But I lie there awake for a long time, listening to every inhale and exhale. Waiting for the ghosts in her mind to resurface.

I tell myself she's safe… but for how much longer?

18

LUNA

I wave my hands when Yakov comes at me with a second plate of blinis and eggs. "I'm full. I swear!"

"You barely ate anything," he argues. "You're eating for two now."

"I don't think that's true. The baby is still teeny."

At fifteen weeks, the baby is just a little over four inches long. Mariya downloaded a pregnancy app on her phone and loves keeping me updated on what animal the baby is closest to in size. Last week, it was a clownfish. Now, I'm carrying a gerbil, apparently.

"It will stay teeny if you keep skipping breakfast." He narrows his eyes at me. "Eat."

Outwardly, I groan. Inwardly, my heart is bursting.

Yakov has been protective of me since the moment he found out I was pregnant. But ever since Dr. Jenkins gave us the all-clear for sex, he has been on another level.

"You know, I think this has less to do with the baby and more to do with you wanting my bump to grow." I fork a bite of blini into my mouth. "It's time to admit it, Yakov. You are turned on by my baby bump."

"I already admitted it. Last night, while you were spread out on the bed in front of me," he says, his voice a deep rumble I feel all the way down to my toes. "And again this morning when you were on top, riding me until you—"

"I remember," I squeak out, suddenly flushed.

You look so fucking good carrying my baby, he said, gripping my hips. *I could watch you do this for the rest of my life.*

Between the guards and Yakov's household staff, there are way too many people in this mansion for me to get hot and bothered in the middle of the kitchen right now.

"So I was thinking this morning," I say, changing the subject, "that the name Olivia is really beautiful."

"Too bad we're having a boy," he fires back, "named Yuri."

"As the person carrying the baby *inside of her body*, I think I would know."

He leans over the island, dark eyebrow arched. "And as the man who *put that baby inside of your body*, I'm positive it's a boy."

So much for not getting hot and bothered in the middle of the kitchen.

"You're wrong. But even if you're not, it doesn't matter to me. I just want a healthy baby."

"I'm right," he insists. "And I want a healthy baby, too. I just also want to live in a house where I'm not outnumbered by females."

I laugh. "Are you afraid of us or something?"

"I'm not afraid of anything, but that doesn't mean I want you all ganging up on me all the time."

"I am *always* on your team, Yakov." I carry my plate over to the sink and stretch on my toes to kiss his stubbled cheek. "Except right now. Because you think I'm having a boy and I'm so clearly pregnant with a little baby girl."

Yakov stretches his hand across my stomach and bends down, biting my lower lip. All the blood in my body pools between my legs. I'm instantly lightheaded and buzzing with desire.

Yakov's eyes darken. "Whatever you're thinking right now, save it for later when we're alone."

I fan my face. "These pregnancy hormones are turning me into an animal. I feel like I'm in heat."

"Well, I have plans right now. But if you want a distraction, I was going to see if you wanted to invite Kayla over."

I inhale sharply. "Really? She can come here? Today? It's safe?"

"She can if you want her to. It's safe."

"I want." I throw my arms around his waist. "Thank you."

Yakov kisses the top of my head and starts to hand me his phone… right as it rings.

He checks the number. I know before he tells me that it's the hospital because his mouth flattens into that familiar disappointed line. "Just a second."

Yakov turns away and takes the call, pacing back and forth as he talks to Nik's doctors.

Every morning around this time, they give Yakov a call to tell him how Nik did over the night. The calls are short, but they linger in the air for a long time afterward. This time is no different.

"Any news?" I ask when Yakov turns around.

He grips his phone in white knuckles, the shadows in his eyes a few shades darker. "It's the same as always. No improvement."

A few weeks ago, I would have searched for the exact right words to say to make Yakov feel better. I would have twisted here on the spot, desperate to hold him, but too afraid to make a move.

Now, I close the distance between us, wrap my arms around his tapered waist, and whisper against his chest, "Are you okay?"

"I'm fine."

"You're always fine," I say softly. "That doesn't mean there isn't something on your mind."

He takes a deep breath. "It's bizarre that my life is moving on without Nik here. He should be here for this. And even though you're still pregnant, he'd be whispering curse words to your stomach and trying to corrupt our kid."

"He absolutely would be doing that," I chuckle. "But you never know… he still might. There's time—"

"The doctor told me not to expect a miracle."

I squeeze him tighter. "Okay. So *you* don't expect a miracle; *I* will. Balance."

"I don't want you to be disappointed, either."

"I don't think I will be disappointed." I lean back to look at him. "Nik should have died that night. Technically, he did. But he's still here clinging on three weeks later. I think that means something."

Yakov shrugs but doesn't say anything.

I wish my hope could rub off on him. The entire Kulikov family are born-and-bred fighters. There is no way Nik is going out without one hell of a fight.

"Does your mom know what happened yet?"

Yakov stiffens. "Not yet."

"Are you going to—"

"I can't," he says sharply. "Not yet. She's... fragile. She was always closest with Nikandr. If I tell her how he's doing, it would make things worse for her. Especially now that she's all alone."

I chew on my lower lip. "I know you're trying to take care of her, but this isn't really your call to make."

"Everything is my call."

"When it comes to the Bratva, yes. But she's his mother. I know I don't know exactly what that's like yet... but I have an idea." I lay a hand over my stomach. "If she finds out from someone else that Nik is in the hospital and then something happened before she could get here to see him, she would be heartbroken."

His face is unreadable. I've gotten pretty good at reading Yakov over the last few months, but there are still times where he can shut me out entirely.

Now is one of those times.

Before I can pry under the surface and figure out what is going on, his phone vibrates.

"I have to go."

"Is it the hospital?" I ask.

"Business," he says. Just before he leaves the room, he adds, "I'll text Kayla the plan and arrange a car for her."

I smile. "Thanks."

He nods, face still expressionless, and leaves.

19

LUNA

I watch from the front porch as the black car carrying Kayla pulls down the driveway.

How long will it take before I don't think about Akim's van in the driveway? Before I stop imagining a line of men in dark clothes advancing on the mansion, guns in their hands?

It's broad daylight. I'm surrounded by guards. Yakov is in his office less than fifty feet away.

I'm safe. My mind knows it, but my body isn't on board.

When Kayla steps out of the car, I shake off my nerves as best I can and meet her in front of the stairs. "It's so good to see you!" I call, bouncing from one foot to the other.

I throw my arms wide, but Kayla steps in for a side hug.

"Wow. That's the first time in years I haven't had to beg you to stop hugging me so I could breathe."

"I don't want to deprive the baby of oxygen," she explains. But she eyes my stomach like I might be packing a bomb under there. "How are you feeling?"

"Good. Great. But let's talk about it inside where the snacks are."

She smiles politely and follows me inside.

It's all very un-Kayla.

I wave my arm over the snack spread. "Cheese and crackers, fruit, and raw vegetables if we're feeling responsible. But between you and me, there are caramel ice cream cones in the freezer for when we start feeling irresponsible later."

She folds her hand on the countertop. "Sounds good."

I nod. She nods. The tension between us is like one of those inflatable men in front of a car dealership. It's flapping around, begging for someone to point it out, but neither of us want to.

"We could go swimming," I suggest.

"I didn't bring my suit."

"I have one you can borrow if—"

"And I might have to cut out early."

"Oh." I sound as disappointed as I feel.

This is the first time I've had to spend with Kayla in weeks. Aside from a few text exchanges and one brief phone call, we haven't had any time to catch up. I expected us to hug and jump and cry in the driveway, gorge ourselves on ice cream, and talk nonstop for hours.

I guess not.

"Where's Yakov?" Kayla asks, looking around like he might be lurking under the dining room table. "His text was pretty vague. I thought he might be around."

"He's around. Just not *around* around."

She frowns.

"He's working," I clarify. "In his office. I think he wanted to give us time alone together."

"Oh."

More tension. More inflatable men flapping between us.

I sigh. "Actually, I think I scared Yakov off by telling him he should talk to his mother about his brother, who is still in the ICU and might not make it. I stepped into his family business and made things weird. Almost as weird as things are between us."

Kayla sags against the counter. "That's rough. Because things are *really* weird between us, Loon. What in the hell is happening here?"

Just like that, the tension disappears.

Tears well in my eyes. Kayla's lower lip trembles. And then we crash together in a hug so tight I have to beg Kayla to let me go so I can breathe.

"I've missed you." She squeezes me, swaying us both from right to left. "I've barely heard from you and it has been so scary. There was stuff in the news about Yakov's brother, but nothing about you. I didn't know where you were and you weren't answering your phone and—"

"I should have called you more. Everything was so crazy that I lost track of time. But that's no excuse."

She pulls back to look at me. "It's kind of an excuse. I mean, you were in the hospital. What even happened with that? Was it about the baby or...?"

I wince. "You're gonna want to grab a snack. We have *a lot* to cover."

As quickly and efficiently as I can with Kayla interrupting me every other word to gasp and curse, I tell her what happened with Akim.

"It was scary, but I was only there for one night. Yakov got me out of there as soon as he could."

Kayla drops the carrot stick she's been nibbling on and grabs my hand. "You were fucking *kidnapped*, Loon. That's insane. That one night had a lifetime's worth of trauma. Goodbye to assuming the best in people. Hello to decades of therapy."

I chew on my lower lip. "It's not that bad. I'm okay."

She shakes her head. "Bullshit. I saw your face when I pulled up. You're pregnant. You should be glowing. But you looked pale. You *still* look pale."

"I think the 'glowing pregnant woman' thing is a myth. I've been barfing for three months straight."

"Has Yakov even taken you to see a doctor yet?" she asks, no small amount of judgment in her voice.

"He actually called in a favor with the best OB-GYN in the country. He's on call twenty-four hours per day in case I need him."

Her lips purse. "That's nice of Yakov."

"It's not like he's doing it as a favor to me. This is his baby, too." I cradle my stomach. "It's *our* baby."

"How many kids does Yakov already have?"

I barely manage to swallow my water without doing a spit-take. "Excuse me?"

"Well, I mean… I don't know. He seems like the kind of guy who might get around. And isn't creating little mafia bosses a big deal for men like him? He'll need someone to carry on the proud criminal tradition or whatever."

"It's not like that, Kayla. He wasn't trying to get me pregnant. It just… happened."

She arches her brow. "I don't believe anything in that man's life 'just happens.' He controls everything, Luna."

"Not me," I say confidently. "You just don't know Yakov well enough. He's a good man. I'm happy here."

"You were happy with Benjy once, too," she says softly. My thoughts must be written plainly on my face because she rushes to explain. "I tried to talk to you about Benjy, but you didn't want to hear it. I knew you weren't happy, but you didn't seem to realize it. I'm just afraid this is a repeat of history."

"Denial and ignorance are two different things," I say softly. "I knew I wasn't happy with Benjy. I just… I didn't want to admit I'd wasted years of my life with him. Things with Yakov aren't like that."

"Agreed," she says. "Things with Yakov are way, way different. Because you're isolated in this house and your relationship timeline is on overdrive. You've known this man for a few months and you're already living together and starting a family. It feels like I walked through that front door into some alternate dimension."

Kayla cares about me. I know that. So I have to wrestle down the urge to defend Yakov. Being mad at her won't solve anything. The only thing I can do is let her see how happy I am here.

"You're the one who was always setting me up on endless blind dates," I say. "You and all the girls talked nonstop about wanting me to find a guy. You all acted like I wasn't complete without a boyfriend. Now, I have one and you're still not happy."

Calling Yakov my "boyfriend" feels juvenile, somehow. He's so much more than that.

"Loon," she breathes, "I *never* thought you were incomplete without a man. Fuck men! You don't need a man. You certainly don't need one to make *me* happy. The only thing I ever wanted was for *you* to be happy. And I could tell you weren't. That's why I tried to set you up. I didn't want you to be lonely anymore."

I blink back tears. "I am happy, Kayla. I'm happy with Yakov."

She studies me, her eyes trailing over my face. Then she nods. "Okay."

"Okay? Just like that?"

There's a reason I went on blind dates even when I was beyond done with them; Kayla is not easy to appease. She is determined and she fights for what she believes in. I've never seen her give up a fight this easily.

"Okay," she repeats, biting back a smile. "It's going to take me some time to get on board with all of this. But if you tell me you're happy, I'll believe it until I have evidence to the contrary."

"There won't be evidence to the contrary. I'm really happy here. This is what I want. Yakov is what I want."

"I hope you're right. That's all I want for you, Loon." Without warning, Kayla swats her discarded carrot stick across the countertop and looks up at me under mischievously lowered lashes. "Now, where are you hiding the caramel ice cream cones?"

We take our ice cream out onto the patio. The moment the door opens, Gregory darts between my feet and saunters outside like he owns the place.

"He won't escape?" Kayla asks, gesturing to where Gregory is curling up on the sun-warmed bricks.

"There was only one spot in the fence that was low enough for him to climb and Yakov had it taken out and replaced with a taller fence."

She whistles. "He's even taking care of your cat? You should have started with that. The man is obviously obsessed with you."

I can't stop myself from smiling. "I think Yakov and Gregory are in a love affair of their own now. Even if things go south and I end up leaving the mansion, I don't think I'd ever convince Gregory to come with me. He's Yakov's cat as much as he's mine now."

At one point, that would have bothered me. Now, it feels right. We're going to be one big, happy family.

We lie back in the deck chairs, licking ice cream as it drips down the sides of our cones, while Kayla catches me up on her life.

"… Being head of a project this big was my career goal out of college, but now, it's a big fucking mess. I'm doing my job well, but my job now depends on twenty other people doing their job well. And no offense, but the people I work with are a bunch of fuck-ups. Especially Gary."

"Gary is the guy who keeps his office dark all the time because of migraines, right?"

She snorts. "Yeah. As if working in the dark in front of a bright computer screen is any better. Also, he does not have migraines. At least not as often as he claims. He left work one day with a supposed 'migraine,' but Janie saw him grabbing lunch at the taco place across the street with a blonde in a minidress an hour later."

"*Across the street?*" I whistle. "The audacity of men."

"Astounding," Kayla agrees.

"Speaking of Janie, how is she doing?"

"Good. She just transferred to the marketing department, so I never see her at work anymore. But I went to her house last week for a pool party."

"I didn't know the pool was finished. She's been talking about it for a year."

It's actually all Janie could talk about. She would go on and on for hours about the struggles of keeping a contractor and the price of concrete work. As someone living in a one-bedroom apartment with a two-foot-wide balcony, I could not relate.

"It was a horror story that Janie would love to fill you in on at extreme length" Kayla says, giving me a withering look. "But they just finished it last month. We've been over there a few times to swim and drink. Mostly drink, honestly."

Kayla goes on like that, rattling off weeks' worth of hang outs and gossip I've missed. It's fun to talk with her, but I can't ignore the pang in my heart.

I miss them.

Really, I miss when my life was simple. When I knew what I was doing every day and every person in my life fit into a neat little box with a tidy label.

Now, everything in my life feels like it's exploding out of the seams. I have complex feelings for a mysterious man who sets my mind and body on fire in a way I've never felt before.

I miss my old life, but that doesn't mean I want to go back there. It doesn't mean I want to give up Yakov or the life I've built here with him—the baby I've created with him.

Kayla's laugh dips into a sigh. "You've missed a lot, Loon."

"I have," I agree.

But if I could go back and do it all again, I'd choose this life every single time.

20

YAKOV

Gregory is stalking after a bird that landed on the edge of the hibiscus planter. He's crouched down, shoulders low and tail flat on the ground. Luna and Kayla are laughing, arguing whether they should scare the bird off to save it or let Gregory take his shot.

The late afternoon light cuts across the patio and through my office window. I've been in here for a few hours and I'm running out of tasks. I didn't have much to do in the first place. I just want to give the two women time to catch up.

I would have used the free time to visit Nik instead of stare at a cat through my window, but Mariya is with him now. She told me she wanted some alone time with him. After what the doctor said about how hearing the people he loves talk to him could help, I figured it was a good idea to get her in to see him more often.

Isay escorted her and took two extra guards with him. He still hasn't heard any rumblings from the Gustev Bratva. He swears he's keeping his ear to the ground, and I believe he's telling me the truth; I just don't believe for even a second that he's right.

After everything that has happened, I'm not taking any chances.

I'm still watching Gregory wiggle his hips back and forth while he tries to muster the courage to pounce when my phone rings. I assume it's Isay calling to update me on how things are going, so I don't even look at the screen before I answer.

"Hello?"

Fifteen feet below, Gregory lunges. He misses the bird by a foot, at least, and smashes into the side of the planter. Luna and Kayla howl with laughter as the bird flies off into the reddening sky.

I can't help but smile. Until I hear the voice on the other end of the line.

"Yakov Kulikov. Long time, no see."

For a second, I'm positive it's Akim.

But no, it can't be. He's dead. Dismembered. I shattered his skull and broke his body. There isn't a single fucking way that he is calling me right now.

Then it hits me. "Pavel."

I haven't spoken to Pavel since well before his voice dropped, but I know it's him.

"I've been wanting to talk to you," Pavel says. "Sorry it has taken me so long. Planning a funeral takes up a lot of your time. I've been swamped."

"It takes a lot of guts to call me."

He huffs out a laugh. "If that's a roundabout way of asking how I got your number, I'll never tell."

"It was a direct way of warning you to keep your head down and stay out of my fucking life. That was a lesson your brother learned the hard way."

"From what I understand, Akim never bothered you at all," Pavel says. "You weren't even home when he dropped by for a visit. And afterward… well, I saw the footage. She was alone in that cell."

Luna.

Even the tiniest reference to Luna has my top lip curling in barely contained rage.

"You have to be used to her getting attention from other men, though. You have wonderful taste in women, Yakov. Like I said, I saw the footage."

I don't need to see the tapes to know what Pavel saw. Luna was locked in that cell wearing nothing but her underwear. She was dehydrated and terrified. I want to kill Akim all over again just thinking about it.

"That footage is the first and last time you are ever going to look at her," I growl. "Do it again, I'll rip your eyes out."

He chuckles. "Relax, Yakov. I meant it as a compliment."

"You're still a kid. This feud is almost older than you are. It isn't worth your life."

"Aww. Do you care about me, Yakov?"

I grind my teeth. "I don't want to waste the time cutting you down for nothing other than some bad blood. But I'll do it. I'll cut you down if you try *anything*. Doesn't matter how small. You come near me or my family, you're dead."

"That threat might have been more persuasive a couple weeks ago," he says. "But now, you've murdered the only family I had left. I'm alone in the world and there is nothing you can do to me that would be worse than that."

I hear the heartbreak in his voice. Pavel is playing the big, tough leader. Under it all, he's a devastated kid.

"Don't be stupid, Pavel. This isn't your fight. It never was."

I don't want to kill him. I really don't. I already killed Akim—I got my pound of flesh. Everything else is a nuisance.

"I'm alone in the world… but you aren't. You have your little girlfriend and a new baby on the—"

"Stand the fuck down," I snarl.

"For a man with your reputation, you wear your heart on your sleeve. Did you know that? It's easy to see what you care about. *Who* you care about." Pavel blows out a breath. "I'll see you soon, Yakov."

He hangs up and I spin and throw my phone at the wall. It dents the drywall and clatters to the floor, the screen shattering.

I fucking knew it.

Isay told me Pavel didn't care about revenge, but I knew it was bullshit. Of course he wants to avenge his brother. I would if I were him.

Pavel wants me to suffer. I took someone he cares about, so now, he wants to take everything from me. And that's exactly what Luna is to me.

Everything.

Laughter floats through the window from the patio below. I'm out of my office door and down the stairs before I can even think about what I'm doing. It's all instinct. The protective urge to have Luna in my sights and close is something I can't deny. Not after everything that has happened.

I throw open both patio doors. Luna and Kayla are still laughing, but the sound cuts off as the doors bang off the side of the house.

Luna frowns. "Yakov, is everything—"

"It's time to go." I gesture for Kayla to follow me. "Now."

The two women look at each other, confused. I can't help but look over their heads to scan the fence line. I shored up the perimeter fence once Gregory started venturing outside, but I should install more cameras.

"Where are we going?" Luna stands up and walks towards me. Her shirt is tight and the swell of her stomach is impossible to miss.

Mine. The thought rings through me like a gong. *She is mine and I'll do anything to keep her safe.*

"*We* aren't going anywhere." I pull her close and point at Kayla. "But it's time for her to leave. Now."

"Oh." Kayla blinks at Luna and can't bring herself to look at me. She sweeps crumbs off of her lap as she stands up. "Yeah, okay… I should probably get home, anyway. I need to—"

"We were still talking." Luna pulls away from me, but I keep hold of her hand. "I told Kayla she could stay for dinner. We were going to watch a movie with Mariya."

Mariya. Fuck. I pull out my phone and fire off a message to Isay. **Get my sister home now. Watch your back. Pavel is out for blood.**

Then I message for a car to pick Kayla up in front of the house in two minutes.

"Yakov? Are you listening to me?" Luna asks.

I pocket my phone. "I heard you. But it's time for her to go. There's a car waiting for you out front, Kayla."

Kayla pulls Luna into a hug. "It was good to see you. We'll do it again soon, okay?"

"Hold on, I want you to stay," Luna says back. "Just give me a second and I'll—"

Kayla shakes her head. "I'm always only a phone call away. Do you hear me? No matter what happens or what you need, I'm here for you."

The message is clear: *if this asshole fucks up, I'll come get you.*

Kayla has no idea what she's promising. No one is taking Luna away from me. Not Kayla and definitely not Pavel fucking Gustev.

She is mine.

Hope steps outside, hands folded behind her back. "There is a car waiting for you, Ms. Stevenson."

Kayla and Luna hug one more time, but my mind is racing. Isay is going to bring Mariya home. There are guards stationed outside of Nik's room at the hospital, but I should change them out more often to make sure the men there are always fresh. Pavel was threatening Luna, but it could've been a misdirect. He might want me to batten down the hatches at home while he strikes at the hospital.

I want to believe he wouldn't try to kill a man who is already barely clinging to life, but I know better than to underestimate a Gustev.

Hope sees Kayla out. As soon as the patio doors close, Luna whips towards me. "What on earth is going on? What was that about?"

"She was here all day. It was time for her to go."

"Says who?" she snaps. "You told me you were going to be busy today. It's not like I have anywhere to be."

Not anymore. She isn't going anywhere. Luna isn't leaving this house until Pavel is no longer a threat. I can't lose her like I did last time. I won't.

"It was your idea, Yakov," she continues. "You said Kayla could come over."

"I didn't say she could move in. And you're pregnant. You need your rest."

"That's what that was!" she cries out, flinging her hand to the door Kayla disappeared through. "Being with her and having fun is *restful*, Yakov. She's my best friend."

I should tell her. She needs to know that the Gustev Bratva is as much of a threat as ever. *Pavel Gustev is gunning for you, Luna, and I'm not taking any chances.*

But she's pregnant. More than that, she's pregnant and just barely recovering from the trauma of being kidnapped by Pavel's older brother. What would all of that stress and fear do to her and the baby?

Luna sighs and steps closer. Her vanilla scent swirls around us. "What's going on, Yakov?"

"You need to rest," I repeat.

She frowns. "I don't need to rest. I'm not tired! What I need is for you to tell me why you are acting like—"

"Do you ever just fucking listen and do what you're told?"

Luna jerks away from me like I slapped her. Her lips are parted, her blue eyes wide. She stares at me long enough that I almost crack. I almost tell her that I'm running on three hours of sleep because she had nightmares all night and I wanted to be there to soothe her.

I almost tell her that I'm trying to be at the hospital for Nik as much as I can, but Mariya is tugging on the leash I have her on, and there's only so much I can do to help Nik, anyway. The doctors aren't optimistic and neither am I.

I almost grab Luna and tell her that I can't fucking breathe when I think about how close I was to losing her and Mariya and Nik. I almost lost everyone and I can't go back to that place again. I won't fucking survive it.

Instead, I stare at her. I watch as her face turns cold and angry.

"Fine," Luna finally snaps. "You want me to rest? Great. I'll rest. I'll go sleep in the guest room so I won't be disturbed. Being far away from you would give me some *fabulous* rest."

She stomps into the house, but I don't go after her. Instead, I walk into my office and pour myself a drink. I toss it back just as she slams the guest room door closed upstairs.

There's still time. I could go to her and explain things. I could make this right.

But it's so much easier to pour myself another drink instead.

21

LUNA

I'm grouchy. And it's not just because I woke up in an inferior guest bed without Yakov's arm around my waist.

It's also because, without his arm around my waist, I was in and out of nightmares all night. I woke myself up three different times panting and crying with the very beginnings of a scream caught in my throat.

Each dream started out the same: Akim walking through the cell door, his face twisted in a vicious smile. But with every step he took towards me, he became less and less distinct. The edges of him blurred and faded away until he was a faceless shadow. Just as I started to think he would disappear entirely, the shadow lunged for me and the entire world went dark.

Part of me wishes I had cried out in my sleep. Yakov would have come to me, I know it. No matter how upset we were with each other, he would have crawled into bed, curled around me, and soothed me back to sleep.

Instead, I tossed and turned all night. And now, even though I'm exhausted and sore, the thought of lying in this bed for another second sounds miserable. Especially when I can smell bacon cooking downstairs in the kitchen.

A few weeks ago, the smell of bacon would have made me gag. Now, it sounds heavenly.

I grab a fleece blanket from the end of the bed and pull it around my shoulders before I pad out of the guest room and down the stairs. Bacon first, then shower. That's the order of operations today.

I turn into the kitchen expecting to find Hope at the stovetop, but it's Yakov. He's in a pair of gray pajama bottoms slung low over his hips and no shirt. His front is covered with a white apron, but I can see every ripple of the muscles across his shoulders and back as he turns the bacon over in the pan.

Oh, God—he's fighting dirty.

He looks back at me, face unreadable. "Good morning."

I nod and start to walk around the island to wait for him to finish with breakfast. I'm giving him the silent treatment, but that doesn't mean I don't want whatever he's cooking.

Before I can even take a step, Yakov reaches towards me. "Come here, Luna."

I'm just out of range. I could ignore him and sit down. But I don't want to.

I take a step closer and it's just enough for Yakov to grab my hand and pull me close. I collide with his hard chest and he dips low and presses his lips to my forehead.

"Good morning," he rumbles again, his mouth just next to my ear. "Are you hungry?"

Oh, he's playing real *dirty this morning.*

I nod.

His hand grips my waist for just a second before he gently pushes me towards the table. "Sit down. I'll make you a plate."

I sit down and sneak glances at him standing over the stove. The way his forearms flex as he flips and stirs, the shadow of stubble along his square jaw.

When he slides my plate in front of me, I take a deep, shameless sniff of him. He smells like he always does, spiced and woodsy. It has me hungry for something else entirely, but I smother the fire in my belly and dig into the eggs and bacon.

It's incredible. The bacon is perfectly crispy and the scrambled eggs are fluffy with peppers and onions and cheese mixed in. He even put a cup of fresh berries on the side.

He's taking care of me. *Or taking care of the baby*, I think bitterly.

Will he shut the baby out the way he likes to shut me out? When things get tense, will he stop talking to our child and give them the cold shoulder? Yakov can be so warm and loving and fun, but he knows how to turn it on and off. I don't want my child to love Yakov if he can dial his love up and down at will.

I don't want *them* to live that way and *I* don't want to live that way, either.

No matter how many nice breakfasts Yakov makes, I'm not going to just forget yesterday happened. I'm not going to forgive him until he apologizes and—

"I'm sorry about last night." Yakov puts down his fork and looks at me.

His eyes are unbelievably green. I stare into them and forget for a second what we're even talking about.

Then I remember and lift my chin. "You should be."

I think his mouth tips up in amusement, but it's gone before I can be sure. "You have every right to be mad at me."

"I don't need your permission to be mad," I fire back. "You yelled at me for no reason. And you did it in front of Kayla. I spent all day convincing her that I'm happier here than I've ever been and then you walked in and yelled at me. It didn't exactly prove my point."

Now, I'm positive he's amused. "You're happier than ever?"

I narrow my eyes. "I *was*. Before you sent my best friend away with no explanation and yelled at me."

"That's fair."

"It is?" I blink at him. Then I shake my head. "I mean, I know it is. But you… agree with me?"

He nods. "Before, I was keeping you in the dark because it was safer. You couldn't go back to your normal life once I told you about all of the shit that goes on in mine. But now, there is no fucking way I'm letting you go. *This* is your life, and you deserve to know what's going on. Even when I wish I could protect you from the stress of it."

I swallow down the emotion rising in my throat. "I thought you were playing dirty before with the shirtless chef routine, but that was a real low blow."

"I'm not the one who came down in the world's tiniest tank top and shorts."

"And a blanket!" I shrug my shoulders and the fleece blanket slips to the floor. "It wasn't on purpose. I didn't grab any pajamas before I stormed into the guest room last night. I didn't want to leave to get pajamas and run into you."

"Because you were so mad?" he asks.

"Yeah, that… and because I was afraid you'd force me to forgive you before I was ready."

"Does that mean you're ready to forgive me now?" He grabs both of our plates and carries them over to the sink.

He ditches the apron on the counter and turns to face me, shirtless and even more appetizing than the breakfast we just finished.

"Yes," I croak. "I forgive you."

He smiles and I swear my panties erupt in flames.

"But," I add quickly, "that doesn't mean there aren't still ways you could make things up to me."

His eyes drag over me from top to bottom and back again. "And here I thought cooking breakfast would be enough."

There is no such thing as "enough" where Yakov is concerned. Whatever you want to call it—hormones, attraction, raw sexual chemistry—it doesn't matter to me. All I know is heat pools between my legs and I *want him. I need him.*

I turn in my chair and part my legs slowly. "Breakfast was amazing. But I'm ready for dessert."

Yakov's smile melts away. There's no amusement in the way he's looking at me now. His eyes are dark as he crosses the kitchen and kneels in front of me.

"I was ready for dessert the moment you came downstairs wearing this scrap of cotton." He kisses his way up my thigh.

"They're shorts," I argue, but it comes out breathless. His calloused fingers on my skin are making it hard to get enough oxygen.

He glances up at me as he hooks his fingers around my waistband. "Whatever they are, they're about to be in shreds."

He yanks the shorts down and I gasp. "We can't do this *here!*"

"It's too late." He slides my shorts off and drags my hips to the very edge of the chair. "You parted your legs, Luna. You looked at me with fuck-me eyes."

"I was trying to be seductive! I didn't mean we'd do it right—"

Yakov strokes his thumb over the soaked triangle of my panties and the words die in my throat. I look around to make sure no one else is in the kitchen, but I'm not sure I could stop this even if we did have an audience.

"Consider me seduced." He slips my panties to the side with his thumb. His breath whispers across my center, sending a shiver up my spine.

"Someone could see," I whisper. "Someone could come."

"It's going to be you. You're already so wet." He teases the very tip of his tongue over me. It takes all my restraint to not curl my fingers through his hair and haul him deeper. "Don't worry, Luna. No one except me will see you come apart. I'll take you there so fast you won't know what hit you."

Yakov plunges his tongue into me. He sucks and licks until I'm panting. I stroke my fingers through his dark hair and grind against his mouth.

He flicks his tongue over my clit and slides a finger into me and I drive myself onto his hand so hard I nearly fall off the chair. Yakov keeps me from falling to the floor with his hand and his mouth, stroking my insides and sucking on me until I forget where we are. I am so dialed into his touch that I'm positive nothing beyond this moment exists.

"Yakov," I moan. I circle my hips, unsure if I'm trying to get closer to him or escape. Because it feels like he's undoing me from the inside out.

His finger slides into me faster and faster as he licks me relentlessly. Pressure builds, the first pulses forming deep inside of me. My moans blur together until they're endless, until I clamp my thighs around his ears and fall apart on his mouth.

When he pulls back, his lips are shiny from my release. He kisses me, letting me taste what we just did.

At the risk of being thrown on the table and properly fucked, I grab the front of his shirt and whisper, "I want more."

He looks at the table like he's considering it. Then a growl rumbles through his chest. "Go get in the shower. Now. I'll meet you there in three minutes."

He doesn't need to tell me twice.

I hurry upstairs and discard my pajamas in the corner of his bathroom. I start the shower and am already halfway through washing my hair when the shower door opens and Yakov's hard body is pressed against me.

He cups his hand over my center, driving friction between my thighs.

"I can still feel my first orgasm," I moan, leaning my shampooed head against his shoulder. "It's your turn."

"But you're so wet for me, Luna. My fingers are drenched."

He pulls his hand out to show me, but I feel him tense behind me. I look down at his hand and see why.

There's a smear of blood across his fingers.

It's not a lot. Just a small spread of pink blood.

My face flames with embarrassment. "Sorry. The apps say that there can be bleeding after sex. I should have warned you that it could happen."

He freezes. I'm sure he's disgusted. He must be thinking I'm—

"We're going to the hospital."

"Wait, what? Hold on. I—"

"You're bleeding, Luna. We're going. Not an argument."

"I know, but this is… it's normal. Everything says this can happen. I mean, it could even be that your fingernail scratched me when you were—This is not a big deal, I promise."

He grabs my chin and looks deep into my eyes. "*You* are a big deal to me. Now, get out of the shower and get dressed. I'm going to call Dr. Jenkins."

22

LUNA

I wait in the car, per Yakov's very clear and very threatening orders, while he gets a wheelchair from the hospital lobby. He drove me here himself because he "didn't trust anyone else behind the wheel."

That doesn't mean we came alone. Oh, no—I have an entourage now. Two SUVs full of his men in front and behind me. I feel like I'm the president.

People walking down the sidewalk towards the hospital keep doing double takes. Based on their frowns when they see me, I can tell they were expecting to see someone famous sitting in the passenger seat.

Sorry to disappoint.

When Yakov walks through the double doors with a wheelchair, I yell through the window, "I'm fine. I can walk."

It's the fifth time I've said it and it has just as much impact as it did the first time I said it: none whatsoever. Yakov ignores me, opens my door, and lifts me out of the car and sits me in the wheelchair.

"The bleeding stopped before we even left the house, Yakov. It was just a little spotting. That's normal."

"I look forward to Dr. Jenkins confirming that here in a few minutes."

I groan and sink down in the wheelchair.

In a way, it's sweet. Yakov is concerned about me and the baby. He wants to take care of us. I can see how lucky I am that I have him here.

In another way, it's maddening. I'm telling him I'm okay, but he doesn't believe me. He's forcing me to go to the hospital to make sure his baby is safe. I know he cares about me, too, but it's hard not to feel like the throwaway box holding the real treasure.

Yakov wheels me inside and straight past the front desk to an open exam room. Dr. Jenkins is already inside.

"Come in, both of you," he says, closing the door behind us. "Let's get you checked out, Luna."

"I'm sorry to bother you with this."

"Don't apologize. It's what I pay him for," Yakov says sharply.

Dr. Jenkins nods. "I am here to make sure you and your baby are healthy. It's not a problem to ease your worries."

"*I* don't have any worries," I mutter.

"She had some bleeding," Yakov says, talking over me.

"How much?"

"Enough to cover four of my fingers." Yakov holds up his hand as reference, and I want to disappear.

My face flames as Dr. Jenkins makes his notes. "The two of you were engaging in some sexual activities, then?"

"I performed oral," Yakov says.

He perfected *oral*. But given the fact that I'm about to combust with embarrassment, I keep that thought to myself.

Dr. Jenkins, on the other hand, is an absolute professional. He simply nods and places a blood pressure cuff on my arm. "Have the two of you had any penetrative sex in the last twenty-four hours?"

"Just a finger," Yakov says. "During the oral."

If there is a merciful God, He would kill me now.

"Some bleeding can be normal during pregnancy, especially after sex. There is a lot of extra blood in the area. It could be something as small as a scratch from your fingernail."

"That's what I said!" I blurt.

Yakov narrows his eyes at me. "And I said we would rather be safe than sorry."

"And *that* is what I always say." Dr. Jenkins directs me to lie down on the exam table and lays a small blanket over my lap. "Any concern, big or small, is worth looking into."

Dr. Jenkins lifts my shirt and presses a small wand to my stomach. "This is a fetal heart rate monitor. You've already seen one of these before. I'll just listen to the heartbeat and—"

A whooshing sound fills the room before he can finish. It's a loud, constant rhythm that clips along way faster than any heartbeat I've ever heard before.

"That's the baby?" I ask.

The last time I heard the baby's heartbeat was the night Yakov saved me from Akim. I was barely able to sit still without shaking. So when the nurse told me she found the heartbeat, I couldn't really appreciate it.

Now, my eyes fill with tears.

"That's your baby," Dr. Jenkins confirms. "A nice, strong heartbeat."

Yakov grabs my hand and squeezes. "So everything is fine?"

"Everything is—" The whooshing sound falters. It blurs and overlaps. Dr. Jenkins readjusts the doppler and picks up the sound again, but his forehead is creased.

"Everything is what?" Yakov snaps. "Is it fine or—"

Dr. Jenkins blinks and slaps on a delayed smile. "Fine. Great, actually. Perfectly healthy."

I glance at Yakov and he's eyeing the doctor with the same suspicion I feel.

Something is wrong.

When we walked in here, I felt confident the baby was healthy. I knew Yakov was overreacting. Now, there's a pit in my stomach that grows with every second Dr. Jenkins spends staring at the doppler.

Suddenly, he puts the doppler away. "I'm going to go ahead and get you back to the ultrasound tech, Luna."

"Why? We heard the heartbeat. That means everything is okay, right?"

"This is just a precaution." He's smiling, but it isn't convincing. "You've come all this way. We might as well do a full check-up."

"But is everything okay?"

Dr. Jenkins lays his hand on my shoulder. "Everything is fine, Luna. You have one healthy baby in there."

I blow out a shaky breath. "Okay."

Dr. Jenkins leads us out of the exam room and down the hall. Nurses and other doctors tip their head to him as he passes.

"He doesn't work here, right?" I whisper to Yakov.

"No. He just set up a home base here so he can take care of you."

"How much is all of this costing you?"

Yakov squeezes my hand. "There is no limit to what I'd be willing to pay to make sure you're safe."

I lay my head on his shoulder as we walk. "Sorry I was being stubborn about coming. You were right." I squeeze his arm tighter. "I think... I think something might be wrong. You saw his face back there, didn't you?"

"I did. But whatever it is, we'll face it together." He turns and kisses my temple.

I'm shaking as Dr. Jenkins leads me into the darkened ultrasound room and gets me positioned on the exam table, but I cling to Yakov's words. We can face anything together.

Dr. Jenkins presses the wand to my stomach and stares at a screen I can't see. He frowns as he moves the wand around, tapping buttons on a keyboard.

I want to grab the screen and twist it towards me. I want to scream at him to tell me what the hell is going on with my baby. But I lie here patiently.

Yakov's thumb massages soft circles over my knuckles while we wait.

"I told you you had one healthy baby in there," Dr. Jenkins says, twisting the screen so I can see.

The white blob I saw a few weeks ago already looks more distinctly human. There's now a little nose and pouty lips. Tiny arms shake back and forth.

"Everything is fine." I press a hand to my racing heart. "She is fine, right?"

"Perfectly fine. As far as the gender goes, who knows? It could go either way. Or maybe you'll have one of each," Dr. Jenkins says.

I flush. "Maybe. Yeah. We haven't really talked about—We don't have any plans yet."

"Hopefully, you want at least two," Dr. Jenkins says.

"Why is that?" I ask, still smiling.

"Well, I said you had one healthy baby back in the exam room because I knew for a fact that was true. But I also had a suspicion." He shifts the wand over and suddenly, the screen splits into two. There's a thin line running down the center of the screen and there are two circles on either side. "Now, I'm thrilled to tell you that you have *two* healthy babies."

My smile drops. My entire face is numb.

I stare at the two circles as, somewhere deep in my brain, I realize they are heads. Two heads.

Two babies.

Two healthy babies.

"What are you—"

"We're having twins," Yakov murmurs, putting the pieces of this puzzle together before I can. He kisses my forehead and folds my hand against his chest. "*Blyat'*, Luna. You're carrying my babies."

Babies. Multiple.

"I heard a murmur on the doppler and thought there might be more than one," Dr. Jenkins explains. "I wanted to get you an ultrasound to confirm. But yes, you are pregnant with twins, Luna. Congratulations."

23

LUNA

"Twins." Mariya eyes my stomach like the babies are going to burst through my chest, *Alien*-style. "There are *two* babies in there?"

"That is the definition of twins, yes."

It's been over twenty-four hours since I walked out of the hospital and not only have I come to terms with the fact that I'm having twins... I think I'm over it.

I'm not over the babies, obviously. They are tiny, precious miracles. Every time I think about holding one of them in each arm, I start to cry with joy.

My babies are not the problem. It's everyone *outside* of my womb that is driving me up the freaking wall.

I haven't been alone for even a second since yesterday morning. Before we left the office, Dr. Jenkins told Yakov to make sure I "take it easy." I understood it for what it was: a joke. A generic, throwaway line. Not actual medical advice.

But Yakov hasn't let me lift a finger since.

He carried me into the house, has escorted me to the bathroom each time I need to go, and even cut my steak for me at dinner last night. A few weeks ago, all I wanted was to see more of Yakov. I missed him. Now, as thrilled as I am that we aren't fighting, I would do almost anything for five minutes to myself. To process. To take a deep breath. To pee in privacy.

"Twins are so weird when you really think about it," Mariya says. "Kind of gross, actually."

I roll my eyes. "How is having two babies any different than having one?"

She mutes the TV. "Think about it like a sleeping bag. One person in a sleeping bag? Fine. Two people in a sleeping bag? Hot and sweaty and claustrophobic."

"They're floating in amniotic fluid. They aren't hot and sweaty; *I'm* hot and sweaty."

Like a bloodhound on the scent, Yakov appears in the doorway. "Do you feel okay?"

Oh, no. Not this song and dance right now. "Hello to you, too."

"I can call Dr. Jenkins."

I give him a tight smile. "I'm just warm. Pregnant people get hot," I explain, trying not to sound as frustrated as I feel. "It's normal. I'm okay."

He tucks a strand of hair behind my ear. It should be sweet, but he's staring at my stomach. It feels like everyone is constantly staring at my stomach. *I'm not going to explode, people.*

"She said she's fine," Mariya groans. "The human oven is just a little warm. It's to be expected."

I elbow Mariya in the side. "Hey! I am not just a human oven."

"You're not *just* a human oven, obviously. But you are, definitionally, a human oven."

Yakov reaches over me to swipe the remote out of Mariya's hand. "Out."

"She doesn't have to go," I protest.

He waves me away. "She's stressing the babies."

"The babies are stressed?" I can't actually believe what I'm hearing. I just said I feel like a human incubator and he's worried the *babies* are stressed? I throw my arms wide. "What about *me?*"

"When you're stressed, the babies are stressed," he says simply. "It's one and the same."

I wasn't stressed before, but I am now. I can feel my blood pressure rising. I would walk away and cool off, but Yakov would pick me up before I could take my first step.

The walls are closing in and there is no escape.

"We aren't 'one and the same'!" I yell. "I am a person separate from these babies. I still exist beyond growing them."

"I was joking about the human oven thing," Mariya interjects. "I didn't mean—"

"It's not just you, Mariya. It's *you*," I say, jabbing a finger at Yakov. The words are pouring out of me now, coming too fast to stop. Everything I've bottled up for days spewing out in a heady rush. "I know when I need to call the doctor. I don't need you to decide that for me. I also don't need you to carry me anywhere. I'm pregnant, not crippled! I can walk and cut my food and pee by myself, for fuck's sake!"

The steam is still escaping out my ears, but I already know I fucked up.

Yakov looks taken aback for a single second before he schools his face into an unreadable mask. "Do it by yourself then."

Without another word, he turns and leaves.

With him gone, I expect the feeling in my chest to ease. I take a few breaths, waiting for relief to come. But it doesn't.

"Now, I kind of wish I'd gone upstairs when I had the chance," Mariya mumbles. "That was awkward."

"God, I'm a bitch, aren't I?" I drop my face into my hands. "He was worried about me and I yelled at him."

Mariya snorts. "He has been obsessing over you nonstop all day. I am all about seeing my brother access his inner softie, but it was annoying even for me."

"I just... I cannot spend the next six months letting him carry me to the bathroom."

"Especially since you'll be waaaay too heavy to carry by the end."

I swat Mariya with the back of my hand. "That is not funny."

She laughs anyway. "You're having twins. It's time to face your destiny. You're going to be a whale here in a few months. By that point, you might *want* Yakov to carry you around and do everything for you."

"Maybe. But I don't want it now. I just need to feel... normal."

"I get that, but..." She sways back and forth, teetering on the edge of saying something I know I'm not going to like.

I ask anyway. "But what?"

"I was shot, Loon. Nik is in a coma—" Her voice breaks, but she clears her throat quickly. "There has been an avalanche of shit that Yakov can do nothing about. But you and the babies? He can do something about that. He can protect you and the babies with everything he fucking has. Right now, that's *all* he has."

"Wow," I say finally. "That sucks."

"What does?"

I look at her. "You just confirmed I really was being a bitch."

"Correct," Mariya chuckles. "But between you and me, I think he'll forgive you."

I wake up to the sound of the front door opening.

Mariya went to her room hours ago, but I decided to wait up for Yakov. I assumed he'd come home for dinner, but dinner came and went without any sign of him. Then I figured he'd come home once hospital visiting hours were over, but one glance at the clock tells me they ended hours ago. Probably around the same time I finally gave into exhaustion and fell asleep.

If he went somewhere aside from Nik's hospital room, he really must be mad at me.

There are footsteps in the entryway and I quickly wipe the drool from my chin and run my fingers through my tangled hair.

Yakov walks past the living room quickly. He's little more than a blur. No sign he's going to stop.

When I clear my throat, he jerks to a stop and spins to face me. His face is unreadable. "You should be asleep."

"I was," I admit, gesturing to the nest of blankets on the couch. "I fell asleep waiting for you to come home."

"Do you need something?" he asks coolly.

"I need to talk to you. I *want* to talk to you."

His jaw flexes. The lamp casts his cheekbones in stark relief. "Go to sleep. I don't want to talk."

"Then I'll talk," I rush to say before he can turn away. "Everything happened so fast, Yakov. One baby and then two. You and me. Everything changed overnight. I needed a second to process it all. Then I got some seconds to process and all I did was sit around feeling like a bitch for snapping at you."

His eyes are fixed on some point over my head. "Don't waste your time worrying about me, Luna. I can handle it."

"But I am worried about you. Because this is all happening to you, too. You're going to be a dad. That's wild. I need to give you space to worry and process, too. I was just overwhelmed and amped up on baby hormones. A double dose of hormones, I think, since there are two of them in there. I don't know if that is scientifically accurate, but it feels right."

"I'll ask Dr. Jenkins."

"Or maybe *I'll* ask Dr. Jenkins," I counter, stepping closer. "I'd love to have a little more control over my appointments and when I need to call the doctor. I'd also like more control over other things like… using my own legs." He narrows his eyes and I quickly cross the room to stand in front of him. "You have been taking amazing care of me, Yakov. I'm so grateful. There was a time when I didn't know if you'd even want to be around for me and the baby."

"Of course I'm going to be there for my kids," he growls. "I wouldn't abandon them."

I nod. "I know that now. And I appreciate everything you've been doing for me and for them. Truly. But I also need to feel like a capable human. I need to be strong to give birth to two babies. I need to keep exercising and using my body. That's part of a healthy pregnancy."

He reaches out and touches my cheek. "You were bleeding."

"And Dr. Jenkins told you it was normal," I remind him. "I'm okay. Our babies are *okay.*"

He's holding himself so rigidly that I know he's fighting all of his instincts to pull me close and not let me go.

I slide my hand down his arm to his wrist. "What if I promise to ask you for help when I need it? Like, when I'm ginormously pregnant and my feet are swollen, I'll probably be begging you to carry me around."

His mouth is pressed into a stubborn line, but he can't keep the spark out of his eyes.

"I look forward to hearing you beg," he says softly.

I walk around him and pull the sitting room's pocket doors closed. Then I flick the brass lock into place and turn to face him. "Why wait? You could hear me beg now."

He assesses me coolly. "Beg for what, specifically?"

I put my arms around his neck and draw close. Our bodies slide together as I press onto my toes and kiss him.

He kisses me back, but his hands stay down at his sides. He's holding himself away from me in a way he usually doesn't. So I grab the front of his shirt and pull him with me until my back is pressed against the wall and I'm pinned in by his body. "Please," I whisper between kisses.

"You were bleeding yesterday," he says again. "*Yesterday.*"

"That was normal."

He presses his hand flat to the wall next to my head and pushes himself away. "You need more time to rest."

I hear Mariya's words in my head. *He can protect you and the babies with everything he fucking has. Right now, that's all he has.*

I don't want to take that away from him.

But I'm also physically aching to be close to him. We fought and now, I *need* to make up. That might just be the pregnancy hormones talking, but I don't care. I want him.

"I want you to know I appreciate how much you care about me." I stroke my hands from his shoulders to his chest. Then I push, walking him back towards the couch until he drops down onto the cushion. I lower onto my knees in front of him. "I want to show you how much I appreciate it."

I unbutton his pants and slide the zipper down.

Yakov grabs my wrist. "Luna."

"This is what we do after a fight, isn't it?" I ask, making a show of licking my lips. "Let me make it up to you, Yakov. Please. Fuck my mouth."

His eyes go dark. There's a single beat of hesitation before he releases my wrist and lets me free him from his boxers. Before he can change his mind, I drag my tongue slowly along the underside of his cock.

"Fuck," he exhales, fisting his hand in my hair.

He grows in my hand and shifts his hips to the edge of the couch. When I swallow him, the groan he releases comes from deep in his chest.

I have the power to hurt him, but it's this power that gets me off. Knowing I can make him feel good beats everything else.

I take him deep again and again, swirling my tongue around his tip before diving back down. When he's as deep inside my mouth as I think I can take, he gently bucks his hips, sliding deeper, demanding more. And I want to give him all of it. All of me.

I move to slide my hand between my legs, but Yakov grabs my arm. He holds my wrist and slides himself into my mouth in slow, luxurious strokes, taking what he wants from me.

I whimper around him, my heartbeat thrumming between my thighs.

When he slides out, I gasp. "Please, Yakov. Let me come with you. I need it."

Suddenly, he lifts me off the floor and places me on his lap. His finger burns a path down my neck and over my chest. He circles my nipple through the thin material of my shirt. "You promised you would ask when you needed my help, *solnyshka*."

"Help me, Yakov," I breathe, wrapping my arms around his neck. "Fuck me."

His pupils are blown wide as he shifts my shorts to the side and sinks into me inch by inch.

My mouth opens in a silent cry as I take him. When he's seated deep, I drop my head to his shoulder. "Thank you."

Yakov kisses my neck and then fucks me with the softest, gentlest thrusts. His hips barely move, but each shift inside of me sets off fireworks. I feel him everywhere.

I try to set a faster pace, but he holds my hips firm. "I'm in control, Luna. You asked me for help. Let me help you."

He fills me with slow, steady movements. It's a slow build, but I enjoy every second. He strokes my face and looks into my eyes like he can't believe I'm in front of him. Like I'm the most precious thing he has ever held. Then he grips my hips and drags me against him again and again. When my breath catches and release pulses through me, Yakov follows after me, a stream of broken Russian falling from his lips.

He kisses me long and hard. All of the power he withheld comes out in the bruising crush of his mouth on mine.

Then he scoops me up in his arms and carries me towards the door.

"I thought we just talked about me walking on my own?" I whisper, laying my head on his shoulder.

"You couldn't walk right now even if you wanted to."

I take stock of my trembling thighs. He isn't wrong.

He sees the fight in me drain away and smirks. "That's what I thought."

24

YAKOV

"It's good to have you out drinking with us again. It's been too long." Kuzma clinks his glass against mine, beer sloshing over the rim onto the sticky tabletop.

Savva adds his glass to the mix, sending more beer sloshing. "Cheers to that."

I grimace and drain my third drink in less than an hour.

Turns out, giving Luna space is easier said than done.

I can see where she's coming from. If anyone was in my face all the time, telling me what to do and when to do it, I'd kill them. There is no way I'd put up with it.

But that's because I can take care of myself. I can kill any man who comes against me. Luna hasn't seen even half of the horrors I have and she isn't trained for any of this. So when it comes down to it, I'd rather her hate me than let anything happen to her or our babies.

"If Nik was here, it would be just like the old days," Savva murmurs. Kuzma elbows him in the side and Savva seems to realize what he said. "Nik will be back with us in no time, for sure."

"Isay, too," Kuzma adds. "As soon as we've taken out anyone who dares to cross us, we can all go out. Until then…"

Until then, my brother is in a coma that may never end and Isay is on guard back at the mansion while I'm gone. Until Pavel has been taken care of, I'm not taking any fucking chances with Mariya and Luna.

"What's the latest on Pavel?" Savva asks.

"I haven't heard from him since he called the other day."

Kuzma shakes his head. "The fucking balls on that kid, calling you like that. I can't believe it."

"I can," Savva says. "The entire Gustev family has no self-preservation. If they did, they'd stop messing with us."

"That's part of the problem. We've always waited for the Gustev Bratva to strike. Then we hit back and kill them. But each time, someone on our side gets hurt. First, my father. Now, Nik." I shake my head. "No more waiting. I say it's well past time we strike first."

Kuzma raises his glass in agreement. "What's your plan?"

"My only thought is that I'll take out the entire Gustev Bratva if it means keeping my family safe. I'm not going to pull any more punches. If we can't narrow in on a specific target, then we throw everything we have at them until they are obliterated."

Savva leans forward, practically salivating at the idea. "A carpet bombing. I'm down."

"As a last resort," I remind him. "In the meantime, I want you to look deeper into who Pavel is working with. Akim had a weapons dealer, Budimir. See if he's still around. I'd like to talk to him about coming to work for me."

Pavel made it clear that he has nothing left to live for now that his brother and father are dead. Maybe that's true. But if I had to guess,

I'd say there are still ways I can hurt him. Cutting him off financially won't go unnoticed.

"Are we trying to hurt him or kill him?" Kuzma asks.

I smirk. "I don't see why we can't do a little of both."

Kuzma smiles and his teeth flash in the dim lights of the bar. "That is music to my fucking ears."

The mansion is dark when I get home. It's nearly midnight—later than I planned to stay out by a few hours. But Savva and Kuzma had a lot of ideas for how to take Pavel out.

Plus, it was nice to drink with my men and pretend for a few hours that everything was fine. It was the exact kind of thing Nik would have roped me into the second he saw me carrying Luna around the house. He has a way of knowing when I need to unwind.

Or, he *had* a way of knowing. Not even his doctors know if he still has that. Or anything else, for that matter.

I peek through my bedroom door and see Luna asleep in bed. Silently, I pull it closed and slip downstairs and into my office. I don't want to wake her up. Not when she hasn't had a full night's sleep since I carried her out of Akim's cell.

She wakes up multiple times per night screaming and reaching for me. Each time she jolts awake, it's even more motivation to make sure I end Pavel as a threat before he can attack. Luna has endured enough already.

It's why I haven't told her about Pavel, either. Not directly, anyway.

She's pregnant with twins—with my children. I'm not going to add even more to her plate. I'm not going to make her carry stress and responsibility that belongs to me and me alone.

I'm going to protect her from the fear of Pavel the same way I'll protect her from Pavel himself.

At my desk, I make notes on some of the ideas Kuzma and Savva had back at the bar. Then I go over the documentation Nik compiled months ago on Akim's weapon's dealer, Budimir. The man was responsible for a staggering portion of the Gustev Bratva's profits. Severing that connection was my original plan for destroying Akim. Then he kidnapped Luna and shot my siblings, giving me no choice but to murder him at the earliest possible convenience.

Since I killed Akim, Budimir has gone underground. I'm not sure if he's trying to avoid being associated with Akim, especially while the police are sniffing around his death, or if Akim's death was the out he'd been looking for. That's what I need to figure out. If Budimir is still working with Pavel, severing that connection is still a valid option.

I'm trying to decipher Nikandr's chicken scratch handwriting when Luna screams.

It's not the usual slow build of her nightmares—whimpering into crying into screaming. It's a full-bodied scream that echoes through the house.

I jump up and sprint for the door so fast my chair tips over behind me.

Luna is still screaming when I make it to the top of the stairs. Mariya is standing in the open doorway. "It's a nightmare," she says. "There's no one in there with her. I checked."

"Go back to bed," I say a bit too gruffly. "I'll take care of her."

Luna is still screaming, so Mariya doesn't argue for once. She goes into her room and I shut our bedroom door behind me.

Luna is tossing back and forth. The comforter is shoved down around her waist and her back is arched. I lie down on the bed and wrap my arm around her. "I'm here, Luna. It's me."

I wasn't there the night Akim took her. I wasn't there to stop her from being thrown in a cell and tormented. I wasn't there the *one fucking time* she really needed me.

But I'm here for this. To fight the invisible monsters in the dark. To hold her hand while she suffers.

Her screams start to taper off immediately, but she's still tense. Her breathing is erratic. There are tears pouring down her cheeks.

"I'm here with you. I've got you."

That does the trick. Eventually, she curls against my chest and eases back to sleep.

I can't undo what Akim did to her. All I can do is hold her through it.

But I'll die to make sure no one gets the chance to hurt her again.

25

LUNA

I close my eyes and try to ignore the prickle on the back of my neck. That sickeningly familiar itch along my spine, like someone is watching me. I've been feeling it for days. Every time I step outside or even get near a window, I'm positive I feel eyes on me.

It's paranoia. I know that.

I was kidnapped from this house. I watched Mariya get shot in the front yard. So of course my body is still on high alert. Especially now that I'm pregnant and more protective over myself than ever before.

Still, knowing it's paranoia does not make it any easier to relax.

That's why I'm sitting by the pool, forcing myself to get my tan on and not think about my chances of being attacked or murdered.

I could tell Yakov how I've been feeling, but he's finally giving me more space. Sure, he saw me cutting an apple this morning and insisted on doing it for me so I wouldn't, in his words, "give myself a c-section." But to be fair to him, my knife skills in the kitchen are lacking and that apple was unusually firm.

But sitting by the pool and relaxing is something I'm more than capable of doing on my own. I don't need any help with that. This mansion is well-secured and I am safe here.

As soon as I sink into a comfortable position, the sound of a rock skittering across the pavement behind me sends me bolt upright.

I spin around, my heart in my throat and my hands in a sloppy defensive position. Mariya stops a few feet away, eyebrows raised. "Whoa."

I blow out a breath. "Sorry. I was dozing off and you startled me."

"Mind if I join you or are you going to give me a swift roundhouse kick to the side of the head?"

I pat my bump. "My days of roundhouse kicks are over. Actually, they never started. I dropped out of middle school karate after one week."

"That's fine. I can fight well enough for the both of us." Mariya throws a few air punches.

She's kidding, but my mind flashes back to the night she was shot. To watching her fight three grown men with guns in the front lawn. It was impressive—right up until the moment when a bullet tore through her shoulder and she crumpled to the ground.

Maybe I should learn how to fight. Yakov will never let me train while I'm pregnant, but once the babies are here... It would be nice to feel like I have some ability to protect the people I love. Mariya is very much included in that list.

Mariya clears her throat loudly, still throwing air punches.

"I saw you," I say. "Very impressive. The wind is terrified of you."

She raises her left arm into the air, rolling the joint at the shoulder. "Hello? Notice anything newly healed and cleared for light use?"

I gasp. "Your arm! You got your cast off?"

She grins. "No more cast and no more sling. I am officially healed. Except for the nerve damage and the many more months of physical therapy ahead. But otherwise, I'm healed."

"Mariya, that's amazing. I'm so happy for you."

"Me, too." She flops down in the lounger next to me. "There was always an itch just around my elbow that no pencil could reach. Plus, my cast was hard to accessorize."

"Do you have a lot of outings planned that require accessorizing?" I ask. "Because I've been wearing nothing but leggings and bathing suits for weeks."

"It's different for you. You're in a disgustingly romantic relationship and pregnant. I'm still on the prowl."

I snort. "You're on the prowl? *For what?*"

"I'm going to ignore the disbelief in your voice. Just because my brother has me on house arrest doesn't mean I'm a nun."

My eyes go wide. "Are you dating someone?"

"Who would I be dating, Luna? Like I said, my brother has me on house arrest."

"But you said you aren't a—"

"I just meant that I have needs, too, okay?" Her face flushes and I realize with a start that Mariya is embarrassed. It's the first time I've ever seen it. I don't hate it.

I bite back a smile. "That makes sense. I'm sure it's hard spending all this time at home."

"The only place I've been in weeks is the hospital. And Nik's hospital room isn't exactly brimming with hot guys. Which is probably good now that I think about it," she mumbles. "I am an ugly crier."

My heart squeezes. Mariya has been crying next to her brother's hospital bed while I've been trying to gather the courage to sit by the pool.

Before I can stop myself, I reach over and grab her hand. "Are you okay?"

"I'm fine. Really. It's just hard to see Nik like that. That's all it is." She blinks and I can almost see her cool mask slipping into place. "That and the fact that I have to live vicariously through that shitty reality yacht show you got me hooked on."

I'm too delighted to call her out for changing the subject. "Are you finally caught up on the newest season?"

"I know why Lydia refused to disembark with Richard when the yacht made port in Capri, if that's what you mean," she says with a smirk.

"Because she's been having an affair with the captain!" I blurt. "Can you believe it?"

"Absolutely. Yes, I can." Mariya nods, a wistful smile on her face. "I want a boy to tell me that I have eyes bluer than the Mediterranean Sea."

"You do!"

"Thanks, but compliments from you don't really do it for me." She grimaces. "I need to go dancing. I'm starting to feel like we are due another jailbreak. What do you think, Luna? Wanna sneak out and go dancing?"

I snap my head towards her. "Don't even think about it! The last time we tried that was traumatic enough. Was getting kidnapped not enough excitement for a lifetime?"

"Relax. I was just kid—"

"Your brother is going through enough without you causing trouble. If you snuck out, he'd have to track you down and then kill every man who even dared to touch you. It would not be pretty. So no sneaking out. *Ever.*"

"Kidding," Mariya finishes. "I was kidding! Jeez, tough crowd."

"What are you two talking about?" Strong hands slide over my shoulders. I jolt before I recognize it's Yakov standing behind me.

"And the crowd just got tougher," Mariya mumbles. She pushes herself to standing. "We were talking about nothing. Absolutely nothing. Definitely nothing that has anything to do with you."

"You live in my house. Everything you do has something to do with me," he retorts.

"Not this." Mariya backs toward the house. "I am going to go to my room now. It's my favorite place to be. I'm very happy there. Could stay there forever."

When she finally ducks inside, Yakov turns to me. "For a girl raised in the Bratva, she's a shitty liar."

"It really was nothing. And I already took care of it, anyway."

"If it was nothing, there would be nothing to take care of." He sighs. "If Mariya has a problem, she should come to me. You have enough going on."

"I'm fine. Mariya can talk to me. I want to be there for her."

Yakov looks towards the house, lost in thought. Then he blinks out of it. "You didn't eat any lunch."

I squint up at him. "Is that a question?"

"You're eating for three now."

"Tell them that," I say, patting my stomach. "I've been nauseous all day."

It could be the pregnancy. It might also have something more to do with me being on edge nonstop, twenty-four hours per day. It's almost like constant stress isn't good for the human body. But who can say?

Yakov bends down and scoops me into his arms before I can even try to resist.

"Where are we going?" I ask.

"Bed."

I'm instantly wet. But when we get upstairs, Yakov actually takes me to bed. He pulls one of his large shirts over my head and settles me under the blankets.

"I thought you might try to seduce me," I admit, sighing into the mattress.

His head is propped up on one arm, looking down at me. From this angle, he's all sharp lines and chiseled edges. "I considered it."

"What changed your mind?"

"You looked tired." He runs the pad of his finger under one of my eyes and then the other. "You haven't been sleeping very well."

I saw myself in the mirror this morning. I don't have under-eye bags; I have under-eye luggage. Under-eye moving trucks.

I press my palm to his cheek. "Neither have you. I know it's my fault."

He shakes his head. "It's mine."

My heart cracks a little. Is he ever going to forgive himself for not being there that night? He saved me. The only reason I'm here right now is because Yakov killed his way through Akim's house of horrors and got me out.

But for him, it all comes down to that one failure. The one time he wasn't there when I needed him.

"Yakov, it's not your—"

"Go to sleep, Luna." He says it gently, but there's no misunderstanding what he means. *This conversation is over.*

I'm not ready for it to be over.

Any of it. Not this conversation. Or hours spent in bed with Yakov. I don't want any of this to end, but it all feels so fragile. Like anything could rip it away.

"What happens next?" I ask suddenly.

"After sleep? Waking up, usually."

"I mean, what does the future look like? For us?" He frowns and I'm struck with the realization that this was not the right time to casually bring up "the talk." I ramble on, trying to salvage the situation. "Our relationship hasn't exactly been conventional. We have a lot going on right now with the twins coming and managing the fallout from killing Akim and everything, so I don't want to put any pressure on you. I just want to know what to expect."

Yakov looks at me like I'm speaking in tongues. "We're going to get married and raise our kids, Luna. What else would we do?"

He says it so simply that it takes my breath away.

I know Yakov cares about me. He's made that clear. But marriage has never come up. I kind of assumed it was off the table. Nothing about Yakov says "traditional."

Benjy and I dated for years and he still recoiled every time the M-word came up. I never would have been the first to say it to Yakov. Mostly because I would have been happy just to live in this house with him. But this…

"You want to marry me?" I breathe.

Yakov brushes my hair off of my forehead. "I want to do everything with you, *solnyshka.*"

26

YAKOV

Luna is asleep when I find her. I'm not surprised. She spent most of last night in and out of nightmares. For some reason, she sleeps easier during the day.

I almost don't want to wake her.

Then again, the sight of her spread across our bed makes me want to wake her up even more. I want her to see what is coming next.

When she asked me what our future held last night, it hit me like a fucking truck. I realized immediately that I didn't want a future without her in it. She's the mother of my children and the only woman I've ever had this kind of bone-deep connection to. There is no version of reality where she and I don't end up together.

So I proposed. Sort of.

I plan to do a better job of it the second time around.

"Luna." I squeeze her shoulder. "Wake up."

She blinks up at me, her blue eyes bleary. "Hmpf? Yak... Is everything okay?"

"Everything is fine. But you need to wake up and get dressed."

"Where are we going?" She yawns. "I was sleeping."

"It's a surprise."

Instantly, her eyes snap open and her mouth curves into a shy smile. "What kind of surprise?"

"The kind that you'll have to wait and see."

She rises onto her knees, moving more gingerly than normal with her growing bump. "Are we going out? Should I bring a jacket? Or a purse? Oh my God," she groans. "Clothes. Do I have to wear real clothes? The only things that fit me right now have elastic waistbands. Will I need to dress up?"

"Whatever you want to wear is fine."

She takes in my charcoal suit slacks and knit cream-colored polo. "Of course you look amazing. How am I going to compete with that? I don't even know where we're going. Just give me a hint so I can—"

I press a finger to her lips. "Put on a dress, Luna. I'll meet you downstairs."

She exhales, her breath warm against my skin. Then she kisses my finger and spins for the closet.

She kissed my finger. It's not like she dropped to her knees and unzipped my pants. And yet, the night hasn't even started and I'm already hard as a rock.

Just another sign I'm doing the right thing. No one has ever gotten to me the way this woman does.

The only reason I even kind of want to pump the brakes is Nikandr. Lying next to Luna last night with this plan coming together in my mind, I told myself that if it was the right time, Nik would wake up.

It was stupid—I know better than most that life isn't some fucking fairytale. Still, I thought that there would be some sign that this is what I should do. After all, Nik should be here for these kinds of moments. My life is moving forward and my brother is supposed to be here to witness it; he's supposed to have a life of his own.

But his doctor called this morning and gave me the same news I've been getting every day for weeks.

No change.

I've come to expect it. Each time my phone rings, I brace myself for the worst. *No change* is better than the worst. That doesn't make the words hurt any less.

I lean against the banister at the base of the stairs and drag a hand through my hair. I can't live my life based on signs from the universe or fucking *vibes*. I'm in charge of my own destiny and I want Luna standing next to me, regardless of what else is happening around us.

As the thought enters my head, there's movement at the top of the stairs.

Luna is standing there in a blue sundress the same shade as her eyes and I'm half a second away from dropping to one knee right now. Fuck the rest of the night—I know what I want and it's already right in front of me.

She glances down at herself nervously. "Is this okay? It's kind of casual, but—"

"It's gorgeous." I climb the stairs and grab her hand. "*You're* gorgeous."

The waist of the dress sits just under her breasts. My attention bounces back and forth from the low-cut neckline to the obvious swell of her stomach.

Fuck, the sight of this woman carrying my child makes my blood stir.

Her cheeks flush pink as we walk downstairs together. "Is it fancy enough?" she asks. "I still have no clue what we're even doing."

"That's good, since it's a surprise."

"Good for *you*, maybe. I'm going out of my mind." She laughs. "It's been so long since I've gone anywhere that I think I've forgotten how."

In another life, I would have taken Luna everywhere. I lost years of my life escorting women I couldn't give a fuck less about to galas and weddings and countless other pointless events. It was all a show. A way for people to climb some pathetic social ladder and try to get close to me.

But with Luna on my arm, they wouldn't have dared get too close.

We would have fucking ruled.

We still will, once Pavel is dead. Then I won't have to hide her to keep her safe.

Luna tugs on my arm. "Come on, Yakov. Give me a hint."

"Okay. One hint." I lead her into the kitchen and stop so we're facing the patio doors.

All she can see through the doors are the string lights crisscrossing over the patio, but she still gasps. "Yakov!" she breathes. "What is all this?"

"I said one hint. That was it." I tug her forward.

"Is this all for me? Did you do this?" she asks. "When did you do this? I was out by the pool just a couple hours ago. How did you—"

Her voice cuts off when we step through the doors.

Lights wind up the base of all the trees around the patio and the usual patio furniture has been swapped out for an intimate table and two chairs. Candles sit in the center of the table, flickering in the breeze.

Luna turns to me with wide eyes. "You did all this for me?"

I shrug. "Are you surprised?"

"Yes… and no." She loops her arm through mine and smiles up at me. "You keep the romantic part of you hidden pretty dang well, but I still know it's there."

I slide her chair in and a server approaches with two champagne flutes between his fingers and a bottle in his other hand. Luna eyes the bottle and looks back to me, concerned.

"Sparkling grape juice," I whisper.

She stifles a laugh as the waiter pours us each a glass.

Luna smells the first course coming before it even hits the table. "Fresh bread." She turns to watch the waiter carrying the warm baguette across the patio towards us.

"With honey butter," I add.

She leans in close, her eyes locked on mine. "Whatever you have planned for the rest of the night, cancel it. You've done enough."

I laugh, but then she takes her first bite of warm bread drenched in softened butter, and I don't think she was kidding. She moans.

I have to readjust the front of my pants. "You're making it look like I never feed you."

"I've been craving this all day. When I woke up today, I was telling Hope how I was ready to kill for some good bread. How did you know?"

"I know everything, Luna."

Especially when Hope passes helpful information like that up the chain of command.

Luna is polishing off the baguette when the main course comes out. "Braised lamb shank in a rosemary and red wine sauce," the server explains.

When he's gone, Luna sniffs her plate.

"The alcohol cooks out."

"And how do you know that?" she asks.

"Because I threatened the chef within an inch of his life if he gave you anything that could hurt our babies," I say. "Everything here is safe. I'm taking care of you."

She grins over her glass of grape juice. "That you certainly are."

We eat and talk until our plates are empty and taken away, replaced with dessert. But I'm not paying attention to the food. I'm fixed on the woman across from me.

The way her hair shimmers gold in the candlelight. The way she lights up when she laughs talking about the reality dating show she got my sister hooked on.

When my father died, I watched my mother crumple. I saw what it looked like to be left behind, and I decided then and there that I was never going to let myself be broken that way. That's what love is, after all. You break your heart and give it to someone else to carry. When they're gone, you're fucked.

Love is loss.

It's also the woman sitting across from me.

It's Luna sleeping and fucking and laughing in my bed.

She's the mother of my children and there isn't a single person on the fucking planet I'd rather break my heart for.

The box is on the table between us before I have time to think about it.

Luna is smiling, a bite of rhubarb and apple crumble in her mouth. "What's that?"

"Open it and see for yourself."

She slides her plate out of the way and reaches for the box. Her fingers are trembling. Part of her already knows the truth.

Still, when she opens the velvet lid, her eyes go wide. "A ring."

"An engagement ring," I specify. "I figured we should make it official."

She looks from me to the box and back again. The only part of her moving is her eyes. It's like she's frozen.

I pluck the box out of her hand and pull the ring out. It's an oval-cut diamond set in a circle of smaller stones.

"This belonged to my mother," I tell her, turning the ring over in my fingers. "Before that, it was her mother's ring. It's been in my family for generations."

Luna claps a hand over her mouth. My name is muffled between her fingers. "Yakov."

"When my father died, my mother gave me this ring and made me swear I'd wait for the right woman." I grab her left hand, the ring poised at the tip of her finger. "I know that woman is you, Luna."

Her blue eyes are glassy with tears. She's blinking them away as fast as they fall. "Yes. Yakov, yes. I'll marry you."

I press the ring onto her finger and bring her knuckles to my lips. "It wasn't a question, *solnyshka*."

27

LUNA

We make it from the patio to our room somehow, but it's a blur. He carries me up the stairs and I am so distracted by his lips and the dirty promises he's whispering into my skin that I don't even consider complaining.

Yakov closes the door and presses me back against the cool wood. His hands are tangled in my hair, his knee pressed between my spread thighs.

I pull away from his lips, already panting. "You said something about a present."

Yakov doesn't stop kissing me for a second. His lips blaze down my neck to my chest. He shoves the straps of my dress off my shoulders. "What?"

"A present. When we were coming up the stairs, you said you had another surprise waiting for me."

I don't care about the present, but if I don't slow this down, we won't even make it to the bed. Though I'm not sure that's really a problem, either.

He makes a noise of recognition in the back of his throat and slowly moves me towards the bed. By the time he lowers me to the edge of it, his lips have purged every thought from my brain. When he backs away from me, edging towards the closet, I swipe out for his shirt to drag him back.

It's only when he returns with a stack of two black boxes in his hands that I remember what's going on. He hands me the top one. "Open this."

I don't argue. The last time he told me to open a box, he proposed. I have good luck with black boxes.

I lift the lid and pull out a black negligée.

"I saw that and thought of you," Yakov says.

Feeling sexy isn't always easy, especially after months of throwing up and watching my body change. But knowing he picked this out for me, hoping I'd wear it for him—there's nothing sexier than that.

"I better try it on." I unzip the side of my dress and let it fall to the floor. A bra wouldn't go with my dress, so I'm naked from the waist up. "To make sure it fits."

Yakov releases a harsh exhale. "Or you can stay like this. It'll save me time."

I step into the nightie and slide it over my hips. "I didn't realize we were in a hurry."

"We have all the time in the world." Yakov strokes a slow finger down my collarbone and then cups my breast in his rough palm. "I'm just eager to hear you begging for my cock all fucking night long."

His green eyes are hooded as he bends towards me. He brushes his lips softly against mine, but then his hand curls around the back of my head. He hauls me against him with crushing force. I gasp as he slips his tongue between my parted lips.

I arch against him, groaning at the obvious bulge in his pants. We may have all the time in the world, but I'm ready *now*. He thinks he's eager? *Pshhh.* He doesn't know the meaning of the word.

"There's more." Yakov pulls away, leaving me stumbling forward from the loss of him. He grabs the second black box and holds it out to me. "Open it."

I'm breathless, desire pooling between my legs. I look up at him. "I don't want more presents, Yakov. I want you."

His eyes darken another shade, but he shoves the box into my hands. "Then open it."

I do as he says, lifting the lid. It's like a treasure chest. A box full of gold. Except... it isn't jewelry.

I pull out a gold, curved shape and press the button at the end. It vibrates to life against my palm.

"Is this—"

Yakov takes the box out of my hands and shoves me back on the bed. He snatches away the vibrator and shoves my thighs apart with his knees.

"It's a twenty-four-karat gold vibrator." He runs the vibration up and down my soaked panties. "Only the best for my future wife."

I'm not sure what's doing it for me more: the toy or the way Yakov is looking at me like he wants to devour every single inch of me.

I drop my head back on the mattress as he presses the toy against my clit. He slides my panties to the side and slips the toy into me, pressing it deeper until it curls against my inner wall. I try to draw my legs together, but Yakov holds me open for him.

"You're already dripping, Luna. I can smell you." He kisses his way up my inner leg as the vibration on the toy shifts into a higher gear. "I want to taste you."

He drags his tongue over my clit, and I nearly arch off the bed. He circles his lips over me, sucking and flicking his tongue until I'm rolling against his face.

"Yakov," I beg, fisting the comforter. "Yakov, I need—I'm going to—"

Suddenly, he's gone.

The vibration is gone and Yakov is standing over me, a feral look in his eyes. "No, you aren't. Not yet."

I know what he wants. He doesn't need to say it.

I slide off the bed and drop to my knees in front of him. His cock springs free when I unzip his pants, and I take him in my mouth like I'm starving for him.

Which, you know… I am.

There's a needy pulse between my legs that he put there. I know he'll take care of it later, again and again. That's what Yakov does. He takes care of me.

I slide him deep into my mouth, my cheeks hollowing around him. His fingers tangle in my hair as he groans.

"This mouth is mine." He thrusts between my lips, pressing deeper and deeper. He grunts out a low curse and pulls back.

I wrap my hand around him, stroking him roughly. "Does that make this cock mine?"

He smooths my hair away from my forehead, grabbing a fistful so he can arch my neck. "What's mine is yours, *solnyshka.*"

He thrusts into my mouth until my eyes water. Until the only thing keeping me upright is his hand in my hair. And I love it.

I love it even more when his breathing goes ragged and his thighs clench. When I know he's on the edge because of me. I speed up, sucking and working my hand around his base.

"Fuck." His hand tightens in my hair. "Luna."

I squeeze his thigh, wordlessly telling him, *It's okay. I want this. Please.*

He's been so careful with me since I got pregnant. I want to feel him lose control. I want to know I was the one to take him there.

His hips stutter once and then he's spilling into my mouth. He holds my head with both hands as I swallow and suck and drink him down.

When he's finished, he lays me back on the bed. He brushes his thumb over my lip and slips it into my mouth, cleaning me up. His eyes are nearly black.

"Did I do good?" I whisper.

He shakes his head. "No, Luna. You didn't."

I frown, confused. "But—"

He curls his hand over my panties and then slips his finger inside of me. "I was supposed to come in here. I was supposed to finish inside of you. But you distracted me with that fucking mouth of yours."

I bite back a smile. "I'm sorry."

"No, you aren't." He arches a brow, looking me over. "But you will be."

Yakov rips my panties and shoves the negligée up over my breasts. His mouth clamps down on my nipple as he drives two fingers into me.

He grabs for something over my head and a second later, the cool gold of the vibrator is pressed against my clit. I arch off the bed as it roars to life, but Yakov stays with me. He curls his fingers inside of me and holds the vibrator close, relentless even as I fight and squirm.

"Wait!" I pant, squeezing my thighs together even though it does no good. Yakov is everywhere. "I want you inside of me. I want—"

"This is about what I want right now," he scolds, his jaw clenched. "And I want you to come for me like my perfect little slut. Hard."

With another curl of his fingers inside of me, I do as he says. I don't have a choice.

There's no finesse to my orgasm, no slow build. It's a wall of pleasure and I smack head-first into it. I clamp down around his hand, riding his fingers as I shatter apart on the bed.

He pulls the vibrator away and when I look down, Yakov has his cock in his hand. He's already hard again. Without a word, he drags me to the edge of the mattress, grabs my waist, and flips me onto my front. He's moving fast, but he holds my stomach up until I can rest on my elbows. Even now, he's protecting me and our babies.

Then he drives every inch of himself deep inside of me.

I arch my back, taking all of him, moaning as he stretches me.

"I don't need to tell you this is mine," he says, stroking out and back in. "This pussy has been mine since the night we met."

I push my hips back against him to take more.

He groans and digs his fingers into my skin. Our bodies slap together, but I can feel him holding back. There's a leash on his desire and I want to snap it.

"No one has ever fucked me like you, Yakov." I grab my breasts, holding them steady as I shake with every thrust.

He falls over me, hitting an even deeper place inside of me. I bury my face in the comforter to muffle my screams.

Yakov grabs my hair and arches my neck, still slamming into me. "Scream for me, Luna. Tell me how good I make you feel."

He thrusts in again and again, touching every one of my nerve endings until I can't contain myself. I fall to pieces, pulsing around him as heat floods all the way to my fingers and toes. My entire body tingles with pleasure and I never want it to end.

"More," I groan. "Don't stop."

Yakov slams into me, but his breath catches. "I love feeling you come around my cock. I love—"

My eyes flutter closed at that last word... *Love?* But Yakov is too busy falling to pieces himself to complete the sentence. I rock with him as wave after wave tears through his body while he pulses into mine. Until, finally, he's utterly spent.

He lays his cheek against my spine and murmurs, "You."

"What?" I ask, forgetting how we got here.

"You," he breathes. "I love you, solnyshka."

28

LUNA

I wake up with a delicious ache between my legs and Yakov's arm around my waist. His breath is warm and even on the back of my neck. He doesn't usually sleep in, but after last night, I'm not surprised he's tired.

I hold my hand up to the morning light pouring through the floor-to-ceiling windows. I didn't get a good look at the ring last night. I was preoccupied with Yakov and all the other shiny things he bought me.

We woke up several times last night, finding each other in the dark. For the first time in weeks, I didn't have a single nightmare. There was no time.

I twist my hand one way and the other. The center diamond sparkles and light reflects off the smaller diamonds onto the headboard.

Yakov's arm tightens around me. "Do you like it?"

"It's gorgeous, but I like the man who gave it to me a lot more."

He kisses the back of my neck. "How did you sleep?"

"That's the one thing we didn't do much of last night."

A dark chuckle vibrates through his chest. "We had to celebrate."

"We should *celebrate* more often," I purr.

Yakov's teeth scrape softly over my skin. "These hormones of yours are going to kill me. I need to rehydrate."

"And I should probably sleep," I admit. "I'm exhausted."

"Perfect. You sleep while I go get some work done."

He starts to slide away from me, but I flip over and reach for him. "You're leaving?"

"Duty calls." He strokes a finger down the center of my palm. I feel it everywhere.

"Will you be back when I wake up?" I whine.

"Probably not. But I'll be back by tonight."

I stretch my arms over my head, arching my back off the bed. "That's okay. If I get bored, I'll use the new toys you got me to keep myself occupied."

In an instant, Yakov is over top of me, his strong hand banding my throat. "The only time you're permitted to use those is when I'm there to supervise."

"Is that an order?" I ask, biting back a smile.

"I can make it a threat if you're going to test me."

I stretch up and kiss him. "I'll be a good girl."

He exhales harshly and mumbles, "You're actually going to kill me."

I watch as he slips out of bed and grabs his clothes for the day. I've never seen a more beautiful naked person. Every inch of him is hard and sculpted. He's like a painting come to life.

I'm going to marry him. The thought sends warmth through my chest and I can't help but smile.

Yakov stops in the bathroom door. "What are you smiling about?"

"You're going to be my husband."

He gives me a rare grin. "Spread the news, if you want. My sister will love to hear I've finally proposed. Hope already knows since she helped set things up yesterday, but she was giddy. You can even call Kayla, if you want."

"Does that mean you trust Kayla now? You don't think she's a spy?"

He rolls his eyes. "It means I trust you. If you trust her, then that's fine by me."

Yakov says it like it's not a big deal, but there was a time where I didn't know if he'd ever trust me, let alone my friends. But here we are, engaged and domestic.

Kayla won't believe it.

❧

"I don't believe it," Kayla gasps. "*He* proposed to *you*? Of his own free will?"

I snort. "Do you think I blackmailed him into it or something?"

"Obviously not. He has too much over you. There's no way *you* could manipulate *him*."

"Would you stop saying everything like that?" I snap. "You're using emphasis in insulting ways. You were supposed to say, 'Congratulations, Luna. I'm so happy for you.'"

There's a long pause. Long enough that I glance down at my phone to make sure Kayla is still on the line.

Finally, she sighs. "I'm happy that you sound so happy."

Almost, but not quite.

"I don't just sound happy, Kay. I *am* happy. I'm thrilled, actually. I love him."

"I know you do," she says. "But that doesn't mean he's right for you."

This is not going anything like when I told Mariya. Yakov's sister pulled me into a hug, demanded to see the ring, and asked for a play-by-play of everything Yakov did and said last night. For her sake, I left out everything after the proposal. There's no need to traumatize the poor girl.

"Yakov is not Benjy," I say.

"You say that, but this feels kind of like Benjy," she says. "I've barely seen you for months, we hardly talk, and Yakov clearly doesn't want you hanging out with me."

"That's not true!"

"Which part?" Kayla asks. "Because from where I'm sitting, it's all true."

"Okay, so some of it is true. But the only reason I've been MIA recently is because Yakov was trying to keep me safe. And it's not that he doesn't want us hanging out."

"He kicked me out the last time I was there. With no explanation."

I sigh. "That was... that was not great. I'm sorry about that. But he's having a hard time with what happened and his brother being in the hospital."

"You're making excuses for him the same way you did for Benjy," she says softly.

"The difference is that Benjy isn't sitting behind the phone feeding me lines!" I snap.

Kayla gasps. "He did that?"

I never told her that. I've never told anyone. Now, I remember why. My face flames with embarrassment.

"Things with Benjy were… worse than you know," I say, trying to keep my voice even. "I know you're looking out for me right now, but I need you to know that I would never put myself back in that kind of situation. Not after I fought so hard to get out."

"I didn't know," Kayla says softly. "I didn't realize—"

"And that's okay. The only thing I need you to realize now is that I'm capable of determining when I'm happy. I don't need you to do it for me. Yakov makes me happy and I need you to trust that."

"Of course I can trust that, Loon. I'm sorry."

"It's okay."

There's a long pause before she says, "So do I still get to be your maid of honor or…?"

I cackle. "There's the Kayla I know and love."

When Kayla and I finally hang up after thirty minutes of her walking me through the tackiest wedding trends I must avoid, I'm exhausted.

Partially because I never went back to sleep after Yakov left this morning. But it feels like more than that. I've barely eaten anything all day because of constant nausea and my eyes burn with the need to sleep.

I lie down on the bed and am asleep almost before my head hits the pillow.

When I wake up, the world beyond the windows is streaked with afternoon light and there's a small pink box on the end of the bed.

I sit up immediately. "Yakov?"

I listen, but I don't hear him. His shoes aren't by the closet and his phone isn't on the nightstand. There's no sign of him.

I crawl across the bed and rip the lid off of the box. This time, it isn't a ring or a box of sex toys; it's a necklace. A delicate golden chain with a rose gold pendant hanging from the center. It's beautiful.

"Yakov?" I call again, but no one answers.

He must have stopped by to give it to me, but wanted to let me sleep.

I put the necklace on and reach for my phone. ***Thank you for the gift, Yakov.***

I fall back asleep before he responds.

29

LUNA

I wake up with a gasp, my hands wrapped around my stomach.

"It's okay," Yakov mumbles next to me. "I'm here. It's just a dream."

My stomach twists and I can't catch my breath. "No. It's not—"

"It was just a dream." He tries to press me gently back into bed.

"Yakov," I gasp, twisting away from him. "I'm not dreaming."

Instantly, he's next to me, his large hand on my arm. "What is it?"

Another sharp pain radiates across my midsection. I hunch forward with a whimper.

Yakov doesn't need to hear anything else. He grabs his phone off the nightstand. "You need to get to my house now," he growls. "Bring your equipment. Something is wrong."

He hangs up and comes next to me, pushing me back onto the bed as I try to stand up.

"Stay still," he orders. "Dr. Jenkins is on his way."

"I think walking might help."

I have no idea why I think that, but it's my instinct. Right now, delirious and in pain, instinct is all I have to go on.

Yakov grabs my elbow and helps me walk slowly back and forth across the room. With every lap, the tension in my core ebbs away. I can breathe again.

"Has this happened before?" he asks.

"I felt nauseous all day yesterday, but I didn't think—"

"You should have told me," he snaps. "I would have called Dr. Jenkins sooner."

"I didn't think anything was wrong. It was just nausea. Whatever just happened now was different." A sob catches in my throat. "Do you think something is wrong?"

He presses his hand to my lower back, steadying me. "It will all be fine."

Half an hour later, Dr. Jenkins is next to my bed with a large black bag and a portable ultrasound machine. "It isn't the most high-tech device, but it'll do in a pinch," he says with a nervous smile. "Just lie back and let me have a look."

Yakov squeezes my hand as Dr. Jenkins presses the wand to my stomach.

Instantly, I see my babies. There are two heads visible on the screen with a tangle of arms and legs wiggling around.

They're alive. I didn't realize how scared I was that they weren't until I see them moving.

"They're okay?" I whimper.

"It appears so," Dr. Jenkins says. "I don't see anything wrong. Heartbeats are strong."

"She woke up with cramping. That can't be normal," Yakov snarls.

Dr. Jenkins shrugs. "Actually, it can be. What have you been up to over the last twenty-four to forty-eight hours, Luna?"

I walk him backwards through my day. "I skipped dinner, went for a swim, ate a small lunch and breakfast. Last night, I…" I hesitate, glancing at Yakov. "Well, we…"

"We got engaged," Yakov explains. "Last night, we celebrated. A few times."

Dr. Jenkins frowns at first, but I see the moment it clicks. "Intercourse."

My face is burning hot. "Yes."

"Well then, that could explain it," he says. "There can be cramping after sex. Especially if it is… enthusiastic, shall we say. It also sounds like you may be a bit dehydrated. You need to make sure you're eating and drinking more than normal, especially as your pregnancy continues."

"That's it?" I ask.

He smiles. "That's it. Everything is fine."

I smile up at Yakov. "I guess I made a big deal out of nothing. I'm sorry."

But he isn't smiling. He's staring at the ultrasound, watching our babies kick and wiggle. Then he turns to Dr. Jenkins. "I want you to make a daily house call to check on her from this point on."

Dr. Jenkins blinks. "Daily for the next five months?"

"Yakov," I butt in, "that's not necessary. I'm fine."

"It wasn't a suggestion," he says, a dangerous edge to his voice.

Dr. Jenkins looks from me to Yakov. "I have to agree with Luna. That's really not necessary. Her pregnancy is progressing normally. There's no reason to worry about—"

"There won't be a single reason to worry once you're examining her every day."

The doctor sighs. "Mr. Kulikov, I understand that this can be a stressful experience for the parents, but I am not at all concerned about Luna or your babies."

"Okay. So if something happens to Luna or my children, I will hold you personally responsible." Yakov studies the man. "Are you concerned now?"

Dr. Jenkins goes pale as he nods. "I'll—I'll be back tomorrow after lunch."

Yakov sees Dr. Jenkins out a few minutes later and then comes back with a glass of water for me. "Drink this."

"I'm really okay. I don't think Dr. Jenkins needs to come see me every day. What if we just did once per week?"

He presses the glass of water into my hand and doesn't say a word until I've taken a drink.

"He is in the city to take care of you. That is what I'm paying him for. If I asked him to examine you once an hour, he'd have to do it."

"That would really be overkill," I tease.

Yakov lays his hand on my stomach. "I'm not taking any chances."

I lay my hand over his, twining our fingers together. "I guess I can't fault you for that."

"No, you really can't."

I snort. "Between this overprotective bit and all the presents you've been leaving for me, I should probably stop arguing and start enjoying the pampering."

He frowns. "You didn't dig into your gifts while I was away, did you? I gave you explicit orders to wait until I was home."

"Don't worry, I didn't touch the toys." I reach into the collar of my shirt and pull out the rose necklace.

Yakov squints. "What is that?"

"My necklace. The one you left on the bed for me."

He leans closer, his face going as pale as Dr. Jenkins' just did.

"I texted you about it," I continue.

Without warning, he grabs the necklace and snaps it off my neck.

I yelp, hang at my throat. "What are you doing?!"

"Tell me where you got this," he says, his voice shaking with rage. "Tell me *exactly* where and when you got it."

I huddle back against the headboard. "It was on the end of the bed! I woke up from a nap in the afternoon and there was a box on the end of the bed. I thought it was from you. I thought—"

Before I can finish, Yakov turns and storms out of the room.

I don't realize I'm shaking until I try to stand up. My legs buckle under me and I have to grab the edge of the bed to stabilize myself.

I hear Yakov pounding down the stairs. A few seconds later, the front door slams closed.

I'm still shaking next to the bed when Mariya pokes her head through my bedroom door. "Luna?"

"I don't know what just happened." I swipe tears off of my cheeks. "Yakov just—I don't—"

Mariya grabs my arm and lowers me to the bed. "Breathe, Loon. You're panicking."

I take deep breaths in and out until my heart rate slows. Then I reach for my phone. "I need to call him. Does he think I'm cheating on him? Because I'm not. I don't know where that necklace came from."

"What necklace?" Mariya swipes my phone out of my hand. "You're not calling anyone until you tell me what is going on."

I reach for my neck before I remember Yakov ripped the chain off of me. "There was a necklace. Yesterday, I woke up from a nap and there was a box on the end of my bed. It had a necklace inside of it. I assumed it was from Yakov, but he looked at it like he'd never seen it before."

"Someone left you a gift on your bed and it wasn't my brother?"

I shrug. "I guess. But Yakov stormed off. I have no idea what he's thinking."

"I do," Mariya says softly.

I turn to her and she's chewing on her lower lip. "What is it?"

"Someone—*not Yakov*—left you a gift on the end of your bed and he has no idea who it was." She looks at me, waiting for the pieces to click together. "This mansion is a fortress. Nobody gets in or out without Yakov knowing about it. Especially not in his bedroom."

"He thinks someone broke into the house," I whisper.

All those days I felt the hair on the back of my neck stand up... All those times I felt like someone was watching me...

Someone *was* watching me. I'm sure of it.

The question now is... what do they want with me?

30

YAKOV

"Check the cameras again," I snarl.

My fist is clenched so tightly I'll probably have a permanent indentation of that fucking rose in my palm. But I can't relax. I can't let this go until I know who was in my room—in my house. Until I know who was close to my fiancée without my permission.

Isay scrolls through the footage for the third time. "There's nothing, Yakov. The only movement on the perimeter cameras was when you left yesterday morning and during the routine perimeter checks. No one is on this footage that shouldn't be there."

"Are there gaps in the coverage?" I ask.

"There aren't cameras along the back fence where it meets the drainage ditch. We didn't think we needed them. The fence is so high right there that almost no one could—"

"*Almost* no one could scale it." I let the necklace slip between my fingers and hold it in front of his face. "But someone fucking did. Someone was in my house and I want to know who the fuck it was."

But I know.

Who else could it be?

Pavel Gustev called me personally to let me know he was coming for Luna. The question I need answered now isn't who was in my house, but who let him in.

"I want every person who knows where the cameras are in this mansion in front of me right fucking now."

"You think there's a rat?" Isay asks.

"How else would Pavel know where to enter my property? How else would he be able to dodge every single camera we have and get into my house?"

Rage courses through me like acid. I feel it eating through me. *He was in my house. He was close to Luna.*

Did he leave the necklace on the bed while she was sleeping? The image of some dark figure lurking over her while she sleeps will haunt my fucking nightmares for the rest of my life.

Or at least until Pavel is dead. The date of which is getting closer and closer with every passing second.

"These men are loyal to you," Isay says. "I would vouch for every single man on the security team, sir."

I spin towards him. "Would you? Would you stake your life on their loyalty, Isay?"

His mouth opens and closes. "I don't—I mean, I believe in them, but I wouldn't—"

"If you wouldn't stake your life on it, then don't waste my fucking time talking about it," I growl. "I want them in front of me now. I want to hear it from their mouths so I can smell the lies on them. Whoever it is won't see the next sunrise."

Isay swallows and pulls out his phone, tapping out a message.

Before he can even send it, there's a knock on the door. Kuzma comes in before I can say anything. "You're needed at the front gates, sir."

"It's the middle of the fucking night."

"One of the many reasons we have a delivery guy detained there awaiting your interrogation," he agrees.

I set my jaw. Then I follow Kuzma down the driveway towards the security shack. Before I even open the door, I hear the sniveling.

"I didn't do anything wrong!" the voice says. "I was paid to drop off the envelope. I have no clue what is inside of it. You have to believe me!"

"We don't have to do anything," Savva spits.

The sound of a fist meeting flesh fills the air followed by more whimpering.

When I step into the doorway, Savva steps back. "I should have waited for you to open the envelope, but I wanted to make sure it wasn't dangerous. Then I opened it and I—I couldn't just sit here."

I see a large manila envelope on the desk behind Savva. I grab it and start to pull out the papers inside. But I stop when I see the corner of a bed—*my bed*. I slide it further and see Luna's black lingerie in a pile on my carpet.

Then I see a foot... a leg.

I yank the paper out and find myself staring down at a photo of Luna lying on my bed. She's asleep, her hands curled under her chin, her blonde hair spread out on the pillow behind her.

At the end of the bed is a small jewelry box.

In the corner of the photo is a hand in a black glove.

A stranger in my house. An enemy near my pregnant fiancée. He was within striking distance of my entire fucking future.

My vision narrows and tunnels. All I see is the photo in front of me and the groaning man on the floor of the shack.

I slap the photo against Savva's chest and haul the delivery guy up by the neck. A strangled shout tears out of his mouth, but it chokes off when I slam him against the wall.

"Where the fuck did you get this picture?"

His eyes are bulging out of the sockets, blood vessels popping in his cheeks as he struggles to breathe. I could kill him. *Should* kill him. Anyone involved in getting Pavel inside my fucking mansion needs to die.

But I know terror. The different shades and flavors of it. The terror I'm seeing in this man's eyes isn't because he's been caught; it's because he has no clue what is going on.

I force my fingers to release their hold on his neck. He sinks to the floor, gasping for air. "I don't know anything," he rasps out. "Someone paid me to deliver an envelope to this address. I didn't look—I don't—"

"Who?" I snarl.

He shakes his head and my foot is crashing into his stomach before the words can even leave his lips.

He doubles over with a groan. "I don't know! I really don't know. Please don't kill me. I have a family."

I grab him by his hair. "So do I. And whoever paid you wants to kill them."

His eyes go wide. "I didn't know! I just took the money. I have no idea what's going on."

"You never met who hired you?" Savva asks.

The delivery guy shakes his head so hard his cheeks flap. "I got hired online. There was an envelope in a box with the cash. I picked it up and brought it here. I never even saw the person."

I believe him.

I also believed my mansion was impenetrable. I believed Luna was safe here. Now that someone got inside and made it all the way to her, I have to question everything.

I slam him against the wall, the air whooshing out of his lungs. Then I drive my fist into his stomach once and again.

As he starts to crumple, I pin him against the wall, my voice a deadly whisper in his ear. "If I find out you are lying to me, it won't just be you who suffers. I'll hunt down every person you know and love and kill them in front of your eyes."

He inhales sharply. "I swear, I don't know anything. I promise you I—"

"You'll watch everyone in your orbit die before I pluck your lying eyes out of your head and let you choke on them," I growl. "Do you understand me?"

"Yes," he sobs. "Yes. I'm telling the truth. I don't know anything. I swear."

I let him fall to the floor and kick him towards the door. "Next time, don't accept a job you don't understand."

He scrambles across the floor, tripping and falling over his own hands and feet until he makes it to the grass. Then he lurches into a standing position and runs for the open gate.

As soon as the man is gone, Savva turns to me. "We've been scouring the footage, but there isn't anything—"

I shove past him and tear down the driveway.

No one knows anything.

No one knows how this happened.

But *I* do.

I failed her. I underestimated my enemy and Luna could have been lost. My children could have—

I clench my teeth until they ache, my breath coming out in an angry huff. When I get inside, the anger pounding through me is lethal. If I don't kill the next thing I see, this rage will fucking swallow me. So I turn into my office and lock the door.

The room is dark, but I don't need light for this.

I grab the table next to the door and hurl it across the room. It snaps against the wall, the leg gouging the sheetrock. I lift the leather chair across from my desk over my head and slam it against the wood floor. I turn my filing cabinet on end. I rip a sconce from the wall. I swing my desk lamp into the back of the door over and over until the stainless steel is pulp in my hands and the door is a mess of splinters.

I force the adrenaline out of me by destroying one piece of furniture at a time until there is nothing left. Until the dust in the air burns my lungs and I turn and slam my fist through the wall.

It isn't enough to ease the rage inside of me. It won't be enough until it's Pavel's skull I'm crushing. Until it's *his* blood on my knuckles.

But it's enough that I can focus on what needs to happen next.

I need to get Luna and our babies out of here

31

LUNA

"We're leaving."

The bedroom door flies open and Yakov has a duffel bag in his hands before I can even process what he said.

As soon as the door opened, Mariya shifted protectively in front of me. Even when she sees it's Yakov, she stays planted in place.

"Now," Yakov adds, shoving a wad of clothes into a duffel bag.

Mariya glances at me, looking as confused as I feel. I squeeze her hand and follow behind Yakov as he moves around the room, shoving everything in the bedroom into a bag.

"Yakov, what is going on?"

"I'm packing," he bites out. "Obviously."

"But where are we going?"

"Away."

I blow out a sharp breath. "I need more than that. I need to understand what is going on and why you're—"

Suddenly, Yakov is a few inches in front of me, his hands like iron clamps on my shoulders. "I'm getting you somewhere safe, Luna. Pack what you want to take with you. Now."

Between one blink and the next, he's gone. But I can still see the distress in his eyes. It's burned into my vision like I spent too long staring at the sun.

I've never seen Yakov look scared. And right now, he's terrified. For *me*.

"Where would we go? I thought the mansion was safe. There are guards here. Security cameras. I thought—"

"You thought wrong." His knuckles are white around the straps of the duffel. He throws the back to the ground at his feet. "*I* was wrong. I can't keep the two of you safe here anymore, *solnyshka*. Just trust me."

"Of course I trust you, Yakov," I breathe. "I trust you with my life, but I don't understand why we need to do this."

"We're doing this because he's paranoid," Mariya spits. She glares at Yakov. "I'm not going to spend the next few months in some windowless bunker. I'll fly back to Moscow right now before I let you lock me up again."

I turn back to her, already shaking my head. I want Mariya on my side. Between the two of us, *maybe* we could convince Yakov to slow down, think this through, and let us stay here.

But this is not the way to get what we want. The more Mariya pushes, the more Yakov will dig in his heels. We will literally be locked up if she doesn't stop.

Yakov doesn't even look at her as he dumps my entire top drawer into the bag. "I'm not doing this with you, Mariya. There isn't time. Go pack."

She throws up her hands. "There's never time to explain anything! We are supposed to blindly trust you and go wherever you lead. But I'm tired of it. I'm almost eighteen. You can't force me to do anything I don't want to do."

I wince, bracing myself for Yakov to blow up at her. For the two of them to spiral off into some screaming match that will end with Yakov getting what he wants and Mariya being miserable about it for however long we are all in lockdown.

But Yakov doesn't yell. He turns to Mariya, his dark brows pinched together, and exhales. "They were in the mansion, Mariya. *In my room.*"

Mariya blinks, clearly as stunned as I am at his tone. For once, she doesn't have anything to say.

"Our enemies got into this house and were here with you while I was away." He runs a hand through his hair. "I have to keep you both safe."

"Not me. I can handle myself. If you're going to fight, let me stay and help," she says.

"You *are* helping me. I need you to be there for Luna."

He needs *her* to be there for me?

"But *you'll* be there for me," I blurt.

Yakov looks at me, something I don't understand flashing in his eyes. Then he looks back to Mariya. "I know you can hold your own. I saw you fighting with Akim's men. You've been trained for this life. That is exactly why I need you to be with Luna. I want someone with her who I know will one hundred percent have her back. That is you."

Mariya is looking down at the floor, her chin dimpled as she thinks.

"You'll be there for me," I repeat, stepping forward. "Yakov, you'll be there... won't you?"

If the mansion isn't safe, Yakov can't stay here. He won't send me away while I'm pregnant. Not when he's been so protective over me the last few months.

He's coming with us. He has to.

I repeat the lie to myself over and over again. I'm too terrified of the alternative to even consider what it would look like to be separated from him.

Mariya isn't suffering from the same delusion I am. She lifts her chin and nods once. "I'll do it. I'll take care of her."

Yakov lays a heavy hand on her shoulder and squeezes. "Thank you."

When she leaves, Yakov turns to me. "I'm not going to be able to change your mind, am I?" I ask softly before he can speak.

"Not when it comes to your safety," he says. "Not about this."

I blink back tears. "What about your safety?"

"You said you trusted me."

"I do." I swipe at my cheeks.

Yakov caresses his thumb slowly over my jawbone. "Then finish packing. We leave in fifteen minutes."

32

LUNA

I try to stay awake on the drive.

It's not like I'm great with directions under the best of circumstances and it's so dark outside that it's hard to see where we're going anyway, but having the hood over my head while Akim's men kidnapped me was disorienting. Tonight, I want to know where I am and how to get away if I need to.

But Yakov squeezes my hand over the center console as he drives. The heat is on in the car and the ride is so smooth that, before I know it, I'm opening my eyes as Yakov puts the car into park.

"Wake up. We're here," he says softly.

I've been awake for less than a second, but my heart is pounding. I sit up, looking wide-eyed through the windshield. "Where is 'here'?"

"It's a safehouse. No one but Nik and I know it even exists."

"Thanks for letting me in on that secret," Mariya mumbles sarcastically from the backseat. "I guess I can't be trusted."

"It's Vera and Usev's place," Yakov tells her.

Mariya gasps. "I haven't seen them since Dad's funeral."

"That's on purpose. The less of a connection they have to our family, the safer their house is."

"We can trust them?" I ask.

Yakov grabs my hand and brings my knuckles to his lips. "I wouldn't leave you here if I couldn't trust them. They are good people. They'll keep you safe."

I want to say, You *can keep me safe.* Arguments I know won't work rise up in my mind. Yakov is set on this, so it's going to happen whether I like it or not. And I *don't* like it. I don't care how safe these people are —they aren't Yakov.

But I don't want to make things harder for him. If he has to go off and face some threat, I don't want him worried that I'll be here trying to dig a tunnel to freedom. I'm on his side. If this is what he needs from me… I'll do it.

That doesn't mean I have to like it.

Yakov lets go of my hand and reaches across to the glove compartment. His woodsy scent surrounds me as he pulls two black phones out and hands each of us one.

"My number is loaded into the contacts if you need anything. These are basically bricks, but you still have to be careful. You can't use it for whatever the fuck you want." Yakov narrows his eyes on Mariya in the backseat. "It's for emergency use only. Any contact with anyone outside of me could put you both at risk."

"I doubt this thing can even complete a phone call." Mariya wrinkles her nose as she weighs the heavy phone in her palm. "But I understand. No outside communication."

Yakov grabs our bags from the trunk and leads us up the narrow sidewalk to the house. It's a modest craftsman-style house on a quiet street. The only lamp is at the end of the block, so it's shrouded in shadow. A well-kept garden lines the front of the house just under matching large windows. All the curtains are drawn, only the thinnest hints of light peeking out between the gaps.

As soon as Yakov steps onto the porch, the front door opens. I don't see who is behind it until we're inside a dimly-lit living room and the door is shut and bolted.

A bald man in house slippers—Usev, I presume—looks through the peephole and then asks Yakov something in Russian.

Yakov answers, a short, staccato conversation taking place before a woman with graying hair wearing a baby blue robe walks into the room. It must be Vera. She cups Mariya's face and utters something I don't understand.

Miraculously, Mariya doesn't swat the woman's hands away like I expect. She smiles and gives her a quick hug.

Then Vera turns to me. She pats my stomach, looks directly into my eyes, and asks me a question.

"I don't speak Russian," I admit sheepishly. Apparently, I should learn. I hate being out of the loop. Yakov answers for me. Vera's eyes go wide. She frowns down at my stomach and then holds up two fingers. Yakov nods.

I know they're talking about me and the twins, but I wish I knew what exactly they were saying.

"Vera is a midwife," Mariya says in my ear, translating. "She has never delivered twins before, but she is confident she can—"

"I'm not having my babies here," I blurt. I look at Yakov. "I won't be here that long, will I? This will be over before the babies come. Right? Won't it?"

Vera frowns, wearing the same confused expression I just had on. Apparently, neither of us speak the other's native tongue.

Yakov says something to Usev and Vera and then grabs my hand and pulls me along after him.

We cut through a narrow kitchen with apple wallpaper on the walls and down a set of rickety stairs to an unfinished, concrete basement. The walls are damp. The floor is damp. The *air* is damp. With every step deeper into the house, I feel like I'm being buried alive. There is no oxygen down here.

I've never been claustrophobic but as Mariya pulls the door at the top of the stairs closed and plunges us into darkness, I've never felt more panicked. I'm about to throw myself on Yakov's back and refuse to let go until he carries me out of here when he slides a bookshelf to the side to reveal a keypad. He punches in a code and a door swings open.

"This way," he says, ushering Mariya and I through the door. "In here."

Instantly, I can breathe.

The air is dry and fresh. It smells like cinnamon apples, which makes sense when I see an apple cake sitting on the countertop of the kitchenette to the right.

Straight ahead is a living room complete with a U-shaped sofa and a wall of bookshelves. Beyond that are three doors set into the back wall.

"Not bad," Mariya says. She grabs her bag from Yakov and heads for the door in the back right. She opens it and nods in approval. "This is definitely my bedroom. Dibs." Then she disappears inside.

"What is this place?" I ask.

Yakov leans wearily against the wall. "My father had it built when I was just a kid. Usev is an old friend of his. They grew up together in Russia. He isn't in the Bratva proper, but he's always been sympathetic to my father and our family. You can trust him."

"But why do I have to?" I try to hide it, but my lower lip wobbles. "I don't want to trust these people. I want to be with you."

"You can't. Not until it's safe."

"I thought it was safe. Akim is dead, isn't he?"

Yakov nods. "Akim is dead. Unfortunately, his younger brother isn't. Not yet."

The fire in his eyes is answer enough, but I ask the question anyway. "Is that who was in the house? Is that who gave me the necklace?"

"Pavel," Yakov confirms through gritted teeth. "He is out for revenge because I killed his brother. It makes him a loose cannon. I have no idea what he is going to try."

There are a few fake windows set into the walls that are meant to replicate daylight, but there isn't any real access to the outside world. I'm safe down here. But I feel suddenly exposed. It's the same feeling I got when I was outside at the mansion... like I was being watched.

"Is there any way he followed us here?"

"None." I don't realize how cold I am until Yakov runs his warm hands down my arms. "No one knows about this place and I made sure we weren't followed. I'm the only person in the world aside from Mariya and the couple upstairs who know you are here. You're safe."

"Then you should stay here. If we're safe, you should stay, too." I curl my hands around his neck. I want to press close, but my bump hits him first. Yakov gives me a sad smile and lays his palm against my belly. Then he grabs my hand and leads me to the door in the far left corner.

This bedroom is small but tidy. There's a full-sized bed with a handmade quilt thrown over the mattress and a stack of extra blankets sitting in a rocking chair in the corner. It's nothing like our room at the mansion.

Yakov locks the door behind us and then lifts me to the edge of the mattress. "I can't stay here with you... but I can stay for a few more minutes."

It's not enough. A few stolen minutes with Yakov will never be enough. I need all of him, all of the time.

But beggars can't be choosers. I grab the front of his shirt and jerk him towards me. Our mouths crash together at first, but the kiss immediately softens. I stroke my fingers through his hair and hold him close, tasting and memorizing every inch of him like it's the last chance I'll ever have.

It might be.

I blank the thought out, wrapping my legs around his thighs and pulling Yakov closer. All I have on is Yakov's large t-shirt. The last few hours were so hectic that I barely even noticed my lack of real clothes. He pushes the hem of the shirt up and over my hips before grabbing my panties and sliding them down.

His movements aren't frantic or hurried. He's taking his time with me. But right now, we both want the same thing.

Yakov drops my panties to the floor while I unzip his pants. The hard length of him springs out into my palm and I press him to my entrance.

I lean back on my hands while he slides slowly into me, stretching me around him inch by inch. When he's in me to the hilt, our eyes catch. The only sound in the room is our heavy breathing.

For this second, we are the only people who exist. There is no danger. No safehouse. No need for us to be apart. For the next few minutes, there is only the two of us and the way we've always fit together so perfectly.

I rest one hand against his square jaw. "I love you, Yakov."

"I don't want to hear that." Yakov pulls out of me and strokes back in. "I don't want to hear you say goodbye."

"But I wasn't—"

"You were," he says sharply, filling me again.

I press my palm to his heart. "Then what do you want to hear?"

He slowly spreads my thighs further apart. His fingers clutch around the tips of my legs, his thumb drawing a devastating circle over my clit. I moan.

"*That.*" He kisses my neck as he thrusts into me again and again. "I want to hear you come for me like you're mine. Like we'll be able to do this again tomorrow and the day after and the day after."

"Like nothing is going to change." I wrap one hand around his waist and cling to his lower back as he angles me back towards the bed.

He hits a deeper place in me and I cry out. "Nothing *is* going to change." His thumb and his cock work me inside and out until I can't form words. "It is always going to be like this, Luna. You and me."

Release pulses through me and I feel Yakov follow quickly behind. But even when it's over, I keep my legs wrapped around him, not wanting him to pull out yet. Wanting to stay here with him as long as I can.

"Promise me you'll call," I whisper.

Yakov hauls me against his chest and kisses my forehead. "Every chance I get."

33

YAKOV

The man's skull ricochets off my knuckles and smashes against the concrete wall behind him. His eyes are glazed over, unfocused, barely conscious. But I hit him again anyway.

"Is this knocking anything loose for you?" I ask, holding the man up by the bloodied front of his shirt. "Can you tell me what information you passed along to Pavel now?"

Isay found the man lurking around the perimeter of the mansion after I got back from dropping my sister and Luna off at the safehouse. Which pisses me the fuck off.

I checked my rearview mirror constantly while I was driving. Not to mention the frequent stops I made to double check for trackers. There's no way he followed me all the way from the house back to the mansion without me noticing.

But that still doesn't mean I'm taking a chance.

The man opens his mouth and blood dribbles out. There's a mushy, ugly gap where his front two teeth were just a few minutes ago.

"Tell me what you know," I demand.

He shakes his head. "Nothing. I know nothing."

I channel the rage still coursing through my veins and take another swing at the asshole.

He's a low-level grunt. Someone expendable Pavel probably sent on the off chance he could gather any good intel. At best, Pavel would get the drop on where Luna and Mariya are. At worst, he'd lose a nobody from his ranks.

I let go of the man's shirt and he crumples to the floor at my feet just as my phone rings.

It's a little early for the usual call from Nik's doctor, but it is still later in the morning than I thought it was. Especially since I've already been awake for five hours.

"Dispose of him," I tell Isay, nodding to the soldier. "Leave him where Pavel will find him."

The man starts to scream, but I close the soundproof basement door on his death and take the call.

"This is Yakov."

"Mr. Kulikov." Dr. Tung's voice is oddly formal. After daily phone calls for weeks, I'm used to the comfortable routine we've slipped into. The easy way she tells me nothing has changed and I continue on with my day like it isn't a fist to my fucking chest every goddamn time.

Whatever she's getting ready to say, I know I don't want to hear it. But I ask anyway.

"How did Nik do last night?"

"I know honesty is important to you, so I'll be blunt: not well. We've been weaning him off of the ventilator and he stopped breathing."

I stiffen, bracing myself the same way I would to take a punch to the gut. "Is he okay?"

"We brought him back, but…" She sighs. "I think it's time you came in and had a conversation with me and Nikandr's team about how we proceed from here. Can you come in this morning?"

"I'll leave now."

I hang up and am grabbing my keys when I realize there is dried blood on my hand. I'm not sure if it's from the delivery guy who brought the envelope, punching my fist through a wall, or the grunt I just finished with. Maybe all three.

I drop my keys back into the bowl and head to the shower.

The water is blisteringly hot, but I stand under the spray until my body is numb to the pain. As if maybe it will do something to get rid of the ache in the center of my chest.

There is only one thing Dr. Tung could want to talk to me about: *what am I willing to do to keep my brother alive?*

The answer, of course, is everything in my fucking power. The answer is that I will do anything to keep Nik here with us.

The real question—the one that hollows me out from the inside—is, *Would Nikandr want to live like this?*

"We've done everything that we can for him," Dr. Tung says for the third time. "What happens from this point forward is up to Nik."

"Except it isn't up to him. It's up to me," I spit. "That's why we're here."

Dr. Tung and a man who looks nothing like a nurse and everything like a security guard are standing in front of me. Apparently, even after all of our phone calls, the doctor didn't trust me to take this news well.

"We're here because having a plan in place for every eventuality makes things easier. In the heat of the moment, emotion can be high. It's better to have already made these decisions when you were calm and thinking clearly."

"I'm always thinking clearly."

She gives me a tight smile. "Even if that is the case, Nikandr's care team sometimes have only seconds—less than that—to make a decision. We don't have time to call you and see what you want to do. So if you want us to act with your best interests at heart, now is the time to decide—"

"How is a Do Not Resuscitate order in my best interest?" I wave the paper with the power to determine if my brother lives or dies between us. "I left my brother here so you could make him better. Now, I'm planning his death?"

I knew things were bad. Dr. Tung told me that I shouldn't expect a miracle.

But I did.

Even at my lowest, I always expected Nik to wake up and laugh at me for making such a big deal over one gunshot. I always thought this phase in our lives would fade away and be nothing but a distant memory. Maybe that's why I stopped visiting him as often. Maybe it's why I let myself get distracted with Pavel and the Gustev Bratva. Because I never really thought my last days with my little brother would be spent by his hospital bed.

"I know this is a difficult time for you and your family," Dr. Tung says. "If there is anyone else you'd like to talk with before you make this decision, feel free. But I would urge you to decide quickly."

With that, Dr. Tung and the security guard in scrubs leave, and I reach for my phone.

My instinct is to call Luna. I want to hear her voice right now. It's only been a couple hours since I left her at the safehouse, but it feels like a lifetime.

But I can't call her. Not only would it put her and Mariya at risk, but she's under enough stress as it is. I don't need to add Nik's life to her plate.

Besides, I already know what she'd say. The same thing she already said. *My mother deserves to know what is going on.*

Grimacing, I tap my mother's contact and wait. It rings long enough that I think she might not answer. Then the line connects.

"Yakov?" She sounds hesitant, like she's expecting someone else.

"It's me."

"Wow." I hear something clatter on the other end of the line. "I can't believe—I didn't think—What is this about?"

"I need to talk to you."

"Not for the last couple months, you haven't! None of you have." She sniffles. "I haven't heard a word from any of my children for weeks. Mariya has never been good for anything other than a text every other week, but Nikandr always called. Never you. That's why I'm surprised it's you now. I send my baby girl around the world to live with you and I don't hear a word about how she is doing or—"

"Nikandr is in the hospital." I decide to rip off the bandage. There's no sense letting her waste time ranting. Not when Nik might not have much time left.

"Oh. Oh. Okay," she says slowly. "Okay. But he's alright, isn't he?"

We've all been in the hospital more times than I can count. Broken bones, stabbings, stray gunshots. My mother has seen it all. I'm not surprised she expects Nikandr to be okay. *I* expected him to be okay, too.

I sigh. "No, he isn't. It's… it's bad. He's in a coma."

She sucks in a sharp breath. "For how long?"

"It doesn't matter. I just spoke to his doctor and they are asking me to consider signing a Do Not Resuscitate. They are worried he won't make it."

I'm waiting for the sobbing. For the hysterics and the questions. We've been here before, and I know exactly how she'll react. But there's nothing.

"Hello?"

"I'm coming," she says sharply. "I'll call Artyom and use his jet."

"Who the fuck is—"

"He's always offering it up to me. Ever since his wife died two years ago, he's wanted me to travel with him. He'll see this as a first step."

"You can't fly here. You're sick."

"I'm not sick; I'm old. I feel older than I am, thanks to this life," she mutters. "First, your father; now, Nik. I don't know what I'll do if he —" She clears her throat. "I'm going to be there for Nik. And for you."

"Now isn't a good time. There's a lot happening here. It's dangerous right now."

"It's always dangerous for us. I'm not going to let that stop me from being next to my son before he—while he heals," she corrects quickly. "He needs me there. Don't sign a fucking thing until I'm there with you."

I could stop her. I could call this Artyom fuck and threaten him within an inch of his life not to let my mother on his plane. There are a million different ways I could keep my mother in Moscow and far away from here.

But I don't want to.

The simple truth is, it would be nice to have her here. She brought Nikandr into this world, and she should be here if he has to go out.

I just hope it doesn't come to that.

34

YAKOV

Less than sixteen hours after our phone call, I'm standing on the jetway watching my mother walk down the boarding stairs of a private jet owned by some Moscow real estate tycoon named Artyom. I offered to send mine to pick her up, but she said it would take too long.

In my mind, that was one of the perks. More time to prepare.

The moment her feet hit the ground, she starts making plans. "I'm sure your things are in the main bedroom at the house. It is *your* house now, after all," she says in lieu of a real greeting. "No need to rearrange things on my account. I'm fine taking the guest room, but have Hope strip the linens before I arrive. I brought my own sheets."

"You had three hours to pack and get to the airport. How did you have time to pack sheets?"

She lowers her glasses and looks up at me, the lines around her eyes more pronounced than I've ever seen them. "I didn't pack a thing. You know I can afford to keep a household staff."

Considering I supply her with her disposable income, I do know that. I pay their salaries. Still, bedsheets seem like a deep cut on the packing list.

Sighing, I grab her suitcase and pull her in for a quick hug. She feels frail. Her shoulder blades are sharp and her blazer hangs off her shoulders like it's a size too big.

"Hi, my son," she murmurs, relaxing into the hug. "How are you?"

"Fine. How are—"

"Are you eating enough?" she interrupts. She pinches my arm and tuts. "You feel thin."

I feel thin? She's a walking skeleton.

"I'm perfectly healthy."

"You should be eating more. I thought you had a woman in your life now. Does she cook?"

"Like you said, I can afford to keep a household staff. I still have the same chef Otets hired."

She ignores me. "Not just a woman. A fiancée, apparently. Though I never heard a thing about her."

I load her luggage into the trunk of the car and hold the passenger door open for her. "You must have heard about it since you're bringing it up."

"I didn't hear about it from *you*," she corrects. "I have to get everything secondhand."

"Hearing it from Mariya isn't 'secondhand.'"

She doesn't deny it, which means my guess was correct. I'll have to have a chat with my little sister about what we do and don't share with our mother.

"Besides, I was going to tell you when the time was right. I've been busy."

I close the door as she mutters under her breath. As soon as I open the driver's side door, she keeps talking. "The time was right when you decided to propose. You used the ring I gave you, didn't you?"

"You told me to save it for the right woman. Luna is the right woman."

"She'd better be," she snaps. "It's going to be hard to go back now that she is pregnant with your child. Not hearing about the engagement was bad enough, but now, I don't even know the mother of my first grandchild."

I start the car, my teeth clenched. "I'm sure I have Mariya to thank for letting that information slip, as well."

My mother turns to me, thinning eyebrows raised to her dark hairline. There are strands of gray sticking out that she must have missed during her last dye job. "So it's true? You got this woman pregnant? She's having your baby?"

"*Babies*," I correct.

The way her jaw falls open tells me Mariya hasn't slipped that information to her yet. When her eyes light up, a grin spreading across her face, I know my failure to share is all but forgiven.

"Twins?!" She beams.

I nod. "Twins."

The smile makes her look at least ten years younger. "That's wonderful news. Two babies. Wow. What a blessing. That's a good sign. You wouldn't be having twins if this wasn't meant to be."

My mother has always erred on the side of mysticism, buying into what she calls "signs from the universe." I want to push back. If the universe is sending any signs lately, it's that the universe is fucking done with the Kulikov family. We've been shot at and kidnapped and rendered comatose.

So no, Luna getting pregnant has nothing to do with the universe and everything to do with the two of us being so eager to fuck that we didn't even discuss birth control.

But it's not the time for cynicism. Especially since Luna and I *are* actually meant to be. Not because of some bullshit like fate or destiny, but because she's incredible. She's the only woman I could ever imagine standing by my side.

I *chose* her. She *chose* me.

The universe had fuck-all to do with it.

"Babies are a lot of work, Yakov," my mother warns, shaking her head. "You have no idea. I was so young when I had you. I didn't know what I was doing. It was hard. And you're having two. Two! You are going to need so much help."

"I can hire a nanny."

She snorts. "You can't have a stranger taking care of your children. Not my grandbabies. Babies know their own blood. They can sense it. If you want them to grow up and be loyal to the family, they need to be taken care of by their own kin."

"Babies eat and sleep and shit. They don't know anything about kin."

"You did!" she insists. "I couldn't keep a nanny. You cried and cried unless I was holding you. Same with Nikandr."

She hasn't mentioned him since she stepped off the plane. I'm now sure that was on purpose. As soon as she says his name, it's like the air in the car is sucked out.

Her fingers are thin. The backs of her hands are blue from the veins running so close to the surface. She clenches and releases the fabric of her pants a few times before she speaks. "Has there been any change since we last talked? Is Nik... Is he still—"

"Same," I bite out. "No change."

She blows out a ragged breath and then shakes her head like she's clearing away the thought. "Babies are a lot of work. You'll need some help. *Family help.* Your cousin, Katerina, was always good with kids."

"Katerina's husband runs a hedge fund. I can't hire her to be my nanny."

"Of course not," she says. "She has five of her own kids, anyway. She's busy. No, you need someone with more time on their hands."

I bite back a smile. My mother is many things, but "subtle" is not one of them. She wants me to invite her to stay with us once the babies are born.

It's not a terrible idea. She knows more about taking care of babies than I do. And this whole thing with Nik has made it clear that I should enjoy the time I get with my family before it's gone. I haven't appreciated any of them enough. Not while I've been so focused on taking out all of the threats against us.

But babies aren't the only things that take a lot of work. Being around her is exhausting. We've been in the car for twenty minutes and I'm ready for a break. How much worse will it be when we're living under the same roof again?

Suddenly, she gasps. I almost swerve, worried there's a hobbled grandma with a walking stick in the road.

My mother turns to me. "Please, *please*, tell me you've started working on the nursery already. There is so much to do. You can't wait until the last minute. Especially with twins. Luna is going to be giving birth before you know it. Time flies."

One can only hope.

My mother stops talking as we pull into the hospital parking garage. She lifts her chin and presses her thin shoulders back, but she doesn't say a word.

Not as we ride the elevator up to the ICU.

Not as we sign in at the front desk.

Maybe she's going to try to pull herself together. Maybe this won't be like the last time we were at the hospital. She said she wanted to be here to support me. Maybe that's what she plans to do.

Then she walks through the door of Nikandr's hospital room, pulls back the curtain around his bed, and collapses.

"Nikandr!" She stumbles forward, barely grabbing onto the side of his hospital bed before she hits the floor. I grab her thin upper arm and drag her to the chair next to his bed.

"My Nikandr," she sobs, laying a shaky hand on the bed railing. "I should have been here."

I slide her chair closer so she doesn't fall face-first onto the tile floor, but she doesn't seem to notice I'm even here. She just grabs for Nik's hand and squeezes, talking to him softly in Russian. Fat tears roll down her cheeks.

I back away towards the door. "I'll leave you two alone."

I move into the hallway and press my back firmly against the wall. I repeat today's date to myself again and again, but the memories buried deep in my brain don't care about logistics. They don't care that my father has been dead for over five years.

Right now, I'm back to the night my father died. I'm back in the doorway to his room, watching my mother's knees crack against the tile floor by his bedside, wailing for someone to help him.

By the time she got to the hospital, it was already too late. He'd been dead for hours. He'd been gone since they loaded him into the ambulance at Nik's soccer game, his blood puddled in the dirt parking lot.

She wept and screamed until the nurses asked me to take her away. I tried to pull her towards the door, but she clung to the railing of his bed. I had to pry her fingers away from the plastic and pick her up like a child. When I got her home, she buried herself in the comforter and didn't get up for days.

When she finally sat up, she looked me in the eyes and said, "I never knew I could miss him as much as I loved him."

It was in that moment that I decided to never give that much of myself to anyone. Because I wouldn't survive if they took it away.

I close my eyes and reach for my burner phone. I tap one of only two numbers in the contacts and press it to my ear.

"Yakov?"

Luna's voice shatters through the memory. Instantly, she brings me back. To the present. To now. Where I'm committed to giving everything I am to this woman.

"I needed to hear your voice."

"Yakov," she says again, softer. "I miss you."

It's barely been a day, but it feels so much longer. "I miss you, too."

"What's going on? Have you found out anything about Akim's brother? Do you know when we'll get to leave here?"

I drag a hand through my hair. There's so much I have to do. So much going on. "Nik almost died. I've been at the hospital since I left you at the safehouse."

She gasps. "I had no idea. Is he okay?"

"He's stable. My mother is here now. She just flew in an hour ago."

"So you told her what has been going on?"

I let out a cheerless laugh. "I didn't have much of a choice. The doctors were wanting me to sign papers to not resuscitate if Nik stopped breathing again and all I could think about is what you said—that she would never forgive me if he died and she wasn't here."

"Do you think…" Her voice trails off for a second. "Does that mean you think he's going to die?"

No one has asked the question so plainly. I haven't had to really consider the possibility. But I find myself nodding. "I do. I don't think… It's been months. If he hasn't woken up yet, I don't see why he would now."

"Yakov," Luna breathes. "I'm so sorry. I wish I could be there with you."

"You will be soon. When this shit is all over with, we'll be together again. You'll be safe. Until then, I'll try to figure out what the fuck I'm supposed to do about my mother and brother."

"You'll figure it out." She sounds certain. Right now, she has more faith in me than I do. "You always know what to do, Yakov. When the time comes, you'll know exactly how to handle all of it."

"Have I told you that I fucking love you yet?"

She laughs and it's like a shot of adrenaline straight to my chest. "You've mentioned it once or twice, yeah."

"That's good. Because I love you."

"I love you, too," she says warmly. "I always will."

35

LUNA

I take a single step out of my room and one sniff is all it takes for me to regret it. I clap a hand over my nose. "I can't take anymore apple cake."

"It's sharlotka!" Mariya holds up a steaming forkful. "I just warmed some up. Do you not like it?"

"It smells like sadness."

That probably has something to do with the fact that the bunker Mariya and I are currently calling home smelled like apple sharlotka the night we arrived. For as long as I live, the scent will always remind me of being ripped away from Yakov. Unfortunately, it's one of the only desserts our hostess, Vera, knows how to make.

"Vera is trying to make us feel at home." Mariya frowns. "Which I guess is working for me. Because my mom made this all the time when we were growing up."

"I liked it fine the first night. And it was okay yesterday. But I can't eat anymore." I lay aluminum foil over the cake on the counter and crinkle the edges around the bottom to try to seal in the smell. "It's making me nauseous."

"The nausea is thanks to my nieces and/or nephews and/or niece and nephew," she says.

"Is that what you're going to call them?"

She shrugs. "We don't know the gender, so I'm not sure how to refer to them."

"How about 'the twins?'"

"Oh." Mariya laughs. "Yeah, I guess that works. Either way, the twins are making you sick."

I sit down on the couch cushion farthest away from her and her cake. Which, considering the gargantuan size of the U-shaped couch that takes up most of the living room, is pretty far away. "Or the stress. Are you not losing your mind being locked up down here? You were climbing the walls of the mansion. But at least there we had the pool and the garden. Here, we don't even have sunlight."

Or an accessible door. Or a dessert free of apples.

I shrink down onto the couch. "I can feel the walls closing in as we speak."

"I guess I'm getting used to being cooped up," Mariya says. "Plus, at least here, Yakov gave me some kind of choice. I mean, he would have forced me down here regardless, but he talked to me about it first, you know? He explained what was going on and what he needed from me before just barking out orders. That makes all of this a little more bearable."

When Mariya first showed up on Yakov's doorstep, I didn't think there was a chance in hell of those two hotheads finding any common ground. But somehow, they've managed to grow together. They understand each other better now. Their relationship is healing.

I'm happy for them, but it all just makes me miss Yakov even more.

"None of this is bearable for me." I lay a hand over my stomach, stroking my bump. As I do, I feel a nudge against my stomach... *from inside.*

I gasp and yank my hand away.

Mariya sits up instantly, on alert. "What is it?"

She's taking her duty to look out for me very seriously, it would seem.

"My bump. I felt—I think I just felt the babies—" Another kick from inside my stomach cuts me off. I look up at Mariya with wide eyes. "I felt a kick."

Mariya tosses her empty plate to the side as she scrambles across the couch towards me. She flattens her hands against my stomach, leaning in close like she might be able to hear them chatting away in there.

"Come on, babies!" she coos. "Your favorite auntie is here. Kick for Auntie MarMar."

I snort. "Auntie MarMar?"

She glares up at me. "I have years before they start talking. That's plenty of time to figure out what they should call me. I'm just workshopping."

We sit in silence, Mariya's hands around my bump, waiting. Until finally, there's a kick.

Mariya's hand jumps and she shrieks, "Holy shit! There are babies in there!"

"Pretty sure we determined that with all the ultrasounds."

"Yeah, but... I don't know. Doesn't this feel more *real?*" she asks. "Feeling them actually move in there is so much different than seeing it on a screen."

I smile. "You're right. It is."

But as I stare down at my bump and feel my babies wiggle around, my smile starts to fade. Because these aren't just my babies. They are Yakov's, too. And he isn't here to feel their first kicks.

The happy moment fizzles away and I'm suddenly blinking back tears.

"Luna?" Mariya bends down to look into my eyes. "What's wrong? Are you okay?"

"I'm so happy. My babies are kicking and healthy and that's amazing, but—" I swipe at my cheeks.

"Yakov should be here with you instead of me."

I squeeze Mariya's hand. "I want you here. I don't regret that. But Yakov should be here *with* us. It should be all of us sharing this moment in *our* house, not buried underground in the middle of nowhere."

"We'll all be together again soon. Yakov is going to handle everything and we'll be back in the mansion before you know it."

"That's what Yakov told me on the phone," I mumble. "I'm not so sure."

Mariya frowns. "You talked to him? I thought we were saving the phone calls for emergencies only."

"We are. Does your mom coming into town qualify as an emergency?"

Her jaw drops. "My mother? The one who lives in Moscow? The one who swore she'd never touch American soil again?"

"Unless you have more than one mother, I'm pretty sure that's the one he was talking about, yeah."

"Well, fucking hell," Mariya spits. "I guess no one thought it was important to fill me in. Cool. I'm always the last to know everything."

What Yakov told me about Nikandr is on the tip of my tongue. Mariya deserves to know her brother is doing worse. She deserves to know he might not make it, the same as anyone else.

But... if Yakov wanted her to know, he would tell her. Plus, Mariya is miraculously content being down here in this well-furnished dungeon. I don't want to tell her about Nik and ruin this rare peace she's managed to find.

"The only reason I know about your mother being in town is because Yakov has so much going on. I think he just needed someone to talk to."

"I get it. You two are disgustingly in love. That love comes with the privilege of information. Consider me annoyed, but understanding." Mariya flops back on the sofa and curls her legs underneath her. "You still haven't met our mom yet, right?"

"I haven't been to Moscow, so—"

"But not even a phone call?" she asks. "Or a FaceTime?"

I shake my head. "This whole thing with me and your brother happened kind of fast. There wasn't a lot of time for proper introductions."

"Not that Yakov would be trying to make time for it, anyway," she laughs. "But now that Mom is in the States and you two are engaged, there is no way she's not going to force a meeting. Even if Yakov resists, our mom has a knack for getting her way. Example: when she put me on a plane and had me driven straight to the mansion even though Yakov didn't want me there."

"It's not that Yakov didn't want you there," I start. "It was more about—"

Mariya holds up a hand to silence me. "Save it. I know what was going on. It's fine. Yakov and I are kind of, sort of working through things.

Plus, I'd rather live with a grouchy Yakov than my mother any day of the week."

I wince. "Things were that bad between you two?"

"My mom is stubborn and scared of her own shadow. After everything that happened with my dad, I get it. But she wanted to lock me up inside and never let me live. I do see the irony in the fact that I'm not trapped in this bunker with you, but at least I have you to keep me company. Plus, I know that one day, eventually, Yakov will see me as an adult and let me live my own life. My mother was never going to allow that. So I'm a lot happier here," Mariya says. "I'm sure she's happier with me here, too."

"I doubt that's true."

I don't know exactly what it feels like to be a mother just yet, but I can't imagine anything could ever take me away from my babies. I haven't even met them yet and I love them. I want to be there to watch them grow up and find their passions and fall in love.

My mind spins, imagining the day when they find someone they love and pull away from me… They'll move out of my house and follow that person anywhere, the same way I would follow Yakov anywhere.

Meh. I just felt them kick for the first time less than ten minutes ago, and now, I kind of hate their hypothetical future spouse for stealing them from me.

"What if your mom hates me?" I blurt, the possibility dawning on me for the first time.

Yakov is her firstborn. He's her first baby. Is she going to be protective over him? Will she hate me for taking him from her (not that anyone has the power to take Yakov anywhere)?

"Please," Mariya snorts, "she will love you. You're the daughter she never had."

I arch a brow. "*You're* her daughter."

"And? I said what I said. You are still the daughter my mother never had. You are pleasant. Kind. Instead, she had me: perpetual disappointment."

"Mariya, you are not—"

"I am," she interrupts. "And I own it. It's fine. Give it a few days of knowing her and you'll be wishing she hated you, too."

"Why would I want that?"

"Because Mama Kulikov is *a lot*. Prepare yourself."

36

YAKOV

"Pavel is like a ghost." Savva shrugs his meaty shoulders. "I've done everything I can. I don't know what to tell you."

"What you should tell me is that you have a plan for how the fuck you're going to track him down," I grit out. "Because Pavel *isn't* a ghost. He's a fucking teenager playing *pakhan* and if you can't track him down, then you don't deserve your job."

Savva's eyes widen, but he nods.

I believe he's doing everything he can. But that clearly isn't enough. When my family is on the line, everyone has to go above and beyond.

I turn to Kuzma. "What's the status of checking the security footage? Has there been any sign of how they got inside to deliver the necklace?"

Kuzma glances at Savva and then me before his eyes hit the floor. "The footage is clean. The Gustev lieutenant we took out the other night is the last time I saw anything suspicious on the cameras. As far as my intel goes, we aren't under any threat."

Nothing. Fucking *nothing*.

"I didn't send my sister and the mother of my children away because there isn't a threat."

"I didn't mean there isn't a threat. There is. But—"

"Then find it!" I roar. "I can't bring my family home until I know they are safe, and I can't know they are safe until you do your fucking jobs! Do you have a single useful thing to tell me?"

Kuzma's mouth twists nervously before he adds, "I have been looking into Budimir. A property he owns sold last week, but I didn't lay eyes on him. I don't know if he's—"

"You don't know if he's in the city. You don't know if he's even alive! For fuck's sake." I swipe the Budimir file off my desk and let the papers scatter across the floor. "Have you added the security cameras we discussed?"

"Yes!" Savva says, eager to tell me he's done at least one thing right. "Yes. I finished the install this afternoon. It took longer than expected because…"

I frown. "Because?"

He sighs. "Your mother didn't like the look of the cameras around the fenceline. She thought it was… cluttered. She asked the groundskeepers to take them down after we finished, so they had to be reinstalled."

I stand up and storm to the door before he can even finish. "This meeting is over. Go do your fucking jobs and come back with better news to tell me tomorrow."

I don't see them leave my office because I'm already throwing open the patio doors and stepping outside.

My mother is at the table, a cup of tea and an open magazine in front of her.

"You can't command my staff around, Mother."

"You're telling me!" She snorts. "Things are way too lax around here, Yakov. It's impossible to get anyone to do any work. I make the most basic requests and they can't manage to follow through."

"I haven't had any complaints until you arrived."

She turns to me, eyebrow arched. "That's because you don't have an eye for this kind of thing. Your father didn't, either. It's why I managed the household when he was alive."

"My eye is fine," I say. "The problem is that my men had to waste time installing cameras twice after you had them taken down."

"Oh." She winces. "He really was telling the truth."

"Who?"

"The groundskeeper. He told me that he took down the cameras like I asked, but I could look outside and see that they were still up. I thought he was making excuses just like Hope and your chef, so I fired him."

I pinch the bridge of my nose. "You've been here for less than twenty-four hours. Why in the fuck do you think you have the authority to fire anyone?"

"Because when I see a job being performed poorly, I know that reflects on you and the family as a whole. I was protecting us all."

"Protecting us from better security?" I blow out a breath, trying to rein in the frustration expanding in my chest. "I asked for those cameras to be installed to maintain security. *I'm* protecting us all. I need you to step aside and let me do that."

She crosses one leg over the other and flips through her magazine. "I thought I was being helpful. You're so busy with everything else that I thought I'd take some of the strain off of you. I guess I'm too old and out of touch to be useful anymore."

My mother has always been like this. She complains whenever she doesn't get her way and will go to great lengths to get her way no matter what anyone else says. But she cares about us. More than almost anyone.

Whenever my mother would go off on some tirade and make demands, my father wouldn't shut her down like he would have anyone else. He'd compromise. Sometimes, he'd give her exactly what she demanded.

When I asked why, he said, "When you find yourself a good woman who will stand by you through anything, you give her what she wants. Your mother is a good woman."

I hear his voice in my head as I try to temper my response. "You don't like the food here, you hate the guest bedroom, and you don't like my staff."

"Only because the food is tasteless, the bed is lumpy, and your staff have no discretion. They walk around like they live here. You never should have taken out the servant hallways."

When the house transferred to my ownership, I had the windowless hallways meant for servants removed. If someone is walking into a room I'm in, I want to see them coming. My ego can handle being in the presence of the people I hire to keep my house running.

"If you aren't happy here, then you could go back home. Things with Nik could go on like this for months. I don't want you—"

"You don't want me here?" She lifts her chin, but her eyes are watery. "If you didn't want me here, you shouldn't have called. Of course I'm going to be here for my baby boy."

"I don't want you to be miserable," I finish as if she said nothing.

"Oh. I'm not *miserable*. It's just going to take some getting used to, I suppose. I haven't been back here since before your father—" She sniffles.

"I'll have to learn what it's like to live in this house when it isn't mine. But I'm not leaving. I haven't seen Mariya or met your fiancée. Plus, I have to stay until my grandbabies are born. That's non-negotiable."

In the end, I leave my mother on the patio and tell Isay to rehire the groundskeeper. Dealing with my mother has to take a backseat to everything else. I can't afford any distractions.

I close myself in my office and stay late into the night, Budimir's file and a bottle of vodka on my desk.

Pavel can't get away with making a threat against my family and then disappearing. If he isn't going to show himself and fight me like a man, then I'll start taking out his associates one by one. I just need to figure out who they are first.

I've been putting out feelers and making calls for hours when my phone rings. I have so many irons in the fire that I don't check who it is before I answer, assuming it's someone getting back to me with information.

"This is Yakov."

"Mr. Kulikov?" a female voice says.

Dr. Tung's name is on the screen. I check the time and sit up. If she's calling late, it can't be good. My heart squeezes. "How is Nik? What is—"

"You need to get down here immediately," she says. "Nik is awake."

The drive to the hospital is a blur. I drank more than I thought, so I order Isay to drive me.

I don't even tell him why. I can't.

Partly because I don't know much. Dr. Tung told me Nik was awake and I needed to get to the hospital immediately, but she didn't want to say more beyond that.

The other part of it is that I don't believe it. Not really. I just began accepting my brother's probable death. Now, he's awake?

Isay drops me at the front doors. A night janitor is loading a cart onto the first-floor elevator so I pivot and take the stairs. I sprint up five floors. As soon as I get to the lobby, the receptionist buzzes me in. She recognizes me. She knows what is going on.

I don't bother asking her if it's true, though. I won't believe it until I see him.

"Mr. Kulikov." Dr. Tung is standing at the nurse's station, a cup of coffee in her hands.

"I want to see him."

I start to edge around her, but she follows me. "Of course you can see him, but I want to prepare you for what you're going to see."

"He's awake. That's what you said."

"He's *conscious*," she corrects carefully. "There is a difference. He's still delirious, but his eyes opened. He tracked me across the room."

"Can he speak?"

"He is still intubated, so I don't know yet," she says.

I'm so goddamn tired of hearing that answer from people. "What the fuck *do* you know?"

If she's bothered by my cursing, she doesn't show it. She lays a hand on my shoulder. "I know that you care deeply about your brother and he would love to see you. Go on in."

Nik's room is dark. The blinds are drawn. The only light comes from the monitors behind his bed and the ambient light from the hallway. But as soon as I walk in, I see his eyes on me.

His lids are heavy and his gaze wobbles when he tries to follow me, but his eyes are open. He's looking at me.

My brother is looking at me.

His mouth is still covered in tape and tubing and I want so badly to yank it out and talk to him. Instead, I sit next to his bed and grab his hand.

"Hey, Nik."

He can't respond, but his fingers tighten around mine. He squeezes my hand like a pulse again and again. His eyes flare wide.

"They're fine," I tell him. "Mariya and Luna—they're both fine. Everyone is safe."

His hand relaxes. He sinks back into the mattress. Then his eyes slip closed and he falls asleep.

I stay for hours. Sometime in the night, Dr. Tung and a few nurses remove the tube from his throat. They tell him not to speak, which is made easier by the fact that Nik can't stay awake.

"He's been asleep for months," I say as Dr. Tung tries to tell me this is normal. "How much more sleep could he need?"

"It's the best medicine the human body can get, trust me," she says.

I consider calling my mother and telling her the news, but I don't want to get her hopes up. Every time Nik closes his eyes, I'm half-convinced they aren't going to open again. There's no need to tell anyone about this until I know it's going to stick.

I sit by his bed all night, watching him slip in and out of consciousness. He responds more and more strongly to the sounds of nurses coming and going, but he still won't speak.

"I'm here with you," I tell him every time his eyes snap open. He always looks vaguely panicked, but it passes quickly. "I've been here the whole time, brother. I'm not going anywhere."

My ass is numb from sitting in the shitty recliner by the bed for so long and my neck aches from sleeping at an odd angle. But sometime in the late morning, I finally fall into a fitful sleep.

As soon as I do, I'm jolted awake by shouting.

I stand up and spin around, looking for the threat, before I realize Nik is shouting. His voice is hoarse, but he's slapping his hands against the bed like he's trying to swat a bug.

"Nik!" I shake his arm. "Nik, what is it? You're awake. You're okay."

He turns to me, eyes wide and wild. "I'm not okay," he rasps. "I can't feel my fucking legs!"

37

LUNA

I'm covered in goosebumps, shivering under a blanket that could double as tissue paper.

I don't need to open my eyes to know where I am. I recognize the damp smell. The distant sound of men's voices leak through the cracks in the walls. I don't know how long I've been here, but I know there is no escape. There's a hollowness in my chest, a hopelessness I can't find my way out of.

I'm going to die in here.

When a hinge squeals, I snap my eyes open. The room around me is dark. I raise my hand, but I can't see my fingers in front of my face. I can't see anything.

"Hello?"

My voice echoes like I'm in a cave.

I slide to the edge of the mattress, but when I stretch out a leg to touch the floor, there's nothing there. Just empty air.

"Hello?" There's a frantic edge to my voice now. I hear it like it belongs to someone else. Each word echoes back to me. "Who is there?"

I hear footsteps getting closer and closer, but I can't even feel the floor. Some part of me knows if I jump off of the bed, I'll be falling forever into darkness.

I curl up at the back of the mattress, the cement wall against my back. The footsteps grow louder and louder.

Then, a wicked smile lights up in front of me.

It shifts, growing and morphing and changing. As I blink, the face behind the smile comes into focus and a normal, flesh-and-blood man is in front of me.

He grins. "This can be our little secret, Luna."

I try to jump off the bed. I'll gladly take endless darkness over whatever he promises. But he's there in an instant, blocking my only way out. I can't see his body, but I feel countless pairs of hands wrapping around my arms and my legs. They pin me to the bed and splay me open.

"Look at me," he snarls.

"I can't!" I wail, fighting against the shadows.

A hand grips my chin, forcing my eyes up. "Look at me!"

Suddenly, Akim is standing above me. One side of his face is gone, pulverized and dripping blood down his neck.

He bends over me, his ruined mouth reaching for my skin...

I wake up screaming. There are hands on my arms and I desperately swat them away.

"Luna! It's okay. I'm here."

For one second, I think it's Yakov. *He's here. I'm safe.*

Then I see Mariya leaning over me. Her face is creased in concern and she's shaking me. "Are you okay?"

Embarrassment burns in my cheeks as I sit up. "I'm okay. I'm sorry I woke you up. It was just a dream."

Mariya sits on the edge of the bed. "Based on the screaming, it was either a *very* good dream or it wasn't a dream at all."

"The latter," I grumble.

"In that case…" Mariya leaves the room. I hear her moving around the kitchenette. A second later, she returns with a glass of water. "Drink this."

I take it happily. My throat is parched. "Is this some kind of nightmare cure?"

"I wish, but no. It's just filtered water. I take my job as your watcher very seriously. You need to stay hydrated for the twins and crying can really zap the moisture right out of you."

I swipe at my cheeks, realizing there are tears there.

"Do you want to talk about it?" Mariya asks softly.

I sag back against the headboard. "It's the same stupid nightmare every time. Well, not the *same*. The details change, but the heart of it is the same: Akim or one of his men slip into my cell in the dark and…"

"Did they touch you?" Mariya's voice is so quiet I almost can't hear it.

"They tried," I tell her. "The only reason one of them didn't is because Yakov showed up. He pulled the guy off of me. I got so incredibly lucky, but I can't seem to get my brain to stop playing the *What If* game. What if Yakov hadn't come for me? What if he'd shown up five minutes later?"

Mariya grabs my hand. "But he *did* come for you and he *didn't* show up five minutes later. He kept you safe. He is still keeping you safe."

"I know. I'm so grateful to him for that. It's just hard to relax now that I know what kind of evil exists out there. It's hard to go to sleep at night knowing there are people in the world who would torture and kill me just to get back at Yakov." I squeeze my eyes closed as another tear slips down my cheek. "If they'd do that to me, what would they be willing to do to our children?"

"Nothing," Mariya says sharply. "No one is going to do anything to the babies. Yakov won't let that happen. None of us would. No one is going to hurt you or the twins."

I give her a tight smile, tears blurring my vision. "I know you have my back, Mariya. You've proven that more than enough times. But you can't really promise me something like that. No one can."

Mariya meets my eyes, but she doesn't say anything.

Deep down, she knows I'm right.

I trust Yakov with my life, but that doesn't mean mistakes can't happen. All it would take is one slip-up—one oversight—and I could be dead. Me, the kids. Yakov, even.

He knows it as well as I do, even if he won't say it. Yakov saw his father die in front of him. He knows how quickly it can happen. One second is all it would take for my entire world to slip through my fingers.

Just the thought sends pain lancing through me.

I gasp as every muscle in my midsection contracts. The pain takes my breath away.

"Luna?"

I wave her off, trying to breathe through it. "I'm okay. It's a cramp. Just a cramp. I need to walk it off."

I hold my hand up to her and Mariya helps me stand up. She keeps a tight hold on my arm as I walk back and forth across the small room.

With every step, the pain ebbs away. I take slow, deep breaths until I can stand up straight.

"What in the hell was that about?" Mariya asks.

"Normal pregnancy stuff, I guess." I shrug. "I don't know. It could be the stress."

She eyes my stomach nervously. "Should we call my brother? Is this an emergency?"

I shake my head. "No, I'm fine. We shouldn't worry him over nothing."

"Yakov doesn't get worried. But he does get shit done," she says. "If there is even the slightest chance that this is abnormal, he'd want to get it checked out. Even if it turns out to be nothing."

"He's busy."

Mariya snorts. "Nothing is more important to my brother right now than you and his babies."

She can only say that because she doesn't know how bad things have gotten with Nikandr. If she knew her brother could be days away from dying, she'd understand where I'm coming from.

"I know, but the sun isn't even up yet. Plus, I feel okay." I step back and throw my arms wide. "See? I'm fine."

I spin in a slow circle to prove to her I'm perfectly healthy. But when I spin to face her again, her blue eyes are wide.

"What?" I ask.

"I think we should call someone," she says shakily. "Vera is a midwife. I can ask her for help. Maybe we should—"

"Mariya, what is it?" I ask.

She bites on her lower lip. "Look at the back of your nightgown."

I twist as far as my bump will let me, which isn't very far. It doesn't matter—I can already see exactly what Mariya is talking about.

A red stain as big as my palm.

My heart leaps into my throat. I swallow it back down. "Bleeding can be normal. Dr. Jenkins told me that bleeding could be perfectly—"

Another cramp wraps around my midsection and zings through my lower back. I groan.

"Should I call someone now?" Mariya asks, slightly panicked.

I double over, my palms flat on the mattress. I can't find the words to answer her. Hell, I can't even breathe.

"That's it," Mariya decides. "I'm calling someone."

No. I don't want her to call anyone. I don't want Yakov to hear about this. I don't want anything to be wrong with my babies.

This can't be happening.

Another cramp tightens like a clamp around my stomach and I cry out in pain.

38

YAKOV

Nikandr is sitting up tall in bed. It's the most alert I've seen him—but he still isn't *here*. Not really. His eyes are glazed and unseeing as Dr. Tung moves around the end of his bed, squeezing various toes and tapping his calves.

"Do you feel this?" she asks again and again.

Each time, Nik shakes his head.

No.

Dr. Tung orders the nurses to place compression socks on his feet. "I'll be back to see you again soon, Nikandr. Until then, rest up. You're doing great."

Nik doesn't reply. He just lies back on his pillow, eyes staring straight up at the ceiling while two women wrestle the tight socks over his legs.

He's lost so much muscle mass since he was hospitalized. I could see the difference in his face and arms, but seeing him without blankets makes it even more obvious. He looks the way he did as a scrawny teenager when he grew twelve inches in six months. He doesn't look anything like the man they first wheeled into this room.

Dr. Tung heads for the door, but I cut her off. I pull the curtain around Nik's bed closed and face her. "What's going on?"

"Your brother has better cognitive function than I predicted he would. His speech and comprehension is far beyond what I expected. You should be proud of him. And yourself. I think all of that talking helped him tremendously."

"The talking didn't do much for his legs, I guess," I snarl.

She frowns. "I'm sorry. The bullet passed very close to his spine, so this was always a possibility. It's not something I like to bring up until necessary, especially when I wasn't sure he'd even wake up."

"Now, he is awake and he can't fucking walk."

"For now," she says calmly. "The paralysis could be temporary. He just came out of a long coma, so I don't want to make any determinations now. We'll get him into physical therapy as soon as he's ready and see what can be done."

I want a solution. I want her to tell me that she'll hit a button and fix my brother. But even the merest possibility that he'll walk again is better than nothing.

I sigh. "Thank you."

"Your family has been through a lot the last few months," she says. "Your brother is awake. Try to forget about everything else and enjoy it."

Nik is still staring at the ceiling when I pull the curtain back. He doesn't show any sign that he sees me approaching, but he asks, "What was that about?"

"I was just talking to Dr. Tung about when we're going to break you out of here now that you're finally awake."

"Who?" he asks.

I'm confused for a second before I remember that Nik barely knows Dr. Tung. He just met her for the first time a couple hours ago. She's been taking care of him for months, but he wasn't conscious for any of it.

"Dr. Tung has been with you since the night you got to the hospital. She's been calling me every day with updates about you."

"Thrilling stuff, I'm sure," he rasps. "Tell me: did I take any shits while I was unconscious? I've been thinking about that since I woke up."

Of course Nik is already making jokes. He just woke up from a months-long coma and is paralyzed from the waist down, but he's trying to make light of it.

"Catheter. If you look on the other side of your bed, you'll see the clear plastic bag where it all ends up."

"Glamorous," he mutters. "I had no idea I was putting on that kind of show."

"Why do you think I always sit on this side of the bed?"

Nik goes to lean over the railing to see the bag, but when he tries to draw his knee up for leverage, nothing happens. His legs are as good as dead weights in the bed. He can't reach.

"I'll take your word for it." He sighs, flopping back into the bed.

I lean forward. "Listen, Dr. Tung said that the paralysis could be—"

"How many people have been in to see me?" Nik interrupts. "Was I the most popular patient in the ICU?"

"Do you remember anyone coming in to talk to you? Dr. Tung wasn't sure if you'd be able to hear us or not."

He shrugs. "Maybe it will all come back to me later. Then I'll find out you all left me in here to rot. I probably didn't have a single visitor."

I didn't come see him as much as I should have. Not with Luna pregnant and Pavel on the loose.

"The guards I had posted outside your room day and night were probably great company."

He nods, his eyes fixed on the ceiling again.

"Am I supposed to bullshit and avoid talking about the paralyzed elephant in the room?"

"That would be preferable, yeah."

"Okay." I sit back in my chair. "I can do that. For now."

And for the next couple hours, I do. We talk about nothing. Nik falls in and out of sleep. In between naps, he asks about the scores to playoff games he missed and laughs when he finds out I assigned one of the recruits to take care of his beta fish.

"I'm sure he took good care of the stupid thing," I tell him. "I told him that if that fish is dead when you get home, so is he."

Nik laughs again and it's a welcome sound. I wasn't sure I'd ever hear it again.

After eating half of a red Jell-O cup and watching some game show rerun, Nik sighs. "Well, I've been conscious for five hours now and Mariya isn't banging down the door yet. I guess that means you haven't told her?"

"I haven't told anyone." I pat my pockets and realize I don't even have my burner phone. "Shit. I was in such a hurry to get out of the house when Dr. Tung called that I didn't even bring my phone."

He points to the bedside table. "Your phone is right there."

"I need the burner."

"Why do you need a burner phone to talk to our sister?"

I shake my head. "No. If we're gonna talk about real shit, it's going to be about you getting into physical therapy and learning how to walk again. It's not going to be about... *this*."

"Fuck physical therapy." His voice breaks over the curse word, still rusty from disuse. "Fuck being in denial. I want to know what in the hell is going on. Akim shot me. He almost fucking killed me. If you have to call Mariya with a burner, does that mean he's still alive?"

Nik hasn't even been awake for a day and I'm about to dump Bratva business on his lap. He shouldn't be dealing with this. It's my responsibility. I'm the reason he's here in the first place.

But Nik's brow creases.. "Come on, Yakov."

I drag a hand through my hair. "Akim is dead. But Pavel isn't."

"Pavel?" His brows shoot up. "That little punk is the leader now?"

I nod. "And he's taking shots at Luna. He left a present for her at the foot of our bed and had photographs of her sleeping delivered to the house."

Nik holds up a hand. "You and Luna are sharing a bed again? Looks like Mom and Dad made up. How sweet."

I snort. "You have no fucking idea how right you are."

"What does that mean?"

I have to fight back a smile. "Luna is pregnant."

"No shit!" Nik jolts forward like he was going to stand up. When his legs don't move, he holds his arms out awkwardly instead. "Don't make the cripple beg for a hug."

I lean in and clap him on the back.

"Congratulations, Yakov." He whistles long and low. "You're going to be a dad."

"To twins."

He freezes for a second and then lets out a loud *whoop*. After we convince the nurses who come rushing in that he is fine and they don't need to check his vitals, he shakes his head at me. "Of course you'd knock her up with twins. You can't ever be normal. One baby would be too tame for you."

"Twins might be too wild even for me."

"Nah, you can handle it," he says. "You'll be a great dad."

Nik grins and I can see how much he needed this good news. Something to look forward to.

Something to *fight* for.

Then his smile fades and I see him shift back into business mode. "So where are Mariya and Luna?"

"Safe. That's all I'm going to say here. I'm the only one who knows where they are."

"What's the plan to get Pavel?"

"I have men working on it."

"That doesn't answer the question, brother. *What is the plan?* Give me something to do."

I shake my head. "You already have something to do. You need to focus on getting better. I can handle Pavel."

"The only thing that is going to help me get better is to think about something outside of this fucking room!" he snaps. "You know I can't sit here and do nothing. I'll lose my mind. Put me to use."

I don't want to. Nik needs to rest. Dr. Tung said it's the best medicine for the human body. But I also know that I don't have a fucking thing on Pavel despite all the men I have assigned to the task. I don't know where he is or what his plan is. Until I figure it out, I can't be with Luna.

"Yakov," Nik pushes. "Come on. Just let me make some calls."

I grimace. "Fine. You can look into Akim's old weapons dealer."

"Budimir?" he asks, a smile spreading across his face.

"He's all but disappeared since I killed Akim. If he's still working for the Gustev Bratva, he's way underground."

Nik starts nodding before I'm even finished. "Consider it done. I'll find him and let you know."

There's no doubt in his voice. No hesitation at all. Nik is looking into it; I know he's going to get the job done. He should be looking into physical therapy and dealing with his new prognosis, but I can't deny that it's really fucking good to have him back.

Suddenly, the door slams open. Isay tears into the room, his face pale. "Something is wrong with Luna."

There isn't time to ask questions or think. No goodbyes. I stand up and sprint out of the room.

39

LUNA

Vera and Usev are whispering in the kitchen. The door to the basement is open for the first time since Yakov escorted us downstairs, but Mariya and I are sitting on the steps like bullets are going to start flying through the windows if we set foot on the main floor.

Who knows? They actually might. I don't know anything anymore.

"What are they saying?" I ask, nodding towards our hosts and massaging my bump. The cramps have eased slightly, but anxiety is a tight fist in my chest.

"Vera doesn't have any equipment here to examine you properly and they can't get my brother to answer his fucking phone, either." Mariya slaps her burner down on the stairs. "What is the point in these useless-ass phones if he isn't even going to answer when I call?"

Mariya is annoyed, but I'm terrified. For myself. For my babies. But also for Yakov.

Why isn't he answering the phone? Is it because Nikandr has taken a turn for the worse? Or did he find Pavel? Images of Yakov bleeding out on the ground flicker through my mind before I can stop them.

"I'm sure he's busy," I choke out, breathing through another cramp.

Mariya stares at me before she picks up her phone. "Fuck this. I'm not waiting for him."

Three minutes later, lights and sirens blare down Vera and Usev's street. The couple have disappeared, ducking out of sight while Mariya leads me out to the porch.

"I can't believe you called an ambulance!" I yell over the sirens. "Yakov is going to kill us."

"If I didn't call an ambulance, he might not have gotten the chance! You are bleeding and he isn't answering. I didn't have a choice."

The ambulance pulls along the curb in front of the house, but I don't move. "We can't trust them. They could be working for Pavel."

"*I* called *them*," Mariya argues. "They are here to help you."

"I want to wait for Yakov."

"He isn't answering!" she snaps. "Yakov's paranoia is rubbing off on you. Despite what he tells you, not everyone is out to get us. Some people are just trying to do their jobs."

Two EMTs hustle out of the ambulance, bags and gear in hand. As they approach the porch, I push Mariya aside and hold out a hand. "Don't come any closer."

"We're here about a pregnant woman in distress." The taller of the two glances at my stomach. "That's you?"

I shake my head. "It was a mistake. I'm fine."

I feel vulnerable out here on the porch. The sun is just starting to creep over the horizon, but the red and blue flashing lights are illuminating everything. Someone across the street is standing on their front steps in flannel pajamas.

So much for our presence here being low-key.

"Luna," Mariya hisses under her breath, "let them check you over. Think about the babies."

I am. I'm thinking about the babies, but I'm also thinking about Mariya. There's a reason no one knows she and I are staying here. Calling an ambulance and having our names logged in some first responder database online could ruin everything. Pavel probably has eyes everywhere.

The second EMT steps closer to the porch. "We're already here. If there is any concern at all, we might as well check you over."

"I don't need to be checked over. I'm fine. I need you both to leave."

"We can't leave until we know that you are thinking clearly, alert, and understand your situation. We just need to ask you a few questions to verify all of that. Okay?" the man asks, not pausing for me to answer before he dives in. "What is your name?"

"I'm not telling you that."

He frowns. "What's your address?"

"I don't need to prove anything to you. I didn't call you and I don't want you here. Please leave."

"We can't," the other EMT says. "Not until we ensure no one here is in danger."

"I'm not in danger!" I bark.

Except, I actively am in danger. It's why I'm living in a safehouse in the middle of nowhere. It's why no one—including these EMTs— should be standing on the porch.

Suddenly, a car squeals to a stop in front of the house, almost crashing into the back of the ambulance.

My heart stops. Instinctively, I reach for Mariya, pulling her back towards the house.

Pavel has found us. Somehow, he's found us, and now, he's here to take us away or worse.

I'm about to dive into the house and look for cover when Dr. Jenkins climbs out of the driver's seat. He already has his black medical bag in his hand and is jogging towards the porch.

"There's my doctor!" I blurt, pointing at him. "That's my personal doctor. He can tell you that I'm safe."

Dr. Jenkins nods at the EMTs and then looks up at me. "I got here as soon as I could."

"How?" Mariya asks.

"Yakov."

He doesn't need to say more than that.

"We still can't leave without knowing—" one of them starts to say, but his words are lost in the roar of an engine. Another car tears down the street and ramps up onto the grass.

Before I even have time to panic that it's our enemies coming to attack, Yakov jumps out of the car and beelines straight for the EMTs.

"Who the fuck called a fucking ambulance?" he roars.

Mariya ducks behind me. "Shit."

The two EMTs turn to face him, standing shoulder to shoulder like they stand any actual chance against Yakov.

Without looking away from the men, Yakov jabs a finger towards Dr. Jenkins. "Get everyone inside. Now. Check her over."

Dr. Jenkins ushers me and Mariya through the front door. As it closes, I hear the EMTs arguing that they need to perform an exam, but I know that won't be happening. Not once Yakov is done.

"Where should I conduct the exam?" Dr. Jenkins asks.

He glances down the hall to where Vera and Usev are watching nervously from their bedroom door. They agreed to take us in, but I'm not sure they realized exactly what kind of chaos they were signing up for.

"Downstairs would be for the best," I tell him. For Vera's sake as much as mine.

Once again, we descend the basement stairs, delving back underground. The terrifying part is how much safer it feels. I think I'm getting used to hiding.

Once we're back in our makeshift house, Dr. Jenkins sets up his equipment and begins the exam. I talk him through my symptoms as he checks my vitals. His expression gives nothing away as he pokes and prods at me.

Finally, he presses the heart rate doppler to my stomach. Immediately, the soothing sound of one, and then a second, heartbeat fills the room.

"The babies sound great," he says. "I'm not concerned about them at all."

I close my eyes and take a deep breath for the first time in an hour.

Then Yakov tears into the room. His dark hair is sticking up like he's been running his hand through it. He finds me and our gazes hold, a million emotions passing between us.

He kneels next to me and squeezes my hand. "How is she?"

"Her blood pressure is high, but that could be from the excitement," Dr. Jenkins offers. "The spotting is more concerning than it was the last time given that she is now in the second trimester, but the babies seem to be doing fine."

Yakov nods and kisses my hand. "I got here as quickly as I could."

"It's okay. You're here. That's all that matters."

"No." His jaw flexes. "You had to call an ambulance. The risk that puts you both in…"

"Mariya was scared. Don't be upset with her," I say softly. "She was trying to take care of me."

"I don't blame her."

In true Yakov fashion, I'm positive the only person he'll blame is himself.

"Thankfully, the EMTs are legitimate," he says. "I paid them to forget this address and Isay is looking into scrubbing the dispatch recording."

Dr. Jenkins clears his throat. "I know your privacy is important to you, but I do think having Luna looked over at a hospital could be smart. Even if she doesn't go in an ambulance, it could be smart to go anyway. Just to make sure she's getting all of the care she needs."

Yakov shakes his head before Dr. Jenkins has even finished speaking. "There are too many variables. I can't keep her safe there."

"I understand your concerns, but I have to recommend what I think is best for my patient. I don't have the equipment with me to give her a full exam. I don't see any immediate concerns right now, but things can change quickly."

Yakov's thumb circles the back of my hand as he thinks. "Would having a live-in doctor be a suitable alternative?"

"If they had the proper equipment, yes," Dr. Jenkins muses. "It would probably be an even higher level of care, actually."

Yakov nods. "Then it's settled. You'll stay here with Luna until it's safe for me to take her home."

Dr. Jenkins' mouth falls open. He blinks in stunned silence.

"I'll make sure you have whatever equipment you need," Yakov continues. "Compile a list and I'll get it done."

"I—I can't," the doctor stammers. "I uprooted my family to come here. My wife and kids are in a rental downtown. They'll be waiting for me. I can't stay here permanently."

Yakov rises slowly to his feet. "This isn't a request, Dr. Jenkins. I'm not asking you if you can help, I'm telling you that you will."

A few weeks ago, I would have argued. I would have told Yakov that none of this was necessary and I'd be okay.

But today… I feel good knowing Dr. Jenkins will be close by.

I feel even better knowing Yakov is going to do everything in his power to make sure me and the twins are safe.

So I twine my fingers through his and watch as Dr. Jenkins nods miserably. "Whatever you need, Mr. Kulikov."

40

YAKOV

Dr. Jenkins clears Luna and the babies after an ultrasound with the portable machine Isay rushed over. Then Vera and Usev found the doctor a spare room upstairs. Now, I'm sitting in the living room with Luna curled against my side and Mariya sprawled face-down on the couch.

"The day has just started and I need a nap," Mariya complains. Her voice is muffled from the cushions.

"Luckily, we have nowhere else to be," Luna drawls. "You can sleep all day if you want."

"Yeah. 'Lucky.' We're so lucky to be trapped down here." Mariya spins to look at me. "You wouldn't understand how lucky we are, Yakov. Because you're so busy going places and seeing people and breathing fresh air that I couldn't even get in touch with you. What the hell are the emergency phones for if you don't answer them?"

I sigh. "I should have had my phone with me."

"Why didn't you?" she snaps. "What was so important that you couldn't answer your phone any of the five times I—"

"Nikandr woke up."

Mariya freezes. She doesn't even blink. Luna stiffens next to me, her hand a vise grip on my arm.

"He woke up last night," I explain. "His doctor called me and I rushed to the hospital. I left my phone behind and didn't realize until—"

"He's awake?!" Mariya shrieks, jumping up and down. "Nikandr is awake? He's conscious?"

I smile thinly. "Awake and talking and everything."

Mariya hurls herself at me, throwing her arms around my neck.. Luna smiles at me from the couch. But when our eyes catch, her expression falters.

One look and she knows there's something I'm not saying.

"This is incredible," Mariya is jabbering as she pulls back. "He's going to be okay. Like, really, actually okay. To be honest, I had my doubts. I wasn't sure if he'd—Wow. He's awake."

"He's awake. Once it's safe, you can go see him."

She frowns. "I want to go see him now."

"I know. Nik wants to see you, too. You'll see him soon, though."

"Will I?" she asks. "Do you have a scheme to take out Pavel or is the plan to keep us in this bunker indefinitely?"

"I have a plan for everything, Mariya," I lie. "Have a little faith."

Mariya plants her hands on her hips and inhales for what is sure to be the beginning of a long rant that would make even our mother proud. But before she can, Luna yawns. "I'm exhausted," she blurts, squeezing my arm. "Can you come lie down with me for a little while?"

I nod. "Of course."

Mariya glares after us as we walk to Luna's bedroom. Just as the door closes, Mariya calls, "You can't avoid me forever!"

"But you can avoid her for now," Luna whispers, locking the door.

"I don't need to be saved from Mariya. I can handle her."

"Yeah, I know. But you don't have to do it tonight." Luna kisses my shoulder on her way to the bed. She slips under the covers and rolls onto her side, her head pillowed on her arm. "Can you stay for a little while or do you have to leave?"

How could I possibly walk away from her now?

I shrug out of my jacket and shoes. "I can stay."

I slide in behind her, my arm draped over her waist like normal. Except she feels different. We've only been apart for a few days, but her body has changed. Her bump is growing.

And I haven't been here for it.

Luna presses back against me, snuggling closer. "What's wrong with Nik?"

"He's better. The doctor thought he might die, but he's awake."

"I know," she says softly. "But I also know there's something you're not saying. I could see it in your face. Can he talk? Does he remember who you are?"

I sigh. "His mind is fine. He's doing better than Dr. Tung expected as far as that goes. It's the physical part that isn't coming along as well. Right now—maybe forever—he's paralyzed from the waist down."

Luna curses under her breath. "I'm sorry, Yakov. How is he taking it?"

"Fuck if I know. He doesn't want to talk to me about it. He won't even let me bring up physical therapy."

"He probably needs time. You Kulikov men pride yourselves on being physical specimens. I'm sure this is going to be a hard adjustment for him. Just be there for him and give him time. He'll come around."

I kiss the soft curve of her neck. "Complimenting me and giving sage advice all at the same time. Well done."

"I don't have much time with you, so I have to multitask." She hugs my arm, her fingers trailing over the muscles of my forearm. "I'll also throw in that I think you should tell Mariya what is going on. All of it. She already feels like she's the last to know everything."

"I just want her to revel in the good news for a little while. My brother just came out of a coma and I should be ecstatic, but instead, I'm bogged down in his recovery and whether he'll ever walk again. I just want Mariya to be happy she has her brother back."

Luna nods. "You must trust me to keep your secret if you're telling me the truth."

"I do trust you," I say, realizing exactly how much I mean it. "I've never had someone in my life that I want to share everything with, but with you... I didn't even consider not telling you."

Without me even realizing it, Luna became the person I want to take everything to. The person I want to talk with when anything good or bad happens.

"I want to share everything with you, too," she says, sniffling.

I roll her towards me and tip her chin up. "Are you crying?"

She lets out a watery laugh. "It's these stupid hormones. I'm sorry. It's just... I felt the babies kick for the first time."

"Right now?" I slip my hands down over her stomach.

She shakes her head. "No. The other day. It was so magical and all I could think was how shitty it was that you couldn't be there for it. I wish you could have been there with me."

"I'm here with you now. And when all of this is over, I'll always be with you."

Luna brings her hand to my neck, leaning close. "Promise?"

I press my lips to hers. My intention is just to seal the promise and comfort her, but the moment we connect, she arches into me. Her lips part and she gasps against my mouth.

I grip her hip, digging my fingers into her skin with the effort it takes not to roll her on top of me. "You should rest."

Luna slowly lifts herself up and straddles me. "Dr. Jenkins said I was fine. We can be gentle."

"I have no fucking idea how to be gentle with you," I grit out.

From the moment Luna and I met, there's been something deep inside of me that responds to her. Something instinctual I've never felt before. It has nothing to do with my head and everything to do with my cock and my black, twisted heart.

As if she can read my thoughts, Luna's palm settles over my heart. "You've done a pretty good job so far. I trust you, Yakov."

My aching cock twitches. Luna slides up and down the length, teasing me closer to the inevitable.

Luna has given me her trust and her heart and her body. She has given up her entire life to take on mine, and I'm enough of a selfish bastard that I'll never ask her to reconsider her choice. Because I don't just want this woman—*I need her.*

I shove her panties to the side as Luna unzips me. Her fist wraps around my length for only a second as she presses me to her entrance. One roll of her hips and I'm sliding deep inside her.

She closes her eyes and leans back. Her bump is enough of an intrusion now that leaning forward isn't much of an option. So I grip her thighs and watch her ride me.

Her full lips part and her forehead creases. She looks fucking gorgeous.

I slip my hand under her shirt and roll her hard nipple with my thumb. When she moans, my grip on control loosens. I take her by the waist and guide her down onto my cock again and again.

"Yakov, I can't—I'm going to come." She leans back and plants her hands on my thighs. I look down and see where I fill her.

"It's because we fit together perfectly. Because you're so good at taking me," I pant, driving into her faster.

Her blue eyes are glassy when she meets my gaze. "I don't want it to be over."

There's no danger of that. It will never be over. This thing between me and her… I'll give everything I have to make sure it never ends. To make sure nothing gets between us ever again.

I slip my hand between her thighs, circling my thumb over her clit. Instantly, I feel her clench around me.

"Come for me, Luna."

She tips her head back and releases, chasing the orgasm with every roll of her hips. She bucks and grinds down onto me until I can't hold back. I spill into her, pulsing until we're both spent.

The moment I slide out of her, I feel the loss.

I clean her up quickly and then pull her back against my chest. My hands naturally settle around her bump.

"I wish you could stay," she whispers softly.

"I don't want to stay here with you." She starts to turn around, confused, but I kiss the back of her neck. "I want to get you the fuck out of here and bring you back home. That's what I'm working for. So you and our babies can be free. I—"

Suddenly, my hand jumps.

"Did you feel that?" Luna gasps.

Before I can answer, there's another little nudge against my palm.

Luna gasps again. "Yakov, do you feel that? Can you feel them?"

Them.

My babies.

The twins have been this vague, happy idea since I found out Luna was pregnant. But in one tiny nudge, they become real.

I'm going to be a father. Luna and I are going to be parents. *Together.*

"I can feel them," I murmur, holding her closer.

Luna falls asleep like that, pressed against me, wrapped in my arms. She's still asleep when, hours later, I press a kiss to her forehead and slip out of bed.

41

LUNA

"Everything looks fine." Dr. Jenkins scrubs a hand down his stubbled face. "Your blood pressure is still a touch on the high side, but since I'm here to monitor it closely, I'm not worried about it right now. The babies are growing and Mom is happy. That's the most important thing."

I may be happy, but Dr. Jenkins definitely isn't. Not if the pasted-on smile he's been wearing for the last couple weeks is any way to judge.

The first few days after Yakov ordered him to live here and take care of me, Dr. Jenkins was surprisingly cheerful. He greeted me with his usual warm smile and didn't act like it was an inconvenience at all.

Weeks later, I think the hope of Yakov changing his mind has dimmed.

Now, he plods downstairs once per day, checks my vitals and the babies' heartbeats, and then disappears back upstairs. It only takes him about fifteen minutes each day to look me over. I have no idea what he does with the rest of his time in this house. Unless he can speak Russian, I doubt Vera and Usev are good company.

Maybe that's another reason why Dr. Jenkins isn't much for conversation lately: he's rusty.

"I'm happy enough. Things are good in the dungeon," I say with a chuckle. "But we do wonder what secrets you all are hiding upstairs."

Dr. Jenkins frowns.

"Soundproof ceiling," I explain. "Mariya and I can't even hear footsteps. You all could be river dancing up there for all we know."

He nods but doesn't smile. "No river dancing."

Oof. His conversation skills are even rustier than I thought.

"Are Vera and Usev good hosts?" I ask. "I hope they're taking good care of you. I didn't have much of a chance to meet them before I had to come down here."

"They're fine," he says curtly, slipping his tools back into his black bag.

"Has Vera made you her apple sharlotka yet?"

It might be my imagination, but I think Dr. Jenkins goes a little green. "Plenty. I think it's all Usev eats."

"I wouldn't be surprised. I think it's all Vera knows how to make," I whisper. "She's been bringing us one every other day since we got here. Even Mariya has started throwing them away."

Finally, he smiles. "If I never see another baked apple in my life, it'll be too soon."

Dr. Jenkins offers me his hand and helps me off of the exam table. Yakov had the exam table, along with a hospital's worth of equipment and supplies, delivered the day after the ambulance scare. I told him I did not want to deliver my babies in the bunker, and he assured me it was just in case of an emergency.

I hope it never comes to that.

I walk with Dr. Jenkins to the heavy door that seals off the safehouse from the rest of the basement. "If you're looking for a reason to spend a little more time away from Vera and Usev, you can stay down here for a bit. You don't have to rush upstairs after my appointment."

"I wouldn't want to intrude."

"No intrusion! I can imagine it would be nice to be able to have a conversation with someone. Vera and Usev don't speak English, do they?"

"I'm picking up some Russian here and there. Vera and Usev keep to themselves a lot anyway."

"Another reason why you can stay down here. If you want the company?"

I don't say it, but I know what it's like to be cooped up against your will. Before Mariya and I were on friendly terms, I was miserable. I hate thinking that Dr. Jenkins feels that way because of me.

He grips the door and keeps his eyes on the floor. "Thank you for the offer, Luna, but I don't think that would be appropriate."

"Probably not," I admit, "but since you're living above my ultra-secret safehouse bunker, I think we're past the normal doctor-patient relationship. I don't want to pressure you, but I feel bad that you're stuck here because of me."

"I'm not here because of you," he says softly.

He seems to regret the words as soon as they're out of his mouth. He sucks in his cheek and shifts from foot to foot.

"Yakov," I fill in softly. "I know he's protective, but he's worried about me. He's intense, but it comes from a place of love. He'd do anything to keep me safe."

"I know he would." His voice comes out high and tight. He steps through the door and starts to pull it closed. "I'll be back tomorrow to check on you. Same time."

"Okay. See you tomorrow," I say, but my words are cut off by the slamming of the door.

Mariya pops her head out of the room a second later. "I heard the door close. Is he gone? Is your vagina put away?"

"You walked in on one exam, Mariya. Let it go. It's not like I was in active labor."

"Active labor would have been better," she says, hopping over the back of the couch to sprawl across the cushions. "Dr. Jenkins was two fingers deep in you. It was perverted."

"It was a pelvic exam."

"It was uncomfortable," she fires back.

I sit next to her, my feet propped up on the coffee table. "It was only uncomfortable because you made a joke about me cheating on your brother and I was forced to inform you that your brother is *way* less clinical when he puts—"

"*La la la la!*" Mariya clamps her hands over her ears. "Forget I mentioned it. I will never speak of it again so long as you swear to never mention where my brother *'puts'* anything."

I flash her a grin. "Deal."

Mariya shakes her head like she's scrubbing her brain of the thought. Then she slips seamlessly back into the conversation. "How is good old Dr. Jekyll?"

"Dr. Jenkins," I correct. "And fine, I guess. I told him he could hang out down here with us if he wanted, but he acted like I asked him to do the same thing you just swore you'd never joke about again. He could not have been less interested. I didn't realize hanging out with us could be a threat."

"I'm sure it has nothing to do with us and everything to do with the fact that my brother has Dr. Jenkins' balls in a vise grip."

I shake my head. "What does that mean? Yakov is paying him to be here. It's not like he's being blackmailed."

"I wouldn't be so sure. Dr. Jenkins is one of the best OB-GYNs in the country, right?" she asks. "I doubt he's desperate for cash. Even if he is, he can't be bad enough off that he'd willingly stay here for weeks on end to take care of you. Whatever Yakov has on him, it must be big."

I think about it for a second and then curse under my breath. "When am I going to stop being so naive about how your world works? I just assumed Dr. Jenkins was doing all of this for the money. I didn't even consider—What do you think Yakov has over him? He's still a real doctor, right? He seems real enough."

"I'm sure he's legit. Yakov wouldn't have brought him here if he wasn't. But who knows what Yakov has over him?" she shrugs. "With guys like that, it can be anything: gambling debts, addiction, blackmail from hiring a hitman to kill his wife. Either Yakov has some dirt on him or Dr. Jenkins needs something from him."

"I don't love the idea of the man who is going to deliver my babies having killed his wife, so let's delete that from the list of possibilities."

I lounge back on the couch, eventually wedging a pillow under my lower back. I've had a constant back ache for the last week. I was hopeful it would go away, but I'm more and more confident every day that it's here to stay. Another glorious pregnancy symptom.

I'll take it as long as the babies keep growing and stay healthy. Though some very small, selfish part of me secretly hopes for another pregnancy scare just so Yakov will come see me again. I don't want there to be anything wrong with me or the babies, obviously, but I want Yakov to rush over to see me just so we can spend another night making love. I want to fall asleep with his body around me. It's been so long that I've almost forgotten what it feels like.

He calls every so often. They're brief conversations, just long enough to check on how I'm doing and say hello. They aren't enough, but they're all we can have right now.

Currently, life is all about settling. I can't have what I want, so I try to be grateful for the little glimpses of light.

Right now, I'm grateful for Mariya and mindless television.

Mariya scrolls through the long list of channels. We have as much fun making fun of commercials and random snippets of shows we've never seen as we do actually settling in to watch something from start to finish. Sometimes, I just kick back and listen to Mariya commentate her way through reality television and bad infomercials. It breaks up the silence.

"I think we need more jingles," Mariya decides, jabbing the remote towards the screen. "Commercials are boring now. They try too hard to tell a story or make things emotional. I say, screw that and write a catchy tune. A good jingle about erectile dysfunction would be amazing."

"I feel bad for Dr. Jenkins," I blurt.

"Why? Does he have erectile dysfunction?" She gasps. "How do you even know that?"

"What? No. No, he doesn't. Or, I mean, I don't know if he does." I blow out a harsh breath. "I feel bad because he is upstairs alone and not hanging out with us."

Mariya considers that for a second. "If he was here, I probably would have picked another example for the jingle idea. Like… a whitening toothpaste."

I smile. "Having these stupid conversations with you makes the time go by faster. I feel bad that he's sitting upstairs in the quiet by himself."

"You offered to let him hang out down here. You did your part. It's not your fault he made the obviously wrong choice and refused our company."

I sigh. "Yeah. You're right. I just feel bad."

"And you should. He's missing out on some really incredible discourse." She narrows her eyes at me. "Discourse that isn't *stupid* in the slightest."

"You're right. These conversations aren't stupid at all. Your thoughts on penis jingles are borderline genius." I grab her hand. "But seriously, Mariya, I'm glad you're here. You could be sulky and miserable and make this entire situation worse, but instead, you're the only thing making it bearable for me."

"Ditto, Luna. This is definitely the best imprisonment I've ever had."

I frown. "You've done this before?"

"Hunkered down in a safehouse?" She snorts. "Plenty. Loads of times. For loads of different reasons. This time is the most intense, but yeah... I was always too young to know all the details, but when you're part of a powerful family, enemies come with the territory."

I knew that already. I *know* that. Yakov's world is dangerous. People don't like him and they're willing to go after me to get to him. It's easy to state as a simple fact... but the reality is different.

I imagined Yakov and I riding out the storm *together*. Naively, I thought it would be a nine-to-five job. Something he could turn off at dinner time so we could eat a quiet meal and fall asleep next to each other.

So sitting here in a basement bunker with Mariya while Yakov is off doing God only knows what to protect me was never fully on my radar.

"Does it ever end?" I ask.

Mariya doesn't look away from the TV. Whatever show she's watching is back on. "What?"

"The fighting. Does it ever end?" I repeat. "Yakov keeps taking people down, but someone else pops up to take their place. Does that cycle of revenge ever end?"

"I guess not," Mariya admits. "You just learn to live with it."

Can I learn to live like this?

I cradle my bump. *Can they?*

I have the choice, but my babies don't. Is this really the life I want to bring my children into?

42

YAKOV

I pinch the bridge of my nose, but the tension in my skull doesn't ease. It's been a constant, simmering pressure for weeks now. Since the last time I saw Luna.

"All I'm saying," my mother continues, "is that Oksana and Tati are not trying to destroy our family from the inside. Inviting them over for tea isn't going to put us in any risk. They have nothing to do with the Gustev Bratva."

"That we know of," I grit out for the third time. "We don't know friend from foe right now. That is why we aren't inviting people over."

She crosses her arms, her pearls bouncing off her diamond tennis bracelet. She's dressed to impress for an afternoon tea that absolutely won't be fucking happening. "If you keep this up, we won't have any friends left. Friendships need to be tended, Yakov. They are like plants. If you leave them unattended, they start to look like that mess of a garden in the backyard."

"Next time Mariya and Nik get shot and the mother of my children is kidnapped, I'll be sure to leave written instructions for the gardeners."

"Why have a staff if you need to leave instructions?" she asks. "They should know what to do. You should fire and replace them."

"I've been a little fucking busy, Mother."

"Which is exactly why I need some company," she retorts, circling the conversation back around. "I'm lonely in this big house all by myself."

I'm tempted to suggest she go back to Moscow, but she's made it clear she isn't going anywhere. Not anytime soon, at least. I could have her removed if I truly wanted, but my father would roll over in his grave if I had my guards escort my mother out of the house she raised me in. There are some lines even a *pakhan* shouldn't cross.

My phone rings and I answer it quickly. No matter who is on the other end of the call, it has got to be better than this conversation.

"This is Yakov."

"Mr. Kulikov?" Dr. Tung says in her usually clipped efficiency. "I'm calling about your brother—"

"What's wrong with him?" I ask, heart already in my throat. Worst-case scenarios flash through my mind. *He's unconscious again. He flatlined. He's dead.*

"Who is it? Is that about Nik?" my mother asks.

"Nothing is wrong with him. Well, aside from the paralysis, but—" Dr. Tung sighs. "I thought you should know that Nikandr is checking himself out of the hospital."

"What the hell does that mean?"

"It means that he will be leaving the hospital this afternoon and will no longer be under my care or supervision."

"Unacceptable," I snap. "Check him back in. He hasn't finished physical therapy."

"That's what I told him. He didn't take my advice and I don't actually have any legal capacity to detain him. Nikandr is ready to leave, so he is checking out today."

"How am I just finding out about this now?"

"I shouldn't even be telling you this much, but he is technically still in my care and you are still listed as his contact information," she says. "But give it two more hours and I won't be able to tell you anything about Nikandr's situation. He'll no longer be my patient."

"He can't just check himself out," I snarl. Even though he apparently very much can.

My mother leans in closer. "Who is checking out? Is Nik coming home?"

I turn away from her and press a finger into my other ear to focus.

"He is an adult," Dr. Tung is saying. "This isn't a prison or a mental facility. As I said, I don't have any legal means to keep him here against his will. He wants to leave and he plans to."

"The fuck he will," I spit, hanging up without bothering to say goodbye.

"Is Nik coming home?" my mother asks again. "Was that the doctor?"

I don't answer her; I'm too busy dialing Nik's number. The asshole lets it ring ten times before he finally picks up.

"You can't change my mind," he chimes breezily.

"Check yourself back in right this fucking second, man. You aren't leaving."

"Am, too," he fires back. "I can't stay here anymore, Yakov. I'll lose my mind if I don't get out. I can't eat any more dry meatloaf or shitty, off-brand gelatin. And I'm tired of being woken up every two hours all night long. I want to sleep in my own bed."

"A bed you can't fucking get in and out of on your own," I remind him under my breath.

I want to add that he also won't be able to defend himself if the Gustev Bratva decides to strike, but Nik still doesn't like to talk about his paralysis in any real way. He finally started going to physical therapy, but he won't let me see him in a session. The longer this denial of his goes on, the more I'm sure Luna is right: Nik is embarrassed.

My mother is circling around me, trying to hear what's happening. "If Nik needs a place to stay, tell him to come here. I'll have Hope get his room ready. I can take care of him."

I put my hand over the phone. "His room is upstairs."

"So? It's always been upstairs."

"But he hasn't always been paralyzed from the waist down."

She frowns. "That's a minor issue. We can solve that."

"I don't need anyone to solve anything for me," Nik interjects, clearly having heard the conversation. "I'm a grown ass man. I can take care of myself and I don't need anyone's permission to discharge myself from the hospital. I already checked."

"You may be a grown man, but I'm your big brother. More importantly, your *pakhan*. I can make your life hell if I want to. Keep defying me and you'll end up shoveling coal in a mine in Siberia."

"Might be tough without the use of my legs, but I'll do my best." He cackles hysterically to himself.

"Tell him to come home," my mother whispers. "We can take care of him here."

I wave my mother off, but it's not a terrible idea. I could arrange full-time care for him here at the mansion. It would also be a lot easier to monitor Nik's recovery *and* murder Pavel if Nik was under my roof again.

"Nik, I'm fucking serious. You can't be alone right now. Someone needs to be there to monitor you."

"Are you speaking as my *pakhan* or my big brother right now?"

"Both," I say. "You can discharge yourself from the hospital, but if you do, you're coming to live with me."

My mother claps her hands. "Nik is coming home!"

"And Mom will be there, too," Nik adds under his breath. "Fuck me. A grown man living with his mother again."

"Take it or leave it," I say.

After a beat, Nik curses. "I'll take it."

Nik is propped up in the hospital bed in the sitting room. Every few minutes, he uses the remote to adjust the headrest or to lift his feet. "Where did you find a hospital bed on such short notice?"

"The hospital."

"They just sold it to you?" he asks.

"I didn't ask to buy it. They just didn't dare stop me when I had it removed from a hospital room and loaded onto a truck."

Nik snorts. "That sounds about right."

Considering the donation I made in Nikandr's name, the hospital can spare a single bed. I didn't have any trouble hiring an in-home care team to take care of him, but acquiring the bed on such short notice was a problem. Like all problems I encounter, I solved it my way.

"How is my baby boy feeling?" Our mother swirls through the doorway and reaches for Nik's hand. Since he got back, she's been fawning over him worse than any of the nurses at the hospital. It's driving Nik insane.

"I'm fine." He pulls his hand back gently. "How are you feeling? Was the traveling hard on you? You could go take a nap, you know. If you need it."

She kisses his cheek. "You're so sweet. Worrying about me. No one worries about you once you're old. I'm not used to all the attention. But I'm fine. Perfect now that you're here, actually. The only thing that would make it better is if Mariya was here with us. And Luna, too, of course."

My working theory is that being back in this mansion with her children is somehow winding back my mother's biological clock. She is bouncing around the house like she's fifteen years younger, at least. I'd be happy for her if it wasn't so fucking annoying.

"You know why they can't be here," I say. "It isn't safe."

"It's safe enough for Nik to be here. I don't see why it's not safe enough for the girls."

I can't explain this to her again. Every time I explain why my sister and pregnant fiancée can't be here with me, it's like tearing open a wound. It's admitting that, on some level, I've failed.

I can't keep the mansion safe enough.

I can't protect my family in the ways I wish I could.

I can admit that shit to myself, but I don't want to fucking say it aloud *again*.

Thankfully, I don't have to.

"It *isn't* safe enough for me," Nik clarifies. "It's not safe enough for any of us."

Our mother frowns. "Then we shouldn't be here."

"If we leave, we could lose the mansion," he explains, understanding the stakes without me ever having to explain a word to him. "If we go underground and stop hunting him, Pavel will be free to track us all down. He'll be free to find Luna and Mariya."

"Then we hide with them," she proclaims. "We all go to the safehouse. Then when he attacks, we're all together."

"All together in a fucking hole in the ground," Nik fires back. "No one wants to attack from a valley. You want to be on the mountain. Yakov knows we need to maintain our position here while we hide our most vulnerable at the safehouse."

Our mother lifts her chin. I can see the war inside of her, wanting to argue, but also taking pride in not being listed amongst the vulnerable. She is, of course. Luna is pregnant and I'd still bet on her in a fight over my mother. But if I sent my mother into an underground bunker with Mariya for any length of time, both of their lives would be in jeopardy.

Eventually, she turns and leaves without saying a word.

"I just earned you an hour of peace before she recharges," Nik mumbles. "Use it wisely."

Sometimes, I forget just how much my little brother has grown up. Just how much he has learned. But he's wrong—there is no peace. Not when Luna is hiding and Pavel is hunting her.

How much longer before Pavel figures out where she is? How much longer before he gives up hunting Luna and goes after Nik or our mother instead?

He got through my state-of-the-art security once before. He could do it again.

I feel like I'm being drawn and quartered, pulled in every direction. No matter which way I go, something else falls apart. For the first time in my life, I'm worried I can't do it all.

The question is, who is going to die if I fail?

43

LUNA

Dr. Jenkins doesn't say a word as he steps through the door of our bunker and places his bag on the exam table. If I thought he was cold before, he's become downright icy over the last week. I'm getting used to the silent treatment.

Every day, he comes down to check on me, moving through the process on autopilot. The only reason I know my blood pressure is still a little high is because he brought me a prescription last week. I had to directly ask what it was for before he explained himself. If I hadn't, I'm not sure he would have told me anything.

The time for inviting him to spend time with me and Mariya is long over. Dr. Jenkins isn't happy being trapped here and he isn't afraid to make that known.

He straps a blood pressure cuff on my arm and presses two cold fingers to my inner wrist. I sit patiently while he counts, staring down at his watch for the time. I'm waiting for him to silently slip the cuff off and reach for the doppler the way he usually does…

But he doesn't move.

Dr. Jenkins' brow furrows. He refits my blood pressure cuff and presses his fingers to my pulse point again.

"Is… is everything okay?" I venture.

He stares at his watch. I can see him counting in his head.

"Dr. Jenkins?" I can't stay quiet. Not when his brow is creased like that. "Am I okay?"

Suddenly, he drops my wrist and digs into his bag for the doppler. "I fucking knew it."

I've never heard him curse before. Cold shoulder aside, he's always been professional.

Until now.

"What did you know? Am I okay?"

My heart is pounding in my chest. I swear I can actually feel my blood pumping through my veins. My blood pressure is probably astronomical. That can't be good for the babies. And the stress about the babies is probably making my blood pressure even higher.

I take a deep breath, trying to break the vicious cycle of anxiety before it can spiral out of control.

Dr. Jenkins shakes his head and lifts my shirt over my bump, pressing the doppler to my stomach. "I should have demanded he send you to a hospital the night I showed up here. That's what you need. A fucking hospital."

He finds one of the twins' heartbeats, but I can't focus on it. I can't feel anything except icy dread pooling in my gut. "You said I was fine. Every day, you've said that I'm okay. Were you lying? Is something wrong?"

His jaw flexes. When I met him, Dr. Jenkins was clean-shaven. Now, he has a beard. There's a patch of gray on his chin. "What do you think? I'm trapped here in this house trying to care for a high-risk pregnancy."

"High-risk?"

"All multiples are high-risk," he explains impatiently, quickly finding the second heartbeat and then pulling my shirt back down. "Your blood pressure is getting higher every day."

"But I'm taking that medication like you told me to. I thought it was supposed to help."

He shrugs. "And I thought I'd be back with my family within a week. But here we are."

"What are you—" I blink back tears. "Are my babies okay?"

Dr. Jenkins runs a hand through his hair and looks down at me. His shoulders sag. "Yes. Yes, they're fine. I'm sorry."

"What is happening?"

"You are okay right now," he says. "So are the babies. I'm—I'm sorry, Luna. I shouldn't be telling you any of this, but I can't talk to anyone else. I'm losing my mind here."

I grab his hand with both of mine. "It's okay."

I trust Dr. Jenkins. Even now. He's a good man in a bizarre situation. The only reason *I* can hide out in this bunker without falling to pieces is because I love Yakov. I know Yakov has my best intentions in mind, so when he told me I needed to live here, I agreed without question. I can't imagine how much harder all of this has been for Dr. Jenkins.

"It's not okay," he says gently. "I need to get you to a hospital and under the care of another physician. I can't do this anymore."

"We can make this work for you. I'll talk to Yakov. I'm sure we can figure out a way for you to still treat me while also being able to see your family. I'll talk to him."

"I'm going to call and tell him you need to get to a hospital," he says, ignoring me. "I'm sorry, Luna, but I'm done."

This is what I wanted, isn't it? I wanted an emergency to get Yakov here so I could see him. But now that it's playing out in front of me, I want nothing more than to make it all stop.

"You can't. Yakov is dealing with so much already. I don't want to worry him."

"I think he should be worried!" he argues. "Your high blood pressure could turn into preeclampsia. It could put you and your babies at risk."

"But you—you said I was fine. I thought you just wanted to leave. I didn't think—" I close my eyes, trying to sort out the jumbled mess in my brain. "You said that I would be under better care here at home with a dedicated doctor. *You* said that, with the right equipment, this setup could be as good as a hospital."

He just shakes his head. It feels like I'm talking to a brick wall.

"Just give it a few more days," I beg. "I don't want to worry him. Let's see if my blood pressure lowers. In the meantime, I'll talk to Yakov about letting you see your family."

"You aren't going to convince that man of anything," Dr. Jenkins spits. "And he'll see right through it if we try to lie to him about how you're doing."

"I know Yakov has made some threats, but he's a good man. You don't need to be scared of him."

"I'd be stupid not to be!" His eyes are wild and scared. "I know what your fiancé is capable of."

I recoil. What does that mean? Does Dr. Jenkins know about the Bratva? Is he speaking from personal experience or from what he's overheard?

"Why did you agree to work for him, then?" I ask. "Why are you here if you're so scared of him?"

Dr. Jenkins pulls out his phone with a sympathetic grimace. "You're my patient, Luna. As your doctor, I have to do what's right for you... and for me."

He presses the phone to his ear and closes the door behind him before I can even get up off the table.

44

YAKOV

When my phone buzzes, Gregory bolts out of my lap like he's been electrocuted. The cat hisses and darts under the chair where he's spent most of his time since Luna left.

"You're gonna have to toughen up if you're gonna survive in this house," I warn him, swiping up to take the daily call from Dr. Jenkins.

Before I can even answer, he's talking to me. "I'm not going to be held responsible for your disregard of your fiancée's needs. I'm telling you that she needs to get to a hospital. If anything happens to her now, it's not on me. I've done my part."

"What the fuck are you talking about, Jenkins?"

Nik's eyes snap open at the sound of my voice. His physical therapy session this morning tired him out. He's been dozing for the last hour, but he's wide awake now.

"Luna's blood pressure is high," Dr. Jenkins explains tersely. "It has been high for weeks. The medication isn't lowering it, and I can't in good conscience keep her here any longer. You need to get her to a hospital."

"That's why I have you there. That's why I found all of that fucking equipment. So you could bring the hospital to her."

"I can't work in a vacuum," he protests. "I need to talk to other doctors and run tests. I'm a good doctor, but I can't replace an entire hospital staff. I don't have a phlebotomist down here or a fully-functioning lab."

"Do you need a fully-functioning lab?"

"Yes. Er—no. Not *here*. You need to take Luna to one. You can't fit the entire world down here in this bunker. She has to get out eventually. I'd prefer it to happen before you lose one or both of your babies."

In different circumstances, I'd kill Dr. Jenkins for the way he's talking to me. For even suggesting that something bad will happen to my children.

As it is, all I hear is that my family isn't safe.

I've made mistakes before. I won't make one now.

"I'll be there soon," I grit out.

I hang up and Nik is already raising the head of his bed so he's sitting tall. "What's wrong?"

"Luna's blood pressure is high. Dr. Jenkins is worried about the babies. He wants her to go to a hospital." I shake my head. "But I can't keep her safe there."

"Not long-term, but maybe just for today?" Nik suggests. "You decimated the Gustevs when you raided that house to get Luna out."

"We took out a lot of men, but I didn't get final numbers. I was distracted."

"The lack of movement within the Gustev Bratva's own territories says enough. They're running low on manpower. I've been making calls and putting out feelers and no one has seen a fucking thing from Pavel in weeks. Isay even managed to track down Budimir. He has cut all ties with the Gustevs and is working for Dima Baranov now."

"That's what Isay told me. I would have liked to have been the one to steal Budimir away and land that financial blow, but at least someone did it."

"Someone who doesn't also want us dead," Nik adds.

"There's that, too," I agree. "Dima Baranov may not be a close friend, but he has never been my enemy. I'd rather him have the drop on illegal arms than almost anyone else. But the most important thing is still that Pavel is weaker now than he's ever been. It might be why he disappeared after delivering his threats: he didn't have the strength to follow through."

"I think you have an opening," Nik says. "If it was my call to make, I'd get your woman and your babies to wherever they can get the best care."

"It's not your call to make," I snap. Then I sigh and relent. "But it's still really fucking nice to hear your perspective."

"Miss me more than you expected?" he says with a laugh and a waggle of his brows.

"Something like that." I head for the door. "I'll get to the safehouse and see how she's doing. I'll make the final call when I get there."

Nik nods. "Text me when you decide. I'll arrange safe transport."

I get into my car and practically fly to the safehouse. I've had to stop myself every day for weeks from driving there on sheer instinct. The desire to be close to Luna is almost a compulsion at this point.

It feels good to let myself give in after so much restraint.

Still, even as I swerve around traffic and slam the gas pedal to the floor, I check my mirrors. I look to make sure I'm not being followed. I take a few random exits as a red herring for anyone who might be trying to tail me. By the time I pull up down the block from the safehouse an hour later, I'm confident I wasn't followed.

Which is why I don't see the first shot coming.

I'm two steps away from my car when a bullet whizzes past my shoulder. The sound echoes off the houses, making it hard to tell exactly where the gunman is shooting from. So I drop to the ground while I pull my gun from the holster.

Another bullet buries itself in the dirt a few feet ahead of me. I track the line back to a row of shrubs across the street and fire.

Instantly, two men fly out of the foliage, scrambling for a nondescript van parked in a driveway down the street. The cowards laid in wait and are now trying to retreat.

I don't fucking think so.

I army crawl forward and lunge to my feet, chasing after the men. I don't recognize either of them. They're young, wearing dark clothes and hoods.

I fire again, hitting one of the men in the ankle. He screams as his leg buckles, but he keeps going, dragging it along behind him.

His friend isn't so lucky. I hit him in the back of his left shoulder. He stumbles forward and my second shot catches him in the neck. He manages a few more steps before he collapses face-first into the ground.

The limping man sees his friend fall and runs faster. He doesn't even consider going back to help him, not that it would do any good. It was a guaranteed kill shot.

The last remaining gunman limps away, firing a few wild shots over his shoulder, but they all go way wide. I hear glass shattering behind me. Hopefully, the asshole didn't take out an innocent bystander firing blindly like that.

I leap over the dead man in the grass and land on one knee. I bring my gun up and take aim at the runner. But the asshole still on his feet dodges to the right. I hit him, but it's a thigh shot on the same leg I already hit. He cries out again, but he keeps moving. Then he leaps into the van, drags his ruined leg in the door behind him, and tears off down the road.

My shots ping off the van like pebbles, so I know it's armored. I don't need to catch the license plate as it speeds out of the neighborhood to know who I have to thank for that surprise.

Pavel knows about the safehouse.

As soon as the van is out of sight, I turn and sprint for the house. I need to get to Luna.

I just hope no one else beat me to her.

45

YAKOV

I clear the first floor with a pathological focus. I don't respond as Vera and Usev fire questions at me in Russian, asking about the gunshots and who is outside. I don't acknowledge Dr. Jenkins, either, who raises both his hands in the air as I stride, gun first, into his borrowed room.

No, I make sure the house is empty and then I move to the basement stairs.

She's safe. If she wasn't, Usev and Vera would know. Dr. Jenkins would know.

Luna and Mariya are okay.

I repeat the words to myself again and again, but I don't believe them until I throw the door open and see Luna sitting on the couch.

She's in a white summer dress, her hands resting on her belly. Her blonde hair is longer than I've ever seen it. It falls in waves down to her elbows.

She looks like a fucking goddess.

Healthy and safe.

When she sees me in the doorway, she starts to get up, but I reach her before she can. I drop to my knees in front of her, my hands on her face. "Are you okay?"

"I'm fine, Yakov. I'm okay. I told Dr. Jenkins not to worry you." She strokes her fingers through my hair. "I feel okay. Everything is fine."

"Holy shit." Mariya circles her finger at me. "Is this all about the blood pressure?"

I keep my hands on Luna, but turn to face my sister. "It's about the two gunmen I just fought off on my way inside."

Her face pales. "He knows."

"He knows," I grit out. My hands are shaking with rage. "How the fuck he knows, I have no fucking idea."

"Pavel?" Luna asks, looking from me to Mariya and back again. "He knows we're here?"

"It was the paramedics," Mariya breathes. "This is my fault. I called that ambulance and—"

I shake my head. "I took care of them. They didn't talk. I made sure of it."

I tied up all of the loose ends. I kept a tight lid on this safehouse. So how in the hell does Pavel keep getting the jump on me?

Luna gasps at something over my shoulder and I'm instantly on my feet with my gun aimed at the door.

Dr. Jenkins is standing in the doorway with his hands raised over his head. "I just came down here to check on you."

I lower the gun. "I'm not the one in danger. I'm fine."

Luna's hand slips down my shoulder. She squeezes and I wince. "No, you're not. You're shot, Yakov."

Luna holds her hand out for me to see. There's blood on her palm.

"It's a graze." I shake her off. "I don't even feel it."

Dr. Jenkins closes the door behind him. "Because you're in shock."

"I'm not in fucking shock. I've been shot before."

"Shock is a physical state as well as a mental one. You're too amped up on adrenaline to feel anything right now. But if you sit down, I'll examine you."

I shake my head. "We need to get out of here. Now. One of the gunmen got away. He's probably relaying what happened and getting ready to come back with more men."

"You can't face them all on your own." I narrow my eyes and Luna holds up her hands. "You can't face them all on your own *with a bad arm*. Give me your phone and I'll text Isay for backup. While we wait for them to arrive, Dr. Jenkins can look at your arm."

"I don't take orders," I remind her icily. "Especially when your safety is on the line."

Gently, Luna curves her hand around my jawline. Her blue eyes are wide and pleading. "It's not an order, Yakov. It's a request. Please let Dr. Jenkins look you over. I can't lose you."

I pull her close, my lips brushing against the shell of her ear as I sigh and relent. "Only for you, *solnyshka*."

I give Luna my phone and tell her to text Nik. "I want as many men as the mansion can spare to be sent to the safehouse to escort us out of here."

Dr. Jenkins rolls up my sleeve and inspects my "gunshot wound." Like I suspected, it's nothing more than a graze. Dr. Jenkins cleans it up and slaps a bandage on my arm.

As soon as he's done, I point to Mariya. "Get packed. Now. We're leaving immediately."

"Where are we going?" Mariya asks.

"*You're* going home," I tell her. "Nik is out of the hospital and back at the house now. Mom is there, too."

She stamps her foot. "What the hell? No one tells me anything!"

"I'm telling you right now."

She waves me off. "What about Luna? Is the mansion safe for her? I don't want to leave without her."

I turn to Dr. Jenkins. "You said Luna needs to be seen at a hospital?"

He starts to nod. "I'm concerned about her blood pressure and the lack of response from the medication, so I think—"

"I don't need to go to the hospital," Luna interjects. "Dr. Jenkins told you that I could have even better care at home with the right supplies and money. You have the money, don't you?"

I snort. "Obviously."

"So what's the problem?" She slides closer and runs her hands up my arms. "I want to be at home with you, Yakov. I want us to be all together. A family."

It sounds too nice. It might be as close to picture perfect as my life will ever be—me, Luna, and the rest of my family under one roof. Soon, the babies will join, too.

But it can't come to pass quite yet.

"The only reason those gunmen didn't tear through the front door and charge down here and kill us all is because of you. Because you showed up and saved me. The same way you've been saving me since the night we met." She flashes a watery smile. "I don't want another secret safehouse. *You* are my safehouse, Yakov. Being with you is where I feel safe. Being with you is where I want to be."

She is tugging on every single one of my heart strings. It's making it very fucking hard to maintain my resolve.

"I already have a staff of nurses working around the clock to take care of Nik, so I'm sure they can look after you, too," I concede.

Luna bites her lower lip to hide her smile. "Yeah?"

"Yeah, but—" I grip her chin and force her eyes to mine. "—if things get worse or there is any concern at all about your health or the babies—"

"I'll go to the hospital without argument," she finishes. "I'll check myself in, I swear."

I press a kiss to her full lips. "Then it's a deal."

I turn back to Dr. Jenkins who is still looking paler than usual. Apparently, the good doctor isn't used to having firearms pointed at his face. "You can return to your rental, but I still want Luna and the babies examined daily."

He dips his head. "Done. I'll keep a close eye on her."

"It won't matter. Everything is going to be great now that we'll finally be together." Luna wraps her arms around my waist and presses her cheek to my ribs.

Luna feels safe with me. She trusts me to take care of her.

That is exactly what I plan to do.

46

LUNA

I'm home.

Those words circle my mind again and again as the car makes its way up the long drive towards the mansion. It's all I can think. *I'm home.*

So much has happened over the last six months, both in this mansion and outside of it. At one point, I would have given anything to get out of this house and back to my normal life. Then I was ripped out of it, kidnapped and locked away, and all I wanted was to get back.

This is my life now. This mansion and these people. Coming back here feels like coming home.

Finally.

Yakov glances over at me from the driver seat, one hand balanced casually on the wheel. "You're happy."

"Can you tell?" I don't bother to hide my smile. I couldn't if I tried. "This is all I've wanted since the moment I left."

He shifts the car into park. "Me, too."

Suddenly, Mariya leans into the front seat. "Because I'm the nicest sister in the world, I'm going to lead the charge and give you all ten minutes of alone time. Fifteen if a fight doesn't break out. Actually," she reconsiders, her chin dimpling, "if a fight breaks out, I can guarantee twenty minutes."

I frown. "What are you talking about?"

"When you figure it out, you can thank me later." She slides out of the backseat, calling over her shoulder, "You're welcome!"

I turn to Yakov. "Do you know what that's about?"

"My mother."

Oh. Right. I sit up a little taller like the woman herself might be looking at me this very second. "I almost forgot about her."

"Continue to forget about her," he recommends. "We'll cross that bridge when we get there. For now, I'm going to take you inside and get you settled."

"Settled?" I open the passenger door, but Yakov is there to help me out before I can put one foot on the ground. "Did you turn the bedroom into a yoga studio or something while I was gone? I didn't take much with me when I left. I should still be pretty settled."

"No yoga studio. I can pull off a lot of looks, but yoga pants aren't one of them."

I scan him from head to toe and there isn't a single item of clothing that wouldn't look impeccable on him. "Agree to disagree."

He smirks but continues on. "I had the staff move our bedroom downstairs."

I blink at him. "But we just left the safehouse a little over an hour ago."

"Correct."

"So… in one hour, your staff moved our entire bedroom?"

"For the sake of their jobs, they'd better have. I don't want you worrying about the stairs as the pregnancy goes on. Plus, you're closer to Nik's nursing staff this way." He wraps an arm around my lower back and pulls me close. "I think you'll like the room I picked."

Yakov leads me through the front door and straight to the library. Hope is inside, straightening the comforter on the four-poster bed. When she sees me, she beams. "Sorry, finishing touches. There are still some clothes upstairs that need to be brought down, but I'll take care of it once you're settled."

She tries to slip past me, but I pull her in for a hug. "It's so good to see you."

She squeezes me for a moment, then steps back, her eyes falling to my bump. "You, too, sweetheart. We all missed you."

Hope pulls the sliding doors closed behind her, leaving us alone.

I spin in a circle, taking in the tall shelves and the windows overlooking the garden. I love our bedroom upstairs with the floor-to-ceiling windows and attached bathroom, but being surrounded by books isn't a bad option by any means.

"Well?" Yakov asks in amusement. "Is it to your standards?"

I arch a brow. "I just spent the last few weeks in a windowless basement that reeked of apples, and now, you're worried about my standards? This is a big upgrade." Yakov's face tightens and I step closer, pulling his hands against my chest. "I didn't mean it like that."

"You shouldn't have needed to be there in the first place. He never should have gotten past my security."

"It's not your fault, Yakov. And I appreciate everything you're doing for me. Everything you've already done. I know you're only trying to keep me safe. I don't blame you for any of it."

"I'm the reason you're in danger, Luna. If you'd had babies with some other man, you wouldn't have spent the last couple months in a basement." He grits his teeth. "I would've had to kill that man for laying a fucking finger on you, but other than, you would be safe."

"*I'm* the one who walked up to *your* table that night at the restaurant," I remind him. "Whatever happened after that, *I* chose *you*, Yakov. Even now, knowing everything I know, I'd do it again. No regrets."

He pulls my hands to his lips, kissing my knuckles. It's tender, but it isn't enough. I stretch onto my toes and kiss him. My bump makes things awkward, so Yakov picks me up and places me on the edge of one of the bookshelves.

I circle my arms around his neck. I fall into his soft lips and the feeling of his hands on my body. Without meaning to, I arch against him, spreading my legs and pulling him in closer. He's hard against my inner thigh and every other thought and worry flies out of my head. The same way it always does when I'm with Yakov. Nothing else beyond this moment exists.

I swirl my tongue into his mouth and moan. Yakov's hands tighten on my hips. He digs his fingers into me like he wants to tear me apart.

Then, slowly, he pulls away.

"Luna," he growls, a warning in his tone. His hands slide to the outside of my legs and he pushes them closed. "We can't do this now."

"What?" I pout, breathless. "Why not?"

His eyes fall to my chest and I know he can see my pointed nipples through my thin dress. I'm sure he can smell the arousal on me. My skin is flushed. It was just a kiss, but I feel drunk.

He leans forward and scrapes his teeth over my neck, finding my ear. "Because my mother is sitting in the room next door."

Shit. I forgot again.

I shake my head. "We can be quiet."

"I don't care if they hear us, Luna. You sound so pretty when you're screaming my name. Let them hear." His tongue flicks over his bottom lip as he stares down at me. "The problem is, I don't want to be interrupted. I'm going to need hours before I'm ready to let you go and we don't have that kind of time."

"Oh," I squeak. My body is on literal fire. "If you're trying to talk me down, you're doing a bad job."

He smirks. "I also think you should meet my mother while you can still walk in a straight line."

Heat pounds between my legs, but my head clears slightly. I step back, straightening my dress and tucking my hair behind my ears. "Do I look okay?"

"Good enough to eat." Yakov grabs my hand and pulls me against his chest again. "The first of many things I plan to do to you later."

My face flushes and I have to force myself to back away from him. "Is there anything I should know?"

"You should know that, as my future wife, you are more powerful than anyone else in that room. What they think of you doesn't matter. *They* should be trying to impress *you*."

"That's nice, but it isn't going to help me in there. It's your mother, Yakov. Of course I want to impress her."

He sighs. "Then tell her how much you love your engagement ring. It's a family heirloom and she's precious about it. That should do the trick."

Yakov grabs my hands and leads me to the sitting room next door.

A hospital bed takes up half of the room and I'm relieved to see that Nik is in the room alone. Then I actually see Nik and my relief evaporates.

His face is so gaunt compared to the last time I saw him. He's lost so much weight. He's tucked underneath a blanket, his hands folded in his lap. From the moment I met Nik, he took up so much space. He was always laughing and bouncing from foot to foot like he couldn't contain the energy buzzing inside of him. It's strange to see him so still. So small.

Then he turns around and the same old wide smile splits his face. "Holy shit, Luna. You've really let yourself go."

Just like that, he's the same old Nik.

Yakov flicks him in the back of the head as I slap his shoulder. "You try growing two babies and see what you look like," I snap at him playfully.

"I wouldn't look nearly as graceful as you," he says. "You look gorgeous."

Yakov flicks him again.

"Ouch!" He rubs the back of his head. "That one was a compliment!"

"How about you don't look at her, just to be safe?" Yakov warns.

I stand next to Nik's bed. "How are you doing?"

"You're home and Yakov will finally stop moping around the mansion with his tail tucked between his legs, so I'm doing great."

Yakov told me Nik doesn't want to face the reality of his situation. Maybe it's time he did. But before I can press the issue, a middle-aged woman with long black hair charges into the room heading directly for me.

"There she is!" she sing-songs, pulling me into a hug.

I look over her shoulder at Yakov, confused. *Who is this woman?* I want to ask. But there can only be one answer. Even if that answer makes no sense.

Yakov described his mother like she was elderly and on the edge of death. But this woman is tall and lean. And based on the grip she has on my shoulders, strong as hell. She doesn't seem frail to me in the slightest.

I slap a smile on my face as she steps back. "Hello—"

I have no idea what to call her. "Mom" is not an option. Neither is "Yakov's mother," but that's all I have to work with. Somehow, we've made it this far without me ever once hearing her name.

It doesn't matter, though. Because she grabs my left hand and bursts into tears.

"Oh my gosh." I pat her shoulder. "Are you okay? Is everything alright?"

"What did I say about crying, Mother?" Mariya drawls from the doorway. She rolls her eyes. "So dramatic."

"This ring has been in my family for generations," she sobs, her hands shaking around mine. "When I gave it to Yakov, I hoped he would give it to a good woman—someone who would take care of him."

"I can take care of myself," Yakov mumbles behind me.

She ignores him and pats my cheek. "I know that woman is you."

I don't even know her first name, so I have no clue how she can know that. But I smile and nod anyway. "It's a beautiful ring. I love it."

Her face lights up. "That's great. Because I thought we'd design the wedding around it. A sort of old world elegance. I'm thinking silver flatware and cool whites. They will look best with your skin tone."

"She's pregnant with his twins. I think that excludes her from wearing white to the wedding. Maybe black would be better," Nik says, earning him another flick to his ear.

"Or," Mariya chimes in, "Luna can wear whatever the hell she wants. It's her wedding, after all. She should be the one to plan it."

"She will be the one to plan it, but I'm always here if you need help," Yakov's mother offers, squeezing both of my hands.

"Thank you. We haven't even talked about a wedding ceremony yet. I kind of forgot about it with everything else going on."

I regret my words instantly because she whips around to look at Yakov. "You need to set a date, Yakov. All of the best venues will be gone if you don't figure it out well in advance."

Yakov squeezes her shoulder and directs her over to the couch. "We'll take care of it. Don't worry."

Mariya edges past me, whispering in my ear as she goes. "I hope you didn't want to plan your own wedding. She'll never let go of those reins now that she has them."

"I don't care, as long as she likes me," I whisper back.

Mariya snorts. "You say that now, but give it a week. She'll be driving you crazy."

47

YAKOV

Nik is sitting up in his hospital bed when I walk into the sitting room, a cup of coffee in his hands. He looks back over his shoulder at me. "Someone is an early riser. Couldn't sleep?"

The sky is still dark and the house is quiet. Luna was asleep when I crawled out of bed—a feat worthy of a medal, in my humble opinion. The fact I'm even conscious after what we did last night is a miracle.

"I could have slept for days," I admit.

"So could I. You two weren't exactly quiet last night." He tips his head towards the shared wall between the sitting room and the library. "If you're going to fuck your fiancée against the bookshelves while I'm living here, pick literally any other wall than this one, okay?"

Luna and I got to talking about the night we met and how I kissed her against the shelves. We couldn't resist a little reenactment.

"Was that all you heard?" I ask.

"Not even close, but the other three rounds were a lot more muffled, thank fucking God."

I wince, but as last night replays in my mind, I don't even feel bad. It's been weeks since Luna and I have been alone together. It was like a race against physical exhaustion to play out each and every one of the fantasies that took root while we were apart.

I devoured her just like I promised I would, spreading her wide and burying my face between her thighs. Then I slid her to the edge of the bed and drove into her, her legs draped over my shoulders. While she was still coming down from that orgasm, I carried her to the bookshelves where we gave Nik's bedroom wall a good shake. Finally, I spun her around and took her from behind, whispering every dirty thought I'd had for the last few weeks in her ear until I exploded inside of her.

I'm half-hard now just thinking about it. Maybe I should go back to bed and see if Luna is awake. Morning sex sounds appealing.

"I was about to work out, so are you going to keep daydreaming about your woman or did you have something you wanted to say?"

Nik always had a way of being able to read my mind. But I ignore that and arch a brow. "Working out?"

"I hate to be a male cliche, but every day is arm day right now." He points to the dumbbells on the floor next to his bed. "So tell me what this is about so I can get to it."

"I wanted to talk to you. Alone."

"Okay," he says cautiously. "About?"

"Business. The path forward with the Gustev Bratva."

He relaxes noticeably. "What are you thinking?"

"I'm thinking that we're fucked," I blurt. "Not *fucked* fucked, but things could be better. I've had to hire a shit ton of outside security to cover the mansion and we lost more men than I would have liked during Akim's attack on the mansion and my attack on the house where he was keeping Luna. Plus, you're down."

"Maybe forever," he grumbles, poking at his legs.

"At least on the front lines, anyway," I agree. "But with all of that against us, I don't like the looks of a full-on war with Pavel Gustev right now. Not when I don't even have any accurate reports of how many men he's currently operating with."

I can see the information churning in Nik's head before he nods. "You're not wrong. Things have been better."

"This continual fight with the Gustev Bratva has worn us down, understandably. If we're going to finally put this feud to bed—which we absolutely fucking are—I think it might be time to call in some backup."

Nik frowns. "We don't have any more backup. We've called in all of the backup."

"That's what I want to talk to you about. I'm considering bringing in some outside help."

"An alliance?" His eyes go wide. "We've never done that before."

"We've never needed to. But we've also never been in a years-long feud like this. Especially not with a heartbroken child with nothing to lose. Pavel is a loose cannon. We can't assume he's going to make the safe call and pull his men back to regroup. He's willing to die and take as many of his own men down with him as necessary. We have to assume he's going to attack tomorrow. Today. Right fucking now."

"And when he does, we need to be ready," Nik finishes thoughtfully. "Do you have anyone in mind?"

"Dima Baranov."

"I knew you'd say that," he mutters, pinching the bridge of his nose.

"I've been thinking about it since we found out he snatched Budimir away from Pavel. Having that black market connection to more firepower could be helpful, even if it is a friend-of-a-friend situation. And Dima isn't afraid to poke the bear. He'd be down to fight."

"Because he's also a loose cannon," Nik points out. "Dima would probably destroy Pavel purely for fun without even considering whether it's beneficial to him or not."

"Seems like a good quality to me."

"Unless he turns it on us."

"So we don't let him turn on us," I suggest. "We make sure he stays a friend. Or we kill him before he becomes an enemy."

Nik goes quiet for a while, mulling over all of the information in his head. I sit back and let him. After a few minutes, he throws up his hands. "I want to say no, but I don't have a better idea."

"There's the excitement I'm looking for," I say sarcastically.

"Sorry, but it's hard to drum up excitement when I know you probably already have a meeting scheduled with Dima and I'm going to be stuck here in this fucking bed." He looks up at me, eyebrow arched. "I'm right, aren't I? You've already put out feelers to meet with him?"

I nod. "I'm meeting with him in two hours. But if you had a good argument against it, I would have canceled."

"And I'm staying here while you meet with him?"

"I wish you could come," I tell him. "But it's too much of a risk right now. I don't want anyone to know that you're—"

"Helpless and trapped in a bed," he snaps.

"Recovering," I correct, clapping him on the shoulder. "You can come with me once you're more mobile."

Whatever that may look like.

Nik's jaw flexes. Then he jabs a finger at me. "Stay alert and don't trust anyone but yourself."

"I never do."

"I'm serious," he adds. "Scope out the site before the meeting and make sure Dima comes alone. Don't let yourself get cornered. You have too much to live for."

I smile. "Don't worry, little brother. I'll take care of myself."

"Un-fucking-likely," he grumbles behind my back.

Two hours later, I'm standing in the hollowed-out remains of an old bowling alley with Dima Baranov.

I kept my promise to Nik. I showed up to the meeting an hour early, scoped out the site, and watched as Dima arrived. I made sure he came alone and unarmed.

Now, we're standing across from each other and he's wearing a suit and smoking a cigar like he's a mobster from a cheesy old movie. As if the air in here isn't toxic enough. I can hear rats scurrying in the rotting walls.

"I'll do whatever you want so long as I'm the one who gets to kill Pavel." He puffs a ring of smoke into the dingy air.

I expected Dima to agree to fight, but I assumed it would take some convincing. His easy acceptance feels like a red flag. I can hear Nik in the back of my head, warning me off.

"You don't even know why I want him dead. You're willing to make an enemy without any clue why?"

"I don't care why *you* want him dead," he explains. "I care why *I* want him dead. And that's none of your business."

"If I'm putting the safety of my men and family in your hands, it's very much my fucking business," I snarl. "I'm not going into the trenches with you if there's any chance Pavel will be able to lure you out."

"I'm no traitor, Yakov Kulikov. I'll warn you against suggesting I am."

"And I'll warn you against thinking that I'm desperate enough for your help that I'll handle disrespect. We came here unarmed—as a man of your word, I assume you followed that rule—but I don't need a weapon to show you what I'm capable of."

Dima smiles, new respect shining in his eyes. "You're the one here asking for my help."

"I have the manpower to take down you and the Gustev Bratva. But as a leader who isn't a psychopath, I don't want to send my men into a battle they won't come home from. I'd rather share the victory with you and keep more of my men alive. *That* is why you're here. Not because I need your help, but because I'm powerful enough to ask for it."

He blows a smoke ring, letting it disappear in the dusty air before he responds. "You want to share a victory with me? That's good. Because that is my price. You make sure I kill Pavel myself and I'm in."

"But you won't tell me why?"

"What I can tell you is that I have a good reason to want every member of the Gustev Bratva to die a slow, painful death. The more of those deaths I can bring about with my own two hands, the better." He blows another smoke ring. "I can't tell you more than that. Family business. You get it."

I don't like not knowing all of the variables, but Dima is right; I do get it. It's the reason no one outside of our house knows my brother is paralyzed from the waist down. There are some things you keep close to the vest.

"That's all you want? I let you kill Pavel yourself and you're in?" I ask.

"I'm in," he confirms. "I offer up my men and my resources. Whatever you need, you've got it. As long as that little bastard dies by my hand."

"And I'm in so long as that little bastard dies," I say. "I don't care whose hand does the deed."

Dima smirks. "Then it looks like we're in business, my friend."

48

LUNA

Mariya told me to give it a week before her mother—Ofeliya, I've since learned—drove me crazy. That estimate seems conservative now.

It's been one day and I'm losing my mind.

"Yakov should have chosen a room closer to the restroom." Ofeliya takes my lunch tray off of my lap and hands it to Hope. I tried to go to the kitchen for lunch, but it was deemed too strenuous. "Nik doesn't need to worry about a restroom since he has a catheter, but it's a long way for you to walk."

"I don't mind walking," I say quickly. Mostly because I think she might actually try to give me a catheter.

I thought Yakov was protective when I first got pregnant, but Ofeliya is taking it to an entirely different level.

"Sure, but we have to think about what's best for the babies. Your joints and ligaments are loosening up for delivery by this point. One wrong step and you could blow out a hip."

"Dr. Jenkins was just here this morning and he didn't mention that as a concern."

The only problem is still my stupid blood pressure. I didn't tell Ofeliya about it, but she managed to find out, anyway. According to her, I need to start taking cold showers and eating dark chocolate. The medication isn't touching my blood pressure, but surely her old wives' tales are going to do the trick. Or so she thinks.

"Men don't know the things a woman goes through when they're pregnant," she says dismissively. "They are clueless."

I manage a polite smile. "He's a doctor."

"Still." She waves it off and finishes loading up the tray in Hope's arms. "Take this to the kitchen and refill Luna's water."

Hope nods, meeting my eyes briefly on her way out the door. She's been in and out of my room all day, but I haven't had a chance to talk to her once. Not with Yakov's mom ordering her around.

Ofeliya is taking care of me—that's nice, right? My own mother seemed relieved when I was finally old enough to take care of myself. She was never interested in the maternal aspects of being a mom. I should be grateful.

I am grateful, I decide. I'm going to do my best to appreciate Ofeliya's obvious concern for me.

Suddenly, she lunges for the corner of the mattress, her face creased in worry. "Has anyone changed this out today?"

"My bed?"

"The sheets." She runs her thumb over some mascara smeared in the bottom corner. "It's dirty."

I remember when that particular stain was made and my entire body flushes with embarrassment. Yakov was driving into me from behind and I had to bury my face in the bed to keep from waking the entire house.

"It's fine. It's nothing, actually. I don't mind."

"What do we pay these people for if not to take care of things like this?" She shakes her head. "I've been telling Yakov since I got here that he needs to restructure his staff. Before my husband was—When I lived here," she says instead, "I kept the staff on a tight leash. If you don't, nothing gets done. You know what they say: if you want something done well, do it yourself."

I don't see what that particular saying has to do with this situation since we're literally talking about hiring people to help run the house. But I smile and nod anyway.

"After the two of you get married, it will be your job." She delivers that little tidbit like a present. Like my life's goal should be to manage the staff.. "I'll teach you everything you need to know."

I think I already know everything I need to know, actually. I know I don't want to run my house the way Ofeliya did. What I don't know is how to tell her that.

"I'm going to find Hope and have her bring in some new sheets," Ofeliya announces, heading for the door. "Is there anything else you need?"

Before I can answer, Mariya appears behind her mother in the doorway. "The only thing Luna needs is a visit from me and my stack of bridal magazines."

"Actual paper magazines?" I ask, sitting up to try and get a better view.

Mariya fans the magazines out on the bed. "All of your favorite movies existed before the internet. I took a leap and figured you'd like this over a Pinterest board."

I could kiss Mariya. Honestly. Being back in the mansion has been amazing, but I need something to pass the time and keep me from starting a fight with Yakov's mom. There's enough family feuding going on without me starting one on home turf.

But before I can even reach for a magazine, Ofeliya appears between us and swipes them into a stack. "Luna has more important things to do than flip through silly magazines with you, Mariya. She's growing the future of this family."

I hold a finger to stop her. "Actually, I wouldn't mind—"

"Besides, we don't need any of these for wedding plans." She tucks them under her arm. "Marrying into a family like ours comes with a lot of traditions. One of those is that the outgoing matriarch handles the planning. It's my gift to you, Luna."

I blink at her, too gobsmacked to come up with anything to say.

Mariya doesn't say a word, but she doesn't have to. The tilt of her head and the arch of her brow say more than enough. *I told you so.*

Ofeliya pulls the comforter up around my waist and turns for the door. "I'll take care of everything, Luna. You just sit back and relax."

I watch her disappear into the hallway while Mariya's stifled laughter turns into full-on cackles. "I told you. I freaking told you. One day in and you hate her, don't you?"

"I don't—" I kick Mariya's leg from under the blankets and lower my voice. "I don't hate her. I never said that. She's... she's trying to help."

"She's driving you crazy and trying to take over your life. Admit it."

I narrow my eyes at her. "You brought those magazines in on purpose. You knew she'd do that."

"I had a hunch," she admits with a giggle. "I tried to tell you what she was like, but you didn't want to listen. I thought you deserved to know what you're in for."

I groan. "What does a Kulikov wedding even entail? Maybe I can just suck it up and let her do things the way she wants. I mean, it can't be that—"

"The dress she wants you to wear on your big day has a lace headband and shoulder pads up to your ears."

"Oh, no."

"Oh, *yes*," she cackles. "And if you don't kill that cursed dress now, it will live on and haunt me at *my* wedding one day. For self-preservation purposes, if nothing else, I'm firmly on your team."

I sag back against the headboard. "This is too much stress. Maybe Yakov and I can elope. We'll just go to the courthouse and—"

"*Bring shame and humiliation upon the entire Kulikov family. What would Yakov's father say if he were here to see this?*'" Mariya's voice is two octaves higher than normal, her face creased in mock disappointment. "*I knew you weren't the right woman to continue the honorable lineage of this noble family. To the dungeons with you!*'"

"That got a little farfetched at the end. Your mom wouldn't banish me to the dungeons. But I see your point."

"You say that now, but give it another day," Mariya says. "You'll realize there is nothing Ofeliya Kulikov won't do to stick her nose all up in your business. Why do you think I fled the country?"

"It's not like you were on the run. Your mom put you on a plane."

"Exactly! I'm her own flesh and blood and she put me on a plane to live in another country, all because I wouldn't do what she wanted. You really think the dungeon is out of the question for you?" She shakes her head. "Nuh-uh. I don't think so."

I know Yakov won't let that happen, but my hopes for a healthy relationship with his mother feel like they're slipping away.

"You have a big decision to make, Luna, but if you want my opinion, I say you push back and start your own traditions. It's time for this family to update. Which is ironic, since you're flipping through magazines for wedding ideas as if the internet doesn't exist." Mariya reaches under the bed and pulls out another stack of bridal magazines. Slapping her hand on the top, she plops it in my lap. "You might want to keep this batch hidden or they'll end up in the trash, too."

~

I'm still flipping through the stack of magazines Mariya left for me hours later, but I can't process any of the information. The pictures of updos and tulle-covered archways wash over me while my mind whirls.

How am I going to tell Ofeliya I hate her wedding dress? I mean, technically, I haven't seen it, so I don't know for sure that I hate it. But a lace headband and shoulder pads don't sound promising.

Maybe I can pick my own dress and then let her plan the rest of it.

Has appeasement really ever worked for anyone, though? If I let her plan the wedding, will she plan the honeymoon, too? Our first anniversary? Our twentieth?

A lifetime of birthdays and dinner parties and home renovations projects being overseen by Yakov's mother flash in front of me. I don't realize I'm crumpling a page from the magazine until Yakov lays his hand over mine and smooths out my fingers.

"Do you have something against—" He leans forward to read the article headline. "—non-floral centerpieces that I should know about?"

"No, but your mom might!"

He frowns. "Who cares?"

"She does! Or, she might!" I groan. "Apparently, I'm marrying into an important family with long-standing traditions. You never told me about any family traditions."

"Because we don't have any," he shrugs. "Except for the Bratva thing."

"*The Bratva thing*,' he says. Like it's casual." I snort. "Well, while you are off running 'the Bratva thing,' I'm supposed to keep the household staff in line. Your mother is going to teach me everything she knows. And if I don't want to know what she knows, then she'll lock me in a dungeon."

"What are you talking about?"

"That's what Mariya said."

He rolls his eyes. "Don't listen to Mariya. She and my mother have been fighting since Mariya was born. That won't be your experience."

Spoken like a man. Ofeliya was definitely right about one thing: men really have no idea what women go through.

"Your mother told me that she was going to plan our entire wedding. She stole my bridal magazines."

Yakov points to the stack in my lap. "Then what are these?"

"The backups that Mariya bought because she knew Ofeliya would take the first batch!"

"I think you're making this a bigger deal than it needs to be. My mother is a lot, but she'll settle down after a few days. Give her some time."

"How *much* time? Should I let her plan the wedding and hope that's enough time? Or maybe I'll let her birth the twins for me because I'll definitely figure out how to do that wrong, too." I turn to him, eyes wide, as something occurs to me. "Please tell me she won't be in the delivery room."

"She won't be in the delivery room." Yakov grabs my shoulders and squeezes, working some of the tension out of my shoulders. "Just relax, Luna. Everything is going to work out."

I let my head loll between my shoulders as his thumbs work into the muscles at the base of my neck. "Everything? You really think we can take the Gustevs *and* your mother?"

"I'm positive we can." He kisses my neck. "Dima and I are already working on a plan in place to lure Pavel out. Once he shows himself, we'll cut him down. Then we'll deal with my mother."

"You'll cut her down, too?"

"Only if you ask me to," he teases. "Otherwise, I'll probably just have a firm talk with her."

"And if that doesn't work?"

He massages down my arms, working until my fingers tingle. "Different continents exist for a reason. We'll send her to one of the others. Problem solved."

"You make it sound so simple."

"Because it is. There isn't a problem too big for me to handle." His voice is a low rumble in my ear. His hands shift back to my shoulders and around. Suddenly, he's cupping my breasts, rolling my nipples between his fingers. "Like this tension you're carrying. I've never seen anything like it, but I think I have just the trick."

My mouth falls open in a sigh. "Oh, is that right?"

"That's right. I know how to help you release it." Yakov lays me back against the pillows and settles between my thighs. "You just have to trust me."

"I trust you," I moan, curling my fingers through his hair as he thrusts his tongue into me. "With my life."

49

YAKOV

"I can't believe we're letting him into the mansion," Nik grumbles. He's in his wheelchair next to me, watching as Dima Baranov's car parks at the top of the drive.

"We aren't going to show him anything that could hurt us," I remind him. "Dima went through every security screening at the front gate, he left all of his technology outside the fence, and it's not like we're letting him have the run of the house. He'll be in my office and right back out."

"I just don't like it." His jaw shifts back and forth. "We barely know him."

"You're the one who suggested we have the meeting here."

"Because *I* wanted to be there," he grits out. "Not because I wanted *him* here."

Getting a wheelchair-accessible van is at the top of my to-do list. But even if I had one, Nik isn't ready to go out yet.

"Say the word and I'll drive him off the property. I'll meet him somewhere else if you're not ready to—"

"I'm fucking ready to deal with Dima Baranov," Nik snarls. "I'm not ready for the world to know I'm sitting on a set of useless legs."

The physical therapist told me this morning that Nik is making improvements. His toes wiggle from time to time. The connection is still there. Whether it can be repaired fully or not is a question that only time can answer.

I clap Nik on the back. "It is a shame. The only thing you had going for you was that you were younger and faster. Now, I'm the brains *and* the brawn. It's a heavy burden to carry, but since you can't do it anymore…"

For the first time all morning, Nik grins. "You cocky bastard. Teasing the guy in the wheelchair is a low blow."

"It has to be. If I swung at normal height, it would go right over your head."

Nik angles his wheels sharply and runs over my foot. "Be professional, asshole. Dima is coming."

By the time Dima walks through the front door, Nik and I are sober and collected.

Dima, to his credit, doesn't say a word about the wheelchair. He shakes our hands and tips his head. "Take me to the room where the magic happens, gentlemen. We have work to do."

An hour later, I'm at my desk, Dima is lounging on the sofa in the corner, and Nik is rolling back and forth across the room the same way he used to nervously pace.

"You're telling me that you have names of every man who broke into my house the night my fiancée was kidnapped?" I growl.

Dima smirks. "Budimir is a great resource. He dealt in weapons, but the man keeps his ears open. Apparently, Akim had loose lips."

"Now, I'm going to sink some fucking ships. Tell me the names. Now."

Dima rattles off a list, but when he gets to one name, Nik screeches to a stop. "Marat?"

"Do you know him?" Dima asks.

Nik and I look at each other. We both know that name.

"He led the charge that night," Nik grits out. "We saw him on the cameras attacking our sister. He shot her."

"When he was finished, he pulled a bag over Luna's head." My fist is so tight I'm sure my knuckles are going to break through the skin.

"Ooh. Juicy. Then I know something else you are going to love." Dima leans forward, elbows on his knees. "I know where to find him."

I don't wait for more of an explanation. I stand up, keys in my hand. "Tell me where."

In the evenings, the usual Gustev Bratva hangout is a nightclub with loud music and watered-down drinks. Right now, in the middle of the afternoon, it's dead.

There are only four cars outside in the lot and a quick search turns up that one of them is registered to Marat.

I haven't laid eyes on the man himself yet—I've only seen him through the security footage—but I can practically feel him hiding behind the walls of the club.

"When?" I snarl to Isay.

He checks his watch. "Dima and his team just breached the club on 75th less than sixty seconds ago."

As soon as I heard his name, I wanted to tear out of the mansion and destroy Marat. But Nik slowed me down. He made me sit down and come up with a plan. He made me remember why I made him my second in the first place.

Instead of charging into this club to kill one man, we coordinated a dual attack with Dima's men. In one go, we're taking out two of Pavel's clubs and any men inside. Between this and Dima swiping Budimir, the Gustev Bratva is going to hurt.

But right now, my entire focus is on how much I can make Marat hurt.

"When?" I growl again, bouncing from foot to foot.

"I don't know. I haven't—" Isay's phone vibrates and he drops it in his pocket and reaches for his gun. "Now."

We make our way to the back door while three more men move in through the front. There are emergency exits on the sides of the building, but one of them is blocked by a metal dumpster and the other is chained closed. Clearly, Pavel has the fire marshal in his back pocket.

On a normal run, I'd try to pick the lock and sneak in undetected, but today, I kick my boot into the center of the wooden door. The wood splinters around the lock and swings inward on rusty hinges.

I charge in with Isay right behind me. I'd rather it be Nik by my side, but he's back at the mansion coordinating the attack via comms.

We're halfway down a long hallway when I hear shouting and gunfire erupting from the front of the club. I'm making my way towards the noise when a door just ahead explodes open.

A man runs through the door, looking back over his shoulder at whatever he is running from. But he has no idea he's running straight into the real monster.

As soon as he's within arms' reach, I slam him against the wall, knocking his gun out of his hand and the breath out of his lungs. The man's wide eyes are wild and he's already spewing out a string of pleas. But I'd recognize him anywhere.

I drive my forearm against his throat until he's too busy choking to speak.

"Hello, Marat," I growl. "I'd like to talk to you."

By the time I string him up by his arms from the lighting rig above the dance floor, the three other men in the club with him are dead.

"Pavel isn't here," Marat blurts.

"I know."

He frowns, sweat dripping down his forehead. "We don't know where he is, either. He isn't telling anyone."

I tug on the ropes, checking to make sure they'll hold. "I know that, too."

"I can try to help you find him," Marat says, his voice edging on hysterical. "I can call him. No one will have to know that I helped. I'll be a double agent. I'll work for you."

"It would be easy for you since you already know so many members of my family," I say. "Do you remember my sister? You shot her on my front lawn."

The blood drains out of Marat's face. He is sickly pale and trembling. His feet can barely touch the floor. He strains to get his toes underneath him and take some of the weight from his hands.

"After that, you met my fiancée. You must remember her," I say, circling him slowly. "Or maybe you wouldn't recognize her. She did have a bag over her head."

"I'm sorry," he whimpers. "I was following orders. I didn't know who they were."

The lie comes out of him so easily that I can't stop myself. I lunge, driving my knife into his side. Blood flows down the handle, warming my fingers. I give it a twist before I pull it out. "Stop lying."

He screams and then devolves into panicked panting.

"Akim trusted you to carry out a mission to kidnap and murder my family, but you can't even endure a little torture?" I click my tongue. "Goons these days just aren't what they used to be."

I drive the knife into his other side. Blood spurts out, spraying across the smooth dance floor. It puddles underneath him, making it even harder for him to keep his toes on the ground. His hands are bright red from the restraints.

I drag the tip of the knife from his wrist to his elbow. Blood oozes from the thin cut and soaks into his shirt.

"Admit that you knew who they were," I growl.

He's sobbing, tears and snot pouring down his face.

I make the same long cut to the other arm, but I push a little too hard. Blood pumps out of his arm to the beat of his racing heart.

"Admit it," I bark in his face. "You knew who they were. You fucking enjoyed terrorizing them, didn't you?"

"Please," he whimpers.

I press the blade to his neck. Blood stains his collar. "Admit it or you die right now like the coward you are."

"I knew!" he gasps. "I knew who they were. I knew why I was there."

I press the knife in deeper. "And you enjoyed it."

"I was just doing my job."

I can feel the tendons in his neck straining against the blade. "You aren't some fucking paper pusher. You were there to murder and kidnap people. You don't get into this line of work without enjoying it. The same way I'm going to enjoy applying just a little more pressure and tearing through your jugular."

He slips in the blood pooled at his feet and yelps as he falls into the blade. It cuts deeper into his neck, but he scrambles away from it. "Please! I have a family. A wife and kids."

"So do I. And you tried to kill them."

I rear back and plunge the knife into his chest. I drag it down, tracing around bones and carving through organs until he's split wide open. He's trying to scream, but he can't find the air. His voice grows weaker and weaker until he goes limp, still suspended from the ceiling by his wrists.

Isay claps from behind me. "Feel better?"

I survey my work and shake my head. "No. But the fucker got what he deserved."

"It'll send a message, that's for sure. Pavel can't ignore this."

No, he can't. Even if it doesn't lure him out, this man's death will let Pavel know what's waiting for him when he finally does show his face again.

I wipe my blade clean on the bottom of my shirt. "Find the man's family."

"What do I do with them when I find them?"

If I was Pavel, I'd order their deaths. I'd have them brought to me so I could show them what became of their husband and father one by one.

But I'm not Pavel or Akim. I'm not this worthless sack of flesh in front of me.

"Make sure they're okay," I say. "Set them up with some money until the wife gets back on her feet. Her husband was a piece of shit, but I'm sure he still paid some bills."

He's dead. I've taken my pound of flesh. I don't need anything else.

50

LUNA

I'm crouched in the corner of the covered cabana with a book when Mariya finds me.

She pops her head around the curtain that shields me from prying eyes inside the house and nearly gives me a heart attack. "You don't need to hide."

I jolt so hard I drop my book on my face. "Can we not sneak up on the pregnant woman with high blood pressure, please?"

"Sorry." Mariya pulls back the curtains, letting in some much-needed sunlight. I was starting to get cold in the shade. "I just thought you'd like to know that you don't have to hide. My mom is out for the day."

"She went out? Like, she left the premises?"

I didn't even know that was an option. Yakov never explicitly said that we couldn't leave, but no one has gone anywhere since he brought us back from the safehouse.

"Don't get your hopes up. She'll be back later," she says. "Apparently, she *needed* to get her nails done, I guess. For what? I have no idea. It's not like any of us have any plans, God forbid."

"My hopes weren't up. I never said I wanted your mom to leave forever."

"You didn't have to say it. It was written all over your face when she told you coffee wasn't good for the baby and made you a mug of hot lemon water instead."

"I didn't mind that much. She was just trying to be helpful," I mumble unconvincingly.

I had to slip Hope a note and have her bring me an iced coffee in my water bottle. Managing my emotions has been hard enough as it is lately. Subtracting caffeine from the equation isn't going to make it any easier.

Mariya pats my leg. "It's okay, Luna. Let it all out. This is a safe space."

I sigh. "She cares a lot about me and the babies. That's a good thing. I know the two of you have a rough relationship, but I don't want to do anything to make things more tense right now. Yakov is dealing with enough without needing to referee me and your mom."

"Do you know what he's dealing with?" Mariya wonders. "Nik mentioned that they're teaming up with another Bratva, but he won't tell me anything else. Those two never tell me anything."

"Yakov isn't telling me anything, either."

It's the truth, but only because I told Yakov I only want him to tell me what I *needed* to know.

I saw dried blood on the floor of the shower this morning, so I know he's been busy. But it's easier for me to imagine that he sits behind a desk somewhere and places his stamp of approval on plans to rid the earth of his enemies. It's better than imagining him covered in blood and dodging bullets.

Yakov doesn't need the added stress of me feuding with his mom, and I don't need the added stress of worrying that Yakov won't make it to see our babies come into the world. Not when I've made it this far in the pregnancy and have so little left to go.

I trust him not to take on more than he can handle, so I'd rather stay in the dark.

Mariya purses her lips. "I don't believe you, but I know you aren't going to tell me anything, either."

"I'm serious. I really don't know anything. Between being pregnant and now worrying about the wedding that I assumed was still years away, I'm not trying to add more stress to my plate. Whatever is going on, I'm sure your brothers have it handled."

"Well, *I* don't have anything going on here at home. I'm bored," she complains. Suddenly, she sits tall and faces me. "Tell me what you need! Give me something to do."

I shrug. "I don't need anything. Your mom has been taking care of everything around the house and I doubt Yakov would ever let me leave even if I wanted to."

"Considering there is a crazy man after you, I'm gonna have to agree. What would you leave the house to do anyway?"

"Well, I haven't bought anything for the babies yet. I assumed Yakov and I would go somewhere and make a registry, but he has more important things going on right now."

"He's preparing for the babies in his own way," Mariya agrees.

I nod. "A nursery isn't important if the mansion isn't even safe for them. I support what he's doing; I just feel like I'm missing out on some of the fun of being pregnant. I want to buy little outfits and decorate the nursery and do all of the nesting, you know?"

Mariya twists her lips to the side, thinking. Then she jumps up. "I'll be right back."

"Where are you going?" I call after her, but she's already rounding the corner of the pool and jogging inside.

Five minutes later, she presents to me an open laptop in one hand and a platinum credit card in the other.

"What is this? Am I supposed to pick one? Is this like *The Matrix?*"

"Update your references, please. I've never even heard of whatever that is." Mariya balances the laptop on my knee and plops down next to me. "You and my credit card are going to do some nesting. We're going to online shop until you drop."

"No. I can't take your money, Mariya."

"Relax." She waves me off. "The credit card is attached to Yakov's account. It's technically for *extreme emergencies only*, but as soon as Yakov finds out you're the one spending his money, he won't care. My brother simps for you like no other."

"Backdate your references, please. I don't know what that means."

"It means that you can buy as much as you want and he isn't going to care." Mariya presses the card into my hands and reaches for the laptop. "Okay, so what's first on the list? Cribs? Bassinets? Those little sucker things that take care of their boogers?"

"All of the above," I admit. "I don't have anything. We'll need car seats so we can get them home from the hospital. That should probably be first on the list. And clothes. Blankets, too. Oh, and hats! I think babies' heads get cold."

Maybe I should add "reading every baby book in existence" to my to-do list. The last time I held a baby was when I babysat for my neighbors when I was sixteen. And it wasn't even a baby. The kid was three years old and almost potty-trained. I don't know if I've ever even held an infant before.

I shove the laptop towards Mariya. "I don't actually know what I need. Is there a list somewhere? Maybe we should look this up. Or wait until your mom gets back. She raised three kids. She probably knows what to—"

"The last time my mother held a baby was when I was one. She is not a fount of information."

"Yeah, but she still knows more than us."

"We have the internet at our disposal. Everything we could ever want to know."

I reach for the laptop. "You're right. I should look up how to do infant CPR. What if they choke on something? I didn't become a lifeguard because I didn't want to do the CPR training. What was I thinking? If something happens and I don't—"

"I'm pressing pause on this freakout." Mariya circles her finger in front of my face. "Now is a time for mindless buying. No panic attacks, no researching how to get a Lego brick out of your kid's windpipe. Right now, all you are going to do is put everything your pregnant heart desires into a shopping cart and not panic, okay? This is supposed to be fun."

I blow out a long breath and the tension in my chest eases slightly. "Okay. I can do that."

"Great. Because we have a lot of damage to do. First things first, do you know the genders yet?" She pauses, holding up a finger. "I really hope you don't. Because if I find out that you know and didn't tell me, I will have to take my credit card and leave on principle."

I laugh. "No, we don't know yet."

"Thank God. Gender-neutral color schemes," Mariya says with a nod. "Got it. Do you want to find out or are you going to wait until they pop out and be surprised?"

"I want to know. I could have found out a couple months ago with a blood test, but... I don't know. I got scared."

"Worried you'd find out you were having an alien?" Mariya asks in all seriousness.

I elbow her in the side. "No. But I was worried about getting too attached to them."

"They're your babies. You're supposed to be attached."

"I know. But the more I know about them, the more it will hurt if something goes wrong."

"I don't think knowing what's between their legs would soften that blow, Loon." Mariya squeezes my knee. "If you want to know, I think you should find out. Don't live your life in preparation for worst-case scenarios. In our world, the worst case can be pretty damn bleak."

Mariya makes a good point. And as I scroll through page after page of gray and yellow gender-neutral baby clothes, the decision cements in my mind.

By the time Yakov and I are lying in bed hours later, I know what I want.

"I'm going to ask Dr. Jenkins to tell me the genders," I announce.

Yakov drops his phone in his lap and turns to me.

"I didn't want to find out because I didn't want to get too attached to the babies and then be devastated if anything happened to them. But I'll be devastated if something happens to them, either way," I babble. "I figure I might as well get to know them as much as I can now and make the most of it. Just in case."

Yakov nods but doesn't say anything. The silence stretches so I decide to fill it.

"I'm not doing this because I think anything bad is going to happen, obviously. But if it does, I want to know I gave them my all." I try and fail to blink back tears. They roll down my cheeks as I ramble on. "I wouldn't be a very good mom if I held my babies at arm's length so I wouldn't get hurt, right? So I should find out. *We* should find out."

Finally, he takes my hand. "Do you want to know or do you think you *should* want to know?"

"Both," I answer quickly.

"You were pretty set on not finding out before. What changed?"

"Well, I was shopping today and there were so many cute baby clothes, but I couldn't buy them because I don't know what we're having."

"When did you go shopping?" he demands.

"Online. With Mariya's credit card," I admit with a wince. "She wanted to help me get some things for the babies. We didn't go overboard, I swear."

"Unlikely, knowing my sister," he mutters.

"I'm the one who put everything in the cart."

It's not a lie. Mariya was sitting next to me jabbing her finger at everything I scrolled past, but I was the one operating the mouse.

Yakov doesn't look convinced, but he stretches one arm up behind his head and leans back against the headboard. "So all of this is because you saw clothes?"

I sigh. "Yes and no. Some of it is about the cute clothes, but I also just realized that I'm ready to know. I trust that you're going to take care of me and the babies. I'm not... I'm not scared anymore. And I want something amazing to look forward to."

Yakov watches me for a second, his eyes studying every inch of my face. Finally, he grabs my hand and presses my knuckles to his lips. "Then we'll go find out."

51

YAKOV

"Gentlemen," Dima greets, bowing at my office door before he kicks it closed behind him.

He's wearing another suit. This one has pinstripes. As Dima walks over to claim his seat on the couch, Nik looks at me, eyebrow arched.

Dima may have joined our team and helped lead a very successful mission to take out two of Pavel Gustev's businesses in the city, but Nik is not going to let anything concerning the Baranov *pakhan* slide.

I ignore Nik and lean back in my chair. "Pavel is panicked."

"You saw that press release this morning, too?" Dima snorts. "I've been shaking in my boots all day waiting for the 'proper authorities' to come knocking."

The attacks on two of Pavel's clubs didn't go unnoticed. My men cleared out the bodies, but we made enough noise during the violence for the news to go mainstream. Akim's absence lately was noted, too, but there hasn't been any talk about his death. Not surprising considering I had his body all but liquified. It's hard to positively identify a puddle.

The article also included a quote from "an associate of Pavel Gustev" that warned the "bad actors" who attacked his businesses that they would be caught by the "proper authorities" and justice would be served. None of us are particularly scared.

Nik balances on the back two wheels of his chair. "He probably didn't even write it. From what I'm hearing, he still hasn't shown his face. It was probably Akim's old PR team who wrote it up. I doubt Pavel cared enough to fire them and we know he doesn't care about maintaining his family's good name."

"You're right, Nikandr. Akim's former lawyer was the spokesperson in the article according to my sources," Dima adds. "No one could get in touch with Pavel himself."

"You still have your spies in the Gustev Bratva?" I ask.

Dima smirks. "I have spies everywhere."

"You should pull them." Nik drops down to all four wheels and rolls closer. "It won't be safe for them once Pavel finds out you're working with us."

Dima waves him off. "I have time. I wore a disguise during the attack."

"Your skeleton mask was terrifying," Nik drawls, "but he'll find out sooner than later. Your men could die."

"Which is why we should strike again before he does." I kick my feet up on my desk. "Pavel thinks he has the numbers to win in a war. If we were fighting him individually, he would. But now that we've joined forces, we have the advantage."

"So we go for the jugular now," Dima growls, his eyes flashing. "Let's charge through his gates and tear the fucker up."

Before I can answer, Nik cuts in. "We don't know where he is. If we attack without knowing his location, it will tip him off that we've teamed up and he'll be better prepared in a fight."

Dima frowns. "I fucking hate recon."

"That's why Nik will handle it." I look to my brother for confirmation and he nods sharply. "Nik will track down Pavel while we figure out how to take him and the rest of the Gustev Bratva down without starting an all-out war."

"And I make the kill shot," Dima reminds me.

"It's yours. As we discussed."

He grins. "Then this all sounds good to me. Let's plot."

Dima left the mansion hours ago and Nikandr had to go to physical therapy, so I'm alone when I walk out of my office and trip on the mountain of boxes in the entryway.

"What the fuck is this?" I mumble under my breath.

Before the words are even out of my mouth, I already know what it is.

Then I hear laughter coming from the other room. I follow the sound and the trail of packing paper and plastic zip ties until I find my sister and Luna sitting on the floor of our makeshift bedroom. A half-finished bassinet sits between them and they're both holding screwdrivers like they've never seen a tool before in their lives.

"I don't know why the creators of this stupid bassinet think I should know the difference between a nut and a screw." Mariya frowns down at the instructions. "There are no pictures on this thing!"

"We don't need pictures. There are written instructions," Luna says.

"And they all sound like the stage direction for a porno!" Mariya unfolds the instructions further so the page takes up her whole lap. "Everything here is about drilling and nuts and shafts. It's disgusting."

Luna cackles and I can't remember the last time I saw her laugh. *Really* laugh. Her smile lights up her face and I want it to be like this all the time.

When Pavel is dead, it will be.

"Can you not make sexual jokes in front of the children's furniture?" I lean against the doorway as they both turn to look at me. "It's offensive."

"*I'm* offensive?" Mariya waves the instructions in the air. "*These* are offensive. There are a thousand 'that's what she said' jokes in here. Plus, no pictures."

"We don't need pictures!" Luna repeats, snatching the instructions away. "We are liberated women. We can build furniture without a man's help."

"I can't," Mariya announces.

Luna shushes her and frowns down at the instructions. "It looks here like we need to hold the base and tighten the nuts underneath."

Mariya fakes a gag. "Honestly, this project is starting to feel too intimate. I think I should bounce and leave you alone with this—" Her eyes go wide as she catches the name of the bassinet on the box. "It's called a *Grow As You Go!* Are you fucking kidding me?"

That even pulls a laugh out of me.

"It's a convertible crib! A three-in-one," Luna tries to explain. "It grows from a bassinet to a crib and then you can use the rails for— you know what? Never mind. You promised you'd help. When we bought all of this stuff, you said you would, and I quote, 'Bob the Builder the fuck out of this baby furniture.' Where is that attitude?"

"I'll build furniture when I have my own kids. For now, I'm the fun aunt. And the fun aunt gets to skip out on boring shit like this and go watch TV."

Mariya runs out of the room like it's on fire and Luna and I look at each other. She takes in the mess of wood and screws around her and deflates.

"Are you still a liberated woman if I come to help you?" I drawl.

She brightens, hope written all over her face. "Do you want to help?"

"That depends. How mad am I going to be when I see Mariya's credit card statement?"

"We only bought the essentials," Luna repeats again. Her hair is twisted into a messy bun on top of her head and it flops around as she makes her case. "The babies need beds to sleep in and I made sure to order the ones that we can use for years. Until they need big kid beds."

"That doesn't explain the mountain of boxes by the front door," I point out.

She chews on her full lower lip. "Okay... so maybe everything out there wasn't strictly essential. Some of it was for fun."

"Luna..."

"Everything else is clothes!" she admits in a rush. "I bought them enough clothes that they could wear three new outfits every day for the first year and still not run out of clothes. I was very, very bad and I'm sorry."

Slowly, I close the doors to the library and lock them.

Luna tracks my every movement. She curls her hand over her bump, instinctively protecting our babies from the predator prowling in the doorway. "What are you doing?"

"You said it yourself." I stalk closer, dropping onto my knees in front of her. "You were very, *very* bad."

Understanding flickers across her face and she leans back on her hands, her legs stretched out on the floor in front of her. "What are you going to do to me?"

"Punish you," I breathe.

I kiss my way across her calf and up her thigh. I lift the hem of her sundress inch by inch until the lace triangle between her legs is the only thing in my way. I stroke my thumb firmly over the material.

"You're already wet." I blow cool air between her legs and she shifts anxiously. "Not much of a punishment if you're already begging for it."

She strokes her fingers through my hair, tugging on the strands to try to bring me closer.

Instead, I shift up onto my knees and gently lower Luna onto her back. She tries to bite back her smile, but she can't. She grins as I unzip my pants.

"You're excited about this, too?" I growl.

Any chance that I actually try to punish her by leaving altogether disappears when Luna nods and opens her perfect pink mouth.

She takes me in to the hilt, her fingers spread across my thighs. As I pull out, she follows me. She lifts up on her elbows and swirls her tongue around my cock. I wrap my hand around the back of her head and pull her onto me. I work her down and up, down and up.

Luna moans and I feel the vibration at the base of my spine.

"Fuck," I sigh, fisting her hair.

She tips her head back and I slide deeper with a groan. Luna looks up at me, her blue eyes wide and clear, and I stare down into her eyes as I fuck her mouth and it sends me over the edge.

I spill into her, moaning as she licks and cleans every inch of me.

Finally, I slip out of her mouth and she falls back on the floor, panting. I run my thumb over her swollen lips. Then I bend to kiss her.

"Feel free to be bad more often," I whisper.

She laughs, but the laughter stops when I slide down her body and tear her panties away in one tug.

"Now, you're dripping, Luna." I drag my tongue over her opening and her entire body responds.

She jerks and then strokes her fingers through my hair. She pulls me against her, and I let her this time. She's earned it.

I thrust my tongue into her while my fingers pass over her swollen clit. Luna cries out and grinds against my face. She chases her own release and it's incredible seeing her take what she wants.

But it's my turn to show her what she needs.

I pin her hips to the floor, spread her legs, and settle in.

I suck her clit and tease her with my tongue until she's at the very edge of release... then I pull back. Again and again, I take her to the brink of orgasm until she's bucking and crying out. Again and again, right before she can finish, I draw back.

"Yakov," she whimpers, voice breaking. "I'm begging you. I'm going to explode."

"That is the point, *solnyshka*."

She groans, her body fighting against my hold. She's desperate to clamp her thighs around my ears and fuck my mouth.

So finally, after one last tease, I let her.

Luna works both hands into my hair and rides my face. She bucks her hips and arches against my mouth until she quite literally explodes.

When she's done, she sinks into the carpet with her arms and legs splayed like a broken doll. "After that punishment, I may never be good again."

I kiss the soft skin just beneath her bump and smile. "Do what you want. There will always be this price to pay."

52

YAKOV

"When are you and Luna leaving for the gender scan?" my mother asks over the rim of her coffee cup.

She's been dressed and nursing her coffee at the table since I got out of bed before dawn. I'm still sleeping like shit. Luna has fewer nightmares now, but I still can't relax at night. Not when the shadows are full of things I can't yet kill.

I check the clock above the stove. "We need to be there in forty minutes."

She hums and takes a bite of the cold toast on her plate. The disinterested performance is undercut by the fact that it's the third time she's asked about the appointment this morning.

"It was nice of Dr. Jenkins to get you in on such short notice," she muses.

"There's nothing nice about it. It's his job. I'm paying the man enough that he should have brought the ultrasound machine here."

She perks up. "Could he do that?"

"It's not worth the risk. I'm not allowing any outside tech through the gates."

That's true, but with Dima's men bolstering my forces beyond the mansion, I can now have even more guards stationed here at home. The extra guards plus the additional security cameras have made the mansion practically impenetrable. Even if someone did get a bug or a wire through the gates, they'd never be able to get onto the property to do anything about it.

The real reason Dr. Jenkins can't come to the mansion is that Luna doesn't want my mother—or anyone else—at the scan with us. But she made me swear I wouldn't say anything to her.

"Should you even be going? If things are as bad as you make them out, perhaps Luna should stay here."

"Luna wants to know the gender of the babies. I'm not going to deny her that."

"That's sweet, Yakov, but think about the big picture," she argues. "What's the point of knowing the gender of the babies if you all get killed?"

It's a simple hypothetical, but my body tenses. I fist my hands at my side and turn on her. "I'm always thinking about the big picture. All I do is think about the big picture."

"I know," she backtracks. "I didn't mean—"

"*Nothing* is going to happen to Luna or the babies. I am going to protect them."

My mother's expression softens. "I know you will. But accidents happen."

I know she's thinking about my father now. Before he was shot in the chest, I didn't really believe he could be killed. None of us did. He was larger than life. It didn't seem possible that someone could snatch that away with something as small as a bullet.

Now, I know the truth. At the core, we're all fragile humans. Animals. Flesh and blood animals.

"I'm taking security," I tell her.

Isay is at the hospital with a team right now making sure the premises are secured and Kuzma and Savva are going to follow behind us in a second car. They'll stand outside the ultrasound room while Dr. Jenkins performs the scan.

I covered all of the bases. Everything is going to be fine.

Luna walks into the room wearing a sunny yellow dress that hugs her chest and shows off her bump. Instantly, the shadows in my mind burn up and dissipate.

"I'm ready," she beams.

My mother stands up and hurries over to steady Luna's elbow like she thinks she's going to fall. "Are you feeling okay, dear? Have you had enough to eat? You look unsteady on your feet."

"I feel fine. Do I not look fine?" Luna looks at me, confused.

"You look perfect."

My mother starts to lead her towards a chair. "Yakov was saying Dr. Jenkins could bring the ultrasound machine here. Maybe that would be a better option if you aren't feeling well."

Suddenly, I realize why my relationship with my mother has improved so much lately: because she is so busy fussing over Luna that she doesn't have any time left for me.

I swoop in and wrap Luna's hand around my arm. Deftly, I pull her away from my mother and towards the door. "Luna feels fine, Mother."

"Of course you think so. You're a man," she snaps. "You don't know the toll pregnancy can take on a woman's body."

"I'll be with her the entire time. Nothing is going to happen to her while I'm around."

To my own ears, I sound confident. But when I glance down at Luna's considerable bump, it's impossible to forget what exactly I stand to lose.

~

"We never came up with names!" Luna gasps as we pull into the hospital parking garage. Kuzma and Savva are right behind us. They slip into the space next to ours as I park.

"Yes, we did. Yuri and Olivia."

Luna turns to me, mouth hanging open. "You remember that conversation?"

I grip her chin and force her mouth closed. "I remember everything."

"Apparently not or you'd remember I nixed Yuri."

"And I nixed Olivia," I remind her.

She throws her hands up. "See? No names! We are about to find out the babies' genders and we don't even have names."

"We don't need names to find out what's between their legs."

"You sound like your sister," she mumbles. "And it feels like we should have some idea what we're going to call them. I mean, this whole exercise is so we can get to know them, right? What better way to get to know someone than to give them a name?"

I grab her hand and pull it over to my lap. "You're nervous."

She frowns, but doesn't deny it.

"We know the babies are healthy. You just heard their heartbeats at your appointment yesterday."

She blows out a breath. "Yeah. I know."

"And Dr. Jenkins isn't going to hand us their birth certificates today. We don't need to fill out anything official. We have time."

"Not much. I'm twenty-eight weeks today. We're in the third trimester."

Believe me, I fucking know. Lately, it's felt like there's a countdown clock hanging above my head.

"Even once they're born, we can change their names as many times as we want. If we get sick of one, we'll swap it for another."

"We can't just change their names!"

"Luna, we can do whatever the fuck we want." I tuck her hair behind her ear. "But once we find out that you're carrying two little boys and we name them Yakov II and Yakov III, we won't want to change a thing."

She slaps my chest, biting back a laugh. "You're so not funny."

"Who's joking?"

We walk through the parking garage hand-in-hand, Savva and Kuzma trailing not far behind us. The building is covered and no one is going to get within a hundred feet of her. Still, the moment we walk through the doors into the hospital, Luna tenses. Her fingers clamp down around mine like her life depends on it.

"You're fine," I reassure her.

She gives me a tight smile. "I don't have great memories of being here."

Fair enough. The last time we were here, she was recovering from being kidnapped, Mariya was just out of surgery from being shot, and Nikandr was still in a coma. We could never step foot in this hospital again and it would still be way too fucking soon.

I wrap an arm around her waist and pull her close. "I'm here and I'm not going anywhere. You're okay."

She leans her head against me and lets me lead her into the office.

Luna goes through her usual pre-appointment routine without any issues. She pees into a cup and gets her vitals checked. I lean against the wall in the hall, eyeing every nurse who passes. I know none of them are working for Pavel, but it's hard to shake the thought. Anyone who isn't part of my inner circle is a threat as far as I'm concerned.

Once Luna's hand is tucked in mine again, the protective instinct settles. We walk together to the ultrasound room where the technician greets us with a wide smile.

"Why isn't Dr. Jenkins doing the test?" I growl.

The woman shrinks just as Dr. Jenkins steps through the door. "Because my specialty is delivering the babies," he explains. "Lindsay's specialty is running this massive machine. She'll get you a higher degree of accuracy than I could."

Luna lays her hand on my arm and I pull back. *She's safe here.* I can breathe.

"Thank you," Luna says to them both.

"I'll be back once your exam is over." Dr. Jenkins waves as he ducks back into the hall.

Luna climbs onto the table and gets herself situated. The technician squeezes jelly on her bump and reaches for the wand.

"Could you not tell us?" Luna asks, looking to me for confirmation. "Maybe write it down or something? I want to know, but I'm not sure I want to know right now. We might wait and look at it later when we get home."

Home. Every time she says it, something inside of me comes alive. We have a home together. A family.

"Of course." Lindsay nods. "I do that all the time. Just look away from the screen when I tell you to and I'll make sure it's a surprise."

For a few minutes, we get to look at our babies curled up inside of Luna's stomach. It's still amazing to me that they're real people in there. In just a couple months, they'll be in our arms. Growing, breathing human beings that we created.

"Can you believe it?" Luna breathes, squeezing my hand.

They're a tangle of arms and legs inside of her now. I can't imagine how they could get any bigger.

I shake my head. "I really can't."

"Okay. Close your eyes," Lindsay announces. "I'm going to do some investigating."

Luna closes her eyes, but I stare down at her. I trace the lines of her face that have become as familiar to me as my own over the last seven months.

I knew the night we met that there was something special about her. But I never would have guessed it would lead me here, to this moment and this life. I never imagined this for myself, but now that I have it, no one is going to take it away.

"Okay," Lindsay says after a few minutes. "It's safe to look now. I've got what I need. I'll write it down for you and leave it with Dr. Jenkins to pass to you on your way out."

The technician leaves and Luna cleans up. A minute later, Dr. Jenkins reappears with an envelope in his hands. He dips his head in greeting, but his expression is tight. Tighter than it should be given the good news he's holding in his hands.

"You know what? Just tell me," Luna blurts with a grin. "I can't wait. Tell me right now."

Dr. Jenkins smiles softly. "There are some things we need to discuss. Do you want to do that now or after you hear the good news?"

Luna frowns. "What do we have to discuss? Is it bad news?"

"Tell me now," I snap, my hackles rising. "Are the babies okay?"

He waves us both down, speaking slowly and evenly. "Your babies are healthy as can be. There is no immediate danger to the babies."

I don't miss the caveat. *No immediate danger.*

"What the fuck does that mean?" I growl.

Dr. Jenkins turns to Luna. "The urine sample you left this morning contained some protein. Luckily, your blood pressure read lower today than it has for the last few weeks. If it had still been elevated, I would have had you admitted to the hospital immediately."

"No," Luna breathes, backing away from him. "I don't want to stay here."

"I'm not going to force an admittance," Dr. Jenkins continues. "However, given your history of high blood pressure and the protein I detected this morning, I would recommend that you elect to stay for observation."

Luna shakes her head. "No. I can't stay here. I can't—I'll be okay at home."

I squeeze her hand and face Dr. Jenkins. "What's the risk?"

"Preeclampsia. Left untreated, it can lead to fatal outcomes for both the mother and the—"

"Then fucking treat it," I spit.

"Luna is already on medication for her blood pressure, but the protein in her sample is cause for concern. It could be something as simple as dehydration or it could be—"

"I didn't drink enough water yesterday," Luna cuts in. "I know that's it. I was distracted with getting the nursery ready and I didn't hydrate. I'll be better."

"It could also be a sign that her kidneys are damaged," Dr. Jenkins continues, talking directly to me now. He knows I'm the one he'll answer to if anything goes wrong with this pregnancy. "If she chose to be admitted, we could keep her here for a few days to make sure symptoms don't get worse. If she remains stable, she'll be released. If things go downhill…"

"Then what?" Luna presses.

Dr. Jenkins offers a sympathetic smile. "We would induce labor."

Luna goes white. "They're too small. It's too early."

I feel the familiar ache in my chest. The same one I felt when I heard Mariya was in the hospital. When Nik dropped to the pavement. When my father took his last breath in my arms.

I can't lose Luna. I won't.

"Is it serious enough that you think early labor is likely?" I ask. "Or are you being cautious?"

I threatened Dr. Jenkins' life if anything happened to the babies. I understand the man being careful. But if Luna is going to be miserable just because Dr. Jenkins is afraid of me, that defeats the entire purpose.

"This would be a precaution," he admits. "Like I said, her blood pressure has gone down over the last couple weeks. Still, the protein is a cause for—"

"You'll come to the house and check on her twice per day," I order him. "In the morning and evening, you'll examine her and make sure everything is fine. If need be, we'll move to three times per day. That way, Luna can be comfortable at home and, if anything changes, we'll catch it quickly."

Dr. Jenkins doesn't look thrilled, but he doesn't argue. He nods and then holds out the envelope. "I'll see you tomorrow morning, Luna. Until then, here's the good news."

Luna stares down at the envelope like it might start talking. After Dr. Jenkins leaves us alone in the room, she's still staring at it.

I pluck it gently out of her hands. "Opening it might be more effective than staring holes into it."

"Yes. Open it. Please." She chews on her lower lip and shifts from foot to foot. Her hands rub nervous circles over her bump.

I slide my finger under the flap and start to pull out the results. Then I stop and turn to Luna.

"Yakov, open it! What are you—"

I grab her chin and force her eyes to mine. "What's in here doesn't mean anything to me. The only thing that matters is that you and our children are safe. If *anything* changes—no matter how small—over the next few days, you're going to tell me and I'm going to rush you to the hospital. Do you understand me?"

Luna pushes my hand away and stretches onto her toes. She kisses me, lingering there for a breath. Then she smiles. "I swear. Now, open that damn envelope."

I chuckle and pull out the sonograms. There are two, each one labeled clearly with silver marker.

"Well, I was right," I say, handing her Baby A's sonogram. "Boy."

There isn't any disappointment at all. Luna's face lights up. "A boy. We're having a boy."

"We are." I hand her the second sonogram. "But it turns out, you were right, too."

"A girl?" She snatches the black and white picture out of my hand and holds it up, looking back and forth between our babies.

Baby A and Baby B.

Our baby boy and our baby girl.

Luna's shoulders start to shake and I lean down to see her face. "Are you crying?"

She laughs through the tears, swiping at her cheeks with the backs of her hands. "I'm just so happy. This is everything, Yakov. This is my whole world now."

53

LUNA

I'm halfway across the room, tiptoeing to freedom, when the double doors to our makeshift library bedroom slide open.

Ofeliya swoops in and then stops, frowning at me. "Where are you going?"

"Bathroom," I answer quickly. Even though I just went to the bathroom fifteen minutes ago. A fact Ofeliya knows since she insisted on escorting me there.

I keep telling everyone that protein in my urine hasn't affected my legs, but they don't seem to hear me.

She arches a brow and suddenly looks exactly like an older version of Mariya. "The door to the nursery is locked. Even if you get out of this room and make it there, you'll never get inside."

I groan and slouch back to the bed. "I just want to have a peek. What if I chose the wrong color for the accent wall? Or what if Yakov and Mariya mixed up the buckets and are painting the ceilings the wall color and vice versa? It could be a disaster."

"Your instructions were clear and Yakov is a smart man. He knows what he's doing," she says.

"Normally, I'd agree, but how many walls has he painted in his life? He might be out of his depth here."

Part of my nesting process involved drowning in paint swatches and staying up most of the night to design a color scheme that incorporates both babies into the design. I settled on a muted dove blue for the paneling on the left side of the room and dusty rose for the right with a nude color on the remaining walls and ceiling.

Then I suggested hiring some painters and Yakov turned into a territorial caveman. His hackles were raised at just the idea of strangers we didn't know walking through the front door.

It became clear the options were to let him and Mariya do the painting or leave the nursery white.

"Last time I checked… one," Ofeliya says.

"Only one wall is done? They've been in there for hours!"

Yakov's mother pulls the comforter over me and places a mug of tea on the bedside table. "This is a recipe from my mother. Decaffeinated black tea flavored with a little orange, a little lemon, a dash of vanilla, and some cinnamon. It's so much better for you than all of that coffee."

If only she knew my iced coffee was in the tumbler six inches away.

"Thanks for that. Sounds yummy. Maybe I'll drink it while I take a walk upstairs just to peek in and—"

"No," she interrupts. "The paint fumes aren't safe for you."

"I'll just peek in and—"

"You'll stay here and wait for a full forty-eight hours." She pats the blanket in around me, sealing me into the bed like a tomb. "You need to be resting anyway. You heard what Dr. Jenkins said this morning. You need to stay off your feet as much as possible."

Oh, I heard him loud and clear. So did Yakov. I tried to take a shower after Dr. Jenkins left and Yakov physically carried me to the bathroom and ran me a bath instead.

Honestly, I didn't even mind. At least when he was around and being absurdly protective, I had someone to talk to. Now, he's busy and his mother is plying me with books and television and tea, but I'm bored to the point of tears.

Ofeliya is about to drop down into the chair next to my bed for what is sure to be another rousing hour of game shows when I say suddenly, "I think I'll lie down and take a nap. I'm feeling a little tired."

"Good idea." She flicks off the lamp next to the bed and pulls the curtains closed. "You rest and I'll double check that Yakov and Mariya are following your design for the nursery. Don't worry about a thing, Luna. I'll make sure they aren't slacking on the job."

Good, I think. *Sic her on them and see how they like it.*

Ofeliya isn't so bad, really. Mariya said I'd go out of my mind within a week of living with her, but if anything, I've gotten used to her. Being overbearing is how she shows love. It's better than the radio silence I get from my own mother.

Still, it's best if Ofeliya spreads her love to everyone in the house evenly.

While she's gone, I can find some social interaction elsewhere. As soon as the door closes, I turn my lamp back on and grab my phone out of the bedside drawer. I punch in Kayla's number by memory.

"Luna?" Kayla answers, sounding breathless. "Are you okay?"

"I'm fine. Should I not be?" My heart clenches. "Are *you* okay?"

Would the Gustev Bratva ever go after Kayla? I don't think so, but why else would Kayla be in trouble?

"Me?" she asks like there might be a third party on the line. "I'm fine. Why wouldn't I be?"

I chuckle in sheer relief. "I don't know. Why wouldn't *I* be fine? You're the one who answered in a panic."

"Oh." She blows out a breath. "I just haven't heard from you in so long. When I saw your name, I assumed something was wrong."

"It hasn't been that long. I just texted you…" I try to think back to how long it's been since I've talked to Kayla.

"Two weeks ago," she says like she has the receipts in front of her. "And I haven't actually heard your voice in over a month."

"Really?" I can't even count back the days in my head. The last six months have been a blur. The only way I can tell time is passing is because my bump keeps growing.

"Did you need something?" Kayla asks curtly.

So much for an uplifting chat with my best friend. I guess I came to the wrong place.

"Yeah. I wanted to talk to you."

"Just to chat?"

I bite back a groan. "Yes. Just to chat. I know I've been busy, but it's not like we aren't friends anymore."

"Well…" Kayla's voice trails off.

"Well what?" I push. "Are we not friends?"

"I love you, Loon, but I never hear from you. It's hard to be friends with someone who is barely in your life." She sighs. "I get it. You have a lot going on and things aren't safe, but… Well, I can't sit around and wait for you to decide you want me in your life. Either I'm in or I'm out."

"You're in! Obviously you're in."

"Am I?" she asks. "Because I used to see you all the time. Now, I've seen you twice in six months. I've talked to you six times, *if that.* You're like a ghost."

I want to argue, but she isn't wrong. I can't even be mad at her for feeling this way. I miss her, too. It's why I called.

"I want to tell you that it will get better starting now, but I can't," I admit. "Things are complicated and I'm not sure when it's all going to get sorted out. But when it does, you're going to see me so much you'll get sick of me."

"Not possible," she mumbles.

"Believe me, you'll be begging for some time apart. Especially since I'll be coming with two babies in tow and cramping your childless style."

There's a beat of silence before Kayla responds. "I cannot wait to squish their little faces. I bought matching knitted newborn hats from a craft fair last weekend. I had to haggle with the seller because the price on these teeny tiny hats was outrageous, but they're so cute."

Tears well in my eyes. Even when Kayla was upset and questioning our friendship, she bought a gift for my babies. She was still thinking about me. Still planning for a future where we'd be friends.

"Those sound adorable."

"They are. And the matching gloves have little bear paws on the palms."

"Matching gloves?" I laugh. "I thought it was just hats."

"I may have bought each of them a full knitted outfit. And I may also already have plans for a fall photoshoot. I know it's a bit played out for twins to wear matching clothes all the time like those creepy girls from *The Shining*, but I mean, come on... how could I not?"

I couldn't wipe the grin off of my face if I wanted to. "Well that all sounds great. Especially since I don't need to worry about them being like the girls from *The Shining*. A matching brother and sister won't be nearly as creepy."

Kayla gasps. "What?! Did you find out? You're having a boy and a girl?"

"We just found out yesterday."

She squeals. "Luna, that's amazing! I can't wait to meet them. I'm going to hang up and buy them so many cute clothes."

"I'm sure Yakov will love that. The stuff I've ordered has started arriving and he already thinks I've lost my mind."

"He can think I've lost my mind, too. I don't care. As if you don't have enough room in that mansion for some baby clothes," she snorts. There's a beat before she asks, "Is Yakov excited?"

"I've never seen him so happy," I tell her truthfully. "He is going to be such a good dad."

Kayla goes quiet for a second. I'm sure she doesn't believe me, but it's only because she doesn't know him. Once she does, she'll see I'm right. "That's great, Loon. I hope you're happy too. You deserve that much."

"I am, Kay. Truly. I'm—" I swallow down the lump in my throat. "I'm the happiest I've ever been."

"If that's true, then I'm happy for you, too. All I want is for you to be happy."

It is true. Every word of it. Even after being kidnapped, locked up, almost killed, and now pregnant, I wouldn't change a thing.

Yakov is worth all of it.

I wake up as Yakov climbs into bed. I slide closer to him, nuzzling my face into the woodsy scent of his neck. "What time is it?" I whisper.

"Late." He kisses the top of my head.

"I haven't seen you all day."

"Mariya and I wanted to finish painting. It took longer than I hoped."

"It's done?" I lift my head. "Can I see it?"

He gives me a firm look and holds up two fingers.

I groan. "Forty-eight hours for one glimpse of the room? You and your mother are running a prison camp, I swear."

"If my mother hasn't driven you crazy enough, you could call your mom."

"Do you think I should?" I ask.

He shrugs. "She's going to be their grandma. I'd understand if you wanted to have her around."

Being around Yakov's family has been nice, but it's always poked at a bruise I didn't even realize I have. My family has never been close the way his is. My mother doesn't fawn over me and my brother has never cared much what's going on in my life. I texted him that I was pregnant a few months ago and he never responded.

"I want her around, but I also want her to be different," I explain. "I want her to *want* to be here."

"You don't think she does?"

I shrug. "It doesn't seem like it. I haven't heard from her in months. And when I did, it was only because *I* texted *her*. If she actually wanted to be part of my life, maybe I'd care more about her being part of our kids' life. But as it is..."

"She has no clue what she's missing," he finishes. Yakov lifts himself up on one elbow and looks down at me. The chiseled line of his jaw is even more apparent in the dark room.

I reach out and stroke my finger over his cheekbone. "How come you get to keep looking like that while I look like this?" I poke at my bump between us.

"You look gorgeous."

I snort. "I feel like a whale. Even my socks are too tight now. I'm afraid they're going to cut off my circulation."

Yakov palms my bump and then strokes his hand over my hip and down my thigh, trailing fire in his wake. "Do I need to prove to you exactly how attractive I find you? Because I will. I'm dead tired from painting all day, but I'll make that sacrifice if it will make you feel better."

Heat pools between my legs, but I gently pat his chest. "As nice as that sounds, it's okay. I'm just feeling a little homesick."

"This is your home now, *solnyshka*."

"I know. It is," I agree. "I'm not homesick for a place, but... for a person, maybe? For people? Is that even a thing? I called Kayla to tell her about the babies and it hit me how much my life has changed in a short amount of time. Sometimes, I miss who I was before."

His face is unreadable and I hurry to explain myself.

"I could never ever regret you or our babies, but I was ripped out of my life without any chance for closure. One day, it was there, and the next, it was gone. It's hard to say goodbye when things happen suddenly like that."

Yakov's jaw clenches. "I know what that feels like."

"Your dad," I breathe. "Of course you know what that's like. I wasn't even thinking."

"I didn't realize that's what I'd done to you."

I roll onto my side and rest my hand on his cheek. "You didn't, Yakov. Please don't ever think that meeting you and coming here was a tragedy. It wasn't. It's the best thing that has ever happened to me."

His brow is creased and I stretch my thumb up to smooth it away.

"I'm serious," I tell him. "I choose you over everything. Every time. No regrets."

His green eyes are fierce as he nods. "I believe you. But one day, I'm going to give you the closure you need. Soon, this will all be over and you'll have the freedom that you used to have. You won't be a prisoner in your own home and you can see your friends as often as you want." His thumb strokes over my cheek. "But first, I need to make sure you're safe. You and our babies are all I care about. I can't lose you."

"You won't."

His mouth tips into a small smile. "I love you, *solnyshka*."

"I love you, too, Yakov."

Yakov pulls me against his chest and I close my eyes.

I know Yakov is doing everything he can to protect our family. I trust him. I just can't help but wonder if it will ever be enough. Will we ever be safe outside the walls of this mansion?

And if we aren't, can I stay hidden inside forever?

54

YAKOV

If hell exists, it's full of flat-pack furniture.

I've been sitting on the nursery floor hunched over the instructions for a children's dresser for two hours. *There are only three drawers. How hard could this be?* The handles are multicolored pompoms, for fuck's sake.

But underneath the frill there are also one hundred individual screws. I should hire whoever designed this fucking thing. It's a masterclass in torture.

"I'll tear down a wall and build a fucking closet," I snap, wadding up the instructions. "That'll be easier than this."

I'm about to get up and find a sledgehammer. Then I remember Luna's face when the package arrived. The way she lit up explaining to me that she had little baskets that would fit inside the drawers to organize their onesies and booties and whatever the fuck else babies need.

She has plans for this dresser. Hopes.

Grumbling, I grab the crumpled instructions and smooth them out on my lap just as my phone rings.

I wedge my phone between my chin and shoulder as I wrestle with the tissue-thin paper. "What?"

"Good to hear from you, too, my friend."

The voice stops me cold. I stand up, glancing at the door and window like he'll appear any second. "Why are you calling me, Pavel?"

"I want to meet with you."

I bark out a laugh. "Would you like me to handcuff myself beforehand? Or maybe I'll save you the trouble and put a gun in my mouth."

"I want it to be civil," Pavel says. "It will just be two *pakhans* handling business."

"Whatever business you need to discuss, you can do it over the phone."

"Don't be so afraid, Yakov. I won't hurt you."

"I'm smart, not scared," I fire back. "Smart enough not to get lured into a death trap by a little poke to my pride. Say what you need to say before I hang up."

Pavel sighs. "I want a truce."

"Of course you do. Because I'm winning."

"You think I care about a couple of clubs?"

"You're the one calling me and asking for a truce," I remind him. "That's the act of someone who knows they are losing."

"Losing what? Do you know why we're fighting, Yakov? Because I don't. This isn't our fight. It never was."

"Spoken like a man with no other options. If you had a way out, you wouldn't be asking for a truce."

We have him exactly where we want him. If Pavel had pulled this humility schtick a couple months ago, things would be different.

"I have a way out. Plenty of them. But I'm trying to take the path with the least amount of bloodshed. If we don't change course, a lot of good men are going to die."

"Don't play noble now," I snarl. "Not after you broke into my mansion and threatened my fiancée. Any unnecessary bloodshed will be on your hands, not mine. I was going to let you slink away and carry on your family's battered name, but you couldn't let it go. You didn't know when to keep your head down."

"You'd just killed my brother. I was grieving. Isn't there some kind of window for that sort of thing?"

"That window snapped shut the moment you took that picture of Luna. I don't take kindly to threats against my family."

"What about promises of safety?" he asks. "If I promise to never touch another member of the Kulikov Bratva without provocations, would you agree to the same for the Gustev Bratva?"

Fuck no. Never. Not when I know what Pavel is capable of.

"Based on what? Your word?"

"It's all I have," Pavel says.

"And it's mud at this point, don't you think?"

"I never made you any promises, Yakov. Up to this point, you've dealt with my father or my brother. I saw how going against you turned out for them. I have no interest in following in their footsteps. I never wanted any of this, anyway. I never even thought I'd be in this position. I didn't think Akim could—I thought he would lead until we were both dead. But here I am." He sighs, sounding decades older than he is. "I'm the only member of my family left and I want to take a new path. I want to choose peace."

Bull-fucking-shit.

It's a nice story Pavel is spinning here. If I had even an inkling that a word of it was true, I'd consider it. I want peace. I don't care about Pavel.

But I care about my family.

Pavel wants me to back down so he can rise up when I least expect it. He wants me to lower my guard so he can strike. But I will not back down until Pavel is dead. I won't stop fighting until the entire Gustev Bratva is dismantled from top to bottom, never to rise again.

I'm going to destroy them and scatter the ashes to the wind.

Nik is rolling back and forth across the room. My phone is flat on the desk between us.

"He wants peace the same way I want to shake his hand." Dima's voice comes through the speaker in crackles. Wherever he is, his service is shit.

Nik frowns. "I take it that means you don't want to shake his hand?"

"Not unless I'm shaking it to make sure the fucker is dead," Dima growls.

"Then we're in agreement about the truce," I say. "Great."

"What did you tell him when he suggested it?" he asks.

"I agreed to it. I told him I wanted a fresh start. What I didn't tell him is that my fresh start involves the entire Gustev Bratva being wiped off the map."

"And *his* fresh start involves *your* destruction," Dima points out. "There's no way that little punk is actually looking for a truce. He's trying to get you to lower your guard."

"He's young enough that I wouldn't put it past him to think he could just call me up and broker peace, but you're probably right." I sigh.

Nik is looking down at his phone. Then he turns it so I can see. "Whoever lowers their guard loses the war. Doesn't look like Pavel is lowering his guard."

I tap on the screen to expand the picture. It's from an unknown number. The photo is blurry like it was taken through a dirty window, but I can see Pavel standing in front of a group of men. They're in a bare, shadowy corner of some room.

"When was that picture taken?"

"What picture?" Dima asks from the other end of the line.

"It's a picture of Pavel meeting with his inner circle," Nik explains. "A source just sent it to me. It's time-stamped five minutes ago."

"Location?" Dima demands.

"A warehouse downtown. They run underground poker games there. High-stakes shit. Oligarchs waste their time showing up, so it's big money. I got a tip about it and have been watching for a while, but—"

"I'm watching it right now," Dima interrupts.

Nik and I look at each other.

"You're there right now?" I ask.

He hums in confirmation. "I'm posted up outside. I've been watching cars filter in all morning. I got the same tip as Nikandr, apparently. I had some free time so I decided to do some surveillance. I figured it would be a good next target."

"And now, we know Pavel is inside." I stare at my brother, watching as he rolls back on his wheels. He's balancing in the chair while I wait for him to understand what I'm suggesting.

Suddenly, Nik's wheelchair drops to the floor, eyes wide. "We can't pull together an attack like this right now. There isn't enough time."

"This might be our only chance."

"He could go underground again if we don't strike," Dima agrees. "Even now, it's pure fucking luck that Pavel is inside. I never saw him walk in. I have no clue how he got in there."

Maybe he's been sleeping there. It would make sense why no one has seen him around the Gustev Estate. He's lying low, sleeping in some hollowed-out warehouse like the rat he is.

"If we want this to end, this might be our best shot for a good long while."

Nik's lips press together. He knows I'll do this with or without his approval. Still, I'd like him to agree. He can't charge into the building the way I know he wants to, but he can stay here and be our eyes. He can support me in every way he can.

"Fine," Nik relents. "But if we're going to slap together this plan, we might as well go big. We should split the remaining forces and take out Pavel's last club on the other side of town. With this hit, you're declaring war. You want to take out as many of his men as you can to hinder their counterattack."

"Makes sense to me. I'll send my men there right now," Dima says.

I nod in agreement. "Dima and I will hit the warehouse and go for Pavel. Everyone else will take out the club. He won't see it coming. Not so soon after our truce."

"I'll stay here and coordinate information." Nik tries to sound cheerful, but I know it's eating him up inside that he can't come along.

Selfishly, I'm glad he can't. I almost lost him once; I'm not ready to do it again. Plus, knowing he's in the house with Luna and Mariya is a weight off my mind.

I grab my phone and speak directly to Dima. "Don't move in until I'm there. Understood?"

"Understood. I won't move unless I think Pavel is getting away."

"Not even then. If you try to take him out on your own, you could die."

"Then I die," he muses. "So be it."

Again, I wonder what the fuck Pavel did to Dima to warrant this kind of undying hatred, but it's not my place to ask. As long as Dima is on my side, nothing else matters.

"Try not to die and I'll be there within the hour." I hang up and turn to Nik. "I'm going to find Isay and deliver the plan in person. I don't want to risk a leak."

Nikandr nods, but his gaze is unfocused. He's deep in thought. Suddenly, he turns to me. "Watch your back, Yakov."

"Dima has been nothing but faithful."

"Up to now," he agrees. "But things could change. Especially as you get closer to actually taking out Pavel."

"I can handle Dima."

"I believe that… so long as you stay vigilant. I won't be there to watch your back, so you have to do it yourself. Don't trust him. Don't trust anyone."

I reach out and clasp his hand, bending down to pat him on the back. "I trust you, brother. You have my word."

Nik claps me on the back once. Then I leave.

I have a rat to kill.

55

YAKOV

The Gustev soldier's windpipe crunches in my grip. He spasms, choking for air he'll never get. I hold on until he realizes it, then I let go and he sinks to the floor in a puddle of blood that doesn't belong to him.

Dima slashes his knife across the neck of another man only ten feet away.

"Where the fuck is he, Dima?" I roar.

My voice echoes off the high ceilings of the warehouse. Fifteen minutes ago, Dima wouldn't have been able to hear me over the screaming and gunfire. Now, the room is almost silent, save for the sound of boots splashing through blood.

"He's here," Dima pants, almost to himself. He's ripping across the room, turning over bodies to see their faces. "He has to be here."

A man behind me moans. Without looking, I fire a single shot to quiet him.

No survivors. It's what I told myself when Dima and I kicked down the doors and stormed the building. This feud between my family and the

Gustev Bratva ends today. There will be no one left to pick up the mantle. No one left to avenge anyone.

A fresh start.

But Pavel isn't here. I know it.

We killed our way through the building, tearing down Pavel's unprepared soldiers, but Pavel himself never showed.

He isn't here. Maybe he never was.

Kuzma and Savva walk out of a back room. Kuzma's hair is matted with blood and Savva is carrying a limp man by the arm.

"Anything?" I call.

"This guy has some information. Repeat what you said to—" Savva looks down at the limp man and groans in disgust. Then he drops him to the ground. "He fucking died."

"What did he say before that?" I bark.

"He said Pavel was never here." Kuzma kicks the dead man's leg. "He said they were ordered here this morning for a meeting with some lower-level lieutenants."

I spin to face Dima, who is listening in with lethal focus. "I saw the photo of Pavel and his men. Nik showed it to you. *They were here.*"

"It was just a photo. It could have been faked. Maybe we were wrong about the location. Maybe—"

"Maybe your brother doesn't have his fucking facts straight," Dima hisses. "Maybe Nikandr needs to step down and—"

The words die in his throat as I close the gap between us and press my gun to his temple. "Keep talking and you'll be dead before you finish that sentence."

Dima growls, but he raises his hands in a small surrender. "I'm as pissed as you are, Yakov. He was supposed to be here."

"And my brother doesn't have anything to do with him not being here."

"Nik is a good man," Dima admits through gritted teeth. "I didn't mean what I said."

Slowly, I lower my gun. "If you question my brother again, it will be the last thing you ever do."

He dips his head as a show of respect. "You're a good brother, Yakov."

I ignore the compliment and step back. "You were the one on patrol, Dima. If Pavel escaped, it would be your fault."

"If Pavel was here, he'd be dead on the floor somewhere. I had eyes on every corner of this fucking warehouse. He didn't escape," he insists. He spins around, scanning the walls like he expects to see Pavel scaling them. "He was just never here."

Dima's phone rings and he answers. Every word out of his mouth is clipped. He hangs up less than a minute later.

"Our men took the clubhouse," he says loud enough that the entire room can hear him. "A few of Pavel's men escaped, but most of them are dead."

"No Pavel?"

Dima clenches his jaw. "No. No Pavel. But we took the clubhouse. Pavel's numbers are decimated."

"But Pavel is alive."

A failure. A fucking failure. This entire mission is a waste.

Pavel knows Dima and I are working together by this point. Whatever advantage we had, it's gone.

"He's alive with significantly fewer guards to protect him," Dima fires back.

"It doesn't matter how many of his men are gone if Pavel is still alive." I gesture to the bodies piled up around us. "Pavel is willing to sacrifice these men. He doesn't fucking care about them. *He doesn't need them.*"

Dima frowns. "He can't lead without support."

"He doesn't want to lead." The air smells like rot and iron. Blood is leaking into my shoe, squelching under my sock. "He wants revenge. And we've just made it even more personal."

56

LUNA

"Do you want to watch something?" I ask, holding the remote out to Yakov.

He waves it away. "I don't mind the silence."

That makes one of us.

I never thought having Yakov at home would be a bad thing, but I can't stand the tension. Every time our bedroom door opens, he jolts. He says he doesn't mind the silence, but I don't trust him as far as I could throw him. Yakov turns towards every little sound, no matter how insignificant. Car doors slamming, hinges squeaking, footsteps in the hall—all of it demands his full attention. And there's no rest for him. I know he isn't sleeping. The dark circles under his eyes prove that.

It's been like this since he got home a few days ago. He walked through the door without his shoes or socks, but the hem of his pants was stained dark.

Blood. Maybe my senses are enhanced because of pregnancy, but I could smell it on him like old pennies.

I tried to ask what happened, but he didn't want to talk about it. I respected that. Partly because I was too exhausted to argue. He isn't the only one who hasn't been sleeping well.

Between new nightmares and the return of my nausea, I can't get any rest.

There's a soft knock on our door and Yakov sits upright in bed. His hand is fisted at his side, one leg thrown over the side of the bed like he's ready to jump into action.

Then the door opens and Hope is there with a dinner tray. "Dinner," she squeaks out. "I brought something for Luna to eat. I can bring a tray for you, too, Mr. Kulikov, if you are—"

"I'm fine," he bites out, leaning back in bed. But he can't quite force himself to relax completely. His back is still rigid, his hands balled up on top of the comforter.

Hope nods and walks around the bed with my tray.

The entree is covered with a silver lid, but I can already smell it. Garlic and butter. One tiny sniff and it's like someone is shoving dried basil straight up my nose.

My stomach turns and I try to breathe out of my mouth. *If I don't smell it, I'll be fine.*

This tactic didn't work with lunch. I took one whiff and ran to the toilet to get sick. But it will work now. I am the master of my own body. I can control myself.

Hope lays the tray on the table next to my bed and then swivels it across my lap. She lifts the lid, unveiling my chicken and pasta.

Steam rises up, making my already clammy skin even stickier. I force air out of my mouth, but I can't avoid the smells wafting in front of me.

My stomach rolls. Saliva gathers at the back of my throat. My body clenches, ready to expel every bit of the not-a-fucking-thing I've eaten today.

"Here's some water," Hope says, pouring me a glass from a pitcher. "Ofeliya has some more tea brewing for you. Once it cools, I'll bring it and—"

Before poor Hope can finish, I shove my table tray away and bolt for the edge of the bed.

Yakov is there before my feet can even hit the floor. "What is it?"

"Sick," I gasp.

Instantly, he scoops me up and carries me to the bathroom. He holds my arms with strong hands and lowers me to the tile floor as I heave again and again and again into the toilet.

Nothing comes up. There's nothing *to* come up. I haven't eaten all day. Hope has probably noticed, but whether she's said anything to Ofeliya or Yakov yet, I don't know.

Yakov holds my hair back, his hand stroking down my back. "Are you sick?"

"I'm okay. It's just nausea. Normal."

Is it? Should I still be getting sick this late in pregnancy?

"Get the food out of here, Hope," Yakov calls through the bathroom door. Then he grabs a washcloth and cleans off my face with warm water. He helps me brush my teeth and rinse out my mouth.

"I can brush my own teeth," I say softly.

"But you don't have to," he says, echoing something similar I said to him months ago.

So I let him help me. For the first time in a few days, Yakov seems at ease. Helping me gives him some place to deposit all of the nervous energy that has been eating him up.

He cleans me up and then leads me to the bathroom door. He lets go so he can open the door for me. And as he does, I catch movement in the bedroom.

It's fast. A flash of color. Barely enough to register. Certainly not enough to give me pause.

I walk through the door and into our bedroom just as Yakov shoves into me *hard*.

And gunfire erupts.

I drop to my hands and knees, catching myself before I fall on my stomach. It could be three shots. Maybe more. They ring in my ears as I try to understand what's happening.

"Who the fuck are you?" Yakov roars.

Another shot goes off and I scream. I clamp a hand over my mouth. I don't want to distract Yakov. I don't want him to worry about me. Not when he's in a fight for his own life.

A man is standing near the double doors. He raises his arm to fire again, but Yakov kicks his hand. The gun flies out of his grip and smashes against the wall, firing again before it hits the floor.

The man lunges for the weapon, but Yakov beats him to it. He stands up, the intruder's own gun pointed back at him. "Who the fuck are you?"

The man looks from the gun to the door.

"Don't waste your time," Yakov growls. "You're not leaving. But you knew that already, didn't you? You knew the moment you set foot on my property that you wouldn't leave alive."

Who would accept a mission like that? Who would die just to try to kill me? It doesn't make sense.

Yakov slowly lowers the gun to the dresser behind him. "But if you answer my questions, I might let you live."

Pick up the gun! I want to scream. *Kill him!*

"Yeah, right," the man snorts.

Then he lunges. He's trying to get to the door, but Yakov snags his arm. Deftly, he spins the man around so he's facing the bed. Yakov twists his arm back and up.

The man is only a few feet away from me. He looks younger than I'd expect an assassin to look. He can't be older than twenty-five with a buzz cut and a tattoo behind his ear.

He meets my eyes for a second before his face creases in pain.

Yakov drives his arm up and a sickening snap reverberates through the room.

"Fuck!" the man moans, sagging.

"Tell me who you are and how you got into my house," Yakov barks. "Now!"

Where is Nik? Or Isay? Kuzma? Savva? Why isn't anyone coming to help?

I consider running for help, but I don't want to distract Yakov. I also don't want to leave him alone with this intruder. I know there isn't anything I can do to fight the man off, but I still can't leave. Not when Yakov is in danger.

"I work for Pavel," the man manages. He's panting against the pain. "Pavel sent me. *To kill her.*"

His eyes meet mine again and they are dark. A depthless black I've never seen before. He looks at me like I'm not even human.

Yakov jerks him away from me, spinning him again so his face is smashed against the wall. "Tell me how you got in."

"No," the man coughs.

"Tell me how you got in or you'll die now," Yakov snarls. "Tell me now or every member of your family will be dead before your body is cold."

The man turns his face just enough that I can see the corner of his bloody smile. "What family?"

He has no one. Just like Pavel. The man doesn't have any family so he has nothing to lose.

Yakov sees that, too. He knows there isn't another option.

Before I can look away or plug my ears, Yakov grabs the man's head and twists. His spine snaps with a dull, wet sound. Then he drops to the floor.

His body is still settling into the carpet when Yakov grabs my hands and pulls me to my feet. He walks me past the man's body, shielding him from my sight, and leads me to the hallway. As we go, he barks orders at some of his men who are sprinting down the hallway toward our room. They scurry off to deal with the body, but Yakov's focus stays fixed on me. He leads me to the sitting room next door and sits me down on the couch.

The room is quiet compared to the chaos of the last few minutes. For once, I'm okay with this silence.

Yakov places his hands on either side of my face, turning my head from side to side to inspect me. "Are you hurt? Are you okay?"

"I'm okay, Yakov. I'm—Are you okay?"

"I'm fine."

As soon as I know he's alright, the reality of everything washes over me. The enormity of what just happened hits me like a blow to the chest. I inhale sharply… and start to weep.

Tears pour down my face. I bury my face in Yakov's chest and soak through his shirt.

"Everything is okay," Yakov says again and again. "You're safe. I'm going to keep you safe."

I'm crying so hard I can't catch my breath. Crying so hard I can't see. The only reason I know Yakov is still with me is because his hands are smoothing up and down my arms.

My stomach tightens as I gasp for air. Every muscle in my body seems to tense at once. When they finally relax, I gasp for air.

"Am I hyperventilating?" I rasp. "Is that what this—"

Before I can get the words out, another wave pummels me. My stomach tightens again. This time, I press my hands to my bump and it's hard as a rock.

"Yakov. My stomach." I groan as a pain I've never felt before wraps around my lower back. "I can't breathe."

Yakov lunges to the hallway. "Hope! Call Dr. Jenkins. Get him here! Now!" He's shouting orders like normal, but there's fear in his voice.

I look up at him through watery eyes. "Am I okay? What's happening?"

Maybe I was shot and didn't realize it. Is that possible? I don't see any blood. I didn't—but the rest of that thought is lost in another burst of pain as my stomach tenses until I'm sure I'll be ripped in half.

Yakov holds my hand and rubs circles into my back until Dr. Jenkins pushes through the door.

"What's going on, Luna?" Dr. Jenkins asks, pulling a stethoscope out of his black bag. "How are you feeling?"

"How are you here already?" I croak.

"I was coming for our regular evening appointment." He presses the cold stethoscope under the neckline of my shirt. "Hope called when I was parking. How are you—"

"She was attacked," Yakov blurts, cutting him off. "A man broke in and tried to shoot her. I took care of him, but now…"

Dr. Jenkins nods calmly. When another wave of pain hits me, he lays his hand on my stomach.

Then he jerks it back like I'm on fire and turns to Yakov. Dr. Jenkins is always so calm, but his eyes are wide now. "She needs to get to a hospital. *Now*. She's in labor."

57

YAKOV

Luna looks gray under the fluorescent lights of the emergency room. Her hand is limp around mine—but for the first time in hours, she's finally asleep.

When the ambulance carrying us screeched into the hospital parking lot three hours ago, I was sure we were about to meet the twins. Luna was screaming with every contraction, gripping my hand until I thought my knuckles would snap.

But they gave her some injection to delay labor. Slowly, the contractions ebbed away. Now, they're gone and she's exhausted.

I reach out and brush a stray strand of blonde hair from her forehead.

I almost lost her.

Pavel sent someone into my house. Again.

He got past my security. Again.

I couldn't keep Luna safe. *Again.*

Rage is coursing through my veins and I have to slide my hand away from Luna's before I accidentally break her fingers. My hands tighten into fists at my side as I pace back and forth across the oppressively small room.

The medication stopped Luna from going into labor for now, but there's no guarantee how long it will hold. She could have the babies within the week. Within the day, even. Meanwhile, the mansion might as well be open to the public. Apparently, anyone off the street can waltz right into our bedroom.

My jaw is clenched so tightly my molars must be dust.

I reach for my phone to call Nikandr and try to talk through some of the shit rattling around in my head, but my service is spotty. Each time I try to call, the line disconnects.

I can't leave Luna alone here to make a call. So I fire off a text instead. **Luna is stable for now, but it could be any day. We need to find Pavel now. He needs to die.**

Nik responds a minute later. **Focus on Luna and the twins. I'll take care of everything out here.**

I know I can trust Nikandr. He's ready to lead. He knows what to do. That doesn't make it any easier to sit here and do nothing.

But that's exactly what I do. *Nothing.*

I drop down into the chair next to Luna's bed, take her hand, and wait.

I jolt awake to the sound of Luna screaming.

I grab her hand with both of mine and whisper softly in her ear. "You're okay. I'm here."

The nurses don't even bother coming to check on her this time. It's been like this every couple hours for two days.

"It's me, Luna. You're safe. I'm here with you."

Luna blinks up at me. Her pupils are blown wide, darkness eating away at her blue eyes. Her knuckles are white from squeezing my hand so tightly.

"Yakov?" she breathes, easing down into her bed. "Yakov, I'm—I'm okay. You're here. It was a dream. I'm sorry."

"Stop apologizing."

"But I'm sorry." She rubs her tired eyes. "I don't know why this keeps happening."

"Because you're fucking terrified, Luna. For good reason."

Because of me.

Every time Luna wakes up screaming, the guilt digs in a little deeper. It has taken root in my chest and it shows no signs of leaving anytime soon.

Her forehead creases. "But you're here with me. You haven't left for days. You're sacrificing so much to be here for me."

"Being here isn't a sacrifice," I growl. "Taking care of you isn't a burden."

She gives me a tight smile. "I know, but I feel awful. You're doing everything you can, and I still can't even get to sleep. I'm sorry."

Am I doing everything I can? Nik has been reaching out to every contact we have, old and new, to find Pavel. But he hasn't seen or heard anything. Dima has been doing the same thing on his end. Still nothing.

I want to be out on the streets hunting Pavel down. I want to tear through every hole and dark corner where he could hide and fucking sniff him out.

I also want to be here for Luna.

It's been a few days and she still hasn't gone into labor. Dr. Jenkins says it's a good sign. We might actually make it to her due date. But he still wants to keep her here for observation. Usually, I'd push back. Luna isn't comfortable here. She wants to be home.

Then I consider taking her back to the mansion and all I can see is that man standing in our bedroom, a gun aimed at her head. I press a kiss to her knuckles. "Don't apologize, Luna. Don't stress about anything. You're taking care of yourself and our babies. That's all I could ask."

She picks at the lunch tray a nurse left for her an hour ago before she eventually falls back asleep.

I slide the tray table away and drop down into the recliner next to the bed. I've slept even less than Luna has the last few days. My tank is empty, but I don't see any chance to refill it in my near future.

So I sink down in the chair and take what I can get. I close my eyes and drift off, settling into a half-sleep for all of five minutes before my phone buzzes.

"Fucking never ends," I mumble, wrestling my phone out of my pocket.

Nik is calling again. I pick up and manage to snag a tiny bar of signal.

"Did you—my text?" he asks, his voice cutting out.

"I haven't gotten anything," I say. "Did you text?"

"—breaking up. Watch your back."

Instantly, I sit up. On instinct, I check the door to make sure it's clear. The room is empty. It's just me and Luna up here.

"What's going on?"

"Someone in the hospital—working for Pavel." The static on the line is getting louder. "I just—figure out more."

"You're fucking breaking up," I growl. "I can't understand what—"

"Don't let your guard down, Yakov. Don't let Luna—"

The phone beeps as the call drops.

My heart is thundering in my chest. I knew it was a possibility that Pavel would invade the hospital, but I hoped it wasn't true.

Adrenaline chases away the last of my exhaustion. I turn my chair towards the door and stare at every nurse, doctor, and patient who passes by. If any of them want to get to Luna, they're going to have to kill me first.

When a figure finally appears in the doorway an hour later, I'm on my feet and blocking their path before I even realize who it is.

"Is everything okay?" Dr. Jenkins asks.

I ease back. "Nikandr heard a rumor about a threat. I'm not taking any chances."

"Understandable." He tips his head towards Luna. "I'm here to check in on her. How has she been sleeping?"

"Terrible up until now. This is the first time she's slept for more than thirty minutes all day."

He peeks around me to see Luna asleep in her bed. "Then my exam can wait a little bit. I don't want to wake her up now that she's finally resting. I'll wait in the nurse's lounge and come back in an hour."

Before he can leave, my phone buzzes again.

It's Nik. His name flashes on my screen, but when I swipe up on the call, it disconnects.

"Fuck!"

"Everything okay?" Dr. Jenkins asks again.

Nik's name flashes again just a second later. Again, I swipe, but it disconnects.

"My brother is calling, but I don't have any service in here."

I type out a message, but a red error symbol pops up next to it. I can't even text now.

"I can stay with Luna while you go take your call," Dr. Jenkins offers. "I can hang out in here as well as I can in the nurse's lounge. It's no trouble to me."

I clench my jaw. I haven't left this room in days and Luna hasn't been out of my sight since we stepped through the hospital doors. I don't want to start now.

But my phone keeps ringing. Whatever Nik has to say, it's important. It could be the difference between life and death. Between protecting Luna or failing her.

"No one gets through the door," I growl, jabbing a finger into the doctor's chest. "I want the door locked and I don't want anyone else, no matter who they are, getting inside. Got it?"

Dr. Jenkins nods solemnly. "I won't let anything happen to her. She'll be safe with me."

Luna is still sleeping. Her chest rising and falling in slow, even breaths.

I'll only be gone for a minute. She'll be fine.

I step into the hallway for the first time in three days and Dr. Jenkins locks the door behind me.

58

LUNA

I wake up as the door closes.

It's the first time in a few days that I haven't woken up with Yakov's hands around mine, his voice in my ear trying to calm me down. I blink into the dim room, but Yakov isn't in his usual post by my bedside. He's not here at all. Instead, there's an unfamiliar figure locking the door.

My heart jolts. I sit up so fast I get lightheaded. My vision swirls. By the time it comes back, Dr. Jenkins has turned to face me.

"Oh." I sigh and fall back in my bed. "I thought you were someone else."

Pavel, maybe. Somewhere in the darkest part of my mind, I thought it could be Akim, even though I know that isn't possible.

Dr. Jenkins nods and drops his bag on the desk in the corner. He turns his back to me as he digs through it.

"Where is Yakov?" I ask.

"He had to take care of something."

I frown. Yakov hasn't left my side in days. If he left—especially while I was asleep—it must be important.

"Did he say what it was?" I press. "Is everything okay?"

Dr. Jenkins turns so I can see his face. He's smiling, but he doesn't meet my eyes. "Everything is totally fine. He asked me to watch over you while he's gone."

Yakov trusts Dr. Jenkins. That means I should, too.

"Sorry. I'm on edge, I guess," I admit with a laugh. "It's probably why I keep having nightmares. I can't relax even when I know I'm safe."

Dr. Jenkins slides a few things into the pockets of his jacket and then turns to me. He reaches over my bed for the blood pressure cuff. "Post-traumatic stress is normal after what you've been through." He slides the cuff up over my bicep and pumps it with air. It constricts around my arm until it's just on the edge of painful before it finally releases. Dr. Jenkins is staring down at the reading, but his eyes are glazed. He's not looking at his watch like usual.

"Are you feeling okay, Dr. Jenkins?"

He blinks and smiles, still not meeting my eyes. "Yes. I'm fine. I was just thinking that, once you have the babies, I can suggest medication to help with your nightmares."

"Really? You think there's something that could help?"

He hums softly. "Of course. An anxiety medication. Maybe a sleep aid."

"That would be... amazing. I sort of accepted that this would be my life now. I guess I should have expected you'd have an answer. You've helped me with everything else so far."

He gives me a tight smile and turns back to his bag.

The silence stretches out between us. My heart monitor beeps along in the background, keeping the time as Dr. Jenkins roots around in his bag. When he turns back to me, his hands are empty. He flexes them at his side like he isn't sure what to do.

"Are you going to check the babies?" I ask.

He blinks and turns to me. Our eyes meet for just a second before he looks away again. It's the first time he's looked at me since he walked in the room.

"Sure. Yes," he says like the idea just occurred to him. He reaches for the heart rate doppler. "We can do that."

I pull my blanket over my waist before I lift my hospital gown. Dr. Jenkins presses the doppler to my stomach, moving mechanically through our routine. When he finds a heartbeat, his face creases.

"Sounds good," he mumbles.

I can hear the heartbeat. It sounds exactly like what I've come to expect. It sounds healthy. But doubt churns in my gut.

Something is wrong.

"My blood pressure was okay, too?" I ask.

"Healthy. Perfect."

I frown. "It wasn't high? And the babies' heartbeats sound okay?"

"All good," he mutters. "No problem at all."

"I hear you, but you don't look like everything is okay." I lean forward and lay a hand over his wrist. "If me and my babies are okay… are *you* okay? Is your family alright?"

Dr. Jenkins jerks away from my hand like I just burned him. "Fine. My family is okay. Everything is fine, Luna. I'm just tired."

He's allowed to be tired. Everyone is allowed to have a bad day.

But this is more than that. I know it.

Yakov isn't here.

Dr. Jenkins is acting strange.

Something is wrong.

I hear Yakov's voice in my head like he's whispering in my ear. *Get out. Now.* I've come to trust my intuition, but this doesn't make any sense. I spent weeks in a safehouse with Dr. Jenkins. He has been coming to check on me two or three times per day for so long now. If he wanted to hurt me, he's had more than enough opportunities.

Dr. Jenkins goes to his bag again, rooting around inside.

I sit up and lean forward as far as my belly will allow. And I see that Dr. Jenkins isn't looking in the bag for anything—he's hiding his phone from me, tapping out a message.

Something is wrong.

The beeping from my heart rate monitor picks up. If Dr. Jenkins notices, he doesn't say anything. He's too focused on his phone.

Who is he texting? I don't want to stick around to find out.

Slowly, I slide my feet to the edge of the bed and grab my IV pole. I stand up on shaky legs.

I need to get to the door. I'll open the door and step into the hall. I can see nurses passing by the door right now. Someone out there will save me.

Save me from what? I'm not really sure. But something is wrong and I need to get out. Now.

I only manage two steps before Dr. Jenkins whirls around. He's looking right at me now, his brows furrowed. "Where are you going?"

"Bathroom," I lie. "I need to pee."

He looks down at his phone and then back to me. "I'm almost done with my exam. Lie down while I finish."

"I can't hold it. You know how the third trimester can be." I try for a smile, but my face is tight. My entire body is clenched, anticipating whatever is going to come next.

"I'm almost done," he repeats. "Lie back and—"

"You're here until Yakov gets back, right? We have time." I take another step. "I'll just pee and—"

"Sit down!" Dr. Jenkins roars.

I flinch back, the monitor behind me blaring my alarm into the quiet room.

"Sit down," he says again with forced calm. "I'm almost done here."

Get out. Now.

I take another step, but Dr. Jenkins is between me and the only way out before my foot even hits the floor. He looks into my eyes and he doesn't look tired; he looks *anguished*. Everything about him is sagging like he's aged a decade in the last ten minutes.

"I'll scream," I warn. "If you don't move, I'll scream."

He shakes his head slowly. "It won't help. Fighting will only make it harder."

"Make what harder? Dr. Jenkins, I don't know what is going on, but Yakov can help. *We* can help you."

He reaches for me and I pull back. But he doesn't grab me, he grabs my IV pole. Between one blink and the next, he reaches into his pocket and pulls out a syringe. With practiced fingers, he injects the syringe into the tube of my IV.

"What are you—"

"I'm sorry," he says, looking deep into my eyes. "Forgive me, Luna. Please... forgive me."

I shake my head. My vision is going dark around the edges. I feel dizzy. "Forgive you for…"

I can't move my lips. Can't move at all. My eyelids get heavy. As they close, I feel arms around my back lowering me to the bed.

Then… nothing.

59

YAKOV

As soon as Dr. Jenkins locks Luna's door, I sweep the floor.

My phone keeps buzzing. Nik is trying to get in touch with me. But I can't leave this floor until I know there is no threat.

The nurses at the station are the same women who were here at this time yesterday. Nik already ran background on them. They're cleared.

Then I walk the halls, looking into each room as I pass. I recognize the other patients on the floor, so I make quick work of it. The two empty rooms at the end of the hall get a thorough scan to make sure no one is lurking inside.

It only takes a few minutes, but it feels like hours pass. It doesn't help that Nik keeps calling. The only time the vibration stops is when I walk into the stairwell, but that's because this is the worst spot for reception in the whole building. I take the stairs two at a time down to the main lobby and step out through the sliding doors.

It's the first time I've felt the sun on my face in days. I take a deep breath, trying to enjoy it before this next round of shit hits the fan.

Then my phone vibrates.

This time when I answer it, Nik's voice is clear.

"Get her out of there right fucking now, Yakov!" Nik yells. "Can you hear me? Am I breaking up? Get her out! Now!"

I'm on the phone with Nik, but my phone is blowing up. Text after text after text comes through. I look down at the screen and see that they are all from Nik. All the messages I couldn't get in her room, apparently.

"What the fuck is going on?" I ask as I open the text thread.

"Can you hear me?" he gasps.

"Yeah, I'm outside. The signal in Luna's room is terrible." Over the last couple days, it seems like it has actively gotten worse.

"Get her out!" Nik yells again… just as I read his messages.

He's texted me twenty times. Each time with the same message.

It's Jenkins.

It's Jenkins.

It's Jenkins.

It's Jenkins.

It's Jenkins.

My stomach hollows out. For the first time in my life, I'm frozen.

No. It can't be. He wouldn't.

"Yakov?" Nik barks. "Can you fucking hear me?"

"I can hear you. I can—What are you talking about? What did Jenkins do?"

I ask, but I already know.

I know how Pavel's men were able to get past my security. Why they were waiting to ambush me at the safehouse. No one outside of my family knew where Luna and Mariya were staying.

No one...

Except Dr. Jenkins.

"He's the man on the inside, Yakov," Nik says, desperation laced in every word. "Jenkins is working for Pavel."

It's how the intruder got into my house even after I'd updated all of the security. Dr. Jenkins wasn't at the house moments after Luna was attacked by sheer coincidence—it was a plan. He *helped* the attacker get through the gates.

"He's with her," I whisper.

"What?" Nik asks.

But I'm already barreling through the double doors and sprinting for the stairwell.

"Jenkins is alone with Luna right now," I growl. "I left him with her. I told him to take care of her. I fucking trusted him."

"You have to get her out," Nik says. "I'll call Isay and—"

The beep lets me know the call has dropped. I shove my phone in my pocket and hurtle up the stairs as fast as my legs will carry me.

I trusted that asshole and the entire time, he's been working to kill Luna.

Now, I'm going to kill him.

I get to Luna's floor and stop at the nurse's station. The woman behind the desk smiles blandly, but it wipes clean when she really sees me.

"I need the keys to room 721. Now."

She frowns. "The door shouldn't be locked. You should be able to—"

"Keys!" I snap. "Now!"

If I knock, I'll just alert Jenkins to the fact that I'm back. He could carry out whatever he has planned before I get inside.

If he hasn't already.

I shove the dark thought away as the nurse shakily hands me the key. "It's the same key for every door on the floor," she says. "You can bring it back to the desk when you're—"

I don't hear the rest of the sentence. I'm already around the corner and running for Luna's door.

I don't stop to look through the glass. There isn't time. I shove the key in the door, turn it, and throw the door open.

Dr. Jenkins is next to Luna's bed. She's asleep, her hands folded on top of the blanket. That's all the information I have before I ram into the man's shoulder. The air whooshes out of him as we connect. I shove him back and pin him against the wall by the neck.

"Yakov, what the hell are you doing?" Dr. Jenkins groans. "What's happening?"

For a second, I think I made a mistake. Maybe Nik's information was wrong. Maybe Dr. Jenkins is on our side.

Then I notice his right arm shift.

I twist to the side and slam his arm against the wall. His fingers are clamped around a syringe. If I hadn't stopped him, he would have plunged it into my back.

I pry the syringe out of his hold and press the point of the needle to a vein in his neck. "Waste my time with lies and I'll empty this in your bloodstream."

Whatever is in the syringe, it's not good. I can tell by how quickly the color drains out of his face. His lips are pale. He's terrified.

I glance back at the bed and Luna is still sleeping. We've made enough noise that she should be awake.

My heart squeezes painfully. I take the pain out on Dr. Jenkins, twisting his wrist until I hear a snap.

"What did you do to Luna?"

"She's alive!" he winces. Sweat is gathering on his forehead. "I gave her something to put her to sleep. I didn't want her to be awake for what came next. It was a mercy."

I twist his injured wrist more. Tendons pop, a sample of what's coming. There won't be any mercy for him.

"Who are you working for?" I snarl.

His eyes dart around the room. He's searching for an escape, but there isn't one. There's not a chance in the world that he walks out of this room. It's possible he doesn't even make it through the rest of this conversation.

"I trusted you," I growl, anger I can't contain bubbling up in me. "I asked you to look after Luna and my babies and you were going to murder them. You sick fucking bastard."

The doctor's face crumples. He sags. I'm the only thing keeping him from falling to his knees.

"I'm sorry," Dr. Jenkins sobs. Fat tears roll down his cheeks. "I'm sorry, Yakov."

"Save your apology. Choke on it, for all I fucking care. What I want to know is who you are working for and why." I drive my arm deeper into his sternum. I want to feel his ribs shatter like dried sticks. "I want to hear you try to explain yourself."

He shakes his head, tears rolling down his neck. "I'm a hypocrite. I'm a worthless hypocrite. I'm so sorry, but... My family. He has my family. I didn't have a choice."

"There's always a choice."

"Is there a choice for you?" he asks. "I tried to hurt Luna. I was going to kill her. Do you have a choice in what happens to me next?"

No. He has to die. There is no other way.

Dr. Jenkins must see the answer on my face. He nods sadly. "That's what I thought. There is no choice, Yakov. Not when it comes to the people we love. I had to try to save them. *He* has them. Pavel. He has my family held hostage. To get them back I had to... He wanted me to..."

"You were going to kill Luna."

His head sags between his shoulders. He stares down at the floor. "I didn't want to, but I didn't have a choice. I'm sorry."

"You gave her something to put her to sleep. So what is this?" I press the point of the syringe into his neck.

He flinches back with a whimper. "Please."

"Answer the question."

He squeezes his eyes closed. "Something to stop her heart. She wouldn't have felt a thing."

My hand is shaking with the restraint it takes not to plunge this syringe into his throat. Not yet.

"What about the babies?"

"I'm sorry," he sobs. Snot and tears pour down his face. "They all had to die. Luna and the babies. It was the only way Pavel would give me my family back. He wanted me to take yours. But I didn't want Luna to suffer."

"How long were you planning this?"

"Since the night the ambulance came to the safehouse. I—I never wanted to—" He swallows, his throat bobbing against the point of the needle. "I never wanted any of this. He forced my hand."

"All the times you tried to get Luna to go to the hospital, it was so you could carry out your plan. It was so you could get her alone and then escape without being seen."

"I'm sorry!" he moans. "I'm sorry. I didn't want to. I didn't want to do any of this."

"Is that why you helped the attacker get into the mansion? Because you were too much of a coward to do it yourself?"

His lack of response is enough of an answer.

I lean in close. "If you had asked me for my help, I would have saved your family."

"He said he would kill them if I told you. He said—"

"I would have saved them," I repeat, pulling the syringe away.

Dr. Jenkins' eyes go wide. He can't believe it. I'm letting him go.

"I would have saved them and you'd be alive to see them again. Instead..." In a flash, I empty the syringe into the base of his skull, hiding the injection point beneath his hairline. "Let's see if this medicine is as painless as you claimed."

He gasps, but the drug is quick. His eyes roll back in his head as his legs give way.

I look down at him, meeting his eyes one final time before they close forever.

60

LUNA

My head is swimming before I even open my eyes. I feel like I'm swimming towards consciousness, fighting against a current that wants to drag me back down. I'm so tired. Maybe I should let it. I'll sleep a bit more and then—

"Luna?"

The voice is deep and close by. I peel my eyelids open, blinking against the blurriness in front of me.

"Luna?" The voice is closer now. A hand grips my arm, squeezing. "Can you hear me?"

The shape next to my bed has the same dark hair as Yakov. The same square jaw. The same deep voice.

But it isn't Yakov.

"Nik?" I try to sit up, but my head swims.

Nik presses my shoulder back until I lie down again. "Don't sit up. Give it a second."

"What's going on? Where is Yakov? Where am I?"

I'm still in the hospital. I can tell by the speckled drop ceiling and the beeping of the monitor behind me. There's an IV in my arm. The tape around it pulls uncomfortably against my skin. I don't remember it hurting before. Did someone move it while I was sleeping?

"Wow. I'm out of it," I admit with a soft laugh. "How long was I asleep?"

"Eight hours," he mutters.

I snap my attention to him. "Really? How? I haven't slept that well in… I don't even know how long."

"You needed the rest."

"You're not wrong." I turn my head from side to side. It feels like it's full of wet sand. "Weirdly, I don't feel very rested. I feel worse than I have in a while. Maybe my body is accustomed to running on no sleep. It doesn't know what to do with actual rest."

I'm joking, but Nikandr isn't in a joking mood. There's a first time for everything, I suppose.

"Is this the first time you're out of the house in your wheelchair?"

He nods. "My physical therapist said I can sit up in the passenger seat now. It'll make it a lot easier to get around. Plus… Yakov needed me."

His eyes shift to the floor and all of my radars start going off.

Something is wrong.

The thought brings back a hazy memory. Me trying to get out of bed. Trying to get to the door.

I frown. "Where did you say Yakov was?"

"I didn't."

I stare at him, waiting for more. "Nik… where is he?"

"He had to take care of something. He asked me to sit with you until he gets back."

The words echo somewhere in the back of my mind. Again, a foggy memory rises to the surface. Those exact words coming from someone else…

"I had a weird dream, I think. Yakov was gone, but Dr. Jenkins was—"

As soon as I say his name, Nik's face changes. His hand tightens to a fist in his lap and his jaw clenches.

"It wasn't a dream, was it?" I whisper.

Nik's jaw works back and forth before he forces the words out. "Yakov got to you in time."

The memories come back faster now, clicking into place like photos in a slideshow. "Dr. Jenkins," I breathe. "Is he…?"

"He won't be a problem anymore," Nik answers curtly.

That can only mean one thing: Yakov killed him. Dr. Jenkins betrayed us all and tried to hurt me and so Yakov killed him.

How many times is Yakov going to have to save me from the brink of certain death?

Without warning, my body contracts. Every muscle in my midsection tightens until I can't breathe. Can't speak.

"Luna?" Nik rolls closer to the bed. "Luna, are you okay? What's happening?"

I can't speak through the pain. All I can do is shake my head. *I'm not okay. This isn't okay.*

Nik rolls to the door and yanks it open. "We need a nurse in here!"

Finally, the pain eases. I groan. "Contraction. That was a contraction."

I know what they feel like now. I've been through this before.

Nik curses under his breath and opens the door again. "Or a doctor! A fucking janitor would be better than nothing. Now!"

Another contraction is ramping up. I feel it coming. I grit my teeth. "Where is Yakov?"

Nik wheels around, rolling closer to the bed. "Pavel was holding Dr. Jenkins' family hostage as blackmail. It's why he attacked you. Yakov went to save them."

The information is coming at me faster than I can process it. Someone is going to have to explain the last twenty-four hours to me in slow, exquisite detail when this is all over.

"Yakov went to save Dr. Jenkins' family?"

Nik nods. "He didn't want them to suffer."

I grab Nik's hand, squeezing as the contraction crests.

"Fuck, that hurts," Nik grumbles. When it's over, he shakes out his hand.

"Sorry if I don't feel bad for your pain," I snap. "I'm going through something here. *Without my fiancé.*"

"He's doing the right thing."

"Fuck the right thing! I want him to be *here!*"

It's true—I want Yakov here right now. But I also love that he's saving innocent people. Underneath all of his threats and bravado, Yakov is a good man. He's noble. It's why I'm glad he's the father of my children.

I'd also be glad if he was here to witness them being born.

A nurse comes in and pulls my blankets back. She takes one look under my hospital gown and blanches. "I'm calling your doctor."

My doctor... Dr. Jenkins.

I look at Nik. "What the fuck are we going to do?"

"Another doctor," Nik announces. "Find another doctor. *Any* doctor."

"Mr. Kulikov told us to defer to Dr. Jenkins for—"

"Well, *this* Mr. Kulikov is telling you to forget that and find someone else," Nikandr interrupts. "Dr. Jenkins has left the building."

She rushes out of the room and comes back with the charge nurse. Together, the women shift me to a gurney.

"We're taking you to labor and delivery," the charge nurse explains. She's wearing bright pink scrubs and has a yellow stethoscope. She doesn't look like the kind of person who would try to poison me and my children, so I take it as a good sign. She looks to Nik. "Are you the father?"

Nik winces. "No, but I texted him. He's coming as fast as he can."

"Tell him to hurry," she says. "Her contractions are close together. It could be anytime now."

They roll me out of the room and into the hallway, but I'm not ready. My babies aren't ready. I'm barely thirty weeks along. They're too small.

I reach out my hand and instantly, Nik squeezes it. He rolls next to me, a wan smile on his face. "These babies are Kulikovs, Luna. Do you know what that means?"

Yes—it means they're in danger.

"They're fighters," Nik answers. "You are going to give birth to two healthy babies and you're going to do it with Yakov by your side. He'll be here any second. Do you hear me?"

I nod, trying to believe him. "I hear you."

"Good." He looks straight ahead, following my gurney into a large elevator. "Because I cannot watch you give birth. I've been through enough."

Despite everything, I laugh.

61

YAKOV

Dr. Jenkins' wife—widow now, I suppose—has more questions than I can answer. I hold up a hand to stop her. My voice is muffled through the mask. The less she knows about who I am, the better. "Leave the city. Go home."

She looks around the dank basement Pavel had her and her children locked up in. The guards Pavel left to watch over them are dead in the doorway. They never saw me coming. "Where is Howard?"

At this point, he's deep in the bottom of a decomp barrel at the clean-up shed. In a couple weeks, he'll be sludge we can dump down a sewer drain.

It's more than he deserves.

"He's gone," I tell her. "Don't wait for him. Leave and never come back."

I turn away from her, mounting the steps. She calls after me, but I don't stop. I saved her life, but I don't owe her any explanations.

I leave the house and climb in my car. Three blocks later, I pull my mask over my head. My phone vibrates in the center console.

It's Nik again.

After what happened with Dr. Jenkins, I couldn't trust anyone else to stay with Luna. I needed my brother to be there with her so I could leave.

Luna is in labor. Hurry.

I'm over an hour out. Closter to ninety minutes if traffic doesn't cooperate. I drop my phone and slam on the gas.

The rest of my drive is a blur. I'm not sure if I stop at traffic lights or follow road rules. The only thing I know is that I get to Luna as fast as possible. By the time I reach labor and delivery, I'm dripping sweat and breathless.

Nik is rolling back and forth in the hallway, pacing outside of Luna's room.

"Has it happened?" I gasp. "Did I miss it?"

When Nik sees me, he almost melts in relief. "You didn't respond. I thought you were dead."

I ignore the unintentional insult. *As if Pavel's men could kill me.* "Is Luna okay?"

"She's sleeping," he explains. "They gave her an epidural or something and I guess it slowed down the contractions. I'm not really sure. They think they might be able to keep the babies in for a few more days."

"I'm going to die of a fucking heart attack before Pavel shows his face again." I press my palm to the wall and blow out a breath. "She can't have these babies before Pavel is dead, Nik. They can't be born into this shitshow."

"Then let's lure him out."

I snort. "If it was that easy, I would have done it by now. Dima is stationed nearby with all of his men. They're ready to strike if we can find him, but he keeps sending in cronies to do his dirty work. I don't have a way to draw him out."

Slowly, Nik grins. He holds a phone out to me. "Give this a try."

I arch a brow. "What's that?"

"Jenkins' phone. He got a text from an unknown contact fifteen minutes ago asking if the job is done. The text thread goes back a few weeks." He shrugs. "If I had to bet, I'd put my money on it being Pavel's number."

I snatch the phone away and scroll through the thread. The messages are innocuous. They don't give anything away. That's on purpose. But they're vague enough to raise an eyebrow.

What time?

Meet at the place.

Don't forget what's at stake.

"It has to be," I breathe. "It has to be him."

"What are the chances he knows Jenkins is dead?" Nik pulls the phone out of my hands and types out a message. "More importantly, what are the chances Pavel will show up if I text him as Jenkins and say we need to meet?"

"It's the best chance we've had so far. I'll tell Dima to get here now. He and his men are already in the area."

Nik nods. "I'll tell Pavel to meet you in the morgue."

"The morgue? That's a little on the nose, don't you think?"

Nik smirks. "I figured it would save you all some time. I'm ready for that bastard to be cold and dead."

Nik sends the message and hands me the phone.

I look past him towards the birthing suite. I want to see Luna. I want to kiss her forehead and let her know everything will be fine. But if I go in there, I'm not sure I can leave again.

"Text me if there is any change with Luna," I order.

Even if there is a change, I can't come back until Pavel is dead. I'm going to kill him or die trying. Nik seems to know that. He reaches out and clasps my hand.

I pull him close and clap him on the back. "Take care of my woman, brother."

"You know I will," he says.

I leave Nik outside of Luna's room. No matter what happens next, I know he'll take care of her. Now, I need to go take care of Pavel.

62

YAKOV

Fifteen minutes later, Dima is tucked in a corner of the hospital lobby wearing a pair of jeans and a t-shirt. Much less understated than his usual suit and cigar. He winks at me as I take the seat two away from him. "I'm undercover."

"You might be undercover for nothing. Pavel hasn't responded."

"Maybe not, but my men saw a black car with tinted windows pull into the employee entrance five minutes ago."

"Were your men spotted?"

He shakes his head. "Give me more credit than that, Yakov."

I hold up a hand in silent apology. "My fiancée is upstairs about to give birth. I'm not taking any chances."

"Fair enough." Dima pushes himself to standing. "In three minutes, follow me. I'll head down to the morgue and see if our friend has decided to show his face."

I tense up. Dima is my partner. I chose to work with him. But sending him in alone to what could very well be the final battle is a risk.

"I'll go first," I offer. "Pavel knows I'm in the building. If he or his men see me, it won't blow anything."

"We made a deal," Dima growls. "Pavel is mine. I get to kill him. If he's down there waiting to jump one of us, I want it to be me."

"If he jumps me, I won't kill him. I'll hold him for you until—"

"Either I go first or I leave." His voice is firm, but his expression softens. "I hate giving an ultimatum when one of the options isn't death, but that's where I stand. I like you, Yakov, but I'm not helping you for nothing. I *will* make that kill shot."

"It might be a trap."

He shrugs. "All the more reason for me to go first. I don't have a fiancée pregnant with twins upstairs."

I could tell Dima to fuck off. I needed his help to lure Pavel out, but I don't need his help to kill him. Ending our deal now could be the smart move. It's not like I have the best track record with trusting people—I left Luna with a homicidal doctor just a few hours ago.

But Dima and I have come this far together. When this is all said and done, I'd like him to remain an ally.

"Fine. Go," I growl. "I'll see you in three minutes."

Dima grins, almost giddy, and saunters towards the stairwell.

Three minutes crawl by like molasses before I follow Dima's path to the stairs. The stairwell is silent. There's no gunfire or shouting coming from the lower levels. It could be a good sign. It could also be a sign that Dima is partnering with Pavel. They could be waiting for me just behind the door.

I have my gun ready as I slowly turn the handle and pull the door open.

As I do, a body falls at my feet. I jump back, gun aimed at the man. Then I notice that his eyes are closed and his neck is bent at a sickening angle.

"I had to lean that one against the door so I could grab the other one," Dima whispers. He's in the middle of the hallway, dragging another limp body my way. "Hold the door for me, will you?"

He drags both corpses into the stairwell and we stash them in the alcove beneath the stairs.

"Guards," he explains, wiping his hands on his pants. "They were stationed outside of the morgue. I didn't stop to chat, but I think they're with the Gustev Bratva. I'm operating under the assumption Pavel is inside."

"They didn't raise the alarm?"

"There wasn't time. I bashed their fucking heads together. Knocked them both out so I could take them out one at a time." Dima chuckles. "That's what Pavel gets for sacrificing all of his men to our raids. He's left with a bunch of know-nothing recruits."

I look Dima over, trying to decide if there's any way this could still be a trap. Pavel has been willing to sacrifice his men so far. He could have offered up two more to make me trust Dima, just so I'd walk into the morgue confident Dima is on my side.

Dima arches a brow. "Well? Are we doing this fucking thing or not?"

"The rest of the hallway is clear?"

"These are the only two men I saw," he says with a shrug. "I haven't heard anything from my men stationed outside the hospital. Have you?"

I shake my head. "Nothing. Looks like Pavel came with a small team today."

Dima grins. "Because he wasn't expecting me."

I can trust him. I make that decision here and now. The only way to go into a fight like this is with full trust that the person next to you has your back. If I walk in that room unsure if Dima is on my side, I could get us both killed.

The only person dying today is Pavel.

So I hold open the door and usher Dima through. He stops in the doorway. "Pavel is mine."

"Say it again and I'll kill him just to spite you," I snap. "I'm a man of my word, Dima."

Dima chuckles. "Just reminding you."

He moves quietly towards the morgue. By the time we're outside the door, his smile is gone and his jaw is set.

"I go in first to draw his attention," I whisper. "If he doesn't know you're here yet, you can be a surprise."

I can tell Dima doesn't like it. He probably wouldn't mind if I sat in the hall while he handled this all himself. But he made the last call. This one is mine.

"Fine," he concedes. "Yell out if you need help. Otherwise, I'll wait for my grand entrance."

We nod in silent agreement. Then I ready my gun, release a long breath, and push the door open.

The morgue is a long, narrow space. Three stainless steel countertops lie in the middle of the room like metal islands. Matching cabinets cover the back wall and the wall to the right. There are exam tables to the left, surrounded by curtains that hang from the ceiling. Privacy for the dead, I guess. I can't see what's behind them.

The door closes with a soft thud behind me.

The next sound is a gunshot.

A bullet pings off the metal wall behind me and I hit the floor.

"Are you alone?" Pavel yells as the echo reverberates.

I can't see him. He must have been behind the curtains.

I drag one of the tables and turn it over, ducking behind the tabletop. Dima's head peeks through the windowpane set in the door for just a second. Just long enough for him to see I'm still alive. Then he disappears.

If I can get on the other side of the room, it might force Pavel to change positions. He'd have his back to the door and Dima could take the kill shot.

"Did you come here alone?" he yells again.

"Did you?"

He laughs. "I didn't, but if you made it through that door, then you already know that. How long did it take you to kill those worthless fuckers? Hopefully, it at least tired you out so it will make this next part a little easier for me."

"Is that what the men who pledge their loyalty to you get? You serve them up to your enemies on a silver platter?"

"They didn't pledge their loyalty to me. They pledged it to my father, who you murdered. Then my brother, who you *also* murdered."

"Sounds like a string of bad luck for the Gustev family."

"Maybe, but the pattern ends now," Pavel hisses. "I'm not leaving this room until you're dead."

Another bullet pings off the top of the table. The metal dents and deforms around the shot.

"You haven't asked about where Dr. Jenkins is. Don't you want to know what happened when I was in a room alone with him?"

I hear Pavel creep a few steps closer. He might be in Dima's line of sight now, but he needs to be closer for it to be a guaranteed kill.

"Do you think killing Jenkins is going to save your whore?" Pavel taunts. "I may be young, but I'm not naive enough to put all of my eggs in that shaking sack of shit's basket. The man was a wreck. He kept reminding me of his fucking Hippocratic oath."

Waiting so Dima can kill Pavel is getting harder and harder by the second. Everything in me is screaming to flip this table over and charge at the bastard. I don't fucking care if I get shot so long as he dies.

But I grit my teeth and swallow down my rage. "What if I surrender?"

"Surender what?" Pavel asks.

"Myself," I clarify. "I'll surrender to you right now if you promise to leave Luna and our babies alone. You can do what you want to me. But you have to leave them out of it."

There's a beat of silence before Pavel responds. "Slide your gun across the room and show yourself."

"Not until you agree. I'm not moving a fucking muscle until you swear you won't hurt them."

As if his word means anything to me. He could get the agreement tattooed on his forehead and I still wouldn't buy it.

"If you surrender, your fiancée and children will be spared. I won't kill them. Now, get rid of your gun."

I glance at the door. I don't see Dima in the window, but I have to trust that he's listening in. That he'll know when to step in.

Reluctantly, I place my gun on the floor and slide it towards the back wall.

"I know you didn't come in here with one gun. I want all of them on the floor."

I roll my eyes and unstrap the gun from my ankle. I slide it next to the other weapon in the corner.

"That's all I have. I'm going to step out now." I say it loudly, directing the words towards the door so Dima can hear.

Despite Pavel's threats, I know he doesn't want to kill me. Not yet, anyway. He wants to torture me first. He wants to tear me down brick by brick. Shooting me in the head wouldn't accomplish that. So he isn't going to shoot to kill right now.

With that semi-encouraging thought, I slowly stand up.

Pavel is standing just in front of the curtain. He's sporting a patchy beard and sunken-in cheeks and there are dark circles under his eyes. He looks like shit. Nothing like the fresh-faced kid I remember.

As soon as he sees me, he grins. His face twists and his eyes go dark. Forget being a fresh-faced kid—he doesn't even look human.

"It's good to finally see you, Yakov. It's been a long time."

He inches closer and I match his movements. I shift towards the back of the room. If I can work my way around to the wall of cabinets against the back wall, that will put Pavel directly in front of the door.

"It has been a long time," I agree. "Put the gun away and we'll catch up."

He snorts. "I always thought Nikandr was the funny one. Maybe not anymore. I'm sure being crippled is putting a bit of a damper on things."

I shrug. "It could be worse. He could be an orphan."

His eyes narrow. Rage burns beneath the surface. "How do you feel knowing your kids will grow up without their father?"

"At least they'll grow up," I say truthfully. "That is what you promised, isn't it? You won't touch them or Luna."

He wags a finger in the air, his gun still aimed at my head. "I said I wouldn't kill them. That is very different from saying I wouldn't touch them."

I want to charge across the room and smash his skull into the floor, but I take another step towards the back wall. Without even realizing it, Pavel mirrors my movement. With every step I take, he's closer and closer to the door.

"I thought you wanted peace," I growl.

He snorts. "There is no peace for me. Not anymore. There is only revenge."

"You'll sacrifice your life for revenge?"

"I've sacrificed a lot of lives for revenge," he fires back. "It's ironic we're even talking about this, considering *you're* the man who technically sacrificed those lives. You tore through the Gustev Bratva like it was your job."

"I did what I had to do to save my family. What's your excuse?" I snap.

He rolls his eyes. "I've already told you: revenge. It's the only excuse I need."

"If you're doing this because you think it will help you sleep better, you're wrong. Killing your father didn't make me feel better about losing mine. Killing Akim wasn't satisfying, either. Revenge for revenge's sake is never worth it."

"No offense," he drawls, "but I'm not going to take your word on that. Revenge is sweet. It's as good a thing as any to build a life around."

I shake my head. "A year ago, I would have agreed with you. Now, I know the truth."

Luna. Our babies. The life we're building. All of that is better than revenge. I'd let Pavel walk free right now if I knew for a fact he'd never show his face again. If I knew my family would be safe.

"Oh, God," he groans. "If you're hoping I'll spare you because of some sob story, save your fucking breath. Hearing how much you love your little wifey and your unborn spawn is just going to make what comes next even better."

I take another step towards the back of the room. Finally, Pavel is in position.

"What do you think is coming next?" I ask.

He has no idea. All Dima needs to do is open the door and fire. It will be over.

But the door doesn't open. Dima doesn't even peek through the window.

Where the fuck is he?

"First, I'm going to kill you. That will be fun."

"Sure. It'll be a riot." I wave him on. I need to draw this out until Dima can get here. "That's a given. What else?"

Pavel's face twists in amusement. "But the enjoyment I'll get from killing you won't hold a fucking candle to how much fun I'm going to have with your little fiancée."

He'll be dead before that can happen. He isn't going to touch Luna. But I hold myself painfully still. I'm afraid of what I'll do if I let myself move.

"She's sexy, yeah?" Pavel wags his brows. "You don't have to tell me if you don't want to—I'm sure I'll find out for myself—but she's a good lay, isn't she? If she caught your attention, I bet she fucks like a whore."

Dima isn't in the doorway. No one is here to give Pavel Gustev what he deserves.

Except me.

Moving on pure instinct and a desire to keep this asshole as far away from my family as possible, I lunge for him.

Pavel is the only one of us with a weapon, but he doesn't know how to use it. He's been insulated and protected by his family name and the men he so eagerly sacrificed. I lower my shoulder and drive him back into the wall. The gun falls out of his hand and clatters to the floor.

Pavel dives for it, but I twist him to the side and slam him down on the tile.

Now, it's just him and me.

It'd be so easy to strangle the life from this miserable bastard. I made a deal with Dima, but he's taking too long. This can't wait. Pavel needs to die.

Pavel swipes out at me. He flails and grapples, trying to knock me off balance.

"Your father really didn't give a shit about you, did he?" I ask, ducking away from a poorly-aimed blow. "You can't fight worth shit."

Pavel growls and drives his knee up. He narrowly misses kneeing me in the balls, but I flinch. It's enough for him to get some leverage and push me off of him.

I roll over my shoulder and rise to my feet as Pavel scrambles to his. He drops into a ready position, his top lip pulled back in a snarl. "I can fight well enough to kill you."

He lunges forward, but he doesn't even take a step before the door to the morgue flies open. Dima steps through the doorway, gun raised. Pavel spins towards the door just as Dima fires.

The shot tears through his shoulder. Pavel falls, a hand gripping his bleeding limb.

Dima doesn't give him a second to recover. He marches over to him and jams the heel of his shoe into Pavel's wound. He digs in as Pavel screams.

"This is for what you did to my cousin, you fucking useless *mudak*."

Pavel shakes his head. "I didn't know—"

Dima steps on his neck before he can even finish the sentence. Clearly, he isn't looking for excuses or apologies.

Pavel claws at Dima's ankle as his face turns red. His tongue swells out of his mouth. Blood vessels in his eyes and cheek burst, turning his skin a mottled red.

"Sorry for the delay," he grits out, stomping on Pavel's neck with all of his strength. "Another guard showed up. I had to take care of him."

I turn around and see a pair of splayed legs through the open door.

Then my phone buzzes. Dima has Pavel well in hand, so I check it. It's Nik.

Luna is awake and the contractions are back. It's happening.

"Fuck."

Dima turns to me, seemingly unaware of the man suffocating under his foot. "What is it now? More guards?"

"Luna is in labor. The twins are coming."

He lets out a long whistle. "Okay. Then I'll make this brief."

He lifts his foot off of Pavel's neck just long enough for the man to suck in a ragged breath. Then Dima shoots Pavel in the head.

BANG. Then, *echo, echo, echo...*

And then silence.

"You didn't need to rush it on my account."

He waves me off. "That's all the time the fucker deserved, anyway. I'll worry about cleaning up. You need to go."

"I owe you for this," I say, already halfway to the door.

"That's a dangerous thing to say to someone like me." He laughs. "Consider this a baby gift. Go be with your woman."

He doesn't need to tell me twice.

I run for the stairwell and take the stairs two at a time.

63

LUNA

I grit my teeth as another contraction rips through me. "This shouldn't be hurting. What was the point of having that long-ass needle in my spine if this is still going to hurt?"

"It hurts me, too," Nik whimpers. He's been shaking out his hand between each contraction.

I woke up thirty minutes ago to a slight discomfort. Now, I'm writhing in pain, which was not at all part of the plan.

"Baby A is sunny side up," a nurse explains calmly.

"He's a baby, not an egg." *Right?* Maybe the pain is making me delirious.

"It means he is coming out face up. It can make an epidural less effective." She lifts my gown to check my dilation. I shouldn't be able to feel anything, but I feel her fingers between my legs.

"Fantastic," I growl. I turn to Nik. "Where is Yakov?"

His face is pale, but he plasters on a smile. "He's on his way. He'll be here."

"He better hurry." The nurse peels off her gloves. "The babies are coming. I'm going to find a doctor."

I bite back a sob. "This isn't how this was supposed to go. The epidural should be working. Yakov should be here instead of you. No offense."

Nik waves me off. "None taken."

"I should be calm and relaxed. Maybe sucking on some ice chips." I whimper as another contraction builds. My entire midsection cinches until I can't breathe. I feel the urge to push, but I try to fight it. "It's happening." I close my eyes as tears roll down my cheeks. "I can't wait. I'm going to have to push. I'm going to have to do this without him."

Another nurse is laying out blankets in matching bassinets in the corner. She stops and comes over to check me. "Oh. Oh no."

"Don't say it like that," Nik snaps.

She winces. "Sorry, but she's ready to push. This is happening fast."

"No," I moan. "Yakov isn't here. Yakov is supposed to be here. He's their dad. He should be—"

The door to my room slams open.

Yakov jogs towards me, sweaty and with blood splatter on his collar, but he's never looked better. My body is still on fire, but he's here. If I wasn't in excruciating pain with a baby's skull between my legs, I'd stand up and hug him.

Nik drops my hand and wheels away. "About fucking time. My hand is broken."

Yakov ignores him and strokes my hair away from my face. I'm sticky with tears and sweat, but he still kisses my forehead. "Everything is okay. You can do this."

"No, I *have* to do this. There's a difference."

"You have to *and* you can."

"Easy for you to say. You're not the one about to push out twins. Fuuuuck!" I flail my arm out looking for his hand as another contraction starts. Yakov's hand slides into mine and I squeeze.

The nurse props my feet up in stirrups and I could care less that my bare ass is hanging out for the room to see. Nothing matters except getting these babies out of me.

"You can push if you need to," she says. "But wait for another contraction. A doctor is coming soon."

It's too late for that. I don't even have to try to push. My body is doing it on its own, doctor be damned.

I push until my lungs are spent and I'm dizzy. Yakov reaches over my head and then places an oxygen mask over my mouth and nose. I have no idea how he knows what to do, but then again, I'm not surprised. He seems to know how to do everything.

He holds my hand with both of his and leans in close. "What do you need?"

"I need to hear you admit that this is all your fucking fault," I mutter.

He chuckles and curls his hand around my cheek. "This is all my fault. But I promise I'll make it up to you, *solnyshka*."

"How?" I squeak out as another contraction starts.

"I'll change every last diaper," Yakov whispers in my ear as I push. "I'll rock them to sleep in the middle of the night. I'll bathe them and make bottles."

The pain is the worst it's been, but I can see our future like a movie in my head. I can see Yakov with a baby tucked in each arm. The thought makes it all bearable.

I want that. I want that future with him and our babies.

The door opens and an older woman comes in. She introduces herself as my midwife, but they could have an intern between my legs for all I care.

"I can see the head," the woman announces. "They're going to be small little babes. One more push and you'll have baby number one out, okay? Push hard for me, Luna."

Yakov braces himself by my bed, his fingers warm around my hand. "You can do this, *solnyshka*."

As the contraction begins to ramp up, I squeeze my eyes closed and push.

I bear down with everything I have, screaming to the ceiling. It's a primal release of the stress and fear of the last seven months. I let it all go. This is a new beginning. The start to a better future for my babies.

"Keep pushing," the midwife urges. "Head is out. The shoulders are coming."

I can't breathe. My lungs are seizing up. But somehow, I dig deep and keep pushing. Yakov's hand braces my shoulders, helping lift me into the right position.

Just as I run out of air and fall back, a tiny wail breaks through the silence.

I snap my eyes to Yakov and he's staring down at the end of the bed. It's the first time I've ever seen him awestruck.

"It's a boy!" the midwife yells, holding up a pink and purple, slime-covered infant.

"He's beautiful," I sob, reaching for him.

The nurse wraps him in a towel and lays him on my chest. It's an out-of-body experience. I'm staring down at my baby, but it feels like I'm watching a movie. Like someone is going to yell, "Cut!" and snatch him away any second.

"Hey, little man," Yakov whispers, stroking a finger down our baby's arm.

"His arm is smaller than your finger." Tears well in my eyes. "He's so small."

But there isn't time to stare in wonder or panic because another contraction starts.

I groan and the nurse whisks my baby boy away to weigh him and clean him up. I would care a lot more if the contractions didn't hurt so damn much.

We go through it all again like a nightmare on loop. I squeeze Yakov's hand until even he winces in pain. The nurse counts down each contraction, asking me to push until I'm on the verge of blacking out from lack of oxygen.

Then, before I know it, another tiny cry fills the room. This one is watery and weak, but I set my fear aside as the midwife lays the baby on my chest.

"Your little girl," she murmurs.

The midwife and nurse chat quietly in the corner, but I'm fully focused on my daughter. *Our* daughter.

"My girl," Yakov breathes. His face is stretched in a rare grin.

"Have I been replaced so quickly?" I tease in a weak mumble.

"You're my *woman*. No one can replace you." He leans over and presses a soft kiss to my lips. "You were incredible, *solnyshka*."

I smile up at him just as the nurse appears over his shoulder. "I'm sorry, but both babies need to be taken to the NICU."

My heart jolts. "Are they okay?"

"They're doing really well, but they're small. Your daughter has some fluid in her lungs. We need to monitor them closely."

"Can I go with them?" I ask, reluctantly handing my daughter over to the woman.

"In a little bit," she says gently. "You need to rest. Don't worry—I won't let them out of my sight."

I don't have a choice but to trust her.

As soon as she wheels the bassinets out of the room, I turn to Yakov. "Is he gone?"

"Dr. Jenkins or Pavel?" he asks. Then he waves away the question. "Doesn't matter. The answer is yes."

That explains the blood on his collar.

"We're safe?"

He smooths my hair away from my forehead. "You are safe. No one is going to hurt you or our babies. I have guards stationed in the hall. They'll follow the babies to the NICU. You can trust me."

Of course he has it all handled. He thought of everything.

"I do. I trust you, Yakov." I loll my head back and let my eyes flutter closed. Exhaustion settles over me like a blanket. My entire body is heavy.

"Rest." His lips brush over my cheek. "You just gave birth to twins and made me the happiest man in the world. I think that's enough for a day's work. You deserve a nap."

My lips tilt into a tired smile just as I drift off, exhausted and unbelievably happy.

EPILOGUE: LUNA

I crack open the door of the nursery and find Yakov standing between the cribs, looking down at our babies sleeping. It's been his favorite place ever since the twins were finally released from the NICU a week ago.

"You're supposed to sleep when the babies are sleeping," I whisper, wrapping my arms around his waist.

He covers my hands with his. "I'm not tired."

"Impossible. You were up all night with Alina."

Coming home has been a tough transition for our princess. She needed more care in the NICU than her brother, Nikolai. She's not used to lying in a crib. The only way she sleeps peacefully is when someone is holding her or, like now, when she's swaddled close to her brother.

"Not all night," Yakov says. "She settled down after four this morning. I got a few hours."

I press my cheek to his muscled back, hugging him close. "Remember when you wanted to hire a team of nurses to take care of the babies? Where did that guy go?"

"I think 'that guy' is wrapped around Alina's finger," Yakov admits with a grin.

He was insistent for the first couple weeks after the twins were born that we needed an army of nurses and nannies to help us take care of the twins.. But as we spent hour after hour and day after day in the NICU, he started singing another tune. By the end, Yakov didn't even want to let the NICU nurses care for the twins. He wanted to do everything himself.

So far, he's kept all the promises that he made to me during labor. He is always there to change a diaper, make a bottle, and rock a screaming baby back to sleep.

"Well, your mother is living here specifically to help with the twins. She keeps asking me to remind you that you can wake her up in the middle of the night. She'd be happy to help."

He frowns. "Why is she telling you to remind me? She could remind me herself."

"She could, but she knows that I have a way of getting through to you."

Yakov bites back a smile. "Oh, you do, do you?"

I hum, slowly spinning him towards me. I hook my hands around his back and rest my chin on his chest. "You may be a bloody brute to the rest of the world, but for me, you're a great big softie."

He arches a brow even as his hands slide down my waist to my ass. He hauls me close, grinding our hips together. "There's nothing soft about me, *solnyshka*."

Heat swirls low in my belly. For the six weeks the twins were in the hospital, I didn't have space to think about anything else. Yakov and I were so busy taking care of them that the thought of taking care of ourselves was nonexistent.

But now… it exists.

I press my hands to his chest and put some space between us. "You and I are taking the night off."

"Says who?"

"Says me," I tell him. "We are going to ask your mom to watch the kids and we are going to be off-duty for the first time in seven weeks."

"You think my mom can handle everything on her own?"

I roll my eyes. "You know she can. She's better at swaddling Nikolai than I am and she's the only one who can get Alina to burp."

I was terrified of what life with Ofeliya would look like. The woman was overbearing before. What was it going to be like now that I also had two premature infants to care for? But since the moment the babies were born—and especially since they came home a week ago— she has been nothing but a fount of helpful advice and patience.

The first night the twins were home, I practically shoved Alina at Ofeliya, begging her to help me. She could have taken over and made me feel like an incapable mother. Instead, she tucked Alina into my arms, squeezed my shoulders, and assured me that I could do it. She sat with me until one in the morning, soothing me while I soothed Alina.

In my book, the woman is a saint.

"Of course she can handle the twins," Yakov says. "I'm worried about whether she can handle the twins *and* Mariya."

I laugh and have to quickly cover my mouth when Alina stirs. "Thankfully, Mariya isn't here tonight. She's staying with Nikandr at his place."

At first, Mariya was staying with Nikandr to make sure he was adjusting okay to life on his own in a wheelchair. Now, she stays with him because she turned eighteen three weeks ago and can get into a lot more clubs without having to use her laughably bad fake ID. Nik's apartment is in the heart of downtown, which is a lot more exciting than living in "Norman Rockwell's wet dream." Those are her words, not mine.

"Then it looks like there's no reason why we can't get away for a few hours." Yakov dips his head, his lips brushing against my earlobe. "Wear something sinful."

"Sounds like you have a plan," I say, suddenly a little more breathless.

He shrugs. "Plan, twisted fantasies—whatever you want to call it."

I twist one way and then the other, examining myself from every angle.

Eight months ago, this red dress fit me like a glove. It hugged my waist, pushed up the girls so I had the perfect amount of cleavage, and the slit was high without being trashy. It was the dream date night dress.

Now, it fits me like an overstuffed trash bag.

My stomach is lumpy, my boobs are swollen with milk and spilling out of the top of the dress, and the extra padding around my thighs has turned the slit into a proper cutout. My entire right leg is hanging out.

"I can't wear this," I mutter to myself for the tenth time.

The only reason I haven't marched back into the closet to find something else is that there isn't anything else. That and the fact that it's been months since I've walked in heels and I'm feeling unsteady in my stilettos.

Yakov wanted "sinful." It was an order. But the only things that fit me right now are my maternity leggings and the oversized t-shirts I wear to bed. Neither of which are something I can wear to a night out with Yakov. Not when he's going to look immaculate in some perfectly tailored suit.

I'm turned around, examining myself from behind, when the door to the bedroom opens.

"My mother acted like it was Christmas morning when I handed the babies over," Yakov says. "She insisted on changing a diaper herself. Can you believe that?"

Yakov rounds the corner just as I turn to face him.

He's in a pair of dark trousers with a cashmere sweater stretched across his perfectly sculpted midsection. When he slams to a stop in the middle of the room, I can actually see his abs contract.

His eyes trail up and down my body, taking a slow tour of me. His face is unreadable. I feel like a specimen under his microscope.

"I know it doesn't fit the way it used to." I tug at the slit, trying to cover more of my leg. "I don't think this dress is 'sinful' so much as it is 'unlawful.' It's too small. I'm going to change into something more—"

"Perfect," Yakov breathes.

I frown. "What?"

"This." He exhales, shaking his head slowly like he can't believe what's in front of him. "You. I mean... *fuck.*"

I'm still not one hundred percent sure what he means when he crosses the room, grabs me around the waist, and pins me against the wall. His hand strokes up my spine, arching my body into his as he looks down into my eyes. "You look fucking delicious, Luna."

That clears things up.

"It barely fits," I argue meekly.

Yakov slides his hand around my waist to cup my breast. "I can help you take it off."

I can't help but laugh. "I thought we had plans."

He nods as his eyes trace a feverish path over my chest. "We do. Fancy dinner plans. I was going to take you out and let everyone see you on my arm. We were going to dance and then go for cocktails. I was going to take you on a long drive with the windows down."

"That sounds nice."

"Or..." His lips are poised over my mouth, his breath warming over my skin, "I could strip you out of this dress, fuck you until you're too weak to stand, and feed you takeout."

"That... that also sounds nice." I have to force myself to swallow the lump in my throat. "That sounds—I want that. Give me that. Do that."

Yakov's green eyes are almost black as he pinches the shoulder strap of my dress and slides it down my arm. Inch by inch, he shimmies the dress off of me until I'm leaning against the wall in nothing but matching lacy red lingerie and my heels.

He actually bites his knuckle and groans. "Fuck, Luna. It's been seven weeks. Are you trying to kill me?"

Ten minutes ago, I didn't feel confident. I didn't feel beautiful or desirable.

Now, Yakov is looking at me like I'm the most gorgeous woman in the world.

And I believe him.

I lay a hand on his chest and walk him slowly backwards towards the bed. "Killing you would be counterproductive to *my* plans."

He falls onto the bed and pulls me along with him. His hands stroke the backs of my thighs as I straddle him. "And what are your plans?"

I roll my hips against him, grinding down on the obvious erection he's packing. "To—how'd you put it?—to let you fuck me until I'm too weak to stand."

"It seems we're on the same page then."

Yakov rolls me over and kisses his way down my stomach. My skin is soft and loose, but he doesn't pause over my stretch marks or avoid the area. He loves every part of me, inside and out.

He hooks a finger under the lace of my panties and rips them away. I long ago gave up on telling him to stop tearing through all of my nice lingerie. It's expensive, but he always replaces it. Plus, it is really fucking hot.

Yakov parts me with a finger and drags his tongue across my seam. He explores every fold of me while his thumb circles over my clit.

After giving birth, it was hard to imagine anything below the waist would ever feel good again. But this isn't good—it's incredible.

I curl my fingers through his hair and buck against his mouth. Yakov flicks his tongue over my center, every lick sending me closer to the edge. Then he plunges a finger into me.

Instantly, I explode.

My thighs clamp around his ears as wave after wave of pleasure washes over me.

When Yakov crawls back over my body, his lips are slick from my release. He kisses me, our tongues tangling together until I'm breathless.

"I didn't know I could still do that," I admit, flopping back on the mattress.

"Do what?" He curls his hand between my legs. "Orgasm? I'd be happy to prove you wrong again if you want."

I'm still pulsing from the first release, but I'm ready for more.

"I didn't know I'd still want you this much," I explain. "I love being a mom and seeing you as a dad, but I didn't know if—I guess I was worried that this part of our relationship was over. I wasn't sure if you'd still want me."

He rears back, brow furrowed. "What the fuck does that mean?"

"It means that I'm basically a baby machine. I had babies popping out of me and now, I'm leaking milk." I wrap my arms around my midsection. "It's not exactly sexy."

Yakov grabs each of my wrists and pins them above my head with one hand. "Says who?"

"Me. *Cosmo.* Society." I shrug, but it's hard with my arms pinned to the mattress. "Once you give birth, it feels like you lose that other part of you. Your vagina suddenly exists solely to birth babies."

"You're not made solely for having babies, Luna." Yakov presses his knee between my legs, spreading them wide. Then he settles between my thighs, his cock pushing against my entrance. "You were made for *me.*"

He presses into me slowly. I'm tense, nervous about what it will feel like given everything my body has been through over the last seven weeks. But Yakov takes me gently. He stretches me one inch at a time until he slides home deep inside of me.

"See how good you are at taking me?" he growls in my ear. "This is what your pussy was made for. To be filled by me."

He holds my hands firmly above my head as he thrusts into me again and again. I writhe, trying to get closer to him. But Yakov keeps control.

I hook my legs around his back and lift my hips to meet him. Our bodies crash together until Yakov is groaning.

Finally, he releases my wrists and grabs my hips. He holds me steady as he drives into me. His body stutters for a second and then I feel him twitch deep inside of me.

Knowing Yakov still wants me—feeling close to him like this—has me falling with him.

When he's spent, he collapses against my chest. "Thai food and then we do that again, yeah?"

I stroke my hand down his back and laugh. "Yeah, we do that again. And again. And again."

"And again," Yakov adds, nuzzling my neck. Then he draws back, his eyes soft as they look down at me. "Until forever."

Yakov forever... Now, that's a plan.

I grab his face and bring his lips to mine.

We don't order the Thai food for hours and hours.

BONUS EPILOGUE: LUNA
ONE YEAR LATER

Download the Bonus Epilogue for a special wedding, beautiful babies, and more!

CLICK HERE TO DOWNLOAD
https://dl.bookfunnel.com/hn83qkdaf0

Printed in Great Britain
by Amazon